Dimensional Shift
Waters of Babylon

Michelle Stone

Dimensional Shift:
Waters of Babylon

Copyright 2012 Michelle Stone

Published by:
Plettstone

PO Box 5008 – 128
Mariposa, CA 95338
All rights reserved

ISBN-10: 1467930245
ISBN-13: 978-1467930246

Volume 2 in the Dimensional Shift trilogy

Library of Congress Control Number: 2012903952

Prologue

Dr. Akhi Richmond's warm smile soothed Kelt as he opened the video link from the floating city Pacificus. She seemed in an unexpectedly good mood. Even though the command bunker located below the southern Nevada desert was spacious, Kelt did get claustrophobic and a bit depressed from time to time.

"I'm up to here directing too many affairs," Akhi said as she waved her hand across her forehead. "I don't want to manage, but Daddy says I'm good at it."

"So I've heard."

"I'd rather be working on some research, but as you know, working on a new physics theory is not a crucial life sustaining pursuit at the moment."

"No kidding. I wish you could develop a real stargate technology and then we could just scoot off to another planet."

Akhi rolled her eyes at the suggestion and moved on to the messages she needed to relay.

"Kelt, Daddy has assigned me to take charge of the day to day tactical operations of the four cities, on top of everything else I've been working on. He's managing people problems and prioritizing our projects. All of our geeks seem to be self-directed, and we don't have a cohesive strategy to address our long-term problems. It's all very frantic. Everyone is trying to pursue every avenue they can think of, but we're not coordinated. He's trying to keep us alive. So, while he deals with all that, he's asked me to take charge of ops for the time being. The up side to this is that I'll have more excuses to talk to you down there," she said with a wink.

"I understand. Are you up to it, Akhi? That sounds like a lot to lay on you like that. I would assume that he'd give that assignment to some military type. Several qualified people are on board, you know."

"I know, but Daddy doesn't want military people in charge. He's assigned me a very adequate group of advisors, which include those who have military, and logistics experience, as well as others. I think that he wants me to develop my leadership skills, so he's just throwing me into the fray."

"I think it's a good idea."

"Really?"

"Yup. You've demonstrated solid leadership skills on various occasions. We certainly need someone organizing our efforts to a better effect. I'm spending time on some of your papers, though I don't know how long I'll be able to devote time to it. I do have a group of people here in the bunker to take care of now.

"While we're just sitting it out here waiting for the radiation effects topside to diminish, our engineers are working on some project or another. For some reason, everyone comes to me to make a decision or answer a question. I don't get much time for my own stuff."

"I understand… in any case, Kelt, we have an assignment for you. And this is one of special significance. We've found active plant life down south on the Nile River!"

"Akhi, that's amazing! But it's terribly close to the Suez. It wasn't all that long ago that it was nuked. There's some serious fallout throughout that area."

"I understand. Yes, there's substantial radiation in the area, but those plants are there and growing! We still want you to get out there and collect samples. You'll need to go out in spacer EV suits, and follow strict decontamination procedures when you get back. You've still got some canaries don't you?"

Kelt's bunkered team of some two hundred, didn't have real canaries. All they had were some mice and worms. However, canary was the word they used for the animals they would use to test for toxins in the atmosphere. If the canary died, then they would go through more than just the radiation decontamination.

"Yes, we still have some canaries," he said wishing they really had a real canary or two.

"I'm going to send you the coordinates and I'd like you to get out there in the morning. Take a full crew and some equipment to bring back plant samples. Once you've tested that it's safe, we need some of those plant samples transferred to the contaminated lab sphere. We'll do telomere testing with them. There's an intriguing element about this assignment, Kelt."

"Really? What might that be?"

"Aldo and Amy think that the libraries are there. They'd like you to do some ground radar scans and see if there is anything worth investigating. We do see evidence from space of a small, buried structure. It looks to be square, perhaps 3 meters on each side. See if you can discover anything artificially made like a crypt or a hiding place. If you find anything like that, open it and retrieve its contents."

"We'll get it done, sweetie," Kelt said as he blew her a kiss before cutting the video link.

*****

The planning for the expedition was fairly minor. Kelt assembled a full crew and loaded ground imaging radar equipment, digging tools, water, food, specimen containers, and the canaries. They timed the trip from the Nevada bunker for the middle of the night to reach the location in the morning. They went through the time zones very quickly; as they lifted their shuttle above the atmosphere, accelerated, flipped to decelerate, and then dropped to the target. It was a bright sunny day, but scorching death surrounded them everywhere they looked. In fear for their own lives, they now avoided any signs of people. Much of Earth's land had been abandoned, including this and the surrounding desert. Radiation levels were especially high here, and Kelt wondered how effective the EV suits designed for work in space would be to protect him and his team.

3

As Kelt dropped the shuttle near the site, he could see numerous plants of various varieties blanketing a place on a raised plateau above the river. He was elated to see thriving plant life again. Lately, everything he had seen, was either dying or was slated for destruction by the plant viral infection that had blanketed the Earth the year before. He had known the Earth would bounce back from destruction, as it had done so many times in the past. How long it would take had always been *the* question. No one knew for sure. The small plot of vegetation lifted everyone's spirits.

After everyone was buttoned up in their EV suits and he had run their self-diagnostics, Kelt went out with the canaries. His live animals would likely suffer the fate of radiation poisoning, but nothing there seemed to affect them immediately. He then waved the rest of the crew out of the shuttle's airlock. They had all dressed in similar protective gear. He wasn't worried so much about being exposed on site, as much as carrying some new bacteria or virus back with them. No one really knew what new species might be cropping up in this new world. Viruses and bacteria seemed to be the best adapted toward evolution. All of Kelt's crew was perfectly protected against radiation within their EV suits, despite Kelt's anxious concerns. After all, they had been designed for spacers working in the extremes of space,.

For the first half hour, the team performed ground radar testing around the perimeter, which outlined what appeared to be a buried mustaba.

"We've got a small square structure here. It's just short of three meters on each side. From these images, it looks like the bottom third of a pyramid," Kelt advised Scotty, "If there's anything of interest to us here, it would likely be in the center," he concluded.

"Yuppers. It looks like this building is only about a meter high, Kelt. I agree that if there is anything here, it will be easier to attack it from the top. If we're going to do any more radar testing, we'd better move some of these plants, so we don't trample them," Scottie advised.

Their principal dirtside biologist, Dr. Padma Patel, first indicated where she would like to pull her samples. Kelt then asked her to take her plants from the middle of the mound, because that was where he and the crew would resume their radar testing. He didn't want to kill ANY plants. Meticulously, she extracted all the plants in the proposed circle, which included several samples of over 20 different varieties, and left the center open for the radar crew to do their thing.

"Is she careful or what?" Scotty asked impatiently, as Patel meticulously took all the time she needed to protect the plants she retrieved from the site.

"Give her time, Scotty. She's doing careful work. We don't want those samples to die on us," Kelt answered.

"Why do you suppose plants are growing here?" Kelt asked Dr. Patel over the open audio com link.

"I don't know, Kelt, I've never seen anything like this before. These plants are thriving, where nothing else has survived, especially so close to the bombing site of the Suez. This is really quite astounding. I don't recognize these plant varieties. They are very similar to those I've studied from this area, but they are mutated from those varieties, or they are completely new forms of plant life. The radiation has killed everything else around here," she announced.

"In that case, might these plants be infected by the virus?" Kelt asked.

"There is only one way to find out, Kelt. We have to take samples back to the labs and test them," she answered.

After the plant life had been cleared in the center of the mound, the team dug down for what seemed like hours to a depth of about 1.75 meters, before hitting rock. As they expanded the hole, they recognized a large flat stone, which had obviously been designed and carved to cap an opening. Everyone stood, circling the hole with great anticipation. As Scotty levered up the stone just slightly, someone turned an LED flashlight on. Inside, laid a long black stone-like object, with rounded ends about 20 cm in diameter. They lifted the covering out of the hole and could see the object in better light. Kelt watered a rag down and wiped off the dust. There he saw many of the old language characters he had seen Akhi and Amy practicing. It didn't look like a great library, but it was definitely an artifact, anticipated from legend, and found nearly where it had been predicted.

"The artifact was satisfying enough by itself," thought Kelt... but the plants! Living plants were a bloody miracle. They were alive and thriving.

"Okay, team, this artifact is interesting to some of our people upstairs, but at the moment, our first priority should be the plants. Let's make sure we get good healthy samples of each variety collected, and load them on the shuttle. Once we've taken them safely to our Nevada bunker, we'll start testing them right away in our labs," Kelt announced.

While Dr. Patel and most of the crew were finishing up, carefully packing her samples, four men struggled to lift the stone artifact from its resting place. They carefully wrapped it for transport and placed it carefully into the back of the shuttle behind the plant samples.

*****

On the floating city Pacificus, Rick Carter squirmed uncomfortably in the modest plastic chair in his office. He was spending some quiet time to sort out in his mind, schedules, projects, and an undeterminable assortment of requests. What he wished was that he could just listen to a little music and clear his head for a few minutes. However, these days there was no time for that sort of thing. Somehow, he had managed to set aside time when he was managing his corporations before the infection.

"Why can't I have more down time now? I have a fraction of the number of people working for me... and yet, there is so much more to do. I'm being selfish," he castigated himself.

Rick had been the impetus behind the formation of Space Truck. In the beginning, it had been a philanthropic endeavor to help victims of natural disasters. He had purchased two large cargo ships and stationed one in the Pacific and one in the Atlantic oceans. His desire to push technology, and his daughter Akhi's unusual abilities with physics had fostered the incredible developments, which pushed nearly 22,000 people into space, shortly before the viral infection went worldwide. Now the company operated four huge spires or floating cities, two large orbiting spoked wheel space stations, two bases on Mars, and two bases on the Moon.

Initially, Rick had been excited at the new findings dirtside, but he still felt hopeless. They had found a rock with ancient markings. What good could it do? He had no faith in the unbelievable. Within a few years, Earth might be a dead planet as far as humans were concerned. Kelt, who he had hoped would marry his beautiful daughter, was hopelessly stranded down there. Many of his best crews were down there, as well... Scotty, a couple dozen commandos, many scientists, and other specialists. They would have been transferred to the floating cities, had the base not been infected. . He had been reviewing the reports from his microbiologists in the floating city, Pacificus. The situation would eventually become truly and utterly desperate. The dirtside team had a secure bunker to live in and enough food to last ten or twelve years, depending on how much they consumed from their freezers. They also had the means to shuttle around the world as necessary. They were certainly better off than the rest of the world's population, which had nothing. The new plant life at the artifact site was an interesting curiosity, but could in no way be used to repopulate the Earth in time to save his loved ones. Neither, could he fathom the fate of the remaining eight billion people on the planet. In Rick's mind, his astounding feat of saving so many seemed so miniscule.

"Well, I've managed to lift nearly 22,000 people into space," he thought, "We were lucky to get that many. I suppose that should count for something," he murmured. His thoughts turned to his beautiful daughter and his heart weighed heavy for the loss she felt for her beloved Kelt. When Akhi was only four years old, Rick had lost her mother in an auto accident. He knew the pain she felt all too well.

"The oceans are still alive!" Rick exclaimed to himself. "Perhaps all is not lost after all." No one knew why the virus did not affect aquatic plant life, but there were many possible scientific explanations.

"And if the aquatic plant life survives, so will the fish and other wildlife. Some part of humanity will survive the infection," Rick said stoically, with his eyes focused on the top of his desk. "Okay, I'll make sure we look into the ramifications later. Right now, I have other business to tend to." No one answered his comments.

*****

Kelt needed to video link with Aldo right away. Aldo was the first millenarian to present himself to Rick. Amy, his associate of three and a half centuries of age, and Akhi, were also included in the link as soon as he returned to Nevada with the artifact. Dr. Patel, the biologist, was busily preparing samples and slides to send to the sphcrc, dedicated for testing items sent up from Earth. That particular spacecraft had been contaminated with the Earth born virus, and could never be exposed to the four floating cities or two space stations. For that reason, it was kept well clear of the spires by at least 350 kilometers.

Although Kelt was most interested in the new plant life, there wasn't much he could do to help the biologists. The plant samples were being decontaminated, as best as could be done, from the radiation. He knew that the experts under his command would do the job in expert fashion. They were in good hands. His interests as an engineer naturally turned to the old artifact.

"Could it indeed fulfill the promises that Aldo, the millenarian, had foretold? Is this alien technology?" Kelt asked.

Humanity needed a break and as far as he knew, this thing might provide some hope. It appeared to be just a large black stone, expertly carved, and polished. Kelt took numerous videos and stills of the characters that covered every square centimeter of the artifact. The texts had been expertly carved in the old language as confirmed by Aldo Brickman, the expert millenarian onboard the floating city Pacificus.

For some time, Aldo, Akhi, and Amy studied the text of the script via video link from Pacificus. Aldo explained that they could activate the device for personal use by some sort of mental link, or use a com link so that all could see. Since no one, not even Aldo knew anything about telepathic procedures, everyone voted for the slightly longer process to build an interface to communicate with this thing. No one in the Nevada based bunker could actually read the old language.

With Aldo's help in deciphering the instructions, Scotty, the team's electronics whiz, put together the hardware interface in a couple days, by modifying a digital television. His device would not plug into the artifact, but would send commands on a modulated transmission according to the instructions written on the artifact. Oddly enough, the object was able to respond with a common carrier wave, modulated to his standard digital monitor output.

"Unreal," thought Kelt, "How would it know what our transmission protocols are? Maybe there IS a clue or answer in this, which can save us. If there isn't, we're on our own to survive this disaster."

"Kelt, until I figure out how to use this interface effectively, I'll just have to experiment a little," Aldo said.

He started keying in the old characters, which brought an image to the monitor. It showed Akhi on a monitor through Kelt's eyes as he told her how much he loved her. Kelt stood shocked.

"Why is this recent and most private event being broadcast from this thing? And why are these images through my eyes part of the record?" Kelt wondered as Aldo continued testing the commands through Scotty's interface.

Kelt felt a certain violation as he realized his whole life had been recorded in this history. Although he had led an exemplary life, he felt ashamed somehow that his personal life might be revealed for anyone curious enough to look. He wondered what the others might feel about this breach of privacy.

"Let's see, it looks like a storage device of some kind... that was one of the most recent entries," Aldo said, "for now, I'm going to have to sort of work backwards."

"Sounds good, Aldo," Kelt said as he tore himself away from feelings of personal violation and resumed his focus.

Kelt had always thumbed through books and magazines from the back when he first picked one up. It gave him a macro view of what the book or periodical contained. As he would scan books in this fashion, he would generate questions that would later be answered as he started from the beginning. The advantage to Kelt's genius was to pick up that which was most relevant first. He absorbed what he needed from any publication much more quickly with this very non-standard approach.

As Aldo continued to enter commands, snippets of Earth history popped up on the monitor.

"Is the entire video history of the world in this thing?" Kelt queried.

"I don't know, Kelt," Aldo replied flatly.

Aldo scrolled back 600 years or so. They saw old sailing vessels in a harbor in Spain on the monitor. The image, although interesting, held nothing of value or interest among the group.

"Hey! Let's check out the library at Alexandria. Now would that be cool or what?" Scotty chimed in.

"I think I'm learning how this works," Aldo said under his breath.

Aldo scripted carefully and within a few minutes, the famous building was there displayed in its splendor on screen.

"It isn't as ornate as I would have thought," said Akhi.

"There is a list of documents related to this edifice," Aldo said, as he browsed hundreds of titles written in several languages.

"Hey, look, there's a scroll by Hypatia," announced Scotty. "She supposedly had written many books on astronomy, but all were destroyed in the Christian sacking of the library," he explained.

"You read Greek, Scotty?" Kelt asked with amazement.

"Uh, yea, Kelt. I picked it up a few years ago on a whim."

"Greek... on a whim? Really?" Kelt asked.

"Really, Kelt. I learned Russian Cyrillic too!"

Kelt stared at Scotty, sporting a warm and slightly crooked grin.

"What?" demanded Scotty.

"I suppose nothing should surprise me where you are concerned."

Kelt had seen so many skill-sets pop up in this group of people that he had learned just to take it in stride. Surprise? Yes. Incredulity? No.

Aldo and Scotty took a few moments to open the scroll and read the Greek text. Aldo had learned Greek in Hypatia's time. Kelt certainly expected this skill from him. After all, he had lived during that period in Earth's history. Indeed, the scroll had been written by Hypatia, it described the methodology by which she used to track, and measure stars in the heavens.

"This is absolutely unbelievable," said Kelt. "I wonder how much memory this all takes," he mused.

"Petabytes of petabytes, of petabytes," Aldo guessed softly. "We have video, sounds, and written documents, all from the beginning of humankind. The memory structure must be far advanced, compared to the simple binary types that we use in our current computers, I would think."

"So, is this just a giant history book, Aldo?" Kelt asked.

"I'm afraid that it is, my young friend," Aldo stated, "I can find no other functions in the instructions."

"Great. How is human history going to help us now?" asked Kelt. "The world is ending and this promised salvation turns out to be a fat history book. How can this possibly help save us? At any other time prior to the viral infestation of the Earth's land based plant life, this artifact would be considered a treasure of immeasurable worth. How we might have changed our recent past, if we had found this sooner? I suppose it is almost meaningless now," Kelt said.

"Hold on, this looks interesting," Aldo said as he compared several symbols on the artifact and then keyed in another command. I have found a translation function. It seems that the world's languages are contained in the device and we can select the language we want to hear in the videos and other spoken recordings."

"Well, then," Kelt said, "Key up the first entry and let's see what this is all about. I want to see how this "library" is going to save us. Let's all share it in modern day English."

Aldo entered several more commands and correlated internal date computations, and then set the machine to show the first recorded entry.

"This is it. If there isn't a solution here, we are stuck here, dirtside," Kelt thought to himself. "The only comfortable survivors, will be those of humanity in space if this doesn't have an answer,"

Akhi joined him in her thoughts, knowing what Kelt must be thinking, and feeling. She started tearing up uncontrollably for her Kelt.

A video showed a group of perhaps 200 normal looking people standing in front of a shack, set atop log stilts. A woman with gray hair spoke to them in the old language, which was translated to modern English by the device.

"We seeded this world long ago. The library of Earth's history is now safely hidden and protected by Danu and his clan. They have taken ownership of it, and shall protect it where we cannot. Their simple mysticism shall lead to discovery and explanations for the things they do not yet understand. Go forth to all places to observe and learn. Teach your children our language. Everything you see will be recorded in this world's library. Perhaps, someday these people, our other children, will join us."

This was the first entry, dated some 16,000 years before. The libraries, as they surmised, contained the history spanning human development through the eyes of select descendants of these people. The histories included an overwhelming amount of data. They included almost everything that these people and their descendants had seen through their own eyes, throughout so many eons.

One hundred and eighty-six members of the Space Truck spires and Aldo's financial consortium were all direct descendants from this clan. Who were the old ones? Their long-lived descendants, the millenarians, were, for the most part, ignorant of their ancestry. None alive knew what they were. The younger millenarians did not yet know how long they would live. What was the purpose of this history of the world?

How could this artifact help to solve the world catastrophe facing them now? All of the world's land based plant life was dying. A virus was responsible for a massive infection, and the human race was unable to combat it. These libraries only contained what looked to be, just human history.

1- Earth side status

Year 0 NE (New Era)

"So how are things going topside, Scotty?" Kelt asked as he stepped up to the monitor station.

Scott had been monitoring live video feeds from around the world to assess the real news. The nonprofit company, Space Truck, Inc., had placed several of what they called floater cams in stationary elevations at 500 kilometers above the world. The satellites were held in position with small disks, called floaters, built into their frames.

"Well Cap'n," Scotty started, "It looks like all the grocery stores have been cleaned out. All of the distribution centers, as well. There have been a few food riots, but everything is still relatively calm. It doesn't look like too many people are on the roads though," he finalized.

"Yeah, they're still worried about the radiation fallout, but the worst is probably over as far as that goes, for now," Kelt responded.

Kelt Nelby, a young member of the bright and multidiscipline Space Truck research team, had been stranded on Earth, at Space Truck's Nevada's launching port, along with some 200 others, when the nuclear devices were detonated in Africa. The bunker under the site had been planned to house only 100 people, and twenty years of food had been set aside to provide for that number. Within hours, the strong winds created by the nuclear blasts, covered the Earth with the virus. Kelt was just nearing his 20th birthday, yet held command of their bunkered site in the southern desert of Nevada. He sorely missed getting outside to kick a ball around. Now, he tried to devote an hour every day to intense exercise. There wasn't room to play a game of soccer in the underground base in Nevada, where he spent his nights, studies, research, and exercise time. He had set up a handball court, in a room that was about twenty feet by thirty feet, and had a hard time finding anyone to play. No one liked to get skunked all the time.

"Hey Kelt, look at all the boats out on the ocean along the California coast," Scotty said.

"I'm sure that we'll see a lot of that, Scotty, in the coming weeks. It looks like that's going to be *the* place to be if you want to survive what's coming. Not only will they be isolated from really hungry people, but the oceans are filled with life to provide sustenance," Kelt responded.

He shuddered at the thought of how people would necessarily turn to cannibalism, once all food supplies were exhausted.

"That will come within just a few months or perhaps even days. The food hoarding has been significant. Most of the world's population has nothing to eat," he thought.

Little did he realize that it had begun already. The food treasures went to gangs that could overpower individuals and the weak. The best of humanity was sharing with each other, but that would last only a matter of weeks. The current fall harvest in the northern hemisphere had been very small. There would be no more. The infection would kill most trees by spring in the northern hemisphere. The southern hemisphere had collected their final fall harvests six months prior. Indeed, every boat near the coast had been launched.

"Thousands of people must be on those boats. I wonder how many pleasure craft will be coming out from the inland areas," Kelt thought pensively. "We may not be able to do much for the people inland, but perhaps we can provide some aide for these few."

He would send the idea up to Akhi, his beloved soul mate in the floating cities. She might be able to pass it along to the right people. He knew that there were a few social engineering types, and good marine biologists on board, who had been lifted to the cities before the nuclear bombing.

The floating cities of Pacificus, Atlanticus, City A, and City B, were four, three kilometer-long spires, with gigantic spheres spun from a matrix of Buckyballs and ceramic steel. The spheres were pressurized housings used for food farming, engineering, research, and production of new machinery. Kelt and his girlfriend, Dr. Akhi Richmond, along with three other young engineers, had perfected the technology of these floating structures that had managed to save some 20,000 people. The cities remained in the umbral shadow of the Earth. They seemingly floated there supported by Akhi's floater disks, the product of her advanced research, as the Earth slowly revolved around its axis. The reason they never let the cities see the sun, was that the Earth's magnetosphere held maximum protection from the Sun's harmful radiation on its dark side. The decision to park the cities there had been a logical one. The additional benefit derived from the non-orbiting craft, was that Earth provided gravity. It was a simple single solution to two complex problems in space.

With the exception of South America, where the virus had first been noticed, and the areas in Africa that had been wiped out with atomic blasts, the rest of humanity had survived. Many, closest to the nuclear attacks, would die within a few days from radiation poisoning. Perhaps, they were the lucky ones.

"It will still take a few months for the virus to dig in around the world and completely destroy all land based plant life. Most of humanity will eventually die from starvation. Oddly enough, some normality of life still continues. Daily newscasts are still sent out over the airwaves and existing infrastructure," Kelt mused.

The world had been forewarned. Every store's inventory was depleted. People hoarded every food item and all other necessities they would need for the future.

"Hey Kelt, look at this. I've got another broadcast about us on CNN," Scotty informed. Kelt and Scotty both hovered over the monitor as they watched.

".... hoping that the floating cities, high above the world's atmosphere, can somehow manage to save the world," said the attractive blond woman dressed in a bright red outfit with a white scarf.

"She looks nervous, doesn't she Scotty?" asked Kelt.

"Aye, Cap'n, that she does. She's outside, and that's pretty brave for most people with the fear of radiation exposure."

News broadcasts mercilessly bombarded civilization with stock news footage, of the floating cities saving human life in previous natural disasters and their final ascent into the heavens. Their hope was to give others hope. Hope was in short supply. The world would soon descend into utter chaos.

"We'd like to remind people that our government is still intact and the laws must be obeyed," the newscaster continued. *"The White House and Pentagon have assured us that we will find solutions to the problems we face. We'd also like to advise everyone that the short-term radiation threat has now passed and you should check with your employer and return to work. Now, back to you Chuck,"* she finalized.

"Well that's some good news Kelt! The short term radiation has passed us by."

"Yes, it is good news indeed. It's, not much, but something?"

"Aye, Cap'n, that it is."

2- Sky diving

"Rick, my guys are down there," Guy insisted.

Guy Lerner was well built at 5'11" and worked daily not only to keep his muscles in shape, but in the fine art of killing, for which the government had spent millions of dollars to train him. He had grown up in the military, joined the Navy Seals at his first opportunity, and had distinguished himself and country while in uniform. He was now supposedly middle aged, but he was losing the scruffy leathered look he was so proud of. The tough life in the military had hardened him, but had also given him a few gray hairs and sun battered skin. His work onboard Pacificus, the floating city, had not been strenuous by any means. He felt he was getting soft. He was looking younger, much to Rick's chagrin.

"Guy, I can't say that I really need you here. But here, onboard Pacificus, you are safe. I really don't want to lose you either," Rick Carter insisted, as his brilliant gray eyes stared directly at his top mercenary.

"Rick, my squad was abandoned at the Nevada site along with Kelt and Scotty. I've never left my men. We all go in, and we all come out. I have lived my life on this principle, Rick. I can't imagine how you could possibly understand the obligation I feel toward them. It's a military thing you may never understand." Guy stated.

"You consider Kelt and Scotty members of your squad, Guy?"

"Yes, I do, sir. I know you've developed a certain fondness for Kelt, and I have to admit that I have too. I know that your daughter is head over heels in love with that kid. So, after working with him for several months, well, I've sorta gotten... well you know... Rick... well you know, right?" Guy choked up fighting back the emotions he was trained to hide.

"I'm trying to tell you that Kelt needs me more than you do. The kid is more than bright, Rick. He's a real leader with a natural sense for strategy and tactical planning. My team and I are highly trained to handle small incursions or dealing with things like the kidnapping of your virologist some time back. Kelt has a critical mind for the big picture. When we were faced with an overwhelming force in the Mediterranean, he saved our hides. He proved his leadership to us, and we don't forget that sort of thing. He's a natural commander and survivor. You know that your people are sitting ducks at that old converted mine. They have no weapons or other means of protection. All that protects them is that old warehouse covering your huge elevator into the caverns, and that ain't much. I know you meant it to be some sort of camouflage, but it won't work anymore."

"Do you think that they are in any immediate danger, Guy?" Rick asked.

"Rick, they have a food supply. The US government knows they are there. The military knows they are there. Other people know about that base. There is no hiding it anymore. So, my answer would be a most definite, YES." Guy said with determination.

Guy was Rick's intimate advisor in all matters of security and the guardian angel with a lethal sting for his little girl. Rick's paranoia had paid huge dividends in return. Guy Lerner and his commandos had been instrumental in saving Akhi and Kelt… even his own life, along with the newly developed technologies more than once.

"Guy, once you are down there, you will be contaminated. We know that the virus only attacks land based plant life. So, you'll be okay as long as you have a food supply. But you can never come back here, where it is safe. We still haven't figured out a way to clean someone up without killing them," Rick advised.

"Sir," Guy started in his most formal tone, "I don't leave my men behind. I don't care what it takes. I realize that it might be my death sentence. I cannot live with myself knowing that my men are stranded and in danger. Perhaps, you think that they are safe, for the time being.

19

After all, no one is roaming the desert these days. Everyone seems to be moving to the coastlines where the fishing might provide them a chance. But, Mr. Carter, I can assure you the threat is real."

"What about your two team members who are here on Pacificus, Guy? I suppose they want to go with you to certain death, too?" asked Rick.

"Yes sir, they do. We've been sort of a family for years now. We all feel the same way, and I don't think there is anything you can say to change our minds. It's a military thing that I don't think you'll ever understand," Guy repeated.

"Guy, I'm sorry to see that you want to leave us here, but I can't tell you how relieved I am that you'll be down there with Kelt and your team. I've been having a very difficult time abandoning all those people. If there is any way for all those civilians to survive, I'm sure that you and your team shall play a critical role."

"Rick, it would really be nice to have a backup base of operations. I'd really like to get the tcam out of that bunker. There are just too many people who know about it. You wouldn't have a spare base hidden somewhere else would you?" Guy asked.

"I'm sorry, Guy. Everything that we could have used as a backup base of operations is filled with other civilians. I only had the two other facilities on those islands in New Zealand and in the Mediterranean. Nevada is the only site we have where we can keep everyone inside and launch our shuttles and other craft. I look back and can see so many mistakes in my planning. The worst I envisioned was more disasters that are natural. The rain, wind, tornados, hurricanes… you name it, gave me the impetus to make the cities space worthy. I had not actually planned to live in space. I could have never envisioned a worldwide plague. I wish that I could have done more," Rick said with apparent regret.

Guy noticed the big guy's face pale before him as a look of terrible guilt flooded his eyes.

"We'll get it all sorted out, sir. I've got confidence in your research people. Somehow, this will be turned around. I've got to get dirtside with my squad. I'm glad that I've got your support, sir," Guy said firmly.

Guy did have a great confidence in the Space Truck team. He had seen miracles with the new technologies. Granted, nothing had come forth on the biological front, but he still had a feeling there had to be some amazing scientific discovery waiting in the wings they hadn't yet tried.

"Guy, have you thought how you are going to get dirtside? I hate to say this, but... well, you know, we hate to risk our shuttles near the atmosphere."

"Could you strap floaters to our backs?" asked Guy with a grin.

"Now, that we can do. I'm sure we can spare three of them for you and your team," answered Rick.

"You wouldn't happen to have any ray guns or anything like that would you, sir?"

Guy grinned as he asked the sarcastic question. Rick only grinned back knowing that Guy had a full understanding of his policies about weapon development. There were no weapons.

"Rick, we really do need some weapons that have a bigger punch than what we carry," Guy advised.

"I suppose you are right, Guy. I've always been hesitant to develop weapons. Now, we have a very different situation. Let me know what you need, and we'll try and get it for you," Rick said, knowing they had very little supplies, that could produce projectiles for weapons. The forges could produce the weapons well enough, but gunpowder required supplies they held in short reserve.

"Midnight at the Nevada site will be coming round below us in about six hours, sir. I can be ready if you can get some of your people to hook us up in time," Guy said.

"Wow, that soon? Okay," Rick answered as he stood from behind his desk. Rick stepped around the furniture and gave his closest friend a strong manly bear hug, realizing that he may never see him again.

Three hours later, Guy and his two commandos, stood fully fitted in the new EV suits in one of the labs. A seamstress and stress engineer quickly fashioned a Kevlar harness to hold the floaters to their chests. It looked much like a standard chute harness with straps around both legs and tightly bound around the chest and shoulders.

"This just ain't right," Guy thought, "these EV suits are way too comfortable. It just ain't right."

He had been on many missions where he had to use diving gear in the past. In every case, the marine gear always gave him some irritation or didn't fit quite right in certain places. He had come to accept the discomfort as "feeling right." If there was no discomfort, he felt that his senses weren't focused. Those sentiments were quickly lost as the webbing surrounding his chest was cinched tight.

"I can hardly breathe!" Guy exclaimed as the air was forced from his lungs. "Now, that feels right," he grinned. "Boys, we'll need our armor. Since it doesn't look like it will fit over our special flight suits here, just bag it in your duffels with your weapons and ammo."

Just as the three-man team had secured their body armor, a technician came in to the lab pulling a large dolly with three huge Army green duffels.

"Mr. Carter wants you to take this freeze dried food down with you," he said.

"Those must weigh in at 100 pounds or so. We can handle that," one of the commandos said.

"Ah, sir, they weigh nearly twice that. We've packed them very tight. We'll attach them to your floater harness so the floater takes the weight along with your own duffels. We'll just let them dangle below you as you descend. I'll get an EV suit on and take this food out on the shuttle with us when we leave. We'll hook it up before the jump, so you don't have to drag it around," the technician advised.

"Sounds good," Guy said.

It had been nearly five hours to get the team outfitted with their extemporaneous drop gear and loaded into a shuttle.

"They should make these locks bigger," Guy said as he managed to squeeze himself and all his gear through the hole in the floor leading into the docked shuttle.

Although the room above the flight deck was locked down, the flight deck itself held only the vacuum of space. The big airlocks on the flight deck were rarely used. Only high priority maintenance or an emergency would qualify as a reason to bring a full sized shuttle into one. The air pumps could never pull out all the air from the chambers. Some air loss was inevitable. For that reason, the locking collars were the preferred method for shuttle access. It was a royal pain to dock with one, but it was necessary. The spires were not battle vessels. Little thought had been given to reducing docking time, for it was not a critical function.

After the commando team dropped into the shuttle, they stepped aside as the duffels were dropped in. Guy noticed that a pilot was "at the console," with her computing pad firmly velcroed to the dash in front of her seat. She had upgraded her equipment by installing a personal computer gaming stick to her right. Time had been so short in getting the spires off the ground that there had not been time to install quality flight controls. Commercially available computing gear seemed to fulfill the requirements in most aspects. Sure, they didn't provide the precise control and redundancy that any flight worthy craft should have, but there were no other real choices. It was a shortcut that everyone had deemed necessary. The decision had meant more people were ultimately saved.

"I'll never get used to this," Guy thought, "I'd feel a lot more comfortable if these things had a real flight stick, and some buttons to push and control switches."

The technician dropped in behind the duffels and gave the people above him the command to close the lock. The pilot responded by closing the lock on the shuttle.

"My name is Trish, and I'll be your driver today," the pilot grinned, "We have no inflight drinks, meals, entertainment, or attendants... shoot I don't even have a proper rudder to control, but we do hope you enjoy your flight with us. Thank you for choosing Space Truck for your traveling needs," she finished with her tomboyish laughter.

Guy had to admit that she was funny. She was the type of woman who could make you laugh without saying anything. Her remarks by themselves were standard silliness, but matched with her body language, it was hard for most to restrain from laughter. Her remarks only created small smiles on the commandos' stone faces. He could tell they were laughing their guts out inside.

"How low are you taking us, Trish?" Guy asked.

"We'll drop you to 300 clicks before we push you out. There's no need in taking risks in the stratosphere," she responded.

"And how fast will you let us drop?" Guy asked thinking of all the crap he had tied to himself.

"We'll let you drop until you reach the atmosphere and then slow you down to 200kph. We'll have you dirtside within 90 minutes," she replied.

Trish backed the shuttle out of the flight deck and let loose. Guy's stomach lurched as the shuttle started its weightless descent. She quickly brought the shuttle under control, and smoothly allowed the Earth to resume its normal gravitational pull on their bodies.

"Okay men and women, before I let Trish open the shuttle rear hatch, I'd like you to recheck the seals on your EV suits and run a diagnostic check," Commander Barnes, from the Pacificus CIC, commanded over the open audio link.

Guy fumbled as he tried to push aside his armor to see the EV suit's diagnostic panel on his left arm. He noticed his commandos were having similar issues with the devices. Trish fit her helmet in place and started up the onboard vacuum pumps, which pulled most of the air into storage tanks, unbuckled her flight harness, and came to their aid.

"Here you go," she said as she helped Guy loosen his armor enough to check his EV display quickly. "I wish you the best, sir," she said apologetically.

Guy knew what she was thinking. She would be safe. His men may not survive long. After helping with the others, she returned to her seat and buckled in. The research assistant buckled into the copilot's seat.

"We're ready to deploy, Lieutenant," Trish commed to Pacificus.

"Guy," started Commander Barnes, "make sure that your people are connected to each other with the orange straps we provided. We'd hate to lose any of you."

The team quickly checked their emergency straps. Each was connected to two others in a circular arrangement.

"We're good to go, sir," commed Guy to the commander on Pacificus.

"Deploy, and may you have a pleasant trip. My best to you, Guy," Barnes responded.

Barnes was concerned that the cities were losing three very important people. He too understood that they were dropping themselves into the jaws of literal hell. Yet, in his voice, everyone heard only the professional military detachment expected from a commander.

Captain Trish lowered the back hatch, when the pumps had finished their job pumping the interior atmosphere into the internal tanks. Just enough air remained in the cabin to push the trio toward the rear of the craft. Since the shuttle was not in orbit, the crew felt their full weight, and that of their inventory. They dragged the heavy duffels out to the lowered hatch, threw them over the side, and jumped.

Barnes nodded to his pilots in the CIC. They quickly and softly positioned the floaters to fall vertically, and moved the three men into a triangular formation, making sure their spacing did not exceed the safety lines the commandos had attached to each other. Guy felt a slight tugging in his harness as the floaters were configured to bring his team into formation and controlled by a single remote pilot in the CIC of Pacificus.

Guy had never dropped from high altitude from any aircraft. He had known only one pilot who had ejected at 60,000 feet. He had told Guy that it was the biggest rush of his life. Now, here Guy was doing a drop from 300 kilometers.

"This is a record drop, fellas! What a rush!" he screamed to his men in free-fall.

As their armor started to absorb heat from contact with the stratosphere, the CIC pilot slowed their descent slightly. The commandos felt only a slight tug as their fall rate reduced to a constant velocity. At 30,000 meters, the CIC pilots further reduced their speed to terminal velocity, as they entered the thickest part of the Earth's atmosphere.

It had taken nearly ninety minutes, as Guy witnessed the appearance of the large old warehouse below in the moonlit night. Pacificus brought them in slowly and comfortably. As soon as their feet hit the ground, Guy commed the CIC on Pacificus,

"We're down gentlemen. Thanks for the soft landing. Please release control of the floaters. We'll take them inside."

"Acknowledged," answered Barnes.

Kelt and a few of the civilians dressed in EV suits ran out of the large warehouse through the side door. Three personnel pulled dollies to bring in the heavy food duffels. Kelt grabbed Guy's hand in a handshake and then quickly put his left arm around Guy.

"I'm so glad to see you. It's been mighty uncomfortable around here without you. I know that it has been only a few months, but damn, it's good to see you!"

"It's good to see you too, Kelt. Akhi asked me to give you a big kiss for her," Guy said wondering just how that might be accomplished.

"Consider it done, Guy," Kelt grinned back. I'll tell her that I can wait for her to give it to me personally."

As they nimbly escaped the night into the warehouse, Guy asked Kelt about his commandos, Scotty, and the rest of the civilians.

"We're fine so far, but who knows what the future holds, Guy?"

3- Shannon and Amanda

"I am a millenarian," mused Shannon Liberty. She had been shocked the previous day when her teammate Amanda had given her the news. She was told that two millenarians would produce offspring with the long-life trait in every situation.

"But my parents are not like me," she thought to herself with sadness. It was easy to see that they were older and aging every year. She realized that the recessive trait had likely been passed down for several generations before she, the lucky one, had received it.

Both Shannon and her associate Amanda joined Space Truck Inc. after most of the vital dimensional shift engineering had been prototyped and perfected. They played a very small role in keeping the cities running, monitoring, and resupplying the Lunar and Mars bases, or many of the other day-to-day operations. They were the only two people in the population that had been exempted from "other" duties. Their assignment was the most important of all others. They had at first identified the virus and how it reproduced by taking vital telomeres from a cell's genes. The virus would reproduce by division. Once the virus had reproduced a few times and collected the available telomeres, they would escape to adjacent cells leaving one dormant virus behind. The remaining virus stayed in stasis in the cell, as the cell died. Telomeres were critical to cell reproduction and without them, cells could not subdivide.

Knowing that the virus did not affect animal telomeres, and that the DNA sequence of telomeres was fairly simple, they had tried splicing techniques to create new species of plants, with the animal like telomeres. For months, even before the nuclear strikes, this had been one of the two major approaches in an attempt to repopulate plant life on the planet.

"C'mon Shannon, we've got a presentation to do," Amanda said as she quickly gathered her notes.

"Thanks Amanda, I probably would have just kept on working. I haven't been paying much attention to the clock today." She had some new ideas that she was researching and truly hadn't prepared in her usual fashion for the presentation. She knew her material, but she had not prepared slides or notes.

Both young women grabbed their things and hurried to the lift port in the sphere where they lived and worked. The huge 500-meter sphere was locked to a three-kilometer spire. Within the spire were some living accommodations and office space, but it mostly served as a means to get from one sphere to another in the floating city. Kelt had often told everyone that they were building "Brussel sprouts in space," after he learned of his unknown complicity in the design and construction methods of the spheres. This floating city had been named "Pacificus." The second spire built had been dubbed "Atlanticus." Cities three and four had never received names when they were launched. In haste, everything had been moved to space with little formality. Those spires were currently referred to as A and B.

"Have you heard that they want to rename Atlanticus to Atlantis?" Amanda asked Shannon as they entered the tube car, which would take them up to the conference center.

"Yes, I have. You'd think they'd rename spires A and B first," said Shannon.

"Well, it sort of makes sense. Pacificus and Atlanticus received those names primarily for where they were initially positioned as relief craft over the Pacific and Atlantic oceans. Now there's really no need for those names is there?" asked Amanda.

"I suppose not. I think people need some hint of hope or levity, to keep their minds from dwelling on the negative."

"We've got mostly scientists on board these spires and they've got to be fed mentally, you know," Shannon smiled.

"Seriously, Shannon. Atlantis? You do know that city was LOST!" Amanda grinned.

"We're not going to lose this one," Shannon smiled back.

The two biologists rushed from the tube car, to the conference room located near the top of the spire. Inside were a few people they knew, Dr. Akhi Richmond, Rick Carter, Aldo Brickman, and seventeen other scientists and directors, directly related to the effort to repopulate the Earth with plant life. On video link from the Nevada bunker site, were Dr. Kelt Nelby, Dr. Scott Ermy, and Guy Lerner.

Akhi stared with great interest at a new fellow on the other side of the video link, wondering who he might be. She knew everyone in the room and on the link, except him.

"Before we start the meeting," announced Kelt, I'd like to introduce you to Sam Walsh. He, his wife, and little girls came to us a few weeks ago. I told you, Akhi, about him and his family. He's passed the test and is pretty bright. I'd like to have him in on this," he finished.

All the young millenarians had passed the "horse farmer" IQ test and missed the same questions. That is how Rick Carter knew to hire them.

Akhi had been the first test subject when she was only ten, and showing unusual aptitude in physics and music. It wasn't long after, her father sought out the brightest in the universities to receive the exam.

Akhi shot Kelt a glance with questioning eyes. His facial response indicated no, Sam did not know the true reason behind the test. Akhi and her father had decided to keep the secret for the short term. There were some 22,000 people now living in the four spires, their two orbiting space stations, and four bases on the Moon and Mars, who did not know about the millenarians. Older millenarians knew how to handle themselves; they had been forced to do so out of necessity on Earth. They had lived like vampires, in stealth for centuries.

"So, is Sam related?" asked Akhi noting a few similarities between the two.

"We don't know. Maybe we'll find out someday. Right now, it's not important," said Kelt. "It really doesn't matter anymore does it, Akhi? We're all in the same family now."

"I suppose you are right, Kelt. We *are* family now," she concurred.

"Hey, was that the same test I had to take?" asked Guy.

"Yes, it was," Rick affirmed.

"It was an easy test. I should have been able to score 100 percent, but I somehow missed a couple questions," Guy responded.

Yes, Guy was also a millenarian. Rick did not know why he looked older than the others did at his age. Rick himself was in his mid-50's and could easily pass as 30 if he wanted. Guy had the genes; they had confirmed it.

"Perhaps, it was because of the intense commando training in his early years," Rick thought.

All of those in attendance introduced themselves to the others. Working together, in a small population, they would soon get to know each other intimately.

"Shall we get the meeting started?" asked Amanda? Everyone pulled their chairs toward the table and straightened, except for Gary Johnson, well known for being a little odd and thinking very much outside the box. "Outside the box," meant stating the obvious when no one else could or would. Those on video feed just sort of clumped together in front of the video camera.

4- Little time left

"It was fortunate, we had the foresight to lift into space as many seed varieties, and frozen embryos of animals, that could be collected before the nuclear attacks," Amanda told those in attendance.

"Yes," added Shannon, "We didn't have much time, before everything went down the toilet, did we? We were all scrambling, trying to do everything... anything. I'm surprised that we managed as well as we have."

Most everyone nodded in acknowledgement. All had been guilty of pursuing ideas or issuing orders for things that had turned to dead ends. The frantic nature of the lift from Earth had severely stressed everyone, especially those in charge.

"Now we have seed stock and spores from nearly 30,000 varieties of plants. Naturally, food crops would come first to most people's reasoning, but plants usually require the aid of other plants, like mushrooms, grasses, or bushes nearby. You can't just put a seed in an empty field of dead Earth and expect it to grow. Plants need various bacteria to help feed their rootstock, insects to fertilize their flowers, predatory insects to eat those who might eat the plants. The list of requirements to grow a single plant seems endless," Amanda explained.

Of course, every biologist in attendance was well aware of these facts. The physicists in the room, and Guy Lerner with Sam Walsh on video link were unknowns. She wanted to make sure the fundamentals were covered before she moved on.

"During the past year, our priorities have shifted several times as we tried to first kill the virus, contain it, then try to find ways to lift our team members from Nevada Base and decontaminate them. It is now time to reorganize and put our priorities in place," explained Amanda. "Shannon and I, along with dozens of others, have been unrelenting in following up all the little details. Our lab sphere parked 350 kilometers away from us, is serving us pretty well for testing Earth based contaminated materials. It's not ideal, but we are getting good data. We have a couple of shuttles and several flitters servicing the sphere based out of Nevada," Amanda explained.

As she looked around the room, she realized many of the biologists didn't quite understand what flitters might be. Kelt noticed the same thing. In the rush to lift civilians to space, no one had the time to orient them properly, they were all learning as they went. Not even those in charge were fully organized.

"Before Amanda continues, let me show you what she is talking about," Kelt said as he picked up a portable cam unit, and walked out into the underground garage where several vessels were berthed in the Nevada bunker.

"Now, this is a shuttle. We have a few versions of these, but they can all carry people or equipment, and each has a hatch that can be lowered in back. Each has a locking ring on top of the craft that we use to connect to you folks up in space on your flight decks… or would if we weren't contaminated," he said as he scanned a small 12- person shuttle with his cam. "These, over here, are flitters." Kelt walked a few steps and pointed the cam toward a neat row of much smaller craft. "Some of these can carry two people and have some storage space, but most are much smaller, remotely controlled, and are well suited to carry small robots to do various things. Unlike the shuttles, they are more aerodynamic in nature. You can see two swept forward wings, and dual tails on the rear of each craft that help maneuver in air space. They actually do give us some lift even though the installed floaters provide all the momentum we need. Each craft sports an extended nose that runs to a sharp point. When I designed these, I thought it was just an aesthetic feature, but it turns out, we've been able to use those noses on many occasions," he was reminded of the first time he had killed another person. He had been sick about it for days. He still had nightmares about it, but let no one know.

"I hope this answers the unasked question I saw on some of your faces. Are there any other questions about the craft?" he asked.

"Ah, yes," one biologist spoke up, "What is a floater?"

Kelt realized that not everyone on board the floating cities had been exposed to the fundamental dimensional shift technology. With corporate espionage the way it was on Earth prior to the nuclear attacks, Rick Carter had kept a tight lid on every technological achievement. Development teams were often isolated from each other, so that no one could create a complete picture of the task at hand.

"Four members of the original five in the floater development team are here, in conference," Kelt started. "We have Akhi, Gary, Scott, or Scotty as many of us know him, and me. Akhi was the mind behind the advanced physics and the rest of us were sort of, along for the ride," he said as he tried to downplay the significance of his contributions. "To keep it simple, we developed and performed the first production run of these disks that float. We build these floaters into the structural integrity of whatever we need to move with them. All the flying craft, including the spires and spheres, use them," he furthered. "I'm sure that you all now have authorization to go through the summaries of those events to do a little catch up on the subject. The physics are certainly amazing… especially the dimensional shift material with the anti-entropic universe. I'm not kidding, it's pretty fascinating, so, go read it in your spare time," Kelt concluded.

"Well, I'm glad that we've been able to get through these pleasantries," Amanda noted with a small bite of irritation.

The meeting was off to a late start. She realized it was now necessary for everyone to work together. They must have the ability to reach out to other teams for help and advice. They needed at least a basic understanding of how they survived in space.

"The concept of isolating development and research must end here and now. I've talked to Mr. Carter and Kelt. We all agree that there will be no more secrets among researchers. So, if you have advice, data, or ideas to share with another team, do it. If you need help, send out a broadcast to the others. We've got a lot of work ahead of us."

Amanda looked at Shannon as she stood up to do her presentation.

"Amanda and I have made some estimates of the biomass remaining on land. It isn't all dead yet, but it is definitely dying. We can see the results of the virus running wild all around the globe," she explained as she flipped through live images shot from satellites around the world. "We can't say for sure, but we believe that within one year, all plant life will be infected or dead. That seems to fit the pattern," Shannon instructed, as she felt a pang of final realization hit suddenly in her gut. She had so far, denied to herself that this would really happen.

"Now," she went on, "it is extremely important for us to think about the life that remains in that biomass. We absolutely must make sure that enough bacteria, nematode worms, natural viruses, etc. continue to live. For nearly total oxidation of the biomass, we anticipate it will take about 10 years, excluding dead stands of trees. That's when the most of the little critters will have died. We see a few major problems in letting that happen," she advised.

"First of all, vast amounts of CO2 or carbon dioxide will be released into the atmosphere. It is very likely that it could make the air toxic for much of the remaining life after year seven. The second issue is even more disturbing. Once those simplest of life forms are extinct, we may no longer be able to recreate the ecosystem. We simply do not have enough sample variety or quantity of the little critters in our inventories to make it work. Once they die, it could literally take millions of years to repopulate the world. Earth has experienced many extinction level events in the past, and she has survived.

Each time, she has created vastly new life ecosystems." She furthered.

"Now, this is most important, people, we believe the tipping point will happen somewhere between years 4 and 5 of the new era. That means that within 5 years, these simple animal life forms will start dying in such numbers that we'll never be able to replace them. We've got to get viable plants growing dirtside immediately, whether they be edible or not," she said.

"How soon is immediately," asked Akhi.

"I hate to say this Akhi, but we have at most two years, and most likely, only within the next spring season in each hemisphere," Amanda said with a calamitous face.

The mood in the room dropped to a new low in the history of mankind. The news was devastating.

"Have we found out if the virus affects animals or sea life yet?" asked Sam Walsh from the Nevada site.

"So far, we have seen no ill side effects. Aquatic life will likely make a rebound since we seem to be harvesting less from the oceans. All of you down there at the spaceport seem to be perfectly healthy," she added.

"Spaceport… now that's a hoot. All we have is a big elevator into our bunker covered by an old warehouse. We never had time to develop our technology fully," Kelt thought.

"Now, this is also important," added Amanda, "We very likely have a limited life here in the floating cities. We simply do not have the materials or means to feed people for more than 20 years or so. We do not, I repeat, we do not have a viable ecosystem here. Look at the stations we have on Mars and the moon. They are merely smaller versions of the floating cities. We are constantly shipping them supplies that they need. They can't survive without us.

Eventually, we'll run out of raw materials, have crop failures, some disease will pop up, you name it. We do have a good store of food supplies, which could last us ten years all by itself. Our crops can make that another seven to ten years. Our chaos statistics indicate a high probability that we will run into unforeseen problems. We have never

36

had the opportunity to assure ourselves that we can build a self-contained ecosystem. That experience is learned through experience, and it could take decades before we fully understand what we need onboard to be self-sustaining," she said.

"I concur with my colleague, Amanda. I have come to the very same conclusions. We must get the ecosystem engine running again on Earth, within the next year or two. Otherwise, all remaining life on Earth is in serious trouble. This may well be an extinction level event of land based life," Shannon said.

Silent whispers spread through the room at the sudden reality of what Shannon had just said. Nearly everyone figured they could solve the problem in some way. After all, Rick Carter had brought the best of the best on board the floating cities. They had reassured themselves that the cities were fully self-sustaining. Kelt and Scotty stepped briefly away from the cam on Earth to exchange a few sentences with each other. Shannon noted that Gary had immediately picked up a call on his com. He stepped to the corner of the room and whispered. The three engineers were on conference.

Shannon continued when Kelt and Scotty had returned on the video link, and Gary had finished his call.

"Kelt, I know that you harvested some plants growing near the site where the libraries were buried," Shannon said. "How are they doing in your underground bunker?" she queried.

"Those weeds? I suppose that they are doing all right. None of them is edible, or at least none has any real nutritional value. They don't seem to be growing very fast, which is a surprise to me. They seem to be doing a whole lot better, where we took the samples near the old ruins on the Nile," Kelt responded.

Shannon picked up a live video feed from a floater cam hovering above the Nile site at 500 meters. She laid up the image they had first seen several weeks ago, and put the two side by side for everyone to see. It was obvious that everyone was looking at the images and attempting to ascertain the increase in growth. The plants weren't much, just some weeds really, but they were all different new species in the crop. All of the weeds did bear striking resemblance to species that had been wiped out, but they differed in many respects as to size, shape, flowers, and such. They certainly could not be categorized as species that were cataloged.

Scotty spoke up immediately, "For those of you trying to figure out the growth rate, we've already done that. It is seven percent over the past six weeks at the Nile site," he informed the group.

"Hmm, that's actually pretty good considering it is so late in the spring," remarked Amanda, "but letting that crop grow, won't do the job in our time frame. Kelt, can you check and make sure that you've duplicated the environment where you picked up those plants?" she asked.

"Damn, I hadn't thought of that," said Kelt. "Well, that was pretty stupid of me, wasn't it? We've neglected to do a number of things, I suppose. We just put them under some grow lights down here in the bunker. We'll get some of our civilians working on setting up a controlled environment room to mimic the Nile site. We'll set the temperature, daylight, humidity, and lighting conditions, so they are a complete match," he concluded.

"That's a good first step," said Amanda.

"I hate to bring this up," said Gary, "but has anyone considered why and how new varieties of plants just popped out of nowhere around the artifact?"

"We've examined the libraries from top to bottom, Gary. We've put every measuring device we can up next to the artifact and get nothing. We've parked it under the plants we are growing and under newly planted potato eyelets. We've even exposed it to seed laden soil from top side, but nothing happens," Kelt explained.

"That artifact is a mystery and yet its technology must..." Gary said as his thoughts wandered.

One of the other biologists, Henry Wagner, in the conference room spoke up.

"You know, it wouldn't hurt to set up a real biology lab down there. You might even use an existing lab if it isn't surrounded by..." and his thoughts trailed as he thought of people murdering each other for food.

Shannon furthered Henry's thought.

"Kelt, we really need an Earth based lab. Our sphere that we've been using is great, but we really need the human interaction. The robotics just can't handle what we need, the way we'd like. We had originally thought we could lower the sphere and let some of you aboard to perform the tests, but with the situation down there as hot as it is, we don't believe that the sphere would be safe. Neither would you folks attempting to use it. It is obviously rather large and easily noticed."

"I know this is going to be difficult for those of you on the ground, but we need lab space in your bunker. We're going to need the works. I can send you the specs and a complete list of what we need," Amanda said.

"No problem, Amanda, we've done it before, and we have plenty of extra space in this mine," Kelt said as he recalled the lab setups he had performed for Shannon and Amanda in the past. He even knew how to build a containment lab if it came to that.

"We'll need a DNA sequencer as well," Amanda told him. The team had not the forethought to put a DNA sequencer on board the floating lab. The structure of the sphere had been pretty much been designed and built around the electron microscope. The lab sphere had been set up for use in the original infection site in the Amazon. Surprisingly, it had survived the Amazon firebombing and it was still fully functional. Setting up the equipment for sequencing DNA and all its associated computing power in the Nevada bunker, seemed entirely possible.

"You wouldn't happen to have an extra sequencer on board one of the cities, would you?" Kelt asked.

"As a matter of fact, we don't even have a single DNA sequencer here, for ourselves," Amanda lamented. "We had a couple of them ordered and packed when those nukes went off in Africa. We had to leave them behind," she concluded.

"Can't we go get those sequencers? Aren't they just sitting there ready to be picked up?" Akhi asked.

"I'm afraid that the site was overrun with gangs and destroyed in a fire." Amanda said.

"Well, shoot, we don't have to buy a sequencer, do we now?" Kelt said with a slight grin, "We'll just do a midnight requisition," he said.

In the early years of computing, engineers had resorted to pulling parts and completed assemblies from the production lines, when their budgets had been slashed to the bone. This theft was usually done at night and was dubbed a 'midnight requisition'. Kelt had picked up this slang somewhere in his short career. "It may have been with some of the older computer geeks I met at the New Zealand facility," he recalled. Scotty beamed as Kelt had made the statement. He knew full well what it meant, even though Scott remembered the story from common military legend.

"I don't know how busy the research teams are, here dirtside, but I'll call around and try to contact the different labs. If we don't get an answer, we'll drop in at night and pay 'em a visit," Guy said beaming with a smile, finally able to participate.

The meeting went on for another three hours. For the next ninety minutes, Shannon and Amanda held an idea session. Every suggestion anyone made would be put up on a white board without comment. For the next ninety minutes, the committee selected the most viable ideas and passed out assignments to each member, who would go back to their team and start the tedious research that had suddenly taken on a path of mandatory success. They were now fully committed to succeeding or letting humankind fade into oblivion.

The first action item was to spread as many of the new plants from the Nile site to as many different parts of the world as possible. The act seemed a futile hope at best, but it was a start.

40

5- The Artifact

Kelt had been studying the artifact that had now become known as the library of history. Aldo, his mentor had been shuffling notes electronically to him since the artifact was found. Kelt had an unusual way of looking at things, always looking from the top down instead of the bottom up.

His fascination with the old language was with its mathematics. The other students were learning the language as a child might, the mathematics were covered in more detail later. Kelt was going backwards and there was a reason. Physics and mathematics are universally true. While he understood that he was not as knowledgeable in the various fields of math and physics as his closest friends, he could see and understand unusual patterns where they could not. His approach to the macro view was certainly not unique in the history of mankind. However, it was solidly his domain now with the artifact. No one could match *this* expertise. He looked up symbols as he ran into problems he could not understand. He would crash into every roadblock possible before he would go back to the reference materials. He did not want the instruction to taint his growing view in the understanding of the ones who spoke the old language.

After their introduction to the device where they had learned the library only contained the history of the world, Kelt had felt extreme despair.

"I'll never hold my Akhi in my arms again," was his first thought. He did love her unreservedly. He also felt an incredible weight of responsibility on his shoulders to save the world. Not much time was left, regardless what he was told. "Yes, I will do everything that I possibly can to win this battle, but I must discover the secrets of this device. There has to be an answer here." This thought consumed every minute of every day. When he wasn't thinking of his lovely Akhi, his mind was boiling with thoughts of the mathematics. How could they be applicable to his cause? And why were those weeds growing around the device when they found it?

Kelt moved his hand over the obsidian like exterior of the artifact. There was a "direct connection" mentioned on the exterior in characters of the old language. In fact, there were explicit instructions for the direct interface. Until now, no one understood them, for they were purely mathematical in nature. The old language was foreign to modern human concepts of what a language was supposed to be. It was filled with mathematics and physics in normal speech. Everyone had a hard time understanding this abstract intuitiveness of such notions. He had found descriptions in old notes, videos, and through direct contact with Aldo, the oldest of all known living. He had discovered descriptions, formulas, or language for perhaps seventy percent of those symbols in the artifact's instructions, from the materials that Aldo had prepared and hoarded over the centuries.

He understood part of an equation. He could see the answer in his head. It made sense to him in an odd sort of way. He played with the symbols, attempting to resolve their meaning with simple algebraic techniques. This was significantly important, and he knew it. He knew that the library would only let his mind access what they could see on video monitors. He also believed that he might see more, feel more, hear more, and understand its fundamental workings. The first step was the direct connection. That was his task. That was his priority. It was becoming a secret life.

His mind wandered as he tried to sort through his priorities. Akhi, of course would always be first. This task should be his second, and everything else should come in dead last. However, Akhi was secure in the floating cities far above the atmosphere, safe from the raging virus killing plant life on Earth. This task of exploration was always interrupted by the demands of his command. The responsibility had come as a default. He accepted it unknowingly when everyone looked to him for direction.

"I've been pulled away every day to work on other things, and you, you my friend seem to be last on the list," he said as he let his finger trace the shape of the Culinari character. Aldo told him that the character meant a person or perhaps a human.

"Didn't the old ones call themselves Culinari?" Kelt asked himself. The value was used as a constant as it appeared in the equation. "It can't be a constant. It doesn't follow this fragment of the equation," he surmised.

"So, the character translates to human or Culinari or... Wait a minute," Kelt exclaimed verbally. "Culinari is singular or plural. It's just like the word data... that word can be used in a singular or plural way. The word human is definitely singular, so where am I going with this? What is constant about this apparent variable?" Kelt thought deeply about the ostensible incongruities of his thoughts and definitions.

"It's a name," he finally realized. "I am Culinari, and my name is Kelt," he said to the device realizing he would receive no reply. Indeed, he received none. "This is a path worth pursuing. What does this equation fragment do in context? I understand its flow..." Kelt's thoughts wandered wildly with the fragment as he closed his eyes. It pushed itself into his brain, weaving its way, forming synapses, creating new channels for his thoughts to roam where they never had. Finally, he could see it. He could see his own name within his mind. The characters were not there, he had no association with any external frame of reference. A series of four figures or characters in a long sequence, combined in an intuitive, yet complex formula, identified himself to the device. He opened his eyes and could see. He saw his own history of Akhi and himself in the music room back at the Stanford lab. It was as he remembered. It was unlike the monitor image of what he could call up from the external video feed. Everything was three-dimensional. He saw everything just as he had seen it. He was in.

6- Cheetah cubs

Akhi had just finished a very short lunch and she was hurrying to join another meeting on her schedule. It seemed that she was more involved in meetings than doing real work.

"Hello, Pumpkin," Rick opened.

"Hi, Daddy, make it quick 'cause I'm running late for a meeting," Akhi advised.

"Akhi, I perused your schedule. Hand this off to someone else today. I'm sure that waste recycling doesn't demand your attention at the moment. I have an assignment that does."

Akhi slowed her pace wondering what emergency might pull her in now.

"Daddy, I don't know how I can squeeze anything else in."

"Sweetheart, this is important, and I really want you to take on an additional responsibility."

Akhi stopped walking forward and started to pace back and forth in the corridor. She had acquired the nervous habit when she focused her attentions. She had discovered that pacing and thinking brought out her best in critical thought.

"Okay, Daddy. What's up?"

"Akhi, I'd like you to go down to the livestock pens. Amanda Perry is down there and needs to talk to you."

"What is she doing down there, Daddy? What could she possibly want...? Oh, don't tell me that something has happened to the animals. They aren't infected are they?" she asked in anguish.

"No, Pumpkin. She just needs some help with some of them, and I thought you should give her a hand. Take this assignment seriously," he advised.

"Okay, I can meet her in ten minutes or so. I'll go straight there," she responded with great reservation. She just didn't have time to play with the animals. There was too much that currently demanded her attention.

Akhi sent a note to someone to take charge of her meeting, turned around, and headed for the lift in the spire. Ten minutes later, she entered the sphere where the livestock was held. She was ashamed to admit it, but she had never been down here before. As she stepped out into the middle level, she was surprised to see no pens or animals. The entire space had been set aside as storage for grains, hay, straw, and freezer space. The heavy scent of hay permeated her sense of smell. It was pleasant and reminded her slightly of a cattle barn she had visited on her father's New Zealand Island. This barn was spotless in comparison, however. The hay bales were all stacked on pallets. All the grains were stored in large organized containers. The floor had a spotless shine. Everything was packed and stored with efficiency demanded by their current needs. Two men were active, moving hay to a service lift within the sphere, but she saw no one else.

"Gotchya!" Amanda squealed as she poked Akhi on her shoulder from behind. Akhi screamed in laughter, and turned to face her friend.

"Amanda! Shame on you! You nearly scared me to death."

"Geez, Akhi, I never get to see you anymore! Don't you think we should have some fun once in a while?" Amanda demanded.

"Who's got the time?"

"You do, my dear! I talked to your father and he has given you an important assignment. C'mon, follow me." Amanda grabbed Akhi's hand and pulled her to a personnel lift nearby. "We need to go up two levels," Amanda advised.

"Oh, Amanda, what are we doing?"

"Don't ask questions. Hurry up!"

The two young women stepped from the lift, and the smell of the animals was not pleasant.

"Oh, Amanda, it stinks here!"

"You can be such a sissy, Akhi. I thought you were a tomboy."

"Tomboy?" accused Akhi, "I'm no tomboy! Why would you ever think that?" she continued as the pair walked down the aisles making a right and then a left deep into the sphere's zoological level.

"I'm sorry, Akhi. I've just never seen you dressed in foo. Don't get me wrong, you wear your flight suits well, but I've never seen you dressed in anything else. I've never seen a touch of makeup or eye shadow, and your hair is always styled the same way. That screams tomboy to me!" Amanda giggled.

"It's *wash-n-wear* hair, it needs no styling," Akhi grinned deviously.

"I should be so lucky, dear. I spend way too much time on mine every day," Amanda returned.

"Oh, here we are," Amanda advised as she slowed, "Look in this pen, Akhi." The two peered in through the metal grating at two small cheetah cubs lying in stupefied boredom.

"Oh, they are adorable, Amanda!" Akhi squealed.

"Here, sit down and let me open the cage door. Let's play!" Amanda returned. Akhi forgot her cares immediately and anxiously waited to play with the cubs. The two small plush toys just lay there with glazed eyes.

"They lost their mother this morning, Akhi. They haven't been weaned yet. Poor things."

Akhi's wide smile immediately inverted to a frown of concern. A wall of water filled her eyes.

"Amanda, it's not fair. So much has been lost. Was the mother infected with the virus? Will we lose these precious cats too?"

"No, their mother died from injuries sustained during her capture. And… my dear, we shall not lose these cubs, because you are going to take care of them."

Akhi waved her hands in protest.

"Amanda, I don't' have time to wean them! How often do they need to be fed? Four or five times a day?" Akhi demanded.

"At least that, Akhi… perhaps more. It depends on how much formula you can get into them. Now, before you say no, remember that your father has tasked you to do this," Amanda warned.

Amanda retrieved two bottles of prepared formula that had been set on top of the cage.

"Now, Akhi, let's play," she commanded, "Do what I do," she advised as she reached into the cage. Amanda grabbed one of the cubs by the nape of its neck and lifted it out of the cage into her lap. "This one is a male and the other is a female." She stuck the bottle's nipple into the cat's mouth. The cub did not take it. Creamy fluid flowed from its mouth and into Amanda's lap.

"Have you fed them before?" Akhi asked.

"No, this is their first feeding. I've never really been exposed to wild animals."

"Here, let me try, Amanda."

Akhi grabbed the cub firmly by the nape of the neck and pulled the little fellow to her chest. She cuddled and cooed as she stroked the baby's stomach. His eyes came alive as he started to purr. He licked her hand. His tongue felt like a wire brush on Akhi's delicate skin. She winced, but did not jerk. She did not want to scare the cub. Akhi demanded the bottle from Amanda, and she teased it into the cub's mouth where he took it eagerly.

"You're a natural, Akhi," Amanda grinned, "How did you know what to do?"

"I don't know how to take care of animals. I just figured it needed a little love and attention."

"Well, he certainly has taken to you," Amanda said as she directed Akhi's attention to the cub's eyes. He followed every movement of her face as he purred. The bottle emptied quickly.

"How much do they take, Amanda?"

"You'll know when they don't want any more," Amanda replied, "here's another bottle."

Akhi snatched the bottle and switched it quickly, just as the last drops were harvested by the cub's hungry tongue. "Look, he's slowing down now. He's only taken a little of this bottle!" Akhi exclaimed.

A broad smile returned to her face. The rosy color of happiness flushed her cheeks.

"Here, Amanda, you burp him while I feed this baby girl," Akhi grinned as she passed the cub over and reached into the cage. The second cub initially resisted the bottle, but after a few moments of motherly attention from Akhi, the cub succumbed to hunger. She nearly drained the bottle of the formula. "Perhaps, we should get bigger bottles. What do you think?"

"This is all we have, Akhi."

"I understand."

"Do they have names?" Akhi queried.

"No, I suppose that will be part of your job."

"Where will I keep them? I can't come down here several times a day!" Akhi demanded in desperation.

"In your personal quarters, my dear. We have someone who will help you train them, teach you how to clean and groom them, and show you how to prepare the formula."

"I'm not sure that I can devote the time. Really, I've got so much going on that sometimes, I don't know which way I'm going."

"Akhi, remember your lab at Stanford? Do you recall that you were told to take time each day to pursue your musical interests?"

"Sure, but these cubs sure don't look like a piano to me."

"Have you been interested in even looking at a piano lately?"

Akhi's facial expressions turned morose. "The piano reminds me too much of Kelt. We played a lot of music during down time when we were working together. I can't bring myself to sit down and play for my own interests... at least for now," Akhi advised.

"And that is why you get the cubs, Akhi. They need you too. Now before you ask the question that I know is rolling in your eyes, the answer is yes, you have to take them both. We think they'll be happier together. Look, see?" Amanda said as she glanced toward the babies playing cub games on the floor in front of them. "For what it is worth, I've been assigned a young falcon to tend, for many of the same reasons."

"A falcon? You've got to be kidding. I can imagine you showing up on the bridge with a falcon in hunter's garb. Amanda, you have to admit, it sounds like a teaser right out of a corny sci-fi fantasy!" Akhi teased.

"And what about you with your cats, my dear? What will people say about you when you stroll into the CIC with them?" Amanda chided waving her hand toward the playful cubs.

"Well, after they grow up, I would imagine they won't say anything," Akhi barely managed to say before breaking out in boisterous laughter.

"He shall be known as Chanto and she will be Freia," Akhi announced with a more serious royal tone.

"So be it," responded Amanda.

7- Fire!

"Hey Kelt, Guy… c'mon over here and look at this!" Scotty demanded as he was watching the broadcast from CNN.

The video feed showed the Rocky Mountain forests near Yellowstone in a fiery blaze, with choking smoke. The shot was from a news helicopter several miles from the conflagration. As the cameraman zoomed in closely, the group could see men setting fires at the bases of the hills.

"What are they doing? Are they crazy?" Kelt asked.

"They're trying to scare out the game. Armed men stationed at the tops of the hills are shooting everything that comes out of the forest. At least, that's what they said earlier," Scotty answered.

"Those idiots will die," Guy said flatly. "By the time that fire gets to the summit, it will be so hot that they'll be broiled alive.

"These fires were started by local hunters earlier today near Yellowstone National Park…" the CNN anchor droned on.

"Local hunters, my eye, Guy said. Look how many of them are out there. Look at the hundreds of cars and trucks. These people don't have a clue what they are doing. An experienced hunter could take down two or three deer in a day. These are good old fashioned mindless gangs, with a mob mentality."

"Crap!" Look at that! There's ten or twelve guys caught in a hot spot!" Scotty exclaimed as the camera zoomed in on them. Fire surrounded them on the hilltop and quickly engulfed them.

"Why are they broadcasting that?" Kelt demanded, "That is totally inappropriate."

"Why? It sells advertising, Kelt. You know that. And with a disaster like this, no one will censor them," Guy admonished.

The video feed remained active as the men were burned to death.

"Turn up the sound, Scotty," Guy asked.

"... all persons caught setting fires will be shot on site by the National Guard," continued the reporter. "We now go to Seth Hanguard in Oregon. Can you tell us what is happening there, Seth?"

"Yes, Connie, fires have been set in more than two dozen locations. While the hunters are somewhat successful in capturing some of the local game, it seems that most of the animals are perishing in the flames. None of the fires here, in Oregon, is considered contained. According to the authorities, adequate resources are not available to fight so many fires at once."

"We have a similar situation here, Seth. The fires are so spread out and there just isn't anyone left to fight them."

"They'll burn and burn until every tree is a smoldering skeleton," Guy determined.

"That's going to add to our CO2 problem, guys," Kelt started, "I wonder how much CO2 is going to be thrown into the atmosphere from this crap. Will we be breathing next week?"

The question went unanswered.

"... want to remind everyone, that there will be no mercy for these acts of what we consider terrorism. President Crawford has just declared that we are now under Martial Law. The president assures us that these terrorists will be shot on site."

"Connie, we have reports that fires are being started in the south-eastern states as well," Seth added with haste. "We don't have news teams on site, but they are on their way."

"Great. The virus isn't enough. We've got to burn our planet to cinders," Scotty grunted. "I wonder when they'll start bombing each other."

"Soon enough," Guy responded.

Sam had been topside checking the security cams on the building and had returned. As he entered the CIC he blurted, "Damn, guys, it smells like a forest fire topside. Where's the nearest forest from this God forsaken desert?"

"Wyoming, Sam." Scotty answered.

"You have got to be kidding me. Wyoming? That's got to be some fire to be able to smell it from here."

"Take a seat and see for yourself, Sam," Kelt offered.

"Oh, this should be good," Guy started as National Guard troops rolled into an alpine valley in a parade of military trucks and Hummers.

"Do you think they'll open up on 'em?" Scotty asked.

"I can't imagine that they would... would they?" Sam asked. Kelt stared at Guy with the same question written in his face.

"I suppose we'll find out, won't we?" Guy answered.

As they sat in astonishment, several of the hunters started taking pot shots at the guardsmen. A skirmish soon broke out with the guard as it assumed a defensive status. The hunters in the open were mercilessly gunned down. There were more civilians with weapons, than there were guardsmen in the surrounding area, and a full-scale engagement quickly ensued. The fight lasted a half hour with dimwit commentary from the inexperienced anchor. Shortly after the last guardsman dropped from several wounds to his legs and head, the news helicopter was shot down with some sort of missile.

"Did you see that?" Kelt asked in amazement. "Where in the world did they get anti-aircraft weapons?"

"I think that was a grenade launched from an M320," Guy whispered. "Kelt, never forget. We live in the land of the free and the well-armed. I'm afraid that we're going to have to face some real threats soon. We've been very lucky so far.

*****

"Have you been keeping track of what's going on down here?" Kelt asked Akhi.

"I was advised a few minutes ago, Kelt. I just don't know what to say. Are they really killing each other?"

"I'm afraid they are. That's not the worst of it. Our people down here tell me that these fires are going to burn for some time to come. They were started in several locations. Usually, just one fire, started from a single source, can burn hundreds or thousands of acres. But with so many of them... well, we think there won't be much left of the great forests of Montana and Wyoming. Oregon was assaulted as well, from what I understand. Our news reception isn't the greatest. They are only broadcasting a few hours a day now."

"The same is happening down in the southeast, Kelt. There hasn't been much on the networks about it, but we see heavy smoke covering several states," Akhi noted.

"You don't suppose that people in other countries will try anything like this, do you? I mean, if we set the world on fire, we won't be able to breathe... will we?"

"I don't know Kelt. I know that it was a terrible thing to show those people burning to death and then broadcast every detail of the shootout like that, but perhaps, it might serve to show others the fallacy of such actions."

"I hope so. I just wish that we could get better organized down here. The government doesn't seem to want to work with us, and we've had very little luck in contacting any of the research facilities. Everything is just going to... well you know..."

"I understand, my darling."

Kelt smiled. It used to drive him crazy when she called him "my darling." Now it warmed his heart and gave him hope. He had been able to curb his genetic urges and deal with his current situation. Sometimes he wondered if he were normal. Certainly, others he knew couldn't quell their sexual urges so efficiently. Sure, he had feelings, but he knew that there would be a time and a place where he could let go. For the moment, only the longing to be with his beloved burned in his heart.

"Sweetie, have you talked to our climatologists up there about the effects these fires might have on our oxygen supply?"

"Kelt, you know we don't have any climatologists on board any of the cities. I assume you are referring to Amanda and Shannon?"

"Yeah, I suppose so."

"They don't have a clue, my love. They are doing some rough calculations, but I've asked them not to spend more than a few hours on it. All they'll be doing is wasting time, if you catch my drift."

"I do, Akhi. We have no control on what dirtside people will do. We should be working on solutions rather than on projections at this point."

"Hey, Kelt. I'd like to change the subject to something a little more light-hearted."

"Now, that I can deal with. What's up, sweetie?"

"Look here," Akhi said as she bent down and retrieved Chanto, who was demanding attention. She held him up in front of the monitor camera.

"Is that a cheetah cub?"

"It is, Kelt. I have two of them. Their mother died and Daddy asked me to take care of them. I guess he figured that I didn't have enough to do, and needed a hobby or something. Seriously, they have cheered me up considerably. This is the male cub, and his name is Chanto." Akhi bent down and placed the cub onto the floor. Freia immediately jumped toward her in a false attack, and she grabbed her by the nape of her neck. Akhi held her up in front of the camera so that Kelt could see. "This is Freia."

"Those are pretty silly names. Where did they come from?"

Akhi felt somewhat embarrassed.

"I named them, Kelt."

Kelt's face turned red, as Akhi recovered from her sense of humiliation and appreciated his foot in mouth proclamation and resulting shame.

"I don't know, Kelt. The names just came to me when I picked them up. Amanda helped me learn to care for them."

"Are they staying in your quarters?"

"Yes."

"I bet it smells really nice."

"Actually, they are doing really well, Kelt. They are using a litter box, and they groom themselves and each other quite regularly. Yes, you can tell animals live here as soon as you enter the cabin, but it isn't as offensive as you might think."

"I'm very happy for you, Akhi. It is a most welcome diversion, I'm sure."

"They go with me everywhere I go, Kelt. I'm their mother now. Ever since I gave them their first bottle, they've bonded to me, and I can't shake them. Our zoologist says that's pretty normal. He said that I can leave them alone between feedings, but the people up here love to see them so much, I just can't bear to leave them in my quarters. They are truly a lot of fun."

"All I've got down here, Akhi is a bunch of straggler humans," Kelt smiled. "They are all potty trained and regularly take showers," Kelt added with a boisterous laugh.

*****

The fires raged for weeks and as the group had guessed, most of the forests in Montana and Wyoming had burned. In the South East, the devastation was nearly as bad. Fortunately, no other massive fires were started. The rest of the world watched on in horror, as the perpetrators were summarily shot on site by troopers and guard units. With Martial Law still in effect, the president had called on the military to dispense justice. They swarmed the countryside attempting to maintain order.

8- Defensive Action

Will Grayson had just been assigned the helm at City B.

Until now, the CIC had no real structure. Assignments had been made to monitor the spacecraft, and those appointed had performed admirably, considering that none of them had any specific training for the task.

The experts in infrastructure support, those assigned to environmental systems, waste management, logistics, and that sort of thing performed with great efficiency. The others were somewhat lost. There had been no command hierarchy and no training.

Will had served in the army as a commissioned officer, and although he was small in stature, at 5'6", he certainly commanded attention in his demeanor and brilliant stare. He decided that a six-year stint in the military was well worth the price the government paid for his college education. He had no way to pay for college, and the ROTC program promised him both college expenses and an adventure in the armed services upon graduation.

Although he was a genial chap in civilian life, he instantly commanded respect when called upon to lead. While commanding, he did not mince words. He had never dressed down a subordinate, as his subordinates seldom required discipline. His motto was "Soldiers rise to their commander's expectations." His expectations were tough, but reasonable. Soldiers in his command respected his attitude and did rise to his expectations. Will was a natural commander.

There were no official ranks within the Space Truck organization, but it was a need left unfulfilled. So far, Rick Carter had been in charge, but he was not cut out to command space vessels. His expertise was in finance and managing his companies. Rick and his staff decided to reorganize part of the company along military lines. Will had been given the title of "Commander," and all CIC staff was required to address him as sir.

Carter had realized, there was really little to do at the moment. That was of course, based on the assumption that all that was needed was to maintain the cities at their current position of 500 kilometers above the Earth in its shadow. That was accomplished by the computing systems and the network of floaters and locks. Humans would only monitor from time to time. Still, every organization needed a command hierarchy, even if the operations were mundane.

Upon taking command, Will felt the obvious need for defensive strategies because what they had, were none. The cities were sitting ducks. Not only did they have no weapons, but also they had no "eyes" for potential threats.

"Who's going to attack us, Will? What good would it do them? They won't gain anything if we fall to the ground," Akhi insisted.

"I'll tell you who, ma'am," Will started "Anyone… The world is going crazy down there. Just look at those people who started the fires. Do you think they really thought that through? Had they planned, they could have had their best sharp shooters planted in those forests. They would have plenty to eat for a long time. Instead, think of all the deer, buffalo, and other game that was burned to death. That's not even counting the meaningless loss of human life in the fires and in the skirmishes. We must develop defensive strategies. I've talked to Guy Lerner, and he's asked me to talk to you. He passed along some ideas, and I'd like to share them with you to see what we can implement."

"Okay, Will. I understand. What can I do to help?"

"The first thing we need to talk about is the fact that we are up here blind. We couldn't see a threat if it were parked on our proverbial doorstep."

"We can see what's going on, Will. We've got floater cams around the world watching the Earth."

"Ma'am, we have nothing protecting us, though. We need some sort of sensor network watching out for the cities. If they sent us a missile surprise, we might not ever know it is coming."

"I see what you mean. So we need some sort of sensor network watching all around us, right?"

"Right."

"Okay, Will. Let's do this. We can outfit more floaters with sensitive cameras and place them around the cities. Would that work?"

"To some degree, Ma'am. We need Radar, heat sensors, X-ray sensors, the works. Suppose some rock is inbound from the Ort cloud, or what if someone brought down a satellite from orbit in an attempt to destroy us? What would it take to see it, and move the cities in time? Think about the extended range. Imaging technology may not be sufficient."

"I have to admit, I've not thought about those situations. I've been occupied trying to solve other technical problems. Will, I appreciate that you have brought this to my attention with your well-considered judgment."

The cheetah cubs were fighting for attention as one jumped to her lap and the other knocked it off. "Chanto, Freia, lay down!" Akhi commanded. Freia dropped to the floor, and the cubs lay down, one on each side of her feet. "Sorry, Will. I was assigned to take care of these animals. I'll never know why."

Through the video link, Will couldn't see everything as it happened, but he had heard the rumors of her latest assignment.

"I sympathize with you, Ma'am. Everyone has been talking about our chief physicist and her pets. I'm sure it's quite a sight wherever you go."

"It is, and it's a welcome distraction for many. At this moment, they're just a pain in the rear. They want to be fed, and they don't want to wait. I'm sorry for getting off topic… So, we need some sensor arrays. I understand. I have people who can put them together. Let me see…" Akhi scrolled through the list of personnel to find the right people for the task at hand. "Here are two contacts I'd like you to work with. Hold on a sec as I send them notices… they've been working on new projects." Akhi quickly typed the messages, reassigning two engineers and five technicians to build sensor arrays. She also indicated in the message that Commander Will Grayson would be in command of the project. She sent the messages. It had taken but a few moments.

"Will, I'm sending you a copy of the request. The names of those assigned are enclosed. Tell them what you need, ask them for suggestions, and get it done. I will assume that you won't get too involved in the development. Please make sure to delegate."

"No problem, Ma'am. I appreciate it. Now, that's just the first of several issues I need to discuss with you."

"Will… remember how I asked you to delegate?"

"Yes ma'am."

"Do it. Work with the commanders of the other four cities. Keep me posted. I trust you to get the job done. If you need special resources, then pass the request along. I'll take care of it right away or pass it along to someone who can. Will that work for you?"

"Yes ma'am!" Will answered with an upbeat voice. In the army, he'd always had to deal with an endless stack of paperwork and approvals. One time, he had to wait several months for a schematic, as the request was passed up the ranks through the hands of three contractors, and then back down. He had just been given a full command with the ability to work without hindrance. "It's a pleasure ma'am, to work with you."

"Look, Will. You have a job to do. I know little about what it entails. There will be times when you'll need to educate me about what needs to be done. This is not one of those times, you know better than I what you need to do. So, just get it done. Remember, don't spend a lot of time on status reports, a few sentences are fine."

"Thank you, ma'am. You won't be disappointed in me."

"You are most welcome, Commander."

Commander Grayson took great pride in his work. Within just a few days working with the commanders from the other three cities, he had put together a defensive strategy. The people that Akhi put at his disposal had positioned a few dozen floaters loaded with sensors in a variety of distances from the cities. Several were placed directly around the cities, others were sent higher to strategic positions above the orbiting satellites. Finally, seven telescopic satellites were placed well into space for asteroid and meteor detection. All sensor floaters could be configured together to focus on a single object. With their ability to do interferometry, they had tremendous resolution capabilities. For now, they were positioned to cover as much area as possible surrounding the cities.

Will paid particular attention to the orbiting satellites and space junk, as all of these objects were well documented. Free software had been available for years that tracked most of the objects circling the Earth. Knowing it was there, and watching it were two different things. The satellites traveled at tremendous speeds, tens of thousands of kilometers per hour. The floating cities did not. The satellites and space junk sped around the planet well above the cities and were potential lethal weapons.

Defensively, all that could be done was move the cities, should an object come hurdling at them. Certainly, no weapon could effectively deal with such an object. Sure, you could shoot a projectile at an inbound metallic object and break it up, but that didn't necessarily mean that its parts would change their course. Weapons were not needed as far as the four commanders decided, their skills and knowledge in evasion would serve more effectively.

9- DNA sequencer

"Hey, Kelt, I've got us a DNA sequencer!" yelled Guy across the room.

"Really? You've just started your calling. That's a fortunate piece of luck!" Kelt said excitedly. "So, what's the scoop?"

"I called MIT, someone answered, and I asked if they had one to spare. They passed me around a bit and finally I was able to find someone who said we could use theirs. They said they'll even load it for us."

Guy had been using a laser uplink to the floating cities, and from there, a phone call could be made through standard communications methods. Phone calls would not be sourced to their current location.

They had also been extremely careful in their excursions. There had been no activity in daylight hours ever, since the nuclear attack on Africa. The only exception had been when Sam Walsh had come to the door of the abandoned warehouse above the bunker and knocked on the door. Guy had advised that the majority of the spy satellites used daylight imaging equipment. The spook birds could do night time thermal imaging, but their course would need to be carefully managed by the secretive agencies, to image an area from space... and that could be done only as the birds passed overhead in orbit. Pacificus was tracking those and keeping them updated as to their positions. They had reasoned that the CIA or NSA could only manage to watch the bunker site occasionally as a result, and when they did, no one would be home. The bunker was covered by the large warehouse, but the floor served as a giant elevator, to lower their flying craft and materials 100 meters to the underground bunker. All flights were run only at night, hopefully protecting the Space Truck shuttles and flitters from detection.

It was a given that they were paranoid about interacting with people on the surface. Kelt thought about it a moment. He could analyze situations even when there wasn't a situation.

"We need to think about this Guy. The Boston area is still heavily populated. I'd really rather not set down and be mugged, if you know what I mean," he explained.

"I hear you loud and clear, Kelt. I've been worried about going topside for those very reasons. I've just started to reconsider this whole thing. It seems far too easy."

"You know that someone is going to come after us sooner or later don't you, Guy? I mean, they know we were lifting supplies into space from this site. I'd really like to make sure we hold on to all of our assets, including your commandos," Kelt offered.

"I know. I've been worried about the same thing. I used convinced Rick to drop my teammates and myself from Pacificus for that very reason. I felt that I had a duty to protect the members of the team. I know that there will be people after our food, and more importantly, our technology. I can't imagine why they haven't come out for at least a lookie-see."

"I'm sure they'll be along sooner or later, Guy."

"Meanwhile… Hey have we got any floater cams anywhere near the site where that electron scope resides?"

Guy checked the status of floater cams in the vicinity. "We've got one just ten clicks out," he told Kelt.

"Great! Let's move that puppy up toward the site. Once we get it in view, we'll drop down to 1000 meters. That should give us some recon video within a minute or two," Kelt explained.

Guy started to perform the maneuver, and it was only moments before the floater cam brought the building into view.

"Okay, let's just glide directly over to the site. Wc are recording, aren't we?"

"You know better than that," said Guy with a tone of some annoyance. "I know to have that recorder on," he said flatly.

"Okay, Guy, I'm sorry, but I just wanted to make sure."

"No problem, sir."

Kelt hated it when Guy called him sir and he'd address Kelt as sir about half the time. The chain of command had been engrained in Guy for his entire adulthood. His life had depended on that chain of command and his superior officers had earned his respect, so he called them "sir." Guy, 49 years old now, with a few gray hairs and skin tough as leather, considered this young teenager "sir."

Kelt had saved his team in the Mediterranean just last year and in that engagement, Kelt had assumed command and dealt with the mercenary attack with experienced aptitude.

"No, he's not deriding me by calling me sir. I'm his commander, whether I like it or not," sighed Kelt under his breath.

"Please, Guy, don't call me "sir" when we're alone together. You can do it when we need it if you have to. Really, my name "Kelt" and the word "sir" are both just one syllable long, so it's not any harder to say," Kelt pleaded.

"Okay, *sir*," Guy responded with a grin. "Here we go Kelt, we've got a good clean image of the site."

"It looks like we were right, sir. Look at that. We've got ourselves a couple of Army Ranger squads for dinner."

"Yeah, there they go, right into the building. Their conveyance has disappeared as well," Kelt said.

"Conveyance, what's that?" asked Guy. "The vehicles they came in, Guy, their Hummers and trucks," Kelt informed.

"Oh, okay. I'd just never heard the word, sir."

"Okay, that one was a dig," thought Kelt.

"I thought we had a deal with the president, that the military wouldn't get involved in our materials procurement," Kelt said

"Kelt, that was some time back and we have a new president. Look, now that they are in the building, they'll cover every entrance and exit. They'll be invisible, even to the people who might be in there. I wonder what they want from us?" Guy asked.

"I don't know. I suppose they think that we are holding back lifesaving technologies."

"I think it highly unlikely they are there to protect us, Kelt. The way they moved in and took position indicates an aggressive attitude. Ultimately, some higher up may want to seize one of the floating cities," Guy surmised.

"Surely, they know that no one has an easy solution to this world wide problem. Let's scrub this attempt," Kelt advised.

"Acknowledged, sir. Maybe they think we have magic."

"Now that is the funniest thing I've heard all day, Guy... we have magic. I suppose that to many, we do have magic with our technology."

"Boy, we're pretty short on humor around here, if you think that's funny, sir. You know, we should be better prepared down in this bunker. Our defense plan requires us to be on the surface to fight. That is untenable. We have no means of escape other than the elevator to the warehouse, and besides that, we've got all these supplies we're sitting on. Most importantly, we've got the only research lab growing plants that can survive topside... well sort of," Guy explained.

"I know that it is only a "sort of" lab, Guy, but I've got a crew of civilians in there implementing Shannon and Amanda's recommendations. That will come together and we'll make improvements. You are correct. We are lacking in preparations. Our entire organization *is unorganized*. We brought people on board for their skills to save the human race. We're mostly scientists and engineers. We have very few military types onboard. This is a company, not a military unit. We'll be learning as we go. In the short term, we're going to be dedicating resources in a hundred unproductive directions." Kelt admitted.

"Let's get the big guy in on this. He built this facility from an old mine. I know that he's likely thought through some of this," Kelt said.

"You've got a point," Guy responded as he called Rick on his private com.

"Hello Guy, what's up?"

"Good, I'm glad I caught you. I never know where you'll be up there. Can you join us in a video conference right away?" Guy asked.

"Uh, yeah, sure. Let me reschedule my guests here."

The wait seemed to take forever, but Rick appeared on the video screen within just a minute. "Sorry fellas, I've got management issues. It seems that people want to waste my time in naming the other two floating cities. Get this; they want to name city A, 'Richmond', in Akhi's honor for her accomplishments in our dimensional shift technologies and the city B, "Nelby Station", for Kelt, "the savior of humanity." Yes, they have become wildly popular up here, now that they know the specifics of our technical evolution.

"Personally, I'm all for it, but I really don't need to be hassled, even with a pleasant task like this one. Instead of rescheduling with them, I told them that they were in charge of the effort, but that they couldn't waste any of their work time on it. They went away thrilled," Rick explained. "Now, what's up, down there?" Rick smiled as he thought about what he'd just said.

"A person should be shot for saying that. Really? What's up *down* there?" Kelt inquired with a grin.

"Sorry, Kelt. I agree that it is a rather odd question. I'm sorry for the memory lapse. So, what can I do for you gentlemen?"

Kelt briefly reviewed what had happened with the sequencer deal at MIT.

"Rick, we don't know what the government wants from us, but they obviously don't want us to have a DNA sequencer," explained Kelt.

"I know. Look at what happened with President Murlough," said Rick.

"Yeah, President Crawford... that jerk had talked China and Pakistan in to bombing Africa, and for that action, I'm trapped here without my beautiful Akhi," Kelt thought. It was little consolation to him that the prior president Murlough and Leo Galt were trapped on an empty moon base in the Tycho crater with not even a stick of furniture.

"We need to put together some defensive and egress plans, sir," Guy said to Rick.

Rick didn't mind the sir thing. Rick had hired Guy and paid him and his team well. Rick had treated his team of commandos as real people, not expensive weapons. Rick had earned Guy's respect and the feelings were mutual. Guy and his team had been an essential part of getting the technology completed in time and to getting the cities launched.

"I suppose that the first item on your defensive plan is to deal with the government birds in orbit, Guy?" Rick asked.

"Yes, sir, that was going to be my first question. How did you know?" Guy asked.

"Well City A, um Richmond, just had to side step a commercial bird as it fell out of orbit up here. That thing came rocketing in at over 28,000 Kph. It barely missed the city. We think that it was a deliberate act, but we have no idea who it might be. I doubt the news stations would do it. It was their bird," Rick instructed. "We're thinking China or the US. They are pretty much the only two powers left with the technology to manipulate the orbital satellites like that," he furthered.

"Before we move on to talking about the plans, we had better resolve this right here and now. Those spy birds are taking pictures of us here every day, I'm sure of it," ventured Kelt.

"I agree with you, Kelt," Rick said as he observed Guy in deep thought. Rick knew Guy well enough to know that he was thinking through all the aspects of this situation. Strategy and tactics were churning in his mind.

"I think that we should take out all the spy birds and anything else in orbit that could threaten the cities," ventured Guy.

"That would be most of them, wouldn't it?" asked Kelt.

"I was actually thinking all of them, Kelt," Guy responded.

"This has serious ramifications," Rick advised the others. "If we take down their birds, we may only be inviting further attack," he said.

"And you think they won't attack us? They had two full squads of Rangers waiting for us at MIT," cautioned Guy.

"And Rick, we've seen other countries all too anxious to use nuclear weapons. Without the GPS satellites up there, it might be harder to use them accurately," Kelt added.

"Perhaps, Kelt. I don't know exactly how the nuclear missiles work for other countries. I know that the GPS satellites are used exclusively for the US military now. All civilian access is being denied. Other countries have good old-fashioned gyroscopes and machinery to self-determine position… I think. In any case, GPS was designed for the military first. It needs to be taken out for our own security," Guy concluded.

"Well, I suppose that's our first course of action then. We'll take them down, and then I'll have to make a personal call to the president, to China's General Secretary, the French, and the Brits. They are really going to be angry. I suppose that we can replace many of the functions of their satellites with floating birds of our own, under *our* control," Rick surmised.

"They will consider it an act of war." Kelt advised.

"Very well, I'm considering their latest efforts against us, an act of war," Rick returned. "They have acted aggressively against us first. We are protecting ourselves due to their actions. Does anyone doubt at this point that we must do this?"

"I don't see a better solution, Rick," Guy answered.

"Okay, I'll handle that from up here. Do you know how many birds are up in orbit? It'll be like trying to kill a mosquito swarm. I'll have some of our physicists make a quick analysis of those, which can be first used to attack us, and all the military birds. We'll have to find a way to bring them down.

"Sounds good," said Guy.

"Say, Rick, are there any military weapons in orbit?" asked Kelt.

He knew that the US had at one time development efforts of some sort for space-based weapons.

"Yes!" exclaimed Rick. "Why didn't I think of that? Of course, they'd try a simple rock like a communications satellite first, and if that didn't succeed, they'd likely send us a missile. Hold on fellas for a minute, I've got to get someone on this right away."

Kelt and Guy watched as Rick called Akhi, and quickly explained the situation. He told her to assess any threats of orbiting weapons, and they needed a plan to bring all satellites down. It was a lot of work for one person to handle, but there was a complete command and information center, or CIC, crew up there for each city that currently carried a fairly light load. They had enough competent people.

"Akhi, you should manage this. You, of everyone onboard the cities, are most familiar with our technologies. You've also proven yourself as a capable leader. In fact, we have no one else here in the cities to take command of a military engagement since Guy dropped to the Nevada Base," Rick said.

Kelt could hear her protestations audibly over the video link. "Daddy, we have retired military commanders. Why can't you assign one of them?"

"Look pumpkin, I know you can do it. I'll bring them in to advise you. They certainly will have some experience to provide. Look... no one has ever done this sort of thing. You are my first choice," Rick finalized.

"Okay, Daddy. I'll consult with them and work with the commanders of the cities. Let me in on your video link with Kelt and Guy."

"Okay, thanks pumpkin, I know that I'm making the right decision."

Rick terminated the audio link to her. "Kelt, she agreed to take this assignment, but she wants in on our video link to cover the details.

Akhi shortly joined the video link to discuss the plans. "I'm sorry to come in late, guys... um... I mean gentlemen," Akhi started.

"Until now, we haven't used the floaters as weapons by themselves. I am making that proposition now. I see no other way to do this quickly. We can place floaters on the satellites, one by one on each satellite, and then slow them down until the satellites lose their momentum and fall from space. I'll assign some of our computer eggheads to write some macros for floater control, so that all approaching satellites will decelerate in unison. The floaters will be easily recovered and will still be in useable condition for the next incoming wave. We can't get the satellites all at once, so we'll deal with them in waves as they come our way. Oh, and one more thing... I'll assign someone to run a quick check to see if any of those birds were launched after the virus was discovered. They might be carrying that cursed thing. We'll be sure that any floater slowing down anything launched from French Guiana in the past year, or any other satellite since the nuclear attack on Africa, stays clear of us up here. We'll manage to get those floaters down to Kelt. I'm sure that he'll find a good use for them," Akhi said

"And I was concerned that my daughter might not feel up to the task," smiled Rick.

"You should never doubt her abilities," Guy broke out with a boisterous laugh. "You came up with that plan on your feet, Akhi? That's good."

"Um, yes," Akhi responded humbly.

"Very good. Get your people lined up with their tasks and then get back to me to finalize the plans. You'll also want to do some simulation up there before you actually take down those birds. It will help to run through the procedures several times before taking action," Guy concluded.

"Alright guys, I'm sure that we'll have that situation taken care of within the next few days. I'll be making some difficult phone calls after we do this. I think that we'll be able to take on all the traffic and supply imaging to any real research facility, so I think they will probably understand," Rick said hopefully.

"In your dreams, Rick. Even if they have been shooting at us, they'll never accept your explanation," Guy stated.

"I suppose you are right. Nevertheless, we've got to do this. Am I correct?"

"Yes, sir. It's a necessity. We can't worry about what they'll do. We're already facing that as it is."

"Now, I suppose you want to talk about the bunker?" asked Rick.

"Yes, sir, what if we have to leave in a hurry? There is only one way in and out of here. I'm hoping you planned ahead for this. You wouldn't happen to have a back door like you did down in the Stanford lab would you?" asked Guy.

"You know me too well, Guy. That's what I've always liked about you. Yes, there is another way out, and the door is blown outward by explosives in that mountain about a click away. When I purchased the mine, that was the original entrance. It is lightly covered now with a foot of concrete and topsoil with dying vegetation. I'll send you the schematics for the location of the tunnel. Once the hatch is blown, you'll be able to fly all your craft out. I'd really hate to see that happen though," Rick said.

"No kidding, Rick!" Kelt exclaimed, "We've got ten years' worth of food here to feed this little clan we've put together, and we sure would miss it if we had to leave."

"That's why we have plans," Guy advised, "We might have to find a secondary base."

10- Slaughterhouse massacres

"Is that all you do, Scotty? I swear every time I come into the CIC, you're watching cable news," Kelt good-naturedly admonished.

"Hey, I've got the security monitors active right here. There's nothing else going on topside. Besides, I've got my to-do list finished for the day. I'm relaxing in my down time. I deserve that don't I?" Scotty returned with some irritation. "Besides, this thing is way out of control!"

Kelt stepped up to the large screen, so he could better see and hear what was going on.

On screen were four semi-truck trailers surrounded by dead bodies. "

They're the gang that was protecting those trailers, Kelt. The people running around the trailers are the gang that murdered them. Get this… those trailers are loaded with beef."

The news reporter continued her report from the noisy helicopter.

"Gangs have been fighting over these refrigerated trailers for several days now, Greg. I've been advised that after this long without power, the meat they contain is no longer fit for consumption. It's well above 100 degrees here."

Kelt and Scotty watched in horror as the new gang in charge entered the trailers, and immediately left pinching their noses closed, knowing that their efforts had been in vain.

"Oh crap, Kelt. Look what they're doing now!"

The gang members started disrobing their dead opponents. Kelt had a hard time keeping his gag reflex in check, as the bodies were cut into pieces and hauled away.

"We've heard that this has happened at least three times in as many days, Greg." The reporter was sobbing with terror as she made her commentary. *"We are hearing shooting again. Those who have just taken the trailers are themselves under attack from another gang. We have reports that this sort of thing is happening around the world. We would like to ask all people to stay at home. Our governments are working on a solution to this problem."*

"This video is sickening, Scotty. Besides that, no one is working on anything except us, as far as I know. Why do they keep broadcasting this crap? What purpose does it serve?"

"It's the end of the world, Kelt. Who knows why anyone is doing what they do? I'm surprised they're still broadcasting. Wouldn't you rather be with your loved ones, than be a floating target in a helo with a television camera?"

"Scotty, I'd rather be with my loved ones, but you're all I've got," Kelt smirked.

Scott looked up at Kelt. "Now, you see what I mean?"

In a grotesque situation, with cadavers being mutilated, people being shot for food, the two friends found a reason to laugh.

"You do realize that we are being conditioned to accept the worst humanity has to offer, don't you Mr. Scott?"

"Aye, Cap'n. And I don't like it one bit."

11- Kelt breaks in to the Artifact

Long days… long video sessions with Akhi… Kelt was exhausted. He had gleaned more from Aldo's very old notes he had saved over the years. Now, Kelt could easily view the history of mankind through any of the eyes of the millenarians who had furnished the recordings. Descendants of the ancient people had been given the assignment to spread over the world and record the history of mankind.

The artifact was more than a memory device. It held the visions and experiences from so many people. How did it collect that information? Kelt's quest was not to learn the history or relive his own past. It was to escape the data stream and invade the operating system. He must know how the device collected information from its observers. Equations he had found and created gave him newfound hope as he studied them, put the pieces together, along with some educated guesses for values of constants he did not understand.

The work was exhausting. He tried over, and over, and over to find a way to escape the constant data stream of thoughts or visions of the observers. He scanned more of Aldo's notes. He worked through formulas and came up with his own. He learned the meanings of new symbols and experimented.

He lay awake all night, far too long attempting a way through the firewall from the constantly streaming video feeds. Near waking time, he succeeded. The tangled weave of historic threads was before him. He was the operator looking at a list of files, only significantly more complex. They shifted and moved constantly. Everything was in a constant state of flux. Kelt had wondered if he were in a virtual world, but realized that he had stepped deeply into his own mind to make an unconventional access to the library. He did not know it, but this had never been done in the history of the Culinari.

The alarm clock brought Kelt to his feet like a rocket. He stood dazed and confused as he made a point to remember every thought that had led him to that place. He scribbled some notes in gibberish that no one would ever understand. He would return as soon as he could.

12- Language class

Dr. Akhi Richmond's mind wandered thinking of Kelt, as he had been quite disturbed the evening before. It seemed he literally was carrying the weight of the surviving world below, on his own shoulders. He was the one going out to check on people and to find food and supplies for them. It was taking a tremendous toll on him emotionally. "And now, there's this worry about being attacked. I wish that he could just get some rest for a week or two," she thought to herself as her instructor Aldo droned on.

From the ancient artifact Kelt had unearthed, Aldo had guessed that the millenarians were likely direct descendants from those who seeded the Earth. Through the eyes of the millenarians, the artifact had collected the history of mankind.

No one could explain why or how this worked. In the current environment, many things went unexplained. After making their first electronic remote connection, Aldo had neglected to study the artifact's surface any further. Aside from one historian onboard the cities, no one had a real interest in the artifact now called the libraries. History could wait. Study of the old language was still a priority for a select few, because the language may hold important clues derived in science. For this reason, Aldo held daily classes to share his gift.

Unknowingly, Akhi retracted her left hand from the cheetah cubs' attention, as she daydreamed.

"Akhi, where are you today?" Aldo asked as he surveyed the small cheetah cubs playing at her feet. They were becoming rowdy, demanding motherly attention from Akhi. She was lost in her thoughts. Absent mindedly, she lowered her left hand to play with the cubs. They swatted at her fingers and Freia latched on to Chanto's tail as he tried to swat her away.

Akhi turned to look at Aldo with empty eyes and a blank look. She had been shaken out of a daydream, most unusual for her. She had a focused determination to learn and direct her attention on anything she set her mind to. Aldo looked down at her perfect porcelain features. Akhi was now 18 and obviously, she was pining for her beau, Kelt. Memories of him, and their all too brief encounters, penetrated her mind far too often throughout most days.

"Why can I not focus?" she would often berate herself. She had been told that she too was a millenarian, a descendent of the old ones, just before the new era had begun, but had not believed it possible.

"Are you worried about Kelt?" Aldo asked.

"So what else would it be?" she answered as she rolled her stylus lazily around in circles with her right hand.

"He'll be fine, Akhi. We will solve our problems, and you will be able to live together with him for many years to come. You are after all ageless, compared to most here in the cities," he said.

"I know, I know. I have a hard time believing it though," she said as she stuck her stylus in her mouth to consider her position silently.

Akhi was perhaps one of the most brilliant people to have ever graced the planet Earth. She had developed an advanced set of mathematics and physics before she had turned 14. Those ideas had in turn been used to build the technology to lift the immense cities into space, enable the lunar and Mars settlements, and perhaps… just perhaps, save the world. "Save the world? Me?" she thought to herself.

"No, not you Akhi, all of us," Aldo stated.

"What did you say, Aldo?"

"I said that all of us, your team of five at Stanford who developed the lift technologies, your father, your father's other teams around the world, we all contributed to this endeavor. I must admit, however, that you played one of *the* most decisive roles. I suspect that you will be *the* "Einstein" for the next few centuries," he explained.

"But Aldo, I didn't say anything out loud. Did you hear me thinking?"

Aldo stood dumbfounded. He tried to think through what had just happened. Sure, he could sense strong feelings around other millenarians, but had never been able to hear their thoughts. This time, he had. Her words were as clear to him as if she had said them straight to his face.

"I suppose it's possible I did hear you thinking, Akhi. I can't imagine how that might be done."

"Aldo, we've been getting together every day now for the past year, for learning sessions of the old languages, and I would think that you just know me pretty well," Akhi advised.

"No, Akhi, I heard you very clearly. No one knew how old millenarians really lived to be."

Aldo only knew one other as old as himself before the new era and that was Leo Galt. Aldo had seemed to age somewhat more than she expected during the few months that she had known him. Perhaps everyone looked a little older these days. It was not a happy time to be alive.

"The old language is complex; it is woven with intricate overtures of mathematics and physics. Might there be clues or even formulae in the language that enable telepathic communication?" Amy Prichard questioned out loud. Amy was about 360 years old. Like Aldo, she did not know her true age.

"The old language combines what we would consider specialties into daily speech. Doesn't it make sense that as we learn the language that other things are possible? Might we find anything that covers this in the libraries?" Amy asked.

"It somehow seems possible," Akhi started, "but we need empirical evidence before we go wasting the historian's time in the libraries. Remember, the libraries are a history of Earth seen through the millenarians' eyes. Even though we've done an excellent job of translating all the languages and indexing subject material, it is really hard to find the sorts of things we actually need to survive. I know of a few religious people... I know that it's difficult to find many after what is left of the world... who have taken their

79

spare time to search their faith's historical foundations and have come away sorely unfulfilled. Of course, there could be many reasons they didn't find much. But, I digress; we only have one historian working with the libraries. Until we work through our current crisis, it's hard to justify more than that. So, why don't we try some simple tests for a few days and see what we can accomplish together?" Akhi suggested as she swatted at the demanding cubs. "Just lie down, will you both?" she demanded. The cubs quickly lay down on the floor and shoved their faces into their forepaws. Akhi looked down at them and wondered at the effectiveness of her command.

"I think that's a great idea Akhi," said Amy. "Let's try it now. While the moment is still fresh, let's try the very same experiment. So, Akhi, you think the things you were thinking about and Aldo, you do whatever you did to connect with her," Amy instructed.

They had been unable to repeat the test successfully. Akhi had been daydreaming and had been shocked by the sound of Aldo's voice and could not adequately repeat her experience as it had unfolded. She had initiated some form of communication with the cubs, however. She seemed to convey her wishes to them far too effectively. It had happened many times recently, and she had not noticed or reflected upon it until now.

"I do think that this is worth pursuing still," explained Aldo. I know from personal experience that societies forget how to do things. Our people nearly forgot the treasure of the old language. Stories are altered or their meanings distorted by subsequent generations. We have numerous examples available to demonstrate this simple fact. So, may I propose that we add another 15 minutes on to our daily sessions for telepathic experiments? If we can't repeat it within a couple of weeks, we'll move on," he concluded.

"I think that sounds fine. I can rearrange my schedule. I think that we should also bring in our other classmates," Akhi noted.

Aldo had been serving up two sessions a day. Amy and Akhi had to miss the sessions often, so his pace was slower with them, than the other three that attended. The other class consisted of two physicists and a linguist similar in age to Akhi.

"You have a good point," Aldo noted. "They've covered a bit more ground than you two have. It may be that we've already shot this horse and haven't even realized it," he said.

"Shot this horse?" grinned Akhi with a laughing tenor. "Where did that come from?" she asked, now laughing most audibly.

"Oh, I don't know, Akhi. I've lived a long life you know. I can't remember where or why I picked it up. It's just a figure of speech," Aldo answered. "Many who now live in the cities have never seen a horse," he thought to himself with remorse.

13- It's organic

The day had been a long one. The work was taking an enormous toll on Kelt. He had lost some weight and his cheekbones had become a bit more pronounced. He had finished up for the evening and spent several minutes on a video link with Akhi before retiring. He could not sleep. He reviewed his notes and cross-referenced some figures. He saw new relationships forming in a new form of mathematics. "Or is it just a variation of a form of physics that someone has already invented?" he asked himself. "I've got to get in there. I need to know how it works," he demanded of himself.

This night, it was much easier to communicate with the artifact through his mind. He stepped directly into the "file system" level, where he saw the informational feeds of history bending, intertwining, and heaving.

"Every machine has a purpose. This one is to record and present history," he thought "but every machine has background processes that manage the information. That's where I need to go."

Throughout the day, Kelt had wondered how his new ideas would work. "How will the formulas I just put together lead me anywhere?" he asked himself, "I can only try." He had tagged his walk on the island with Akhi, with his index marker the night before. Now, he would look for it upon the woven complex of historical feeds.

"It's strange how organic this looks," Kelt thought as he mentally traversed the "files" of history. He had no perspective of a timeline within these 'files'. There was none. It was dynamic and moving. "How do I find the marker?" Kelt then remembered the long sequence of numbers or symbols that must identify him. "It must be a number in base four," he thought. What identified him was a long sequence made up of a combination of those four unique characters. "There it is!" he screamed with delight within his mind. The tag was there, attached to an individual stream. He entered the stream to verify he had been correct, and he was. There was his lovely Akhi sitting on a beach blanket opening the picnic basket. Kelt knew he had no time to enjoy the recorded memory. He could come back here at any time. In this short experiment, he had gained some new snippet of information. The base four sequence was definitely his. It identified him as a constant where a variable had been noted in the formula.

"I'll tag this moment right now," Kelt thought as he processed the information into the library and watched his own stream as it spun out of the present into the past. He monitored the tagging operation, and caught an almost living thing reach out to place a tag on the thread. Kelt followed the process into the operating system. He took special note to remember how to enter this place.

Other streams of diverse complexity reached out to control threads of processes from random locations. Kelt was looking for patterns, for the big picture. He saw many, but did not recognize them at once. As he observed, he kept seeing the four characters that he had visualized as part of his name, intertwined with complex formulae and equations. The machine operated on a multifaceted scale. While modern computers used ones and zeros in base two, there seemed to be no limits to the numbers of values passed back and forth between processes.

"Kelt had some knowledge of standard processing theory. This bore no similarity. It seemed organic. He could not get that thought out of his mind now. What was it about this vision he had that made it organic? Perhaps it was just the shear scale of values processed at face value. In a binary modern computer, the ones and zeros had values that could be easily evaluated, moved through gates and transistors made of silicon. This was much more basic and at the same time, immensely more complex.

"Is it organic, or am I watching the manipulation of individual molecules?" Kelt asked himself. He wondered, "Is what I'm seeing, real? Or am I just making this up?" He reached into his mind, following a synoptic path he had calculated on the fly, and toggled a neural switch. "Tag

83

that." Kelt waited for the operating system to tag his thought as he stepped back to the weaving history threads. The tag did not appear. "I'm now invisible within the operating system," he noted in awe.

14- Simulation

Akhi opened her door to step into the hallway. Amy Prichard was waiting opposite her door, leaning up against the wall.

"Amy! What are you doing here?"

"I'm waiting for you. I heard we were going to run some tactical simulations today. I was hoping that I could accompany you to the CIC. Aldo and Rick are encouraging me to expand my skill set, so I figured that I might watch and learn if that would be okay with you."

"I wish that you would have asked," Akhi mentioned as she watched the cats follow her through the door.

"Is there a problem, Akhi?"

"No, not really. It's just that I'm worried about establishing some protocols now. I don't want to inhibit independent thinking or action, but I would like to get things organized a bit better. So, I don't really mind if you're there... I just would like to know in advance."

"I understand, Akhi. I'll keep that in mind for the future. Say, are those cubs going with you to the CIC?"

"They go with me practically everywhere now, Amy. They've learned very quickly to behave themselves. I let them play in my cabin so they can get a little exercise. Believe me, my furniture bears witness to their destructive prowess, but when I tell them to behave outside our quarters, they obey without hesitation."

"Hmm, that's very interesting, Akhi. They are either very fast learners or they understand you."

"Come on, Amy, how in the world could they understand me? I had thought that I was just doing a good job in training them."

"Do you always give your commands verbally, or do you think it is your body language?" Amy inquired with interest.

"I had thought they were reading my body language, Amy. I had started with verbal commands, moved to hand signals, and lately, I have noticed that they do whatever I think I want them to do… well, for the most part. Truly, I think that they are just learning to do what I expect of them."

"Say, are you still bottle feeding them? They seem to be growing pretty quickly."

"Chanto, Akhi waved her hand at one of the cubs, ate a can of cat food today. I suppose that within the next day or so, they will be weaned."

"Are you going to keep them when they can eat solid food?"

"A week ago, the answer would have been a definite no, but now, I'm reconsidering. They've become a very important part of my life. I've learned to love them. They are so affectionate. I can't imagine not having them around."

"May I pet them?"

"No problem, Amy. Here… try it with Freia first."

Amy bent down to pet Freia and she was met with a low growl in response.

"Freia, Chanto… Amy is a friend. Treat her nice and protect her," Akhi commanded. Freia quelled her natural instincts and stepped up to lick Amy's hand.

"Owe! That's like running the back of my hand over sandpaper!" Amy exclaimed in a startled voice.

Akhi lifted her raw hands and showed them to Amy. "I've learned to expect it, Amy. They are terribly sweet, but yes, they have a lethal affectionate lick. Okay you two, don't lick Amy. You have other ways to show your affection."

Freia immediately started rubbing Amy's leg with her head. Amy reached out again and started petting the cub's head and scratching her ears. Freia purred wildly.

"I'm impressed, Akhi. There is no way that you've trained them to do these things in such a short time! You seem to have done the impossible," Amy smiled.

86

"So, Amy, how are you coming along with Aldo's instruction?"

"I'm doing very well now," Amy stated confidently. "It has been difficult, but now the math is coming to me very quickly. I understand how most of it works, and believe it or not, I have this incredible desire and ability to design robots."

Akhi smiled. "Good for you Amy. Welcome to the club. Hey, I don't want to be late for our exercise, let's get going."

Amy smiled in acknowledgement and the two women and the cats walked to the lift in chitchat.

*****

The door opened to the CIC and Akhi entered first, with a cat guarding each side. Even though the entire crew of Pacificus had seen her with the cats, they never tired of the sight and all eyes turned to watch her enter. Amy followed her in. The two women took seats toward the rear of the facility. Akhi was in command of the four-city exercise, but Commander Barnes would be commanding those in the Pacificus CIC. For the most part, and hopefully, Akhi would only need to issue top-level commands to each CIC. The commanders would be taking care of the real details in their own command.

Tim Barnes, a linguist fluent in 7 languages, had served in one of the Special Forces units. He was average in size and very well toned. A captivating smile, his ability to relate anecdotal stories, and his mild mannered, but unyielding command style, earned immediate respect from all members of the Pacificus CIC. Commanders of the other three cities had become appreciative of his insights and quick strategic thinking.

He refused to talk of his experiences or even mention the service branch to which he had been assigned. Rick Carter knew his complete history, and Guy Lerner had helped bring him into the company. Akhi had great respect for him, even though nothing of any import had taken place until now. That was about to change.

"Commander Barnes, let's begin the exercise. You have the coordinates of the first four Space Truck test satellites. Let's proceed according to the plan. Each city with one pilot will position a floater in front of their assigned satellite."

"Yes ma'am," he responded as he locked an open command channel to the other city's CIC. "Okay team, let's proceed with the first exercise," he commed to the other commanders.

The Space Truck exercise satellites orbited high above the floating cities. All four had circled the planet and were lined up and approaching the cities overhead. The birds were well spaced, allowing the exercise to focus on one bird per city without expecting the crews to deal with too many procedures or issues at once. The crews needed to learn how to perform these procedures on a single satellite unfettered by confusion, before they could think about the ultimate task; bringing down all satellites.

One pilot in each CIC was assigned to bring a floater in on the same flight path and position it in front of the satellite. Floater control was managed through commercial computers or pads. Each pilot also had gaming flight sticks for a quicker response. A team of computer eggheads had written a number of macros that each remote pilot could utilize for the various procedures they would need to employ. Finding a small object flying at 28,000 kilometers per hour and flying in a floater to sit on it was a very difficult task. The computer macros were essential to the job. Manual control could only be used once the floaters had matched speed and had moved in next to the satellites.

"I sure wish that we could give these people better control equipment," Akhi murmured.

"What do you mean?" Amy questioned her.

"This gaming hardware is just not precise enough. It's unreliable. They deserve better," Akhi whispered.

"Why can't we get them better equipment?"

"We had not anticipated these sorts of issues or potential problems. We have designs for better flight gear, but it is pretty low on the priority list. The gaming hardware works. We're short on raw materials and other projects, so far, have had a higher priority. If we put these at the top of the priority heap, we'd have working models for the entire crew within a couple of days. They aren't necessarily complex, Amy."

"You know, Akhi, it used to be all about money. Now that money is of no consequence, it is interesting to note that there is always a reason to not have what you need when you need it."

Akhi smiled at the clear hint she had received from Amy. Akhi promised herself to put some new flight gear on the projects list with top priority.

As the first satellite cleared Earth's limb, Nelby station started acceleration of its attacking disk. The disk was placed several thousand kilometers out. The distance was needed so that the disk could accelerate to match the satellite's speed.

Even though the disks could accelerate at an almost infinite rate, Akhi had been concerned about the relativistic problems associated with intense acceleration. She had requested that the programmers put a limit of one-fourth the speed of light into their software. Of course, in this exercise, the disks would never need to approach 77,000 kilometers per second. Still, Akhi felt the failsafe, to be quite necessary. Relativistic effects could be extremely dangerous. According to Einstein's theory, an object approaching the speed of light could become infinite in size. The danger from such an object was self-evident. Additionally, the power to move an object at that speed would be infinite. Even though the energy to move the floaters was pulled from the anti-entropic compressed energy from a dead galaxy, it was a resource, which should be guarded. No, the relativistic affects were to be well respected.

"Nelby actual here. Our floater is approaching the satellite... The satellite has been destroyed. The floater is still under operational control."

"Nelby, we want to drop the satellites from orbit, not destroy them," Akhi started on com, "please adjust the use of your macros to place the floater in front of the satellite."

"Acknowledged," Commander Will Grayson commed.

"Atlantis, your go at the next bird as it comes into range," Akhi commanded.

"Atlantis actual... our floater is accelerating ... coming in... okay... decelerating... I'm sorry to report that we've fallen short by a thousand kilometers."

"A thousand kilometers? Figure out what you did wrong over there," Akhi curtly commanded.

"Acknowledged, Pacificus."

"Commander Barnes, Pacificus is up next," commanded Akhi.

"Yes ma'am. Okay, team; let's use a different set of macros. I want this thing to work"

"I think that I can see what went wrong and I've got my macros rearranged, sir," claimed the assigned pilot.

"Do it."

"Pacificus actual," Barnes announced to the CIC's on the other cities. "Our floater is moving in at a slower acceleration... maintaining acceleration a bit longer... okay... deceleration is on the mark. Floater is alongside the satellite!"

The pilot easily moved the floater around to the front of the satellite and moved it somewhat slowly to make contact with the craft.

"Target acquired and floater in place, sir" the pilot announced.

"Very good. From this point, decelerating the floater will slow the satellite and let gravity pull it to the Earth. Let's keep this bird in orbit for further testing," Akhi commanded.

"Commander Grayson?"

"Nelby actual."

"I'd like you to refine the procedures. We've had several failures today. I'd like to run another simulation tomorrow afternoon. Between now and then, work with the other commanders and pilots. Let's refine these procedures. We don't have much time.

"Acknowledged. We have good data on the two failures and the single success. We'll be running exercises for the next twenty-four hours. Every pilot will get some experience here."

"Glad to hear it, commander. Please make sure to bring in the crews dirtside. Many more satellites orbit Earth than we have pilots. We can use everyone we've got," Akhi stated.

"Acknowledged."

"Good work people! We have some experience under our belts and we have learned a few things we should not do. It is your assignment now to find out exactly what we *should* do," Akhi said from her command seat.

*****

"That didn't go very well did it?" Amy asked Akhi.

"That's not correct, Amy. Yes, we had a couple of failures, but we collected some valuable data. Learning what not to do is just as important as learning what to do. I'm very happy with the results," Akhi returned.

"I understand. You make perfect sense. I have a long way to come, Akhi. In many ways, I'm still stuck in the 19th century, when I was born. I have new abilities and a great desire to learn. I'm learning so much and yet have a very difficult time putting it to practical use."

"You'll get it Amy. I have no idea where your skills will ultimately lead you, but I can see your creative mind at work. You have ambition, an ability I've seen lacking in the older millenarians."

"I've noticed, Akhi. Do you suppose that they've lost those abilities?"

"I don't know, Amy. I've seen it in Aldo almost from the beginning. He is generous and kind. He's an excellent instructor. But his imagination falls short and he freely admits it."

"I've noticed that in him as well. I've worked with him for several decades. He has always relied on the advice of competent advisors. A few years ago, he learned to listen to my advice in financial matters."

"I didn't know that Amy! So, you are a financial whiz?"

"Oh, I did pretty well for the consortium," Amy said in a very modest tone.

"Do you have an interest in the arts, Amy?"

"I love to sing, Akhi. In my early years, it was all I had to cling to. The gift of song has carried me through many years of abuse and difficulty. Now I'm learning how to read music and I'm even in the community choir here on Pacificus."

"We have a community choir?" Akhi asked.

"Yes! We also have a small orchestra," Amy smiled.

"Amy, why don't we spend some time together right now? Let's get down to the gym and run the cats around the track? They really need the exercise and quite frankly, I do as well," Akhi demanded. "And then let's grab a bite to eat."

"That sounds great. I need to postpone a meeting I have scheduled. I'll take care of that and go get dressed. I'll meet you in the gym in 15 minutes."

"Sounds good, Amy."

Amy and Akhi split up in the hallway and rushed to their quarters.

15- Telepathy

Aldo met earlier in the day with the five students to accommodate their schedules. He explained what had happened the previous day. He told them exactly what he saw and heard in detail. Akhi followed and also explained the events that led to Aldo seemingly hearing her thoughts. The cheetah cubs were laid out on either side of Akhi behaving like perfect angels. Each was alert, but stayed still with silent obedience.

"Well," said Steve, one of the physicists, "I can tell you right now, that Akhi is concerned about her beau eating frozen Marie Callender potpies that are a decade old."

"What?" Akhi exclaimed. "I don't believe you just did that! How did you do that?" she demanded.

"I don't know, but Jed here, my physics colleague, can do the same thing. Nick, our linguist, can't seem to make it work," he responded. "We've been able to do this for three weeks now. We haven't said anything to anyone because we figured it would make them feel really creepy. You know... in a way where they might want to beat us with sticks or at least ridicule us," he added with a wry grin.

"Can you read anyone's thoughts?" Akhi asked.

"No. We can only do it with millenarians and not all the time. Nick and I have discovered that we can turn on, or turn off our "mental transceivers" at will. When we cooperate, we don't need to communicate verbally," he concluded.

"This is truly astounding," said Aldo. "I never knew that we had this ability, and I wish we could discover how it works," he added.

"It's most useful for accessing the libraries," Nick added. "We don't need translators to understand the many languages used. We don't miss the subtleties missed in translated speech. For example, the word Culinari translates to human for those using the translators. So, we've entirely missed the point that the Culinari were the original people of the old language. That's what they called themselves anyway," he further explained.

"Perhaps it is because you have studied more with Aldo?" queried Akhi. "If that is the case, why then, does Nick not have this ability?"

"Perhaps it is that part of the language that Nick has the most difficulty with," Aldo explained. He looked at the group as they stared back at him with *the* pregnant question. The cheetah cubs seemed to raise their heads in attention.

"That would be the advanced physics," he finally answered.

"If that is the case, this should be a simple process of elimination," started Akhi. "I have been able to enhance my perspectives of physics we are learning from the… what did you call them… oh, yes, the Culinari," she concluded. She also acknowledged to herself that the physics she had been learning through Aldo's lessons had little to add to her own personal research in dimensional shift technologies. Certainly, her skills as a physicist were greatly enhanced by the physics she was learning. This new knowledge led down other paths and away from the dimensional shift.

"So, Aldo, can you recall what you covered with these men in the week previous to their discovery?" she asked.

"Ah, yes, simple and direct reasoning," Aldo said as he looked up his lesson notes and videos of those sessions. "Um, here we have an item of interest. It seems that the topic we did cover for which you may have no knowledge Akhi, is we can best translate as radio waves and transmission', he said.

"Oh come on Aldo, be realistic. I know all about radio waves, how to produce them, how to receive them, how to amplify them. Shoot, I could draw you a schematic right now for a complicated transceiver," Akhi said with an insulted tone in her voice.

"But, Akhi, what are radio waves made of?" asked Aldo.

"I don't know. We have ways to define their properties, how to transmit them, and how to receive them, but, quite honestly, we don't know what they are made of."

"That is what we covered in the physics portion of the old language class you missed," Aldo explained. "The physics explain in some detail, what radio waves, and light are actually made of by formula and complicated speech. There is no way to describe it in English. It could take literally gigabytes of data to describe radio waves completely, where it is done in a few simple statements in the old language. Bluntly, it quite simply cannot be explained in English, it must be described in context, in the old language. Frankly, I'm amazed that I could recall this material from what I learned millennia ago from my mother. I learned all of this by memorization, not necessarily understanding its meaning. I have been able to use a natural sensing capability in the past to identify other millenarians. I never understood how it worked. But, I believe that your two friends here, have readily picked up on a more advanced technique and stored it in a special place in their minds. Can it be that we can send and receive mental messages?" Aldo asked.

"I've come to notice a subtle possibility with my cubs," Akhi noted.

"Yes, it is possible," Aldo clearly heard, but did not know from where the answer came.

"It's Jed, Aldo," Jed sent, as he sensed Aldo's frustration.

"Jed has just been able to communicate with me," Aldo announced, "not only am I the teacher, I have become a student, for I am learning from you. It might be that I can learn to comprehend this material better than I thought. I suppose you *can* teach an old dog new tricks," he concluded. Aldo quickly pulled up the notes and made them available for Akhi, Amy, and Nick.

Akhi, extremely adept at covering new physics materials at break neck speed, scanned it with photographic memory. She focused, flipped that imaginary switch in her brain, and could hear her Kelt thinking about another shuttle mission to the east coast the next day. She then focused her mind to the libraries, set a date to July 6, 1776, and placed herself in Philadelphia. Not only could she see the images from the library, but she could also hear excited people in the streets talking about the new proclamation of independence, announced two days earlier.

"I can do it!" she exclaimed to herself. As far as she knew, she had been the first to access the libraries in a direct connection. With the security conscious paranoia of her father, she decided to keep this information to herself. She might share it later with Kelt on an encrypted link.

The team flew through a few simpler tests of their newly discovered mental abilities. Poor Nick and Amy were still out of the loop. All the others however, were easily able to communicate without verbalization of words.

"I am definitely passing this material down to Kelt," she thought excitedly. "He has to have this. He just has to." The cubs at her feet purred in approval. "Aldo, I think that we should all agree right here and now that this information should not be shared with anyone else, except with other millenarians. The other people might not understand," Akhi demanded.

"Agreed, Akhi," Aldo replied. "Did everyone else get that?" Aldo demanded. The others in the class all silently nodded their heads as they milled over the potential consequences of disclosure in their heads.

After class, Akhi returned directly to her quarters. The cubs were very hungry. They were no longer content to lap the formula that Amanda had provided. They wanted meat. Akhi wondered how this was going to work out as she opened the package of beef. Certainly, the animals were worth saving. Did their lives have more value than that of another human? She watched them batting each other in play after their meal and smiled. They were adorably cute.

They were definitely worth the protein sacrifice. Chanto left play for the corner.

"In the bathroom, Chanto! You know better!" Akhi commanded. Chanto immediately altered his course to the bathroom where his box was. "Wow!" Akhi thought, "I should teach them how to use the toilet," she smiled. A sudden realization hit her, "*I really should teach them how to use the toilet!*"

She leaped to her feet and joined Chanto before he jumped into his box. "Up here, Chanto," Akhi's thoughts demanded as she motioned with her hands. The cub looked at her curiously and then at his box. He looked back to her, and she issued him the same mental command. Chanto sulked to the head and jumped up on to the seat. He didn't quite know what to do with the hole. "It goes in the hole, Chanto," Akhi commanded mentally. Chanto was a little large to reposition himself on the seat, so he jumped down and jumped back up in the right position. Chanto looked at Akhi seemingly to smile as he did his deed. "Good boy, Chanto! That's where you will go potty from now on, okay?" she demanded mentally. Chanto turned his face toward her and licked her arm with his lethal tongue.

Motion at the doorway indicated that Freia was watching. "Your turn, Freia," Akhi sent mentally. Freia jumped to the seat following the same instructions she had heard sent to Chanto. "Good girl, Freia!"

Akhi felt greatly relieved. The cat's hygienic needs had become quite a problem. Cleaning the boxes was a royal pain. They had to be emptied twice a day and sometimes even more. The smell was overwhelming for Akhi's delicate olfactory senses.

"Tomorrow, I'll show you both how to flush the toilet," she sent them with a mental image as she reached for the knob. Freia jumped on the seat and placed her paw on the knob. Akhi helped Freia push the handle down. "Good girl, Freia!" Akhi squealed.

She beamed happiness toward the two cats as they started licking at her hands with their barbed tongues. Akhi walked back into her room and sat on the floor to play with her cats before she called Kelt. They jumped and swatted. Chanto grabbed Freia in his favorite cub play death grip around her head. Freia escaped and playfully went for his throat. This was a happy moment in a time of great unhappiness. It demanded time. Akhi freely gave it.

Kelt received a recorded transmission an hour after class, including the video links that had been instrumental in the most recent discovery. Akhi also shared a brief video note of her own in explanation. Clearly, she was excited, but in her delighted state of mind, she had neglected to tell him of her unrelenting love. She always included a small romantic snippet in their communications. He realized the importance of the discovery and even at the late hour, with a long mission looming this very night, he perused the material.

As a very accomplished physicist and structural engineer, he had designed the various structural elements of the large spheres in which the people lived. He had designed *the matrix* that was used in not only the construction of the facilities, but of the aerospace craft, and most importantly of all, the underlying structure of the floaters and locks that kept them floating in space and propelled their craft. As he read through the information, he was at a decided disadvantage. He was developing his own form of mathematics to enter and research the operation of the artifact, or the intelligence that controlled it. He still did not understand the language.

While he could understand some of the physics, without knowledge of the old language, it did not form a complete picture. He decided he needed to spend time to learn it. Videos were available for 24 years' worth of daily instruction. "Great. Even though the classes were generally only an hour or so in length, I could easily spend two or three years watching the videos," he thought. The video link flashed on his monitor indicating an incoming call.

"Kelt, we also have transcripts… you don't need to watch all the videos. I'm sure you can fly through those rather than watching all those tedious class sessions," Akhi said with a cheek-to-cheek grin.

"I can see that I'm going to have to come up to speed very quickly then," he answered back with full understanding of what had just happened. She had heard him pondering these issues and had called in response.

"Kelt, this is so amazing. I've even been able to communicate with the cubs!" she squealed.

"You're kidding," Kelt said flatly.

"I'm not kidding, Kelt. I told them that they should use the toilet and they did!"

"Really?"

"Really! I've taught cheetah cubs to use the toilet!" she shouted gleefully. "My thoughts are sent to them so that they can understand them, Kelt."

"Mamma Timba, I honor you," Kelt said with wonder still evident in his eyes.

"Mamma Timba?" Akhi asked.

"Oh, it's the nick given to a woman who had trained three baby elephants in an old 2D flick," Kelt answered. "Yes, I like it. I shall call you Mama Timba," he teased.

"No you shall not, Kelt!" she teased. "You sir, shall address me as Queen Timba." She managed to say through her laughter.

"No, Akhi, Mama Timba is the nick."

"Don't you ever tell anyone else!" she laughed.

"Okay, sweetie. I'm so happy for you. You made my day. You can imagine we don't have too much to smile about dirtside. Listen sweetie, I'm going to terminate the link now, so I can review these files. I love you very much," he finished.

"I love you too, Mister Man."

"Mister Man?" Kelt scrunched the question in his face as Akhi terminated the link. "Now I've opened a can of worms," Kelt mused with a huge smile as he cleared his desk in preparation to review the files.

Akhi could hear his thoughts. He had to be able to control this. It was a lacking piece of his ventures into the ancient technology. So, he would learn. This sort of discovery demanded the insights of a team, but he had come so far and lacked the time to bring someone else up to speed with his abilities.

He would tell no one of his ventures into the matrix of the history processor.

16- Planting

"Ready Kelt?" asked Scotty.

"Yuppers."

Scotty and Kelt, along with one biologist and five commandos fully outfitted in environmental suits covered by armor and laden with weapons, would be travelling to the Amazon where the virus outbreak had first been noticed. Guy Lerner would normally go along with the boys. It was his primary duty to protect them. "Those kids have to help save the world," he told his subordinates, "They come back alive, you copy?"

The squad of five resounded with a firm, "Yes sir."

Guy remained at Nevada Base to help with the targeting of satellites and to move hundreds of floater disks into position.

"I hate wearing all this crap," Kelt scoffed, hoping that no one would notice.

"Sir, you know that we have to take full precautions. The EV suit will help keep out possible radiation, and you just need to start getting used to the fact that this armor just might save your life,"

Kelt had worn the EV suits on every excursion since the nuclear blasts, but only now had accepted the fact that he would not only have to wear the armor, but also carry a weapon. Guy had been instructing them for a few minutes each day for the past week. Scotty and Kelt had managed at least to hit the paper targets... not anything inside the rings on the target, just somewhere on the target was good enough as far as Kelt was concerned.

"Yeah, I suppose you are right," he responded directly to the commando. "Procedures must now be strictly followed. I'll just have to suck it up," Kelt admitted.

The commando smiled as Kelt used some of the military lingo. He liked these two boys, even though one of them much younger was his commander on this mission.

The large hangar door opened and after a moment, Scotty plugged in his computing pad and attached it to the Velcro lined dash in front of his pilot's seat. With a few simple touches, drags, and taps with his finger, he lifted the shuttle and floated it out in front of the building. From that position, he started a gradual climb and moved to the two g acceleration rate. The team was used to that acceleration. It essentially doubled their body weight in their seats. It was worse with Kelt at the stick. He'd often do a three g acceleration. No, the commandos much preferred to fly with Scotty.

Of course, there was no real stick in most shuttles. There weren't even any controls. The only switches controlled lights and the access portals. The craft were flown by a laptop or pad computer with a universal bus connection. There were many reasons why the craft had been designed this way. They were cheaper to build, they were piloted by complex communications between land based locks and floaters, and should some enemy steal one, they would have a difficult time figuring it all out.

"Hey Scotty, why is your shuttle so much nicer than mine?" Kelt asked accusatorily. "I've got regular car seats in mine with home center heaters to warm up the cabin. You've got real flight couches and full environmental systems on board!" Kelt added.

"I'm sorry Kelt, mine was made before yours. We couldn't outfit the last batch fully. We just didn't have time before the commies nuked Africa. That's why only this shuttle at Nevada Base is fully outfitted. All the others were basically operational shells back then," Scotty explained.

Kelt had remembered how the engineering teams in the base's caverns, had scrambled for junk and garbage to keep things running. He had let them take care of their assigned tasks on their own. He had bigger problems to consider.

Their mission tonight should be a milk run. No one lived in the devastated area. Those still alive in South America had moved to the coastal regions hoping to get on boats, or at least, live on the coasts bartering with the seafarers for food.

Scotty ascended well above the atmosphere keeping the craft in a constant acceleration, to maintain the simulated feeling of gravity.

"Oh Scotty, you are NOT going to try this maneuver are you?" Kelt asked.

"Why not, Kelt, you do it all the time."

"That's when I'm alone or with you. Our friends here aren't used to it."

Usually, every time they dropped from space, in free fall, their harnesses were what kept them in their seats. A free fall simulated weightlessness. In order to prevent that effect, the craft were usually slowed to let Earth's gravity kick in for the comfort of the passengers. Scotty had mentioned the alternative and he was setting up for it. They quickly reached the drop location as the craft slowed to almost a full stop in space.

"Here we go Captain!" he yelled to Kelt and the crew. The commandos were a tough bunch. They could deal with just about anything. As Kelt looked back at them, their faces were ashen. They did not like the brief conversation they had just heard.

Scotty inverted the craft and started the drop procedure. At no acceleration or even orbital velocity, the shuttle dropped like a rock. Scotty increased the acceleration toward the ground. The maneuver was called floater assist. The crew was slammed into their seats.

"See there, Captain, I told you that it would be fun!"

"I think you're right Scotty, I think that they would rather be slammed into their seat than enjoy a few more minutes of descent. Let's see what the crew thinks when you do the free fall," Kelt said sarcastically.

At an altitude of ten thousand meters, Scotty killed the deceleration and let the shuttle drop. Then, the crew experienced weightlessness. One of the poor fellows in the back had never had zero g training and lost his supper into a bag made for the purpose. He got most of it into the bag. Some of the vomit remnants floated about the cabin.

"Scotty, I told you this wasn't a good idea. You should have just brought us down nice and slow," Kelt admonished.

"Oh, but it is working splendidly!" Scotty yelled as the roar of the rushing air passed over the craft. Four kilometers above the deck, Scotty applied a slow deceleration and brought the craft to within 100 meters above the spot that the biologists had determined would be the best for this experiment. "See there, Cap'n? I just saved us 30 minutes compared to a slow descent from upstairs!" Scotty claimed.

The biologist stepped forward.

"Scotty, first let me say that I'd appreciate it if you'd fly that thing next time without your fancy tricks. I nearly lost it."

"Sorry, ma'am," Scotty sheepishly responded.

"Okay, that's out of the way," she started, "that looks like a good flat spot over there to set down. It's just a short walk from there.

Scotty slowly moved the shuttle to the site and carefully set down. "I love to fly these birds Cap'n, but having a soft landing is more important than doing tricks," Scotty told Kelt in an apologetic tone.

"I'm glad you feel that way, Scotty, because I'd sure hate to lose one of these shuttles. We just don't have any to spare. And please, when we have passengers, go easy on them, okay?" Kelt reprimanded.

"Okay boys and girls, put your night vision on and then your helmets," the lead commando ordered.

"I hate wearing all this stuff," thought Kelt, "I sweat and itch all over the place." Although, the thin suits regulated the temperature even in the extremes of space, Kelt managed to find a way to sweat in them. "I just lose my cool in a tense situation," Kelt chuckled to himself.

"Okay, where too?" Kelt asked Padma Patel, the biologist. Padma had been a green card slave, working for some genetic firm in the bay area when she had come to

Space Truck's attention. Even though she had not passed *the* test, she was an excellent biologist.

"Let's go up slope about 50 meters," she replied. "We want to plant these things on soft ground, with good drainage. We don't want erosion to be a factor in the success of this experiment," she advised.

Kelt, Scotty, Padma, and three commandoes carefully carried wide flat plastic containers, originally made to store sweaters under a bed, out into the night. The other two commandos unslung their weapons from their shoulders and took positions on each side of the group, as they made their ascent. Each container safely held an interwoven biomat and new seedlings from the Nevada site's small but growing population of the new plant life.

"These aren't even as big as a bathmat," Kelt noted.

"It's all we can spare, Kelt. We have to try this," Padma said.

"Here we go, this looks really good," said Padma, "let me test the soil before we plant."

She broke open a small carry case, which included a garden shovel. She dug down to test the depth of the topsoil and was satisfied with the results.

"I now want to make sure we have the right bacteria and soil composition," she said as she pulled nine tubes and solutions from her case. She put a small sample of the topsoil in each tube and then put a different solution in each.

The commandos were getting nervous. They hated exposure in the open. Kelt noticed them nervously watching the perimeter as they lay on their bellies, surrounding Kelt, Scotty, and Padma.

"Scotty, do you have the microscope," she asked.

"Sure, here you go," Scotty said as he passed the small device and a computing pad to her.

"It will just be a few more minutes, gents. I need to prepare these slides and take some pictures," she said.

"I can help with that, Padma, I'm not a biologist, but I do know how to prepare slide samples. I designed some little robots to do the task remotely out here. You may or may not know. I dare say it shall be much easier to do with my own fingers," Kelt said with assurance.

He knelt down and started to prepare four slides of the solution from four of the tubes. Padma had completed her set of five and had examined and taken video of two of them by the time Kelt had finished.

"I didn't say that I could do it fast," Kelt grinned.

"That's okay, Kelt, you've saved us some time. I'm already looking at these specimens and I do appreciate your help."

Padma reviewed the videos for a couple minutes, of each sample on her pad.

"I think that everything looks good," she said, "We've got active cultures of the good kinds of bacteria and a rich chemical mix in the soil."

Padma dug the first shallow hole with a hoe to plant the first mat. It was only a few centimeters deep. She then instructed one of the commandos to dig the other four holes similarly. She showed Kelt and Scotty how to remove the mats carefully by unlocking the end of the container, and just let them slip into place by letting gravity do the work. They carefully pushed soil around the mats and even sprinkled a little bit over the new sprouts, taking great care not to damage any of them.

"Let's go home, Scotty!" Kelt commanded.

The trays were stacked and two more commandos were able to carry their weapons downhill. The trip back was uneventful and the shuttle arrived in its bay well before sunrise.

"Hey Kelt, let's grab some breakfast," Scotty said as he smelled the rich taste of bacon wafting from the kitchen. Kelt just wanted to catch a little sleep, but he agreed to have breakfast with his good friend.

"So, do you really think that we'll get some company?" Scotty asked Kelt.

"Count on it Scotty. I think that Mr. Carter, up there, is going to drop all those satellites today."

"If we had waited, we might be able to better prepare a defense, Kelt," Scotty whispered.

"Commander Scott," Kelt started with a grin, "you've been in tight spots before, I'm sure you'll do just fine."

"Aye, Cap'n, that I will," Scotty answered with a bold laugh.

"The bacon and eggs were delicious," Kelt told Scotty.

"I'm sure glad we decided to raise chickens Kelt. Fresh eggs taste so much better than that powdered stuff we have in the freezer," Scotty replied, "you know I think that I'd miss those chickens if we lost them?" he asked.

"Well, I'm very happy to tell you that I won't be missing the hogs... at least the smell," Kelt said jokingly, "can you imagine what the stench down here might be like? It smells like a sweat locker as it is."

"Yeah, it's getting to smell pretty ripe down here. We've got a couple of engineers spending their spare time on some method to better filter the air."

"Are they making any progress, Mr. Scott?"

"I don't know. I only heard it through the gossip mill. You know that sooner or later, we'll have to leave this place."

"Is that a fact or your opinion, Scotty?"

"It just makes sense, Kelt. We are pretty cramped down here. Our food supplies will only last so long. We'll get tired of staying here. There is any number of reasons to leave this dark hole."

"Well, right now, we don't have any other options that are more attractive, believe me. Guy and I have been looking for another secure site to hide out. It's just that we have so many flying vehicles to hide. He's very concerned that too many people know we are here."

"Couldn't we relocate to one of Mr. Carter's islands? That one down in New Zealand was particularly nice."

"Scotty, it *was* a nice place. It's not so nice anymore. It was once a lush green island. Now it's just a brown heap in the middle of a very big ocean. You realize that was one of the first options that came to mind when I started considering a new location."

"I get it, Kelt. That's one of your favorite places, isn't it? That was the first time you really got to spend special time with Akhi. I'm not making fun of you, just pointing out the obvious."

"Indeed. Yes. The place holds a special memory for me. I do suppose that's why it appeared at the top of my list. Actually, if we need to leave, it might not be such a bad place to go."

"Really? Why is that, Kelt?"

"We have construction facilities on that island, Scotty. The bunker there is filled with a couple thousand potential workers. They're sealed in for the moment, and they are producing some of their own vegetables and fruits with some small indoor farms. If their farms fail, we may pay them a visit. We can certainly use some more equipment. We're short on shuttles... disks... we may need a few solar collectors down the road... you know."

"Yeah, I get it. It's a resource worthy of consideration down the road, but not right now."

"I don't want to break the seals on that habitat until it's absolutely necessary, Scotty. There may also be issues with ocean going vessels in the area, but those are becoming much less of a problem. Piracy is certainly taking its toll. The pirates themselves don't have the wherewithal to make it on their own. Once their victim pool diminishes or learns to fight back, they won't last long on their own."

"It's not a very good time to be alive, Kelt, is it?"

"We don't have much of a choice, do we?"

"I suppose not."

"Kelt, I hate to cut you short, but I need to get back to the lab. I'm working with people on Pacificus to develop our spacecraft further. We didn't really ever get a chance to build real spacecraft."

"I tell you Scotty… I'm going to get myself out of these planting trips. There's no reason for me to go on another. We have plenty of people here who can do that sort of work. I have some serious problems to solve, and I'm not getting enough sleep as it is. From now on, I'd like you to organize these expeditions. Whether you go with them or not, I'll leave up to you."

"I've got the same problem Kelt. We have several shuttles that need work and we have a list a mile long for little construction projects. I really need to spend time where my skills are most needed.   I'll make the assignments to take out the little plant rugs and file summations for you to peruse. I need to get over the doom and gloom crap and get to work on the machines, Kelt"

"No problem. I know that the biomat plantings are just tests. I certainly hope that no one is hoping that they will save the planet."

"Well, Kelt… those plants might spread around the planet within the next million years or so. Maybe ET will show up then and have a nice green place to set up house," Scotty replied.

"Cute, but not funny. I do appreciate your attempt at some levity, though. I hate these depressing conversations. I suppose we need to talk about these things once in a while. There is some catharsis in doing so, but I wish we could provide results that are more upbeat. We don't have much to look forward to."

"Kelt, you do. Her name is Akhi."

"Don't remind me, Scott. Yes, I have to admit that she is the only motivation I need. I was speaking more in terms for everyone else."

"I know, Kelt. Hey, let's get out of here."

The two friends returned their trays to the kitchen. Kelt hit the sack and Scotty ran off to the lab.

17- Bridge training

"Great work, gentlemen and ladies. We're up to eighty percent efficiency," Commander Barnes proclaimed as Akhi and Amy entered the CIC with the cheetahs in tow.

"Eighty percent, Commander? That's excellent progress in just one day!" commented Akhi.

"It was mostly in the computer macros, ma'am. Once we got our acceleration figures worked out and implemented into these systems, these simulations have been much more effective."

"What about the other twenty percent, Commander Barnes?"

"May I talk to you in my quarters?"

"Of course, commander."

Akhi stood and walked with the commander to his office located just off the CIC in a narrow corridor.

"I hope you don't mind if the cubs come with us. They are hopelessly attached to me."

"No problem, ma'am."

The four of them entered the office and Barnes closed the door. He offered Akhi one of the two seats in front of his desk and he took the other. Barnes hated the formality and power game of sitting behind his desk, especially when it came to discussions with his superior. He had no problem reporting to Akhi. Although she was still very green at command, he recognized her potential. Her decisions were quick and more often than not, very well reasoned.

"I didn't want to say this in front of the rest of the crew, but we have a couple of problems that I'd like to address. First, this gaming gear is not adequate. There's just too much slop in the sticks if you catch my drift. We're flying remote objects thousands of kilometers an hour. A slight error, which is common in these sticks, can mean an offset of a hundred kilometers or more for these pilots."

"I understand commander. For some time, I've been worried that we've been devoting all of our resources to just food production, and attempting to resolve the crisis dirtside. I realize that we have many other important tasks that are not getting the proper priorities. Would you please make a list of your recommendations for exactly what you need? Our engineers already have some designs and I'd appreciate it if you would look them over. Do you have paper and pen?"

"I've got my com unit."

"Give Dave Sutton a call. He's in charge of the machine shop over on Atlantis. They've been building a series of telescopes the astronomers want. Our astronomers figure that we should take your sensor strategy to the next level. They want to spread hundreds of these small telescopes throughout the solar system. Collectively, with interferometry, we'll be able to see anything the size of a basketball anywhere in the system, provided we know where to look.

I noticed there were equipment issues when we ran the first simulation, and I've already given him a heads up. Certainly, his project can be put on hold for a few days. We'll get you your flight sticks."

"Thank you, ma'am. I suppose you'll be able to provide similar equipment to our folks in the Nevada bunker as well?"

"I'm sorry, Commander Barnes, but we've suspended all drops to the bunker for the moment. We are extremely concerned for their safety. We dare not make any drops to them. I'm sure you are aware what's going on dirtside."

"Yes ma'am, I do. It's the dirty little secret, which no one wants to talk about, but everyone does anyway. Yesterday, I watched a US Army unit take out a National Guard patrol for their MRE's. The Army had a tank and the guard unit only had rifles. We have the good guys killing the other good guys now. It's certainly discouraging to say the least."

"Well then, you can understand why we are keeping those 200 plus people underground where they can't be seen. They are doing projects at night, but they are in control of the situation, so far. They have eyes on the ground. Sure, we help out with imaging from our floater cams, but they alone should be making these kinds of decisions."

"Well, it's not that much of a problem, I suppose. They only have three people down there that can really fly these things with any accuracy. They've done pretty well too, considering their equipment. Quite honestly, I'd trade those three for 10 of my crew in the CIC."

"I suppose that's the other thing you wanted to talk to me about?"

"Yes, ma'am. These are the greenest people I've ever commanded."

"They are civilians, Commander. Each one has specific skills that are keeping these cities alive. The time they spend in the CIC is their free time as volunteers."

"I understand... It's just that... well I shouldn't be venting my frustrations on you. We both understand this problem and I'll just have to spend more time training with them."

"Very good, Commander. I understand your feelings and I'm glad that you came to me with this. It seems as though you've come to your own solution without my advice. I don't want to discourage you from coming to me at any time when you feel the need. I know that sometimes, you can reach a decision just by talking to someone else. I've learned this through my own life's experience. I can't tell you how many times I've discovered the solution to a complex problem, just by explaining it to someone else... even if they didn't understand a single word," Akhi grinned.

"I'd rather that you come to me first, before going to someone in the CIC or one of the other commanders. We can't let fear spread through the crew. Is there anything else, Commander?"

"No, ma'am. Thanks for letting me bend your ear. And double thanks for the authorization for more appropriate flight control equipment!"

"That's what I'm here for, Commander. Don't forget it."

"That's not likely ma'am," Barnes grinned.

As Akhi stood, the cats who had been sitting on either side of her stood and heeled on her left and right as she left the small office.

"That woman is amazing," Barnes thought "When she's a couple years older and those cats are grown, she'll cut a most imposing figure.

18- Satellites down

The door to the CIC opened and Akhi motioned the cats to enter first. She pointed to Commander Barnes and mentally instructed them to go sit in front of him. "He's part of our family," she sent to them mentally.

Obediently, the cats approached Barnes and sat right in front of his chair. They stared into his eyes, begging for attention.

"Go ahead, give them each a little scratch or pat on the head, Commander. I'd like them to get to trust you."

Commander Barnes reached out and scratched each cat around the ears and on the top of their heads.

"Good kitties," Barns chuckled.

His actions prompted a strong purring response from each of the cats.

"They won't lick me will they? I've heard they have pretty wicked tongues," he asked.

"Don't worry. I've instructed them to lick no one but me."

"You know, ma'am, sooner or later we're going to have to establish some formal protocols of some sort here on the bridge. For example, you should be a captain or admiral and have some official posting."

"If you want to call me by title, you may use "Doctor," Akhi grinned. "I actually earned that title. I believe I have a way to go before I can feel comfortable being called Captain. However, the posting is real. I am in tactical command. All that aside, Commander, are we ready to bring those satellites down?"

"Yes ma'am. All of our pilots are in their positions and ready to go."

"How many remote pilots do we have tonight, Commander?"

"Three hundred eighty seven, ma'am. Some of them are in other quarters since the CIC bridges aren't large enough. They are all linked in. They'll do fine."

"Well then, we've certainly got our work cut out for us, gentlemen. That means that each pilot is going to have to bring down over thirty satellites each. Once we start this project, we cannot stop until it is over."

"We are well aware of that, ma'am. The kitchen facilities have provided sandwiches, drinks, snacks. We have wet towels, and priority to the restrooms, will be given to the pilots. We are ready to take as long as we need to bring those birds down."

"Very well, Commander, I'll take the lead if you don't mind. Please take command of your people.

"Nelby Station, are you ready?"

"Nelby actual, ready to go ma'am."

"Atlantis?"

"Atlantis actual, all present, and able."

"Richmond?"

"Richmond actual, ditto here. Let's bring 'em down."

"Commander Barnes?"

"We're ready as you know, ma'am."

"Very well team, we'll have several hours of intensive work. Let's get busy."

Akhi moved front and center on the deck and stood firmly, facing her crew and cameras providing a live feed to the other three CIC's.

"Is everyone wearing their EV suits?" she asked.

"Yes ma'am. All crews throughout the cities are suited up," Commander Barnes returned.

"You have an accurate count?" she asked.

"Yes ma'am. All 18,571 suits are powered up," he said as he checked the numbers on his screen.

"Are our shuttles launched?"

"Yes, ma'am, half of them are outside and clear of the cities."

"Good. At least half of them will be safe, no matter what happens," Akhi nodded.

Each floating city had been designed for 5000 occupants each. Not all crewmembers had been able to make it up to the cities before the nuclear attacks below. Foresight had provided some room to grow and supplies to lengthen the spires and create new habitat spheres. A train of standard shipping cargo containers sat close to the cities with raw materials to expand, should the need arise. Akhi was concerned about that supply train. It was a huge easy target.

Even though the cities held a relatively permanent position above the atmosphere, in constant darkness, they were significantly lower than satellites in orbit. The birds above them traveling at orbital velocities were potentially very lethal.

So, she and her crew had managed to scrape up 387 qualified "pilots" who could fly the floaters. The most threatening satellites had been given priority for the tactic they would employ.

"That's it," she commenced, "Accelerate your floaters to your first satellite on your lists. The orbital vectors are each programmed in your individual stations."

Of course, everyone knew the drill. It didn't hurt to have a cool commander keeping everything in sync and reminding people of the correct sequence of maneuvers, especially with so many civilians serving on the team.

"Then, move your floater in front and park it on its nose." She referred, of course not to the nose of the satellite, but to the side most forward in its orbital path

"Akhi, we've just identified a missile platform!" yelled Gary, her engineering associate from the Stanford lab. "It was dark, but it has just lit up," he said.

Akhi recognized his terminology. "Lit up" meant that the electronics had been powered on and activated. Up until that point, the craft had never been seen or identified. Most of the satellites they were targeting were in easily obtainable databases that NASA had unwittingly provided. Akhi wondered why the CIA had not unwittingly provided their database. It had been her hackers' responsibility to obtain the data. Akhi was upset with their inability to get a complete data set.

"What I wouldn't give for some sci-fi sensors," Akhi mused, "In those flicks, they could see another ship across the full solar system. Here we are flying nearly blind as a bat," she thought. "Are they getting ready to fire?" asked Akhi.

"I don't know, but it looks like they're warming up for a shot at us, and we haven't brought down a single satellite. What's up with that?" he exclaimed.

"Do we have any available floaters nearby?" she asked everyone in the five linked CIC's, which included the three pilots in Nevada.

"We've got one on a comsat just a few kilometers lower in orbit," came the response from someone in the now cramped CIC.

The floaters were still controlled with simple PC's and software that encrypted signals in bursts to the craft. Each floater had its own identifier and an attached DC (dimensional conduit), which would allow them to control all of their remote devices in real time. Originally, the floaters had been designed to be commanded by short, low powered microwave bursts, but they had discovered soon enough that real time access was essential. The loss of a second or two in response to commands would not allow them to do what they were doing. That was when Akhi had let the secret out of the bag with the "direct connection" aspect to the floater technology. It had to be done. The pilots now had upgraded flight sticks and the efficiency had risen to 93 percent.

"I need someone who's farther away than that, so we can get enough acceleration. Anyone positioned at least 30 Km away? We need to hit that thing hard, not just slow it down."

The other pilots understood what she was talking about. A few hundred meters would not give enough acceleration to create the required velocity to slice through the platform.

"Okay, Akhi, I can confirm that the missiles are being prepared to launch," Gary said.

"I've got a floater over here that we can hit at 26,000 Kph," volunteered a pilot named Wang.

"Hit it quick!" commanded Akhi.

The pilot seized control of the disk floating in front of his assigned satellite, and pushed the floater to accelerate at 10 g's toward the missile platform. Tension in the CIC increased as just a few seconds ticked by. Everyone wondered if they could take out the missile launching system in time. Just as the first missile had started its rocket motor, the disk blasted through it, and the platform.

"Great going, Mr. Wang," Akhi said, "bring your floater around and drop that wreck back to Earth before one of those warheads detonates,"

"They are nukes, ma'am," warned Simms. "Drop them from orbit," she commanded. "They won't detonate unless they are armed and they'd be foolish to do that again to themselves once they hit the ground," she said and hoped secretly that she was right.

Wang positioned the floater in front of the largest remaining piece of the platform, which contained the warheads and slowed the floater so that the orbital momentum of the platform was lost and it started its descent to Earth.

"Okay team; let's drop as many as we can, as soon as we can. This is a coordinated effort, so look sharp people," Akhi commanded. "I'm spending too much time studying commando tactics," she thought silently and then reconsidered, "I suppose, right now, that is a good thing."

"The satellite I was assigned is coming in on a vector straight toward us," yelled Wang.

"How would they know to bring that bird down to hit us?" questioned Akhi. Not bothering to listen for an answer, she quickly assessed that no one had anything nearby to hit the satellite on collision course with Pacificus.

"It's going to hit us in the teeth," shouted Wang. The forward momentum of the satellite was Earth bound. The best tactical move was straight up.

"Pacificus flight, accelerate 90 degrees at 3 g's," Akhi ordered. At three times their normal weight, the crews were slammed into their seats, many fell to the floor, and laptop-computing pads spread everywhere as the city started immediate acceleration from a dead stop.

It was too little and too late, the satellite hit the primary forge sphere near the bottom of the spire. It felt like a minor earthquake from the CIC. Akhi watched in horror as external videos showed several dozen crewmen sucked out from the fairly large hole in the sphere's hull.

"How many do you count?" she asked the officer at the video screen.

"It looks like there about 60 or so, ma'am," he replied.

"Get an emergency team down there right away to extract the survivors and injured," she commanded.

"Raise all cities one hundred kilometers," Akhi ordered. "That should throw them off," thought Akhi.

As the numerous satellites were dropped from orbit by slowing them down with Space Truck floaters, others had either been able to slip through or appear from nowhere. Three comsats slammed into the cargo container train far below them.

"I hope they didn't get any of our stored oxygen," she said.

"It looks like we've lost some extruded aluminum and raw plastics," one of the crewman advised as he surveyed the cargo train's inventory map.

"Move that train south in latitude out of the orbital plane at 1.5 g's," ordered Akhi, "and keep it on the move for the duration of this mission." She had realized that was what ground based radar had been tracking. The spires were made mostly of a carbon Buckyballs and ceramic steel. There was very little in the spires visible with ground-based radar. The cargo containers on the other hand, were big flat steel surfaces. They reflected radar most effectively.

"We've got a second missile platform lighting up!" yelled Wang.

"How many could there be... and more importantly, why didn't we know about them?" Akhi demanded. "Anyone at the right distance to hit that platform?" Akhi shouted.

Three hands went up. All sent their disks toward the platform. "All spires, evasive 45 degrees up, north above the orbital plane!" shouted Akhi, "lets put some distance between the spires and the supply train." A missile launched from the platform.

"If anyone can put a floater in direct path of that missile do it now!" she ordered. Four floaters came to bear and one lucky pilot managed to lock his floater right in the path of the missile. The missile had not succeeded in achieving enough velocity to do any damage to the disk. The missile crumpled its nose into itself and fell from space.

"Damage report from our forge?" Akhi demanded.

"It looks like we've lost a total of 69 people. We have a couple of dozen severely injured," replied CIC Commander Barnes.

"Please make sure to assign someone to follow up on the losses. Find out who they are, and if needed, notify families," Akhi ordered.

"Yes, ma'am," Barnes responded.

Akhi checked with Commander Barnes to make sure there were no more imminent threats.

"We've got an AWACS circling below the cargo train," Barnes noted.

"That means that we are fighting the US military, doesn't it, Barnes?" Akhi noted with great sadness, "the land that I love," she added as she thought of the song she had learned as a child that contained those words.

"Barnes, send down a disk to blind that plane," Akhi ordered.

Barnes commanded one of the pilots who had control of a floater, the right distance away to accelerate his small disk to 24,000 Kph, just as it slammed into the supporting elements of the AWACS radar structure. The large AWACS dish ripped away from the plane, and took out the tail section of the aircraft as it sheared away. The plane started into an uncontrolled roll as it tumbled dirtside.

"They'll not be able to get out of that," Barnes noted.

He had answered her question as to whether or not the crewmembers would be able to parachute to safety. With the strong forces pulling the craft as it tumbled and its weakend structure from the floater attack, the plane broke its back on the way down. As the two sections fell to Earth, Akhi did note one parachute deploy. She had now joined the club, she had killed real live people and was sick to her stomach. Her thoughts wanted to dwell on that devastating fact, but she refused to relent.

"Okay people, let's bring down the rest of them," she commanded. There would be many more rounds this day with the pilots she had available to clear the skies of satellites.

*****

"Kelt, are you awake?" Kelt had been soundly sacked for only a couple of hours. It was still fairly early in the morning. Sunrise was just underway on top of the bunker, not that he would know for sure without checking a clock. Akhi's voice woke him from his well-deserved rest. He shot up out of bed and looked around the dark room for her. He hit the lights. His eyes stung from their brightness as his irises started to collapse to compensate.

"Are you there, Kelt?" he heard her again. He shook his head attempting to bring his mind to focus.

He finally remembered that Akhi had literally been playing mind games. She had been able to read his mind when he was thinking about her. She had admitted that was the only time she could connect with him in that fashion. She had never been able to send him a message when he was focused on other things. Perhaps he was still dreaming.

"I'm here, Akhi," Kelt thought to himself as he threw on a tee shirt and some sweat pants. "Oh, I'm here sweetie. Why don't you come down and join me for breakfast," he smiled as he sent her the mental question.

121

"Oh Kelt! You heard me, get a vid link up to me right away!" he heard her say.

Barefoot, he started to walk to his screen and nearly tripped as he ran his toes into the foot of the chair. "Owe! That hurts!" he exclaimed aloud.

"I'm sorry darling" he heard her say.

"This is blowing my mind," he said to himself.

"You'll get used to it, my love. Just get a video link established, I want to see you while I talk to you," he heard her clearly say.

The screen came on and he entered her code. There she was before him. Her eyes bore through the screen like a drill going through a peeled hardboiled egg.

"I'm sorry, Akhi, I was up all night placing plantings in the Amazon with the new varieties we found along the Nile. Our dirtside biologist has a list of places where we'll attempt to plant these things, in a feeble effort to bring plant life back. It's a start, but it might take hundreds, thousands, or even millions of years for them to take significant hold. I suppose that it's a start even though it is a very small one. I've only been asleep a couple of hours," he told her.

"I know, Kelt, but I had to tell you right away. Our crew up here brought down almost every satellite that had ever been launched, early this morning. We were attacked."

"They were playing games with us and we needed to poke out their eyes," Kelt responded.

"I know, Kelt, but we lost 69 people in the attack! We found two missile platforms up here with US markings. All those birds have gone down now."

"Sixty nine people, Akhi? Were any of the millenarians lost?" Kelt asked as the realization had suddenly sunk in to his sleepy stupor. "How could that have happened?" he asked.

"Kelt, they flew a comsat into our forge."

"Sixty Nine...," he grieved with true sadness in his heart.

"None of the millenarians were injured. We lost people while I was in command, Kelt. I'm devastated," she cried. Her eyes were red with tearing and her cheeks were partially swollen from hours of agony.

"But Kelt, that's not what I called you about. I knew you were sleeping and I figured the satellite mission news could wait," she said.

"Well, what is it? What is so urgent?"

"There's an Army Hummer approaching the turn off road. They'll be there at your site in about 25 minutes. Aren't your people watching down there?" she asked.

"Hey, babe... I don't know... I have to check into this. Talk later," Kelt said as he abruptly terminated her call.

He called up the code on his pad to put the station on alert. There was no loud klaxon, nor were there flashing red lights. They had set up a code to turn lights on and off repeatedly in the private quarters and cafeteria. All other areas were immediately fully illuminated.

Kelt announced over the speaker, "We've got incoming. Everyone to their stations, please," he commanded through the PA system.

In the very brief planning they had done, they had given assignments out to everyone on site. Each person was responsible to make sure that three others were out of their personal quarters when alarms sounded. The plan had worked. Everyone sleeping had been aroused, grabbed their clothes, and ran to their assigned stations undressed.

As Kelt entered the CIC, he noticed Guy waiting for him. Before Guy garnered Kelt's interest, Kelt shouted to one of the young officers, "Bring down the elevator now. Send someone up to retrieve the elevator remote from the wall. Put a light switch there instead," ordered Kelt.

"But sir," the young officer protested, "the light switch won't work."

"Don't ask questions, just do it, now. Standard power lines don't run out this way. We'd hate to let them know that the lights still work," he instructed the kid as he ran toward the elevator. He was a kid, although he was several years older than Kelt. He hadn't remembered to call down the elevator before he ran off.

"Someone get that elevator down here now!" Kelt shouted with great irritation.

"I'm on it, sir," someone called out, "I've called it down.

"Guy, what's the status?" Kelt asked.

"I'm sorry, Kelt, but I too was up all night. Our CIC staff saw the Hummer coming in, but didn't give it a second thought since it was only one vehicle," Guy said apologetically.

"So, what do we have in the air?" asked Kelt.

"On that front, we are pretty good, I think. While you were out last night, I lifted all the floaters we have and 4 of the small flitters. Not everyone has passed flight school to carry people, but any sorry ass gamer can fly a floater," Guy explained.

"What's on the warehouse floor, Guy?"

"It's clean as a whistle," he responded.

Kelt quickly pulled his com unit out of the pocket of his jeans, and called supplies.

"Yes sir, what can I do for you?" the supply manager asked. He had immediately recognized Kelt's call sign and gave the call highest priority.

"Remember that truckload of big screen televisions we got during the lift to the cities?" asked Kelt.

"Sure, they're still here on pallets, wrapped in plastic," he answered.

"Get some people, as many as it takes to get the entire lot to the elevator right now!" Kelt commanded.

"Yes sir, hold on..."

Kelt waited for a few moments as the man yelled several commands to his crew.

"We'll have them all there by the time you bring down the platform,"

"Good," said Kelt "have we got anything else we can't use in stores? If so, bring it all to the elevator as fast as you can, bring in anyone else if you have to. Tell them that we have a situation topside," Kelt concluded.

"What are you doing, Kelt?" asked Guy.

"I want them to think we're not home."

"Oh, I get it now. You want them to think that stuff was left behind because we couldn't use it," Guy surmised.

"Right," said Kelt, "that's what we are doing. The best way to fool someone is to put everything out in front of the store. It might not work, but then again, it's worth a shot."

Kelt did a quick calculation in his head. Once the platform came down the second time, after replacing the elevator control near the doorway with the deceptive light switch, they would have 6 minutes tops to load the cargo. He quickly put his clothes on and ran to the elevator.

The first forklifts had arrived with the pallets of big screen televisions. There were some bringing in long tied up sections of plastic drain pipe, in large containers with hand controlled dollies. And some wise guy had found some floaters and was bringing in a huge double stack supersized pallet of two by six redwood lumber. Kelt looked at Sam and smiled for his ingenuity. That's what they had been designed to do, after all.

"Hey Sam, where'd you find the floaters? Guy told me that he'd sent them all up this morning," Kelt demanded.

"We have a room full of them down that hallway," Sam said as he pointed the opposite direction of where supply was located. Kelt didn't have time to wonder how they had been misplaced.

"Hey people, get down there, and program some of these floaters to bring in some more lumber. The elevator still hadn't come back down yet.

Kelt had wondered if the officer who went up had taken a light switch with him. He noticed half dozen small empty boxes to the left side of the large elevator door's entrance. "He must have called someone to fetch him one each of all the types we have," thought Kelt. "The kid officer had just redeemed himself. He took up six switches to make sure he had one that matched the same size as the elevator control. There should be no telltale paint lines."

The door slowly opened and the officer rolled under the door as soon as he could and handed Kelt the elevator door remote. "I replaced it with a switch exactly the same size sir. Hopefully, they won't notice," he said with a winded voice.

"He must be scared to death," thought Kelt, "He's just been on a four minute elevator ride, up and down. How winded can you get doing that?" he asked himself.

"Okay team, elevator's down. Get this stuff neatly stacked inside. We have precisely 6 and one half minutes." Kelt ordered.

Guy and 5 of his commandos directed traffic to keep everyone from bumping in to each other. They formed up twelve lines. Six equipment lines went in and six lines of forklifts, hand dollies, and empty floaters would come full circle coming out to the left of each cargo line. It was a marvel of logistics to see just how much equipment was actually loaded into the immense elevator.

"How we doing for time?" Kelt demanded as he shouted at a woman who had a video link to a floater cam above them.

"We've got five minutes until they get here, sir," she yelled back.

"Everyone out of the elevators on the double," Yelled Guy to his army of ants, "Just drop your loads, nice and straight, and get out!" The resulting pile certainly did look disorganized as if left in haste.

"So be it," thought Kelt.

The elevator rose back into position just thirty seconds before the Hummer arrived on site. Kelt turned to Guy and asked, "Can we tag that vehicle?"

"Yes sir. We'll drop the bird scat on them when they leave."

Kelt was familiar with the technique. He had worked with Scotty to develop it. A floater rigged with tags would drop directly down toward the vehicle moving laterally in the same direction as it descended. When the

126

floater was only a few centimeters away, a tiny robot would squirt out a gooey sticky mess with a tag in it. It looked just like bird excrement. The floater would ascend skyward keeping track of the vehicle directly underneath it. The occupants would never know that they had been tagged. Some grunt would eventually wash the truck and the tags would go down the drain.

"Did anyone think to tag our door entry keypad?" asked Kelt. He was met with blank stares. "We should have spent more time on defense planning last night instead of taking that trip down south" he sighed.

Five rangers exited the Hummer. All carried automatic firearms and one carried a crow bar. With hand motions, the commander told his team to spread out and check all sides of the building. As they ran to each corner, the man with the crowbar inspected the finger/keypad combination remote to the door.

"We're not getting in with this," he said to his commander.

"We'll take it back with us then. We'll see if there's anything of interest in that device hanging on the wall."

"It's just a common digital security lock, sir."

"We'll take it anyway. You just never know how clever people can be," the commander chided.

"Yes sir," answered the soldier as he pried the digital entry lock from the wall and threw it in his bag.

After a quick sweep of the area and finding no one within sight, the other three rangers quickly ran back to the side door to the old warehouse. They took aggressive attack stances on each side of the door.

"They're not going to get in with that crow bar," Kelt smiled. "A crow bar against that door? It's like throwing toothpicks at a tank," he chuckled.

"Don't worry, sir, they always come prepared," answered Guy with a serious tone. The ranger tried using the crowbar for a mere minute.

"Okay, dig out the C4," shouted the commander.

Two of the rangers quickly retrieved two backpacks from the Hummer. Quickly, the charges were accurately placed. One of the rangers pulled the Hummer around to the front of the building and the others ran around to follow him. They all got behind the vehicle, stooped low, and one of the rangers flipped the recessed detonation switch on the remote. The door instantly buckled and it was thrown half way across the immense warehouse floor.

"Do you think that we can replace that door after they leave, Guy?" Kelt asked.

"No sir. If we do, they'll know for sure that we are here when they come back."

"Well, let's see if our little ruse works for us," Kelt responded.

The rangers carefully entered the warehouse and moved from row to row looking for defenders, but found none.

"It looks like this is just a bunch of stuff they couldn't use sir. Everyone is gone," said one of the rangers.

"Let's just make sure," responded the commander. He walked slowly up and down the aisles, inventorying mentally the items sitting on the floor. "Yes, this is all the sort of stuff, they might leave behind," he thought. He still kept walking up and down the aisles with pangs of doubt churning in his gut. He walked along the walls looking at the floor.

"Naw, there's no way he'll see that this is an elevator. The walls are built out over the opening," Guy said, but there is one thing he hasn't done that I would do."

"And what would that be?" asked Kelt.

"You are about to see, my young friend," he said, as he pointed to the monitor. The commander retrieved a pair of white gloves from his belt.

"Here we go, friends. He'll nail us within about two minutes," Guy announced.

The head ranger put on his gloves and walked up and down the aisles spot-checking the items for dust. There was plenty. They'd been stored for months down in the bunker.

"Okay, now, he's going to take a look for recent prints on the cargo," advised Guy, "he'll be looking for clean spots where the inventory may have been recently moved.

"We carried it in with fork lifts and those little forklift dollies. I hope we didn't leave any telltale signs," Kelt answered.

"It doesn't matter, Kelt. This guy is too sharp. He'll check the floor next," Guy told him.

Feeling satisfied that the inventory seemed that it had been left there, the commander started toward the entry door and suddenly stopped just inside the building's entrance. He turned around to look where he had been. There were no footprints.

"There's dust all over the goods and none on the floor," he ventured out loud. He used his left hand with the clean glove and wiped the floor with it. His glove came back perfectly clean.

"They're here," he announced to his crew. "Let's get out of here," the commander told the others. They moved quickly out of the building, climbed into their vehicle, and left.

Guy piloted the floater down above the hummer and let the bird scat fly.

"Now, we must develop a defense plan or get our hides out of here," Guy told Kelt.

"How long do you think it will be before they come back?" asked Kelt.

"I don't know, Kelt. It's hard for me to understand their motivations. Maybe they think we have a thousand people here with 20 years of food and other supplies," Guy said.

"Well, we do have 10 years of food for two hundred people, Guy," Kelt whispered.

"My point exactly, Kelt. They'll come back. They might think that we have technology they can use. We'll never know. I just wish that Mr. Carter had better planned for this sort of thing," Guy said.

"This wasn't supposed to happen. We weren't supposed to still be here," Kelt said morosely.

"I know, Kelt, I know. I truly wish that you were upstairs with that wonderful girl of yours. The reality is we're going to have to go it on our own," Guy replied.

"Kelt, now that I have thought about it, there is a strong possibility they may attack tonight with a bunker buster bomb. That is their standard operating procedure," Guy flatly stated.

"Guy, I was dreading that we'd be defending ourselves so soon," Kelt responded.

19- Defensive planning

Kelt and Guy spent all day making plans and preparations for the expected attack that might be coming in the night. Defensive tactical planning for a direct assault would have to wait. A bunker buster could easily destroy them.

"I think that a guided bomb is their first choice. We don't have any defensive weapons they can see, and they can't use cruise missiles or anything else that requires GPS navigation," Guy advised Kelt.

"That means they'd use an aircraft to deliver it, wouldn't it," asked Kelt.

"Affirmative, sir." Although the US military hadn't updated much of its equipment for decades, they had made improvements in their smart bomb technologies. Everything could now be controlled from a single aircraft. "The thing is, they'll likely drop it directly down our throats, so, the best tactic is to take out the aircraft long before it gets here," Guy advised.

"Guy, look, for all of my life, I've had great respect for our men and women in uniform. The jerks in charge are the ones who will be mounting this attack. The pilots will only be following orders, I will not have them killed," admonished Kelt.

"Come on, sir, we are fighting for our lives here!" Guy exclaimed with some amazement at the naiveté of his young commander.

"We can do this, Guy, I have some ideas. Before we go any further, let me tell you briefly what I have in mind," Kelt explained.

Kelt then sketched out his plans with Guy on how they could modify some floaters for specific tasks and exactly how they might be used. Guy agreed. Without making any specific plans in their implementation, several floaters had to be built up with the necessary hardware. Kelt had sent a floater disk into the Amazon when the virus first broke out equipped with a full experiment kit and microscope.

"They used floaters to bring down the satellites last night. We can do this can't we?" he asked Guy.

Guy nodded in agreement.

"Scotty, grab some of the machinists and that mining guy and get them into the CIC right away," Kelt mandated over his private com.

"Aye, Cap'n, You talking about Dr. Simmons the geologist?" Scotty asked.

"Yeah, that's him, I just couldn't remember his name," Kelt answered.

"We'll be there right away, Kelt, we're all in the lab right now," Scotty advised. The team assembled quickly within five minutes in the CIC.

"Okay, ladies and gentlemen," Kelt started, "we believe we will be attacked tonight."

"Those guys came in today and just left us alone. They didn't find anything they want. Why would they attack us?" asked Scotty.

"Scotty, you do recall the last words of the Ranger commander don't you?" Kelt asked.

"Aye Cap'n, he said, "They're here. So, why does that mean we will be attacked tonight?"

"Mr. Lerner has advised me that would be their standard operating procedure. They like to take out targets of interest as soon as they are identified, and they'll do it after dark," Kelt informed the group.

"Now we've only a few hours before sunset and I'd like all of our assets in place by then." He then outlined how he wanted some floaters to be enhanced. The machinists would produce all three versions, but the geologist had quite a bit of work to do before the crew could start work on his version. His floaters could be the critical factor in the strategy, but it would take time for him to make some modifications to his mining equipment, so it could work properly at supersonic velocities. Kelt knew that he'd not be able to count on that particular tool to come to bear in certain aspects of his plans. He quickly modified his ideas mentally and talked them over with Guy as a backup contingency.

The construction team went off to the machine shop and labs, where they enlisted anyone who could follow directions in the machining process. Most sat around for a couple of hours, while the engineers whipped up the CAD drawings that would be used in the automated machining process. From a working CAD schematic, all they really needed were operators to position materials in the automated machinery and start the process.

"Has anyone talked to Rick, upstairs?" asked Kelt.

"Yes, I had a conversation with him around O-three hundred," Guy told him.

"So, it's probably old news by now," Kelt said.

"I would suspect so, Kelt. He's really managed to piss off just about everyone who was depending on those orbiting birds," Guy said.

"Just think about it. Everything that the world accomplished over the past seven decades was represented in those satellites. I recognize the necessity of bringing them down to protect us, but I also sense a sort of loss for what seems to be a terrorist act. So, what assessments did Rick have to offer?" asked Kelt.

"His biggest headache is the US military, of course. China was ready to nuke the US, but Rick convinced the General Secretary that the US had no responsibility for the action and talked him out of it. International news stations are dead, but we are prepared to bounce their signals off our own birds. They begrudgingly accepted the offer. Everyone on Earth will be able to use our communications birds in peaceful pursuits. At least, that's what Rick told them, when they talked. You might give him a call, Kelt," Guy said.

Can you give me twenty minutes, Guy? I'll make a video conference. While I'm busy, see if you can pull up the schematics of anything that might be coming our way tonight. You know what I want to do, so let's get our act in order, and prepare instructions for our newly trained pilots.

Maybe Rick can offer some help in that regard," offered Kelt. "Check with Akhi too, she was in command last night. She's got the most experience using floaters as weapons."

"Sure thing, Kelt. That was next on my list, so let's break for now. Let's see… it's about noon, I figure that we're going to have to move our robotic army upstairs, as soon as it gets dark. I don't think that sending these things up during the daylight hours is a good idea, Kelt. They'll wait until midnight or so, before they try anything," Guy said.

"Agreed," Kelt concurred, "I'll see you in twenty."

Kelt put in an emergency video link request to speak with Rick. "Hi, Kelt. I'm truly sorry that we threw you into this mess," he said as he picked up the link.

"How did you know we were in a mess?" asked Kelt, "we haven't had a chance to talk about it."

"It's not hard to figure out. During the night, before we could bring the satellites down, someone else tried to run another comsat through Pacificus. We lost some of the container vessels with supplies, and we even had a couple of nukes launched at us from orbital platforms.

"We were hit this time Kelt, and we lost some people in one of the forges," Rick added.

"Akhi told me about that earlier, Rick. Has the body count risen?"

"It looks like we've lost one of the injured so far. We still have a few locked up in secure sections that we need to get to. We have a very few who were thrown out of the sphere and managed to fall onto shuttles who are in critical condition. I'm afraid that we won't be able to do much with the forge right now. We just don't have enough oxygen in reserve to fill it back up. It's a good thing that we had four of them up here," Rick added.

"The spheres are highly compartmentalized," Kelt said.

"Yes they are, but this brick managed to come in very fast at an angle to penetrate three decks. We didn't really lose that much deck space and air, but reserves are pretty limited up here, if you know what I mean," Rick explained.

"Rick, I'm terribly sorry, I feel like it was my fault for this mess, but I didn't design the spheres for space habitats. I only designed them for the pressure differential that you had on the specification. Had I known we were going into space with these things, they'd have a much thicker skin," Kelt explained trying to avoid sounding negative.

"I didn't really think that we'd ever need to ascend up so high, Kelt. I thought that I had over spec'd those spheres for the intended purpose of bringing aid to disaster victims. I had the specs drawn up so that we'd be able to rise far above major storm systems, and then bring them down to replenish our air supplies at the very least. And since it didn't require all that much more in materials, I figured we may as well build them to withstand space... at least for short periods. I only gave you the numbers that my physicists recommended. I should have been more aggressive with them," Rick responded apologetically.

"Now, I have the complete picture, Rick," Kelt said, "I suppose none of us could have ever predicted the events unfold as they did. It is truly a freakin Greek tragedy."

"It's more than a tragedy, it is the end of the world," Rick reminded Kelt softly.

"Rick, it's not the end of the world as long as I'm alive. We need to take care of this potential raid tonight. Have you been able to talk to President Crawford?" Kelt asked.

"He's not taking my calls."

"That figures, Perhaps he might be a little more willing to cooperate if we are successful tonight."

"Do you really think they'll drop a bomb on you, Kelt?"

"That's what Guy says."

"Well, he would know, Kelt. He's a good man. I'm glad that he's down there to advise and protect you."

"I'm glad he's here too, Rick. I doubt we'd survive the night without his expertise in this situation." Kelt went on to explain the strategies that he wanted to use in the anticipated bombing of the Nevada Base.

"I'm doubly glad that you have Guy down there with you. He really knows his stuff, doesn't he?"

"Yes, he does. Say, you know, we could use some more floaters mounted with thermal detectors and cams above us," Kelt explained, "We might also need to enlist some of your pilots too."

"Tell me what you need and send us the access codes for your disks," Rick returned. They discussed the situation for a few brief minutes to resolve the logistics.

"Hey, Rick, one more thing. Remember those women in the space elevator?" asked Kelt.

"Yes, what about them?"

"Have you cut the line and put that grand hotel in orbit yet? If not, we might have some visitors up there very shortly.

"Ah, no. We've sent them supplies once in a while, but the hotel remains firmly mounted to the ground. We didn't think that anyone would dare enter South America again. Since the hotel is geostationary, it was a little easier for us to come close and push foodstuffs into one of their open airlocks. Besides, putting them into orbit would create some serious problems for them, especially where the plumbing is concerned," Rick answered as he checked the status of the elevator. "Kelt, thanks for reminding me about that. I'm looking at the elevator status right now, and it seems that the car is on its way down."

"What could they hope to accomplish by coming up?" asked Kelt, "they will only find a bunch of pregnant women and their pastor on board."

"There's food," Rick answered. Kelt wondered if he were talking about the women or the supplies they carried onboard. He quickly realized that Rick had meant both.

"Rick?"

"Yes, Kelt."

"Can you drop an eye on who's at the base of the elevator and see who's knocking on the door? I smell a rat," Kelt said.

"Kelt, I'd rather not cut those women and push them into orbit. It doesn't make much sense. They'd lose the Earth's gravitational pull. Think about it, Kelt, what would happen in the "powder rooms." I'm sure that we didn't outfit that hotel with zero g toilets... if you know what I mean," Rick said with a grin.

"Yeah, it doesn't make sense to let them go that way, does it?" Kelt returned smiling. "I don't think that it makes much sense to cut the anchor line. Couldn't we lock a floater just under the car, say at 10,000 kilometers? That would stop its descent.

"I think that is an excellent idea, Kelt. Can you manage to take care of that situation? We don't want to run any risks of contamination with our equipment," Rick suggested.

Kelt thought of everything on his schedule and knew that there was no way for him to deal with this personally.

"I'm not too sharp this morning, Rick. Why don't you just take one of the floaters I'm assigning to Pacificus and drop it at that altitude below the descending car for me? I hate to pass it back to you, but you realize that we've been seriously tasked for time, resources, and manpower down here."

"I know how difficult it is for you dirtside, Kelt. Yeah, I'll pass the info down to Barnes in the CIC. Frankly, I don't know how you few have been able to do so much with so little," Rick said.

"We're doing a lot, but I doubt that we are accomplishing much more than staying alive. I just hope we won't actually have to go out with rifles to defend ourselves. Guy has a team of only 29 commandos. We have other military personnel, but they're not as well trained. The rest of us are all civilians," Kelt advised. "Well, Rick, I need to get back with the team. We need to finish our preparations in case we get attacked tonight. Guy is pretty sure that we'll have to defend ourselves against a bunker buster bomb attack."

"I'm sorry, Kelt. You'd think that this situation would bring us together as a people," Rick said sadly.

"People tend to forget how to be civilized when they are facing starvation, Rick. I'm wondering if we can manage to turn this situation around, what the world will be like. Can those who have turned to murder, or even cannibalism, be trusted? Will the survivors be a bunch of thugs, or thoughtful considerate citizens?" Kelt asked.

"I've not even considered that aspect of this catastrophe. In answer to your question, I'm afraid that most of them will lean toward the "thug" side, Kelt. I'm sorry, but that's the way I see it," Rick answered.

"Well Rick, I need to get back to our planning session. I'll get those floaters assigned to Pacificus. It will take a few days for that car to descend to that point and no one will know how to deal with the situation when it comes to a sudden stop. Problem solved. Right?"

"Right, my friend."

Kelt smiled as he cut the link.

20- Tactical planning

It was 4 in the afternoon at the Nevada CIC as the team met together to discuss the tactical planning of what was sure to be an exciting night.

"I'm sorry I couldn't get those industrial LASERs mounted up for you Kelt," apologized Dr. Simmons. "They are just too big," he explained.

"To tell you the truth doctor, I wasn't sure you could do it in time, but I'd like you to keep working on it. I can see several uses for them," Kelt said. "We learned a lot today from the satellite battle upstairs. I hope those of you pilots, not involved, were able to catch the video clips I sent to you," Kelt said as he noticed nods in the affirmative.

"Okay," Kelt started, "what did we come up with?"

One of the machinists picked up a 50 cm x 50 cm box, reached in carefully with industrial gloves, and lifted out the new floater. "This one hasn't been activated yet, and it is pretty heavy," the man grunted as he lifted the disk out of the box and dropped it on the table. "As you can see, we've made a new covering with your matrix," he said.

Kelt looked at the disk and it was no longer a short squatty cylindrical disk, it looked like a little flying saucer.

"I love it!" exclaimed Kelt.

"We did paint half of them white like you asked, Kelt, but we left the rest black. Let me show you why," the machinist explained. He picked up a piece of paper and dragged its edge along the edge of the disk. The edge of the saucer had been sharpened so that it cleanly cut the paper. "Since Simmons couldn't get us the LASER platforms working in time, we thought that we'd improve on what happened upstairs last night. These things will easily cut through anything we throw at them," he concluded.

Kelt had only considered using the little flying saucers to spook soldiers on the ground. Hovering a hundred meters up, they would be extremely deceptive. They could appear to be kilometers away and much larger than they really were. The saucers in black would be effective cutting tools in the darkness.

"Great thinking gentlemen, we have an additional "weapon" in our arsenal," Kelt approved.

"I only wish we had an arsenal," Guy commented with a wry grin.

"Okay, let's see our next adventure in machining," demanded Kelt.

Scotty pulled his specialized floater out of his box. It too was saucer shaped with a fat bulge on the bottom. Its additional casing kept the mechanical components safe inside until they were required.

"I wish that we had more time to work on this, Kelt, I just don't know what speeds you'll be able to achieve without tearing the legs off," Scotty apologized.

"Well, let's see how it works, Scotty," Kelt said.

"Okay, Well… you wanted to be able to latch on to a jet's exterior and hold on firmly, so we've got these little spider legs that are extremely sharp. The legs are loaded with small explosive charges, so when we come close to an object, we just trigger the little bombs and the little critter sinks its teeth in deep. This floater here will show you how the mechanism will work." A couple of men brought in a sheet of steel 3cm thick and laid it over two small tables. Scotty then placed the bogus floater with the bulge on top of the sheet of steel from his computer. "Ready?" Scotty said.

Without waiting for a response, he remotely set off the micro charges. The six arms of the device sliced clean through the steel and bent outward.

"You'll never get that out of there," he explained, "but from what you've told me, we won't be working with steel either. Right?" Scotty asked hopefully.

"That's right Scotty, we won't," answered Guy.

"Kelt, if we have to, the floater can separate itself from the knife set," Scotty said as he pointed to the razor sharp penetrating legs protruding through the steel. He turned back to his computer, released the spider leg assembly remotely, and piloted the small craft out one meter away.

"That's great, Scotty! We don't want anyone dirtside getting their hands on any of our floaters. We don't want to sacrifice any of them either. I'm sure that we'll need every one we've got sooner or later.

"Okay Guy, why don't you review our plans with everyone? Let's use these black disks with a cutting edge instead of the lasers we had planned," Kelt ordered.

"Of course, sir," Guy answered. He then went on to show several 3D CAD schematics and images of the craft that they might be facing during the night. He pointed out the best places to "attach" Scotty's lethal plaything to the various aircraft.

"Kelt has told me that no one dies and we'll do our best to satisfy his demands. Is that clear pilots?" Guy asked. He had expected the resounding response "Yes, sir" in response, but half of the pilots were mechanics or machinists. Guy's heart sank. He needed complete discipline and did not have it. He knew that he would only be able truly to depend on his own commandos. He pulled Kelt over to the corner of the room and expressed his concerns. Kelt agreed.

"We'll hold the civies in reserve then," said Kelt, "your team will be first on the line."

21- Bombing run

It was just after midnight and the focus was on the US air base north of them. Their eyes in the sky watched carefully as an F-26 exited the hangar. The F-26 development had been abandoned nearly three decades before as a viable aircraft for the military. It had been the last fighter aircraft ever to be designed and built by the US Air force. Between politics and severe recessions, the government could not afford to purchase new military hardware. They maintained what they had.

There were no lights down below but the low light imaging equipment they had was superb. Scotty had been playing with some new software that performed stretching algorithms in real time, which showed every detail from down below. They had even moved a couple of floater cams in above the hangars for a side view.

"Now this isn't the only show in town gents," admonished Guy. I want the other teams monitoring their assigned airspace.

"It's heavy," explained Guy.

"You mean it has passengers on board?" asked Kelt.

"No sir, the plane is heavy, look at the tires. That bird is packing," Guy explained, "It's got some bunker busters loaded for a surprise visit."

Guy motioned to one in his squad by moving his hands quickly across his knees. The commando acknowledged and brought in the little black saucer, accelerating at 5 g's. By the time it had approached the F-26, it was traveling at just under the speed of sound.

"Here we go," said the pilot as he dipped under the back end of the craft. The action happened so quickly that Kelt couldn't see what had been done, but he could clearly see the results. The plane fell on its nose. The front landing gear had been sheared. Several emergency vehicles emerged from surrounding buildings and surrounded the jet fighter bomber. They quickly extracted the pilot, checked for fire threats, and then surrounded the landing gear to assess what had happened.

"So, Guy, do you think they'll pull out another fighter and give it another go?" asked Kelt.

"Yes, sir. I believe that they are thinking that the landing gear collapsed," he responded.

Shortly, Guy was proven correct as another F-26 pulled out of the same hangar obviously carrying a similar load. Guy garnered the attention of two pilots in his team. He quickly drew his index finger quickly across his throat this time. Kelt wondered what that meant.

"No killing, Guy, we still might be able to work together," Kelt advised.

"We're trying to make sure that happens, sir. Just watch," Guy responded.

This time Kelt decided to watch the monitors focused on the plane. Two resounding booms resonated around the air base, as two small saucer shaped craft broke the sound barrier coming in at nearly mach 3 and accelerating. The two tails of the aircraft were sheared completely off.

"Do you think anyone could see what happened, Guy?"

"Naw, it's dark and so are your playthings, sir. There is no way they'll see them coming in."

Kelt felt a joking jab in the comment, but took it in stride. He even smiled as he tried to contain an outburst of laughter rising in his throat.

"They won't see this as an accident," Guy explained, "The sonic booms were a dead giveaway."

"So, you think that is it for the night?" asked Kelt.

"No sir, they will not give up that easily," Guy advised.

"We've got an old stealth bomber coming in from the west, sir. It's lit up like a Christmas tree with all the heat coming off its backside," one of the civies cried from a monitoring station.

"Okay gents, this one is airborne, so we can't just take it out, that wouldn't suit our fine commander's requirements here," Guy ordered.

Until now, the disks had been piloted with simple computing pads and complex macros that the pilots easily initiated. Now, with a piloted target moving at supersonic speed, more intervention than is human was required. The software that the floating cities had developed to bring down the satellites was no good here; the satellites had fixed orbits and were more easily tracked and monitored by computer systems. The macros from upstairs were also nearly useless for the task at hand. Experienced dogfight pilots were needed. Scotty had found a flight simulator game released 34 years prior, and had interfaced it to work in concert with the floaters. He had a real "cockpit" set up for three of Guy's team who had been actual pilots.

The pilots couldn't believe the toys they were working with. There was a cheap joystick clamped to the front of the desk and a pair of foot pedals to simulate rudder control. Of course, the simulator didn't have a stealth aircraft model; the pilots would be pretending to fly an F16. An ancient computer mouse lay left of the joystick. The slop in this gear was almost overwhelming, but the pilots were good enough to compensate. Guy had explained that this situation required real pilot control, in contrast to using macros the night before to bring down the satellites. "There will be humans piloting those bombers. We'll need pilots to anticipate their moves and react accordingly," he had explained.

"Am I going to have to use this thing to use the software controls?" asked one pilot incredulously as he lifted the mouse in his left hand.

"I doubt it," answered Scotty, "I think the stick and pedals will be all you need. I figured it couldn't hurt to be prepared." The pilot nearly swallowed his tongue.

*****

"We're coming up from behind now, sir," advised the flight leader of the three-man crew.

144

"Careful gents, you know where the gas is. Don't let any out or you might make the boss mad," Guy instructed.

The three saucer packages with claws were positioned, two up front on either side of the cockpit, and one just rear of the bomb bay of the stealth aircraft. Guy had figured these would be safe places to avoid a fuel leakage, and still gain a substantial hold on the craft. Hopefully, they wouldn't rip it apart.

"We're in luck with this bird," announced Guy.

"Why's that?" asked Kelt.

"Because sir, it's a flying brick; it needs its own computer to control the engines and flight surfaces. With no tail to worry about, we'll manage to deal with it just fine," he said.

"Okay, the packages are in place. Fire the explosive charges and release control of the floaters to our pilot over here, on my mark, 3... 2...1... mark. The timing wasn't precise, but it worked. The spider like articulating blades sunk into the stealth bomber and latched on. Scotty immediately released the floaters from each of the individual pilots and linked them together with a macro script he had written. All he had to do was punch the enter key on his computing pad.

"Hey, I can feel the plane with this toy!" announced the real pilot assigned to manage the aircraft. "Yeah, they used to call that force feedback," Scotty said.

"Why don't you turn him around, fly him out a couple hundred clicks, and fly him in circles until his fuel runs out. If he hasn't bailed by then, drop the plane so he has the initiative to do so," ordered Guy.

It wasn't long before the pilot of the stealth bomber realized he no longer had control of his aircraft. He didn't know what was wrong, but the stupid controls just wouldn't respond. He sent out a May Day message and bailed out as he approached Los Angeles.

"I assume you can retract those blades can't you? I'd hate to drop them with the aircraft. We could need them down the road," Kelt asked Scotty.

"Yes, Kelt, we were able to improve on our design shortly after our meeting. These have some little servo motors geared pretty low, so that they can retract, but it will take a while to pull them out of the skin of that aircraft," Scotty replied.

"Well, get moving and let's drop that bird in the ocean," Kelt ordered.

"And when you fellas are done throwing rocks in the pond, get those tinker toys back in position," commanded Guy.

"What's a tinker toy?" asked Kelt.

"Forget about it, Kelt," he grinned.

"So, what's next? Do you think they'll send a cruise missile our way tonight?" asked Kelt.

"I don't know, sir. As far as I know, the cruise missiles still depend highly on GPS data from the satellites, and we've taken those down. Now, I can see we can handle whatever they send. Why don't you leave Scotty in command and let's start planning a defensive plan for a ground assault," Guy advised.

Scotty took command of the CIC, and everyone remained on watch until relieved at 6 AM. They would now have to maintain a defensive force ready at a moment's notice.

"It's so unproductive. These people should be working on our other projects," Scotty thought to himself. Indeed, the base had doubled the number of occupants it was originally designed for. That alone decreased the food supply to only 10 to 12 years, depending on how they rationed the supply.

"We're going to die down here if we don't start producing food... and I have an idea," he thought to himself.

Instead of retiring to bed after his shift ended, he made a call up to Amanda Perry, the microbiologist. He needed some help in developing a new food source.

146

22- Carter ruminates

Rick Carter tapped his stylus on his desk looking at his new surroundings. "I'm glad they pulled through dirtside last night. It was tactically brilliant," he thought, "that Kelt…" Rick let his mind drift as he realized just how much he had come to respect him and love him. "Akhi misses him so much… I wish that there was something, anything we could do to bring them back together." The on-board biologists still hadn't been able to bring someone up from the Earth's surface and adequately decontaminate them. The risk of bringing just one virus on board was still a serious threat to their crops growing in the spheres.

When the cities had been locked in space several months prior, his office was spacious; complete with a mini bar, couches, assorted tables and art of various types. His office space had been moved twice since then. Each time the walls closed in on him. He had donated the art to the museums on board the cities. There was very little art to go around and everyone needed to be able to share it, from his perspective. Although the population had not grown, there was a constant need for more space for all of the research, manufacturing, and especially crop farms. The new office had space for his video monitor on a stand, a small writing table, which was mostly used just to hold a cup of coffee, and a conference table that three chairs easily surrounded. Rick did not regret the need for the move, but he did miss the space.

As one of the wealthiest men in the world, before the new era, he had financed the entire enterprise at the beginning. Near the end, he had brought in Aldo and his associates to help fund the last and most expensive phases of the many projects. These, they had managed to implement, and had saved a small slice of humanity from the toxic surface of the Earth. He still kept in excellent shape and was still the subject of many stares from the women onboard. They always stared at his stunning grey eyes with flecks. He mused over the prospects of finding a companion or even a close female friend from time to time. He could not tear himself away from the memory of the love of his life, Akhi's mother who had tragically died in an automobile accident. Akhi, his precious little girl, had nearly died in the same auto crash.

"I've been at this for nearly fifteen years," he thought. He didn't regret his humanitarian and philanthropic work in any sense. "This isn't my responsibility now. I can't run these cities as my own company. It isn't fair to the people. I am not a king and I don't want to be king." Such simple statements, he had thought to himself on many occasions, but they carried significant consequences, which he could not manage. Until now, he had needed complete control and it was hard to consider parting with that power.

He had been especially concerned over the attacks on the Nevada Base the night before. "I must engage the remaining governments," he resolved. "Without their help, we shall all perish," he thought. He was worried sick about the warning delivered by his top biologists, about restoring the world's ecosystem. They had 12 to 18 months to get a significant start in restoring plant life on the planet, before irreparable damage would make it impossible for humanity to survive.

"There is so much to do. We haven't even decided on which calendar to accept. The population had pretty much demanded that, "New ERA" or "NE" be adopted, almost from the outset to measure years.

The Earth was dying quickly. Many on board the large floating vessels went by other calendars from their own cultures. So, as a simple standard, they had begun a new calendar started after the bombing of Africa. For each year, they just counted the days. Most people didn't even know what day of the week it was anymore. There was no sense of season onboard. "Shoot, we don't even have any windows to look through," Rick thought. The large spheres had been spun from thin strands of Kelt's Buckyball/ceramic/steel matrix, atop beamed structures in

148

the beginning of the massive project. They had quickly turned to spinning the same mix inside large balloons near the very end for expediency.

Although both types of habitats were equally strong in their ability to hold the air in, windows were never considered for the sake of expediency. Most everyone had their video link monitors, which could display the exterior of the vessels from many angles. Some bright engineer had come up with the "wall poster," that looked like a spaceport window, but was as thin as a sheet of paper, and just stuck to the wall anywhere you chose to place it. "I'm glad that everyone is still focused on survival, with the exception of the poster," Rick mused with a smile. "Otherwise, we would have had several mutinies by now."

He stared at a considerable number of electronic requests stacked in his computer's inbox. "Well, I should at least tend to these before I address my musings," he considered. The first was a request from the cosmologists and astronomers onboard. They wanted to launch several telescopes to examine the heavens in all wavelengths from microwave, visible, radio, and so on. They had recently been sidetracked for the development of the stations' security monitors. They wanted to get back to their telescopes. He wrote a note responding to the request "Why do you think you are here? Just do it." "Why am I forced to approve all of these decisions?" he asked himself.

The next request was from several religious leaders on board. They were requesting space on each city for chapel and prayer space, for the various denominations of faith. Although Rick was not a religious man himself, he knew that this was a reasonable request. "His people" needed whatever inspiration and support they could garner. "I'm no Moses," he chuckled, "but they should definitely have the space they ask for. They could use some of the conference centers during off hours. Signed and delivered," he said. The next request came from a group of Jewish individuals wishing to readjust their schedules to honor the Sabbath. "Hmm," thought Rick, "We've had too much up time and no down time. My crews really need time off to attend to personal affairs. He drafted a memo to all crews to work with their shift organizers to take a day off, of their choosing every week. "That should satisfy everyone," he thought as he drafted the brief memo.

He was becoming unraveled with all of these non-critical requests. He was overworked for no real reason.

He called the five social engineers he had on staff and linked them together on video feed.

"Look, my friends," Rick started, "I know we don't have a real government here, and I have way too much on my plate to deal with the day to day issues. I really need to be in contact with the remaining governments on Earth. I'd like to pass on the day-to-day issues to you five, as you develop a plan for a long-term government. I realize that sooner or later, a situation will arise. No one is being paid and I'm the default leader. It is untenable."

His associates agreed that government creation was more of a long-term issue, and that as their leader he was burdened far too much.

"I'm going to announce that you five are in charge of day to day issues. Akhi is in tactical command of the stations, but I want you people to handle project priorities and the general stuff that I've been dealing with. Please work with her," Rick announced. "If you don't understand the technical aspects of requests, then bring in the right people and get solid advice. If you still can't come to a decision, then please contact me," Rick continued, "But for the moment, gentlemen, I'm still in charge. We need to be able to make on the spot decisions, which may determine our very lives. So, please, keep your plans for a future government to yourselves' for the moment. Just work on it, okay?"

His team agreed. The current arrangement of what could be considered socialism under a dictator would be the de-facto government until it was no longer tenable.

"I'm going to send out a ship wide announcement to the effect that you five will be managing these sorts of issues from here on out. I'll also be forwarding the majority of requests down to you.

23- Algae Goo

It was still early in the morning for Scotty and he'd been up all night in the CIC, fighting off the bombing runs. He was so tired that he couldn't manage to remember what time schedule the floating cities were on. It didn't matter. He contacted Dr. Amanda Perry, via video link. She had obviously been awakened by the call, as Scotty realized that it was just after 3AM upstairs.

"Hello Scotty," Amanda said as she wiped the sleep from her eyes.

"Amanda, I have a question for you."

"Fire away, Mr. Scott," she responded.

"I just thought of this at the most inconvenient time, but it's really been bugging me. I just have to get it out of my head before I can get some rest. We've been up all night fighting off bombers," he said.

"I heard that you were anticipating attacks down there. You must have been successful in repelling them, or I wouldn't be talking to you, right?" Amanda queried.

"Yeah, the team we have down here isn't a disciplined bunch, but we managed to hold out. That's not what I want to ask you about. Do you have anyone up there working on algae food supplements?" Scotty asked.

With all the research that Amanda and Shannon had been working on, the algae project had been far from her attention. The two microbiologists were still heavily focused on plant reproduction in the face of the killer virus.

"Ah, yes Scotty, there is a team up here working on it. I don't know much about the program, but I do know the marine biologist in charge. She's pretty sharp," she answered.

"I'm glad to hear that. Can you forward me to her com station?"

"I don't know if she's sleeping or not. We are working around the clock... let me try to see if she is available," Amanda stated.

Amanda looked up the number and Dr. Rupa Patel immediately came online. She was working and wide-awake. Rupa immediately recognized Amanda's face.

"What can I do for you Amanda?" Rupa asked.

"I have Dr. Scott Ermy on line from Nevada Base who would like to talk to you.

"THE Dr. Scott Ermy?" Rupa asked with a grin.

"The one and the same," answered Scotty.

Amanda linked the conversation in conference mode, so that all three could see and talk to each other.

"It's nice to meet you, Dr. Ermy," Rupa said.

"Likewise, Dr. Patel. Please call me Scotty, that's what I prefer," he said.

"I would appreciate the same, please call me Rupa," she returned, "So what can I do for you, Scotty?

"Amanda told me that you are in charge of the algae project," Scotty said.

"That's right. I've been working on it for the past twenty years or so."

"Can you make food out of it, yet?" Scotty asked.

"As a matter of fact, we can. Long before we were lifted up here, I had a team of researchers working on alternative food supplies, and this was our primary project. We were successful on Earth and we've managed to put together a complete little ecosystem that can produce a form of algae that we developed several years ago. This little alga reproduces like no other we have ever seen, and we've helped it along in its ability to reproduce," Rupa answered.

Scotty, thinking ahead asked "I realize that we've pretty much lost our ecosystem down here, but if we had one, would that algae produce any hazards if it got out of control?" he asked.

"That was an essential part of our design criteria, Scotty. The algae are perfectly harmless and they will not crowd out other forms of marine life. It needs a special mix of nutrients that we provide, and most importantly those you can buy at any home and garden store," Rupa replied.

"Or you used to be able to buy," she thought to herself. "Without those nutrients, the bacteria die. We also provide a host of necessary bacteria and other little critters, which will help it along as well. It can grow in any stagnant fresh water source as long as the initial water source is clean and we add the required nutrients," she added. "Oh, and there is one more requirement. The little ecosystem we have working, requires live carp in the mix," she finalized.

"Carp?" asked Scotty wondering why a bottom feeder fish was necessary.

"It's just part of our micro ecosystem that works, Scotty. Without them, it falls apart within just a few months," Rupa finalized.

"So, what about making it into food?" Scotty asked.

"It's not rocket science Scotty, but it does require some special machinery such as ovens, conveyer systems, cutting blades… you can follow where I'm going with that. You are well known for understanding the machine end of things," She answered.

"We wouldn't necessarily need machines of that sort on a small scale, right?" asked Scotty.

"You are correct. One or two people could attend to a small pond, harvest, process the algae, and bake them in a conventional oven… or even a sun reflection oven, I suppose," she answered. "A nice side benefit is that the carp can produce a source of protein as well. The fish population must be culled to a certain level depending on the pond size. All the extra fish must be removed from time to time," she added.

"We should get that technology going down here," Scotty said. "People are already killing each other for their food supplies. We've already seen mass cases of cannibalism around the world. It is frightening," he said.

"I completely understand, Scotty. My sister, Padma, is down there with you and I was hoping that we could start building these in the near future. I'm terribly concerned for her wellbeing. I'll send you down a synopsis of the farming and nutrition bar process. I'll also forward the specs on the machinery we are currently using to produce the bars. Let me warn you, they taste a lot like cardboard, but they are a nutritious food source.

"If we were to implement it down here, how could we find the right species of carp," Scotty asked.

"They produce eggs, Scotty, and we've got hundreds of thousands of them up here," Rupa answered.

She was already running through the logistics of transferring hundreds of little portable ecosystems dirt side.

"Scotty, our containers up here are producing well in excess of what we can handle. We are introducing the food bars into the population in a few weeks. I'm sure that most people will hate them, but we too are going to run short on food if we don't do this… at least that's the projection for the long term," she told him. "We can easily prepare some care packages to send down to you," she furthered.

"Great!" exclaimed Scotty. "Figure out how to produce a small "algae in a bottle ecosystem" for us, and we'll work on the mechanical aspects on our end."

"How small, Scotty," she asked.

"I assume you have a whole lot of two liter soda containers up there waiting for recycling? Let's shoot for that size."

Rupa thought through his requirements and based on her experience, she felt that it might be feasible. The algae could reproduce so incredibly fast that by the time fresh carp eggs would hatch, they would have enough to survive in a space the size of a small backyard swimming pool successfully. She had over designed her algae food production systems. Scotty had forced her to think on a smaller scale. She had new hope for her sister in the Nevada bunker.

24- Military moves in

Things had settled down to where Kelt felt he could resume his work in the libraries. The sun had set topside, and Kelt was itching to get out of the cave. He was looking forward to the brief excursion topside for some fresh air. He and Guy were sharing their mealtime in the cafeteria. They still had some fresh food and knew that much of it would run out within the week. For now, they still had potatoes, apples, and onions for a while since they stored fairly well if kept cool. After that, it would be frozen and dehydrated meals plus the meager offerings from whatever they could scrounge or trade. Fishing might be a viable source down the road, but Kelt was not ready to split up his force or expose them in such a way. Still, he did have the urge to get out of the bunker occasionally.

"Guy, we haven't had any problems for well over a week," Kelt said to Guy.

"I know how you feel but they are going to hit us again. That's how they work. I'd really like to keep you here until Rick can resolve things with the president. We haven't had to kill any of their soldiers and they haven't managed to hurt us yet, so there's always the possibility that we can sort through this," he scolded Kelt.

"I hate politics," Kelt responded, "Especially when they're trying to kill us. None of it makes sense to me. We should be working together, Guy."

"I know, sir, but that's how the world works."

"It won't be long before we'll be able to say, "That's how the world used to work," Guy. One way or the other, whether they work with us or against us, this situation will change," Kelt finalized.

"You are right, of course. It will change. Everyone topside seems to want to kill everyone else. Soon, there won't be many left. Let's give it a few more days, okay?"

"Alright Guy, a few more days, we can handle," Kelt said.

One of Guy's commandos quickly ran up to the table.

"Sir," he said looking at Guy with an ashen face, "they're moving in armor and troops."

This man wasn't one of Guy's original crack squad. This was a younger fellow and he was scared to death.

"See, Kelt? I told you," Guy said as he glanced at Kelt.

"Yes, Guy, you did," Kelt answered.

Kelt made an emergency announcement over the internal com. We are under attack, report to your stations immediately. The training drills had been improving the team's efficiency in responding to threats. The CIC was filled in mere seconds with more seasoned pilots and their computing pads. Scotty had made up two more cockpits for Guy's crack members who had real experience piloting real aircraft. He had also been working with the computer science types upstairs to develop useful tactical macros for the small craft.

"We're going to have to raid an electronics store and get some more game controllers," Scotty mused as he watched the crewmen settle into their office chairs. Each of their computing pads was connected to an old computer joystick clamped to the front of their table and a set of foot pedals. These flight systems were then linked to their assigned floaters. Scotty had made some improvements in the software so that these more experienced pilots could be quickly assigned control over any of the floaters in the air. This had been an issue in the previous raid where the inexperienced pilots could not participate at all.

"These guys are experienced in real dog fights," Guy had explained to Scotty. "In a real dog fight, you never really see the enemy, you trust your flight controls," Guy had told him. Scotty had understood the situation quickly. The civilians would naturally fight by sight and would have a hard time relating to the concept. They could use that intuitive ability to paint targets.

They already had good floater cams that could see at night. For a ground-based operation, the civilians could easily position their tracking floaters up to 3 kilometers away and point at the target. With two floaters pointed at exactly the same point, the target was effectively triangulated and painted, and the exact point of attack would be passed on by software to the fighter pilots who could see that information in their flight simulation game.

Now the inexperienced would do the target painting as well as what they called the house keeping; the floater retrieval, running the disks out several kilometers, and on command, starting the return acceleration as control was passed back to the experienced pilots. This gave the men at the stick direct control of an attacking floater or floater group as necessary. In tactical terms, they were effectively flying four or five real attack floaters each. Additionally, they could fly and maneuver the craft at accelerations of several g's. That sort of acceleration would instantly crush a human body.

From an experienced military perspective, it looked like a bunch of people playing games on their laptops. From up top, it would be a blinding dance of death.

"What've we got here?" Guy asked Dave who was on watch in the CIC.

"We've got a battle group coming in sir. We have five M1 tanks, some light artillery, and it looks like two companies of troops. They are 25 clicks out on the main road," Dave responded.

"How about long range guns," asked Guy knowing that some of those big guns on tracks could loft shells tens of kilometers. "We've seen no heavy artillery, sir," Dave answered.

Guy had been worried about the huge Howitzer guns on tank tracks. Space Truck's eyes in the sky tracking had been greatly improved with the coordination of simple software updates and some additional training for those keeping a watch on the surrounding desert. They were still watching the area for hundreds of kilometers surrounding the site for aircraft. His pilots had been training every night in the use of acceleration to make these little flying saucers, with knife sharp edges, into lethal killing machines. The concepts were straightforward but in practice counter intuitive. To attack an object, they had to move the floater away from it, and then accelerate in toward the target at an appropriate rate to attain the needed speed to do the damage. They had built up several squadrons of the flying saucer shaped floaters with cutting edges and another dozen that could clamp onto an incoming bomb or missile.

"I'm proud of this team, Kelt," Guy said.

"Really?" Kelt asked with some sense of amazement. He knew that Guy had some pretty tough standards.

"Yes I am sir. It's only been a few days since the first attack and now we are much better prepared to do battle," Guy explained.

"Let me give the big guy a call to see if he can call this off, otherwise, we'll have a go within just a minute," Kelt said.

Kelt sent the pre-recorded message for this scenario of a ground attack to Rick. Rick was already on the phone attempting to contact the president.

"I'm sorry Kelt, but they still refuse to take my calls. I did leave a message though," Rick said as his face popped up on a vid com link.

"What message did you leave him?" asked Kelt.

"The message that I gave to the operator was: "You'll get the message in about five minutes"", smiled Rick.

"Yes sir, that they will," Guy stated.

"I'd like to try a direct communication with the commander of that attacking force before we start the engagement, Guy," Kelt pleaded.

"Sorry, Kelt, they are using encryption, I doubt that they'll be listening in on an open standard frequency."

"I understand," responded Kelt.

"Very well, gentlemen, let's get underway," announced Kelt. Civies, do you have those tank barrels triangulated?" he yelled. Although several civilians had been assigned to the task, only three teams had been able to move their floaters into position. The other teams of two were responding by flying their disks in from other surrounding grid areas.

"That's a vulnerability we have in our strategy," Guy noted. "When we move them like this from one side of our perimeter to the other, we leave ourselves blind. We'll take care of that first thing after this encounter," he thought.

"We've got the first three in the line locked sir," announced the chief in charge of target painting, a civilian.

"Have we positioned the attack floaters at an appropriate range?" Kelt asked.

"Yes sir," the chief answered, "we'll be breaking the sound barrier on these," he finalized.

"Well then, there's nothing better than the crack of Hell itself to scare them into oblivion," Kelt mentioned to Guy. "Everyone, attention, Guy is now taking control of this battle," announced Kelt, "I'll be coordinating with him, but he is in charge."

The fold up tables had been arranged in a large horseshoe arrangement. In the center of the horseshoe, were two tables with several monitors, showing multiple images from above, and at various angles surrounding the advancing column. One monitor tracking the attacking force, highlighted the triangulated points that were about to be hit in red.

"Pilots," Guy said to the real pilots using their toy controls, "take out the guns on those tanks."

The disks were oriented at ninety-degree angles and spaced out tens of kilometers away.

"Accelerating at 10 g's sir," announce the flight leader.

Dirtside, the loud bangs of vehicles breaking the sound barrier could be heard through the attacking force's ranks. At mach 3, the little vertically oriented disks sliced off the big barrels from the turrets of the three leading tanks. All anyone saw was a brief flash as the big guns

160

were shorn from their mounted positions. Twenty seconds later, the remaining two tanks lost their guns.

"Now we are going to see how motivated these brave soldiers are," Guy told Kelt with some remorse. Guy was ex-military himself. He did not want to kill his fellow Americans. He would do it to protect his own people, now.

Guy and Kelt saw the troop carriers move around the tanks and proceed forward.

"Civies, paint the front wheels on those personnel carriers," Guy commanded.

Even though the targets were moving, the floaters easily kept up, accurate triangulations were calculated thousands of times every second.

"Pilots, level your craft and hit the targets," commanded guy.

The floaters that had taken out the tank guns were being retrieved so others had been already positioned for the attack.

"Kelt, we need to reassess how we can work that retrieval process to attack from the other side. We're losing time here.

"I understand. I'll take care of it, Guy." Kelt answered.

Kelt walked over to the civies and explained that they would need to recover the floaters and move them only the short distance required to attack from the south side of the column. They did not have to move them back to their original starting positions to the north. He also assigned civie spotters to do target painting on the south side of the column.

"We're covered now on both sides now, Guy," Kelt advised, "but that leaves our flanks and rear hanging in the breeze," Kelt added.

"I know, Kelt. I was thinking the same thing earlier. It's been running through my mind ever since. We just don't have enough people if we have a full on assault from more than one direction," Guy said.

The advancing column of troops heard six more deafening claps of the sound barrier breaking. The three front troop carriers lost their front wheels and came skidding to an uncontrolled halt on the paved highway. The dead vehicles disgorged themselves of their crews. The soldiers jumped up on surviving trucks and carriers as the heaps of junk were sidestepped or pushed off the road.

"Take out the next three in the front of the column," Guy ordered.

This time, the floaters came in from the south, the direction they had been retrieved. The vehicles lost their front wheels and nosed into the pavement.

"That's two more personnel carriers and one light artillery unit down," Kelt said to Guy.

"That's right, sir, and it doesn't look like they are going to give up even yet," Guy noted, as they noticed the soldiers, on foot, jumping on vehicles to their rear. The remaining troops on foot were organized into columns and they started a quick march down the road.

"Rick, I know that you are watching the events as they unfold here. Over two hundred troops out there are coming down our throats and they are not giving up. Can you please contact the White House again?" Kelt pleaded.

"I've been trying to get through, and all I've been able to accomplish is to leave a message. We've even routed calls so that they appear as though they are coming from different telephone numbers so the operators will pick up on the lines. I have five people here attempting to contact the commander of that air base north of you. You're on your own, Kelt. I'm really sorry you have to do this. I'm not so sure that I could," Rick stated with great remorse.

"I understand," Kelt answered. "Rick can't give a command to have someone killed. He couldn't even manage to handle that bastard Leo Galt. He could only lock him up tight, in Tycho base, after he had tried to kill his daughter and himself, not to mention me," Kelt mused.

"He's a good man, Kelt," said Guy, as he recognized Kelt's pensive face and read his concerns, "Don't concern yourself with his inability to take command in a life and death situation. He has always been this way," Guy told Kelt.

"I need teams to take out the remaining vehicles and those light artillery," yelled Guy. His subordinates made the necessary assignments.

"That leaves us with several unused craft, sir," Dave advised Guy.

"Good, position the remaining cutters in formation Delta 30 clicks forward of that column," Guy commanded.

"This really sucks," said Kelt softly.

"Better to take them now, before they spread out," advised Guy.

"I know, but it doesn't make it any easier to do," Kelt said.

"I'm with you, sir. I'm afraid we have no other choice. They've had every opportunity to withdraw," Guy said.

"But, Guy, why don't they spread out and take defensive positions? Why is their commander leading them straight down the road like that?" Kelt asked.

Guy positioned a floater cam to show the face of the convoy's leader.

"There's your answer, Kelt. He's just a kid lieutenant. It looks like all the experienced officers have gone home to their families," Guy answered.

All the vehicles had been driven into the pavement nose down. All the tanks and light artillery had been destroyed. Still, a column of brave men and women marched in double time down each side of the road.

"They are good soldiers," Guy said, "They know how to take orders."

"They are also dead soldiers who don't realize their imminent fate," Kelt murmured.

"Okay, take those cutters, pilots, and mow them down," ordered Guy.

"Now our little flying saucers are aptly named 'cutters'," Kelt thought, "That name will stick."

To the east, 30 miles away, 35 of the small craft hovered 1.5 meters above the ground and formed into a triangular formation, covering the entire width of the road and its shoulder. This formation was under the control of one pilot. The lead soldier of the column had been triangulated. Within seconds, two large thunderclaps resounded through the air and the entire column of brave men and women had been destroyed.

"Get some shuttles out there and collect any usable weapons and ammunition, as well as any foodstuffs they may be carrying," Guy commanded to one of his subordinates.

"Yes sir," the subordinate replied sharply. "We'll get some crews put together and be back within a couple hours."

"It's not going to hurt to have a few more weapons," Guy thought.

"Rick, send the president another message," started Guy, "tell him he can bring in two trucks with two unarmed men each to start picking up his "army" at first light. Only two trucks will be allowed within 100 kilometers at a time. Advise him that if we see any weapons, we'll take out his trucks and soldiers again," Guy said over the video link.

"Understood, Guy," Rick said in a cracking voice. Guy cut the link.

"He's a good man, Kelt," Guy said, "He's just got no guts to kill."

"I don't either," Kelt said as he quickly grabbed a nearby wastebasket and lost the contents of his stomach.

25- President Crawford

President Crawford listened intently to an audio feed from his attack force. He heard every word from the lieutenant, tank commanders, and a few others as the battle had unfolded. He also received every message from Rick Carter immediately, as they were received. He refused to respond to Carter.

"Damn! We've just lost our guns on our first three tanks!"… "We've just lost the other two tanks, sir."… "What in the pariah's domain is going on?"… "What's that thunderous noise?"… "We've just lost the front end on our APC!"…

"Ditto, here. What are they using against us?"… "What's that damned noise? It sounds like thunder?"… "We've lost all of our vehicles, sir, what are your orders?"… "Form up, double time down the road to the gravel entrance!"…

Then, he heard nothing but the static of a radio that had been clutched in death with an open mic.

"What's the status of those troops, General?" Crawford demanded.

"I don't know sir. I assume they have all been killed."

"General, we know they have no weapons. How have they done this?" Crawford demanded.

"I don't know sir, I really don't know."

"We should have more experienced commanders in the field, General."

"Who will you send, Mr. President? We have hardly any fighting force left. We have more deserters than people to go arrest them," the general stated.

"Mr. President, Mr. Rick Carter is on the phone. He wants to tell you that your forces have not prevailed. He would like to talk to you personally," the operator said.

"Put him on line one," Crawford commanded angrily.

"Mr. President, I don't know what you are hoping to accomplish here," stated Rick.

"I'm trying to protect our country," Crawford roared.

"From what? Seriously, Mr. President, the world is dying. No one cares about "our country" anymore. All they are worried about is where they are going to get their next meal. That's what we should be working on, together. I encourage you to talk to us, sir. We have some very bright people in these floating cities. We also have some very bright people dirtside. We need to be working, together."

"I don't trust you, you bastard," Crawford stated.

Rick didn't trust Crawford either. During the past few decades, the executive office had been overrun with actors fronting for those that truly held the reins of power. That power structure was gone and had no practical advice to offer. The president could only rely on the military people on hand, in his own protected bunker.

"Mr. President, with all due respect, you have just murdered over 200 men and women with your attitude. We tried everything we could to dissuade them, by disabling their vehicles first."

"I don't believe you, Carter. You couldn't have taken out five tanks and two companies. We've been out to your little private landing site and there's nothing there except an old warehouse. We know you don't have many people down there," Crawford announced.

"Mr. President, you have no idea what we have, or what we can do. You have refused to talk to us ever since this disaster happened. You seem to be as disassociated with the true facts, as your predecessor. Do you know where he is?" asked Carter.

"He disappeared in one of your shuttles, Carter. You kidnapped him."

"President Crawford, I'm going to transmit down to you some videos of the real event. I'll patch you through to Murlough, who is currently our guest at Tycho station. You can find out the truth," Rick said.

"Before we do that however, Mr. President, you'll want to retrieve the bodies of your brave soldiers. We will allow only two trucks within 100 kilometers of our site. Only two men are allowed in each vehicle. No weapons will be permitted. When your men arrive to retrieve the bodies, they will note that all of the vehicles were disabled first. You will find no bodies within them. Your soldiers were marching down the road double time, well ahead of your disabled tanks and trucks, before we had to take them down. That by itself, is proof that we tried to stop this tragedy without taking any life. Once your teams in your retrieval trucks reach the bodies, they will be convinced that we will allow no one within 100 kilometers of this site. When you have the proof you need of everything I've said, you know how to contact me," Rick finalized.

"Patch me through to Murlough," scoffed Crawford.

"Very well, Mr. President," Rick started, "here you go. Have a pleasant conversation with our previous president. Your people have been sent video records of the hijacking of our shuttle by Murlough and his team of commandos. When you are ready, let's talk," Rick said as he enabled the laser link through to Tycho Station.

25- The two presidents

"President Murlough!" Crawford exclaimed as he saw his former commander in chief.

"Yes, it's me, Crawford, what do you want?" Murlough answered.

"Mr. President, we thought that you had been kidnapped."

"Well, we live in some pretty tough times, but I was not kidnapped, Crawford. Please don't call me Mr. President. Crawford, you are "Mr. President" now, and I couldn't wish it on a nicer person," Murlough said with strong sarcasm in his voice.

"How did you get on the Moon? We've known nothing about it!" exclaimed Crawford.

"Do you remember our conversation a couple of weeks before you thought I was kidnapped?"

"Why, yes, you told me that if anything happened to you that I should take out the Suez Canal to prevent the virus from spreading to Europe and Asia" Crawford remembered.

"No, my orders were quite clear. I told you that if anything happened to me that you should take out the Suez Canal as a last resort. Did you take action and wipe out the Suez just because I disappeared, or did you wait until it was a last resort?" Murlough asked.

"Why, no, I convinced China and Pakistan to do it, since they were closer. It didn't go as planned. They wouldn't wait. Not only did they nuke the Canal Zone, but they also took out South Africa."

"And why in the world would you get the Chinese and Pakistanis involved?" Murlough asked incredulously.

"Well, sir, I thought it would be best for them to do it, so we wouldn't be blamed."

"Well, you dope, let me tell you the story," Murlough said, "Remember Leo Galt?"

"I do, sir, he used his television network 24 hours a day to push your candidacy. He also poured nearly one

168

billion dollars into slime campaigns, against your opponent in the general election and against MINE in the primaries! That's how you beat me in the primaries, you bastard." whined Crawford.

"Yes, that's right. I've known Galt for many years. Had it not been for him and his money, I would not have been elected. I was shocked when Galt had been arrested for terrorism in China. I couldn't believe it. I could not conceive that such a loyal supporter of our democracy would commit such heinous crimes for which he was accused. The Chinese sent him off to a prison where he would just disappear. No one comes out of that place you know," Murlough said.

"Yes, I know about that," said Crawford.

"Anyway, Galt somehow managed to convince the Chinese prison guards to pass a message on to me. Galt told me that he had been falsely accused. He told me that Rick Carter was out to get him, and had set him up for the terrorist acts for which he was charged. I believed him. He was, after all, my friend and loyal contributor. The country was falling apart, and, frankly, I needed his money for the next election. We secured his release with China through diplomatic channels. I had to call in every marker I'd ever earned on that deal. The FBI brought him over to Camp David incognito and that's where he hatched the escape plan with me. He told me that if there were any chance to stop the virus, the Suez had to be nuked. He also told me that there was little chance that it would be successful, but at least we had to try *as a last resort*. He promised to get my family and me, along with the secretary of state, up here to Tycho where we could ride this thing out. I was convinced he was telling the truth, and fell for the plan. We pirated two shuttles slated to pick up people on the capitol mall. The secretary and I accompanied Galt with a crack squad of Navy Seals and brought them up to Tycho.

"Tycho station is the perfect spot. It is up and fully functional with only a minimal staff. We can easily take the station with two squads of Seals and bring your family up with the same shuttles we steal," Galt had told us.

"Carter had dropped two shuttles to pick up some very important researchers at the Smithsonian. You know those types, geeks all of them. They were excellent scientists and Carter was looking for the best to help save the world. I thought Carter was full of it. Leo's television network after all, had been pushing his crap against Carter at least 4 times an hour throughout the day. You probably remember how he was accused of trying to take over the world, or how he wanted a communist government, or any of the rest of that slime," Murlough said.

"But it was true! He is a communist!" exclaimed Crawford.

"I suppose right now he is in some ways, you dope. How is he going to pay his crew who are working around the clock trying to save your worthless hide? Well guess what, Crawford, they ripped out everything here, including the chairs and beds, and stranded us here with absolutely nothing. And it's all your fault. Had you not stranded Carter's crew down there... when those nukes were dropped by China and Pakistan... so you wouldn't have to take the heat... well, I think my life would have been different. I'd at least have my family safe somewhere. Instead all we really get to do is keep Mr. Leo Galt tied up 24 hours a day, while we grovel trying to produce food on equipment we can't hope to understand," Murlough explained.

"Why do you have to tie him up?" demanded Crawford.

"Because he's managed to impregnate two of our women commandos. He's got a helluva sense of timing, that one," answered Murlough

"Were they raped?"

"They say that they weren't. Galt sure has a way with people. I just don't get it. I've since learned to ignore his charm."

170

"Why are you trying to wipe out Carter's crews dirtside? Are you even a bigger idiot than I was?" Murlough demanded.

"He wiped out two of our Army companies," Crawford said sheepishly.

"That's because you attacked him, you buffoon."

"Well, you'd have done the same!"

"No I wouldn't"

"But you did, Murlough. You buzzed Pacificus relentlessly from one of our carrier groups, in the Pacific, and then told him that he had to leave US air space after an attempt to help the Koreans resolve a nuclear meltdown," Crawford said with his teeth clenched.

"That was different. We had to protect our political interests, and the PR in favor of Space Truck was overwhelming. He was helping people all over the world. The people were ecstatic. Had we let him drift over Hawaii, our people would have lost confidence in our government," Murlough explained.

Rick Carter knew that it was bad manners to listen in, but he did. This had to be recorded for all of history. It was the Bobbsey twins arguing back and forth like schoolchildren, fighting to tear a choice doll in half rather than share. He knew that what he heard and saw, would become part of human history in the artifact.

"So, what happened to my family, Crawford?" asked Murlough,

"Carter told me that I had condemned them to die with the rest of the world. Do you know what happened to them?" Murlough asked.

"I have no idea where your family is. They aren't with us. Listen, Murlough, things are really bad down here. The government is safe in its bunker, of course. We've got food riots and people eating each other. We've done our best for our military so that we can maintain order," Crawford explained.

"And have you been able to keep order, Crawford?"

"No, I suppose not. We don't know what to do," offered Crawford.

"Well, you are the president, Mr. Crawford. You always were a political hack, you know. You've always done only what you were told to do... and executed it poorly. You've never had any initiative. So hear me clearly, Crawford and I'll tell you what to do. You won't be reelected, so don't worry about an election. We'll be lucky if our country, let alone the world, survives. Carter is attempting to save us all. He's shown me the aftermath video of your crusade against the "great and terrible monster" shack at the Nevada base they own. You have shut down his team's efforts for nearly two weeks, you dolt. Do you have any idea how long we have, until we need to get the ecosystem kick started?" asked Murlough.

"No, sir," Crawford cowered.

"Carter tells me that we have slightly more than a year to get the plants growing again. Sounds impossible, doesn't it?" demanded Murlough.

"Yes, it does, sir."

"So, gentlemen, I hate to interrupt," Carter said as he joined the conversation. President Crawford, are you convinced that we did NOT kidnap the president?" asked Rick.

"You are holding him against his will," Crawford responded.

"He is where he wanted to be. And Mr. Murlough, I did my best to honor my promise to pick up your family, but the planet had already been contaminated by the bombing. All that heat from the bombing sent the virus around the globe. They are still alive, and they are protected under my care in a dirtside base," Rick said.

"Where?" asked President Murlough.

"At the Nevada site President Crawford has been trying to destroy for the past two weeks, Mr. President," Rick hissed.

26- Sequencer, take 2

"Hey Kelt, we think that we can finally get into that company that made those DNA sequencers you wanted," Guy said in their morning status meeting.

Kelt had monitored three teams that had been out most of the night transplanting weed plants around the southern hemisphere. It was late summer there, and soon, the efforts would move to the northern hemisphere as early spring approached.

The weeds were taking hold, but they just didn't reproduce that quickly. Dr. Shannon Liberty had suggested they speed up the reproduction process in the lab, by varying the temperature and lighting conditions to vary the seasons at an unprecedented rate. For some reason, these plants responded well, and within the first three weeks, they had enough plants growing and reproducing, to run little plant mats out every night with four crews in four shuttles. Once they had been transplanted on site, they grew and reproduced at the normal seasonal rate. Soon, they would have a crop of carefully harvested seeds from the underground facility, to start planting in the northern hemisphere as spring rolled around.

"I'm so tired of this, Guy," Kelt said, "We just can't seem to make any progress."

"Don't let 'em get you down, son. We're doing our very best.

"Yeah, I suppose so," Kelt said as he tried to wipe the sleep from his eyes. He had lost some weight and didn't look all that healthy.

"Kelt, you know, you don't look all that good. You really should get some rest," Guy advised.

"Yeah, I'll try to sneak some in," Kelt said with a rasp in his voice. "Hey Guy, I think you are right. I just can't keep this up, I am not feeling well. I'm sorry people, but I'm going back to bed. I'm of no use this morning,"

Kelt said as he stood from the fold up table and left the room.

"Sleep it off, son, we'll miss you, but we'll be fine," Guy said as Kelt shuffled out.

"You say you found us a DNA sequencer, Guy?" asked Scotty.

"We found a place where they used to make them, Scott. We won't know if they have any in inventory or not, if we don't look. The site looks pretty clean. It's near Boston, so we've been watching the site for two days, and we've seen no human activity in the area. I'm pretty confident we can get in there to snag us one," Guy told Scotty.

"Sounds good. Our lab down here is in tip-top shape. All we need for our microbiologists upstairs is to get a DNA sequencer installed. Do you know how big those things are, Guy?" Scotty asked.

"I have no idea."

"Pretty damn big, Guy."

It was going to be a busy week. Guy was going to do this in the daylight. He figured that it would be a tossup as to whether a nighttime invasion would be better, than in the daytime. Both had their advantages and disadvantages in this case. They really needed to see what they were doing with such a large piece of fragile equipment, if they couldn't get one already packed.

"Yup, we're going to need to take a Space Truck out, Guy," Scotty told him. "We can use a general use flat frame and just tie it down and take an easy flight back. Hopefully, we can find one that's crated. That would be a huge help. These things tend to have a lot of interface cables, power, and such… well, you know," Scotty said.

"Yes, I know, Scott, electronics," Guy sighed. He had sorely lacked proper controls for his men, while trying to fly their little saucers with computer gaming equipment. This situation didn't set well with him, for some reason.

"Look Scotty, this looks like their loading docks, and this looks like their storage facility."

"Can you send that floater cam down so we can look at the loading dock door?" asked Scott.

"Uh, yeah, that looks good… just keep going down… there… see that staircase going into the building?" Scotty queried.

"Yeah, I see it," said Guy with great disappointment. Smears of fresh blood ascended the staircase to the doorway of the loading docks.

"Look, Guy, we don't even know if this place has any machines available. They are pretty much made to order. With this blood, I see a real risk here," Scotty said.

"I agree with you, Scott, it just isn't worth the risk. What are we going to do, Scotty? I know that this is important, but we just haven't had enough time or resources to chase one of these down. It seems as though we are able to devote only a couple hours a week, with all this other stuff going on," Guy said.

"It's only going to get worse, Guy. I have a major project coming up tomorrow. Rupa is going to be dropping us a pond scum delivery. Kelt and I are assigning more civilians in replanting these "door mats" full of weeds around the southern hemisphere. You and your team are going north up to that air base to make a drop when I get back, remember?" Scotty said.

"Yes, I remember. We're supposed to deliver the 'ecosystem in a soda bottle' or what you call 'pond scum' stuff to them. I think we'll be all right on that one. The military really wants our help now. I don't know how many are still left on that base. I don't know when things may turn nasty again. At least, they seem like they want to work with us now," Guy replied.

"In the short term, Guy, if we can get people growing these things in stagnant ponds, they might stay alive for another year or two," Scotty advised.

"Yeah, I suppose that starting the project here in the desert and that includes the base north of us, gives us a better chance of getting these things rolling. Most people have moved to the coasts. We'll have less need for security," Guy added.

27- Date stamps

"Akhi, I need to ask a favor of you," Kelt asked her through a video link.

"No problem, Kelt. What's up?" she asked.

"I'm running some experiments on the library. I need you to link up with the library mentally at 11, my time tonight," he explained.

"What do you want me to find, Kelt?

"Akhi, I just want you to continuously make the connection to the same point in time, break it, and repeat the process until I ask you to stop. Try to repeat the process in one-minute intervals. Don't give up on me sweetie; it might take some time for me to figure things out."

"What are you looking for?"

"I'm looking for a time stamp."

"Ah, yeah, I can do that," Akhi answered pensively considering what Kelt was up to.

"Great, sweetie. I love you," he said. Before she could respond in kind, Kelt had cut the connection.

"I wonder what he's up to?" she mused.

*****

Kelt had entered the operating system for several nights in a row now, seemingly making little progress. He had been studying the old language, as he did with most projects, picking out the pieces he needed here and there. He had finally reached the point where he had to start at the beginning of the lessons, which Aldo had prepared over the years, and was now presenting to a class on Pacificus. Kelt had been able to fly through the lessons at an unprecedented rate. Each lesson had required a full hour to present. Kelt now had a fairly solid knowledge of the workings of much of the physics intertwined with the language. What he considered the language part was easily wrapped around the physics.

He was able to go through five to eight lessons in an hour, every day. Within a week or so, he would be at the same level with the language as Akhi and the others. He was already far advanced beyond what they had learned, or what Aldo could even pass on to them in the ancient knowledge of physics. Kelt had attained the impossible. He realized, even the Culinari could not possibly understand the underlying real physical constructs of their computing platform, hidden in the ancient artifact of the history library. Their mathematics was too basic. He had side tracked their natural flow and created his own. It was through his constructs, he better understood the artifact.

He reached in with his mind, and traversed the heaving threads that he had come to refer to as files, until he got to the operating system level. Here, within the library, a maze of complex threads and formulae were thrown into the processing mix in parallel fashion. Sequences of what would normally be known as simple hexadecimal machine codes were thousands and millions of molecules long. He was searching for a small segment in that mass of flow, Akhi's name. He had discovered her name through their mental connections. He had "walked through her open door" into her mind, into a similar place where he had found his name, in his own mind. There, he found the four character sequence that identified her, uniquely wrapped in ancient equations.

"If only I knew the language of this thing, it would be so much easier," he thought, as he watched for the string of symbols that represented her name. He had yet to crack any significant aspect of how the library functioned. Earlier that day, he had read through Aldo's discussion of wave theory. A formula within, held a symbol representing a constant. The group had been using it to connect telepathically with each other, and to the library. He quickly realized that the symbol could easily be replaced with a variable. If he could just find Akhi's name during her access to the machine, the new knowledge might provide a time stamp. Surely, other information would be included as well, but he now knew what a time stamp might look like, with the equations he had developed. With Akhi's identifier and the time stamp, perhaps he could find the system logs. That was where he ultimately wanted to go.

At 10:45 p.m., he finally found Akhi's markers associated with her access to the library. Kelt studied the streams and threads tracing back to find other files with the same sequence. He took note of where he was, and mentally stored several hundred common symbols in his mind. He then could compare the threads, subtracting the elements they all held shared, and with some variation, he found what he was looking for. The sequence seemed insurmountable at first, but he was acutely aware that it could be reduced to a few simple equations that he could remember. He could now accurately date files within the library, by looking at their heaving streaming threads. From this discovery, he transversed the internal layers of threads and streams, to find the system log. This was getting to be too much to remember, so he summarized what he had learned, then broke the link to quickly record the equations and symbols he had memorized, while they were still fresh in his memory.

"Akhi, I've got it, sweetie. You can quit." he sent to her mind.

"Kelt, that was exhausting! It's been well over an hour, repeating this exercise every minute. What are you up to?" she queried.

"I'll explain later, sweetie. I've got to make some notes before I forget," Kelt answered curtly.

Akhi sat stunned, with a great headache for her efforts. She understood he was researching. She understood that he could not break his train of thought for an explanation right now. She would confront him later though. She really needed to know what he was up to.

28- Shuttle Transfer

"This is just a bucket of bolts!" Scotty yelled at the commander in the Nevada CIC.

Scotty had just stepped into the shuttle the machine shop had prepared for the trip upstairs.

"I'm sorry, sir, but your shuttle is still out," replied the CIC commander.

Scotty was extremely upset with the arrangement, but had agreed to take out one of the newer shuttles. Instead of proper flight couches, the cockpits had been fitted with bucket seats from a sports car.

"The seats are firmly bolted to the floor, sir. No one else seems to mind," the CIC commander offered.

"The reclining function could break! I'd hate to run this up to a decent acceleration," whined Scotty.

"Don't worry about that, sir. We've welded them in place. Those seats will not break on you," the CIC commander reassured.

"At least you have heating control of the cabin," the commander reminded Scotty with a smirk.

"Humph," Scotty said to himself as he sat down in the "pilot's seat" and strapped himself in. I can't even adjust this chair to where I'm comfortable, and these home store heaters are junk," he grumbled to himself.

"Nevada, we're buckled in and ready to launch," Scotty commed the officer in charge.

"Very well, sir, we'll raise the elevator and open the garage door for you."

"Wow, it's really wet outside," Scotty said as the mammoth hangar door revealed an exceptionally hard rainstorm in the early dawn. Late winter storms had been extraordinarily heavy this year in Nevada. Scotty and Kelt had wondered how soon weather patterns may or may not change, without the world's active plant life. It may be that it was only anecdotal evidence to be sure, but these new weather patterns could be helpful in getting their weeds to grow.

"Well, we're still a couple of weeks until early spring, I suppose. We should expect a few showers," he explained to his fellow crewmates.

The president had reluctantly called off the raids, and instructed the remaining military forces to give aid to the teams from Space Truck.

"Look," President Crawford had told his dirt side commanders, "they are going to show you how to produce food you can eat. You touch one hair on them, and you'll be shot."

Most of the remaining command, topside, was all too eager to help in exchange for the promised extension to their dwindling food supplies. Some of the older military personnel were concerned about outside intervention, even if it were in their own interests. They had acquiesced to their commander in chief for now. They knew lean times were upon them.

Scotty tapped out some commands on the computer pad he had plugged into the shuttle's universal port. The shuttle moved slowly, one meter off the deck and out of the old warehouse at Nevada Base. Since the truce between Space Truck and the U.S. President, they had decided to try to step up their efforts. This required daylight-flying time. The rain and biting wind pelted the craft heavily, but made no progress in its attempt to buffet the floating craft. With the support of the floaters built into the shuttle's frame, nothing short of destroying the shuttle could move it, if the pilot didn't want it moved.

Scotty and two civilians were dressed in their EV suits. The machine shop had removed the simple bench seating along both sides of the interior, and had attached two long ladders to each side. Military grade webbing had also been strapped in, from the floor to the ceiling, behind the flight crew seating. Since the interior of their shuttles was usually so scanty, modifications like this had been accomplished with little effort. This was their first venture from the base during daylight hours.

"We should have left near midnight. This flight path is going to take us longer," Dan, one of his flight crewmembers, complained.

"I don't know about you, but I was bunked out at that hour," Scotty said, "I really needed the rest. And besides, who's flying this thing anyway?" Scotty scolded, "We'll accelerate fast enough once we clear the atmosphere, and that won't take much time at all," he added.

Scotty pressed some controls on the pad, and the craft started a comfortable one g acceleration straight up. As he cleared the atmosphere, he angled the ship toward the floating cities. At about one-half the distance to the cities, Scotty inverted the craft and started to decelerate. Only during the inversion did the crew feel no gravity.

"That was smooth, Scotty. I only had one second to throw up," Dan said as he started tying a wire around his barf bag. "But it was enough," he added with a green smile.

"Now, let's see, where's our package?" Scotty queried as he approached within 100 kilometers of the cities.

"I've got it located, Scotty," said Arshad, the other member of the crew, "I'm passing you the coordinates now," he finalized.

"Get another barf bag ready, Dan," Scotty grinned as he slowed the craft. Earth's gravity kicked in as Scotty slowed the craft.

"What am I going to need another barf bag for?" asked Dan.

"Why, laddy, for the trip home of course!" Scotty grinned. "Okay, lads, check your EV suits, make sure you've got 'em zipped up tight," Scotty commanded as the crew ran their diagnostic checks.

"You know, Scotty, your Star Trek crap gets pretty old in a hurry," Dan complained.

"I'm sorry laddies but that's life," Scotty said as he stared Dan down.

"Ah there, now I can see it. There's the beacon," Scotty said as he approached the large insulated and pressurized package.

"Okay boys, each of you hook into your ladders in back. I'm going to tip the nose down. Now, don't you complain when I do this, I'm the one who will be facing down and strapped in."

Scotty cracked the hatch ever so slightly, and let the air rush out in a brief violent storm. Scotty held tight to his computer pad. Other than the little electric heaters, which had been midnight requisitioned from a home center store and bolted to the walls, there had never been time to devise real environmental control for most of the dirtside shuttle fleet. Most all the good shuttles were upstairs with the floating cities. They weren't very different in the basic design. They were controlled with a computing pad the same way. They had been outfitted with a few more creature comforts and more importantly, environmental systems. Only one of the shuttles at Nevada Base could depressurize or pressurize their cabin. That was Scott's personal shuttle. Due to the modifications required for this mission, he had to use this one.

Scotty positioned and moved laterally until the opened craft was directly under the care package. He then fully opened the rear hatch and moved within a few centimeters next to the package. Dan and Arshad climbed their ladders and carefully adjusted the package, so that it would slide right into the shuttle.

"Okay, Scotty, lift her up," advised Arshad. Scotty made some easy adjustments on his pad.

"Slowly, okay, slowly, slow down, slow down some more, okay stop," Arshad commanded.

Dan retrieved some snips and cut the 300-meter cable that suspended the package. Up three hundred meters was a floater with a lightweight winch attached. Once Scotty had closed the hatch and moved away from the dangling line, he commed Rupa.

183

"We're good, my dear doctor, go ahead and advise them to drop the winch," Scotty said.

"Thanks … will do," she replied.

The command was sent to the floater and the winch was dropped into Earth's atmosphere. Sure, it was a waste of good equipment, but the floating cities could take no chances with viral infection from below. The remaining floater would be moved high into the UV exposure of the sun, and there it would remain in open space for three weeks or more, before it would be retrieved.

"Let's get back to base," Scotty said has he started one g acceleration toward Nevada Base. "Shouldn't we at least drop down and get some air?" asked Arshad.

"That would waste time, Arshad. Those bottles in that package need to be opened as soon as possible. The goo growing inside needs air too. You'll just need to keep your hood on until we get back."

The shuttle dropped straight to the launch site and slowed carefully before entering the giant hangar. The doors were open, and a throng of volunteers was waiting inside to help unload the cargo. They always had kept the hangar clear with the elevator in the up position. It was a paranoid defensive strategy, which the Nevada Base had long held to be a necessity. They had decided to unload the container precisely upon Scotty's return.

As the hatch opened down to form a ramp, Guy called out the commands. "Roll it out quickly, boys!" he shouted. His squad hurriedly entered the craft, lifted the pressurized container, and put a couple of furniture dollies underneath. Then they deftly rolled the large package out on to the elevator floor. Scotty, Arshad, and Dan finally stepped out. Scotty removed his EV hood and wiped his forehead with his arm.

"Are you hot, Mr. Scott? grinned Kelt.

"No, Kelt, I just felt under a bit of stress, if you know what I mean. That is the first time we've handled a drop, you know," Scotty answered.

"Well, if this works, it might become a standard procedure for the next several weeks," Kelt smiled.

184

The two of them turned around as Guy's team retrieved the two-liter soda containers from the package, removed the caps, and then carefully stacked them in two sets of packing crates.

"One of those sets is for the military north of us, the other is for us," Kelt explained to Scotty. "While Guy takes this shuttle out to the military base, we're going to make a run out to the California coast. I've made arrangements with a few ship captains," Kelt said, "They seem like good people and stand a real chance of surviving, if we can get these miniature farms to them. They've all managed to prepare for this delivery.

"Do you trust them?" Scotty asked.

"Someday, we are going to have to start trusting people again, Scotty," Kelt said. "I'm not sure that we have a choice, really. I don't want to give this stuff just to the military, civilians deserve a chance too," he added.

29- Sea going vessels

From Nevada Base, Tim Lockhart, in command, watched as the now experienced civilians moved six shiny white saucers in a wing formation, into position just outside the military base to their north. Other lethal disks remained high above to swoop in and take care of any potential threats. Three experienced military pilots manned their gaming cockpits. All were ready for the drop.

"I don't want anything to go wrong with this mission," Guy had told Kelt and Scotty as they had drawn up the plans. "This little white cutter wing is just a tactic to help them remember who they are dealing with," he commented.

"Guy, everything looks good from what we can see. Those military types are standing well clear, as instructed," Tim commed.

Guy was in one of the two shuttles assigned to the mission. "Acknowledged," Guy commed back. "Let's drop right in the middle of the ponds," Guy commanded his own pilot and the other of their accompanying shuttle. "Shuttle Two, just follow us down, and put down next to us."

Both shuttles set down softly. "Are we good to go?" Guy asked, as he commed Nevada.

"Still clear, Guy," Lockhart confirmed.

"Alright troops, keep your weapons ready, but let's clear this site quickly," Guy informed both crews.

Guy commanded the pilot of the other craft to lower their hatch. He watched via his pad as a floater cam image unfolded before him. The hatch came down cleanly, and four crewmembers quickly removed a number of crates of open two-liter soda bottles.

"Load 'em up," commed Guy as his troops quickly retreated to the safety of the open shuttle. Only one shuttle would be vulnerable at a time this way. The shuttle closed their hatch. "Our turn, boys. Lower the hatch captain," Guy ordered. As soon as the hatch was down, he and his team quickly moved the crates of bottles out into the open and set them on to the desert floor. The rain had let up, and the sun started to shine through the clouds. "Now that's a nice sweet smell. A good sign for once," he thought with a smile on his face. "Okay, troops, back on the shuttle!" he commanded. He and the other four quickly entered the shuttle, and before they had fully closed the hatch, both shuttles ascended out of sight.

"The packages have been delivered, Mr. Lockhart," Guy commed Nevada.

"Very well, Guy, We'll retrieve our cutters and I'll notify the base commander that he is good to go." Both shuttles had entered the large warehouse at Nevada Base before floater cams showed troops entering the pond area where the bottles had been deposited.

"Welcome back, Guy!" Kelt exclaimed in exceptionally good spirits.

"Kelt, you look much better, I was really getting concerned for you, son," Guy returned.

"Hey look, Guy, we are watching our men in uniform up there following their instructions to the letter," Kelt noted.

They watched for the next twenty minutes, as each two-liter bottle was poured into a shallow trough, lined with heavy home center plastic and 1000 liters of water.

"Each one of those ponds will supply three people nutritious algae bars and fish, once they are working at full strength," Kelt noted. "And let us not forget, they'll produce enough slime and fish eggs every month to start new ponds," he added.

"I can hardly wait," Guy said. "The thought of eating that goo, does not appeal to me, Kelt."

"It will when we get hungry, Guy," Kelt said.

The Nevada Base team had taken about two thirds of the remaining inventory of gooey slime, in a bottle to feed their own tanks. Half of that had been poured into constructed ponds a few kilometers south of the Nevada Base and the other half into large tanks in the bunker. "I can't tell you how this will improve the smell down there, Guy," Kelt smiled.

"I can hardly wait," Guy answered.

"We'll block off those tunnels to reduce the smell. It shouldn't be too bad. So... everything looks good. We have some deliveries to make out on the coast.

"Yes, sir," Guy responded sharply.

Even though he had slackened in his strict military standards of speech, he still was well organized and he recognized the commander in charge.

Two shuttles ascended into the now clearing sky of the morning. One had the supply of opened soda bottles with Guy and two of his commandos. The other shuttle carried eight commandos in addition to the flight crew. A dozen cutter floaters accompanied them in close proximity.

"Move west, young man, move west!" cried Kelt at Scotty, who was at the pilot pad.

"Where did you pick that up, Kelt." Scotty asked.

"Scotty, it's just a piece of trivia I picked up from my personal reading. The author's name was Horace Greeley. He wrote an editorial, encouraging civil war veterans to move west, and take advantage of the Homestead Act. It was a program where the government was giving land to anyone who would farm it, from what I recall," Kelt told Scotty. "It just seems so appropriate now. You know? It's just this time, we are taking the farms to the farmers," Kelt added.

"This is Lockhart, Nevada actual."

"Yes, Tim, how do we look?" asked Guy.

"We've got floater cams in place around those big tankers. They are all lined up as instructed and we see no suspicious activity.

"I assume that they've all completed their artificial ponds?" asked Kelt.

"It looks like they have, sir. Everything looks good for your distribution. Send in our little white friends to do a few flybys, Mr. Lockhart," commanded Guy.

"Well, that got their attention, Guy," Lockhart commed. "They are out on deck, and we see no weapons."

"Have you told the crews of those ships what we expect of them?" asked Guy.

"Yes sir, you'll notice that they are now moving to the bow of each ship. Only two crewmen are moving aft," Nevada returned

"Acknowledged," commed Guy.

"This is looking smooth, so far, Guy," Kelt said.

Guy merely looked at him as a reminder that anything could go wrong.

"Let's make our first drop with that ship," Kelt pointed to Scotty.

Scotty approached the ship's aft, and as he let down the hatch, the other shuttle took up a position 90 degrees portside with its hatch open. The two shipmates at the aft were a bit unnerved to see well-armed commandos pointing automated weapons at them, as they handed out the bottles, but they soon settled down.

Kelt moved aft to the hatch of his shuttle to hand out the containers. As he approached the hatch carefully guarded by his commandos, one of the two men on the ship stepped forward.

"Captain Devin Sherrod, sir," Sherrod said as he put forth his hand to Kelt.

"I'm Dr. Kelt Nelby, Captain. We hope that this will help you and your crew," Kelt answered, "Now, we are putting caps on these bottles as we pass them to you, but make sure that you gently get the contents into your ponds as quickly as possible," he added.

"We will sir. We are so grateful that someone is getting things done. We feel so totally helpless. The only thing that keeps us safe is the size of our ship. No one dares board us," Sherrod said.

"It's also the size of your ship that helped you qualify to get this 'algae-eco'," Kelt answered. "Not only are you less likely to be attacked by others, but you have those big stabilizers. You'll be less likely to lose your ponds in a storm," Said Kelt.

189

"We're working with the instructions you sent us, and we believe that we'll have working covers to help us in that respect within a day or two," answered Sherrod.

"Well, Captain, we've got other deliveries to make. We'll be in touch, I hope," Kelt said in parting.

"Thank you again, sir," Sherrod said as he smartly saluted.

"Nice fellow," said Guy, "and you, son, have just made up a name for the slimiest crap I've ever seen. "Algae-eco? Where in the world did you come up with that?" Guy teased.

"I was going to call it green slime or give it a nick similar to what you guys have been calling it in expletive terms, but we're professionals, Guy. No matter how we treat each other, we've got to present ourselves professionally to the rest of the world," Kelt explained.

"You're preaching to the choir, sir," Guy smiled.

The rest of the distribution went very smoothly, and the two shuttles had finished just as the sun had set.

"This has been the best day since the new era started, Guy," Kelt noted.

"It is well deserved, son, well deserved."

30- Hughes research lab

"Now this looks interesting... Hey Kelt, come into the CIC will you?" Guy commed.

Kelt showed up within a minute. He was going to take a few minutes after lunch to call Akhi. She would understand if there was a delay. He found it difficult to maintain their long distance relationship, especially when everything seemed so hopeless.

"What have you got?" Kelt asked as he scurried into the CIC.

"The Hughes Research Laboratories in Malibu, California, Kelt," Guy answered. "We've called them a number of times with no answer. We figured they were off line, being so close to a major population center and all. For that reason, we decided not to go in personally some time back. We're taking a second look at the labs, to see if we can make some inroads on getting that equipment that your friends upstairs need. Look at this, Kelt," he said.

Kelt looked at the video feed on the monitor.

"Looks like some of your people, Guy," Kelt said.

"Yes, it does. Look at that face," Guy said as he zoomed in on one of the armed specialists, crouched and cautiously peering through the dying bush.

"It's Robert Gunn!" cried Kelt.

Robert Gunn had worked for Aldo before the new era, and had also been best friends with Guy for well over a decade. Gunn had been instrumental in helping the Stanford research team to escape and save their technology, when they had been attacked by overwhelming forces.

"Oh Guy, this is great news! This research lab has never been held hostage by anyone. I mean that figuratively of course. They have never taken government funding nor have they taken on partnerships. They've run their operation just like Rick Carter. Old man Hughes gave the research team a fat wad of cash, and they never had to beg for funding. We have to work with these people," Kelt said passionately.

"Kelt, do you mind if I handle this my way? No questions asked?" Guy formed an impish smile which spread the width of his face.

"No problem, Guy," Kelt grinned. He knew that his friend was up to a little mischief, but he deserved his little moment of respite, or whatever it was. Kelt knew it would be funny in at least some part. There was no doubt in his mind that it would lift everyone's spirits to some degree.

Two hours later, a shiny little white cutter hovered over the security fence at the HRC in Malibu. Attached to its bottom was a 75 cm by 20 cm plastic tube. Floater cams were positioned just off site with very good camera angles. Several commandos noticed the craft float slowly toward the first building where Gunn was stationed. Two of his command raised their weapons to fire.

"Hold all fire!" Gunn yelled, so all in range could hear him. He'd never seen one of these, but had an inkling as to where it came from. He shouldered his weapon and approached the saucer-shaped floater with careful curiosity. Guy sat in the CIC watching his old friend approach the little saucer, with the extended tube attached to its bottom.

"Wait, wait... okay... NOW!" he ordered."

Sitting right next to Guy, and watching the scene unfold on the large screen in front of them, Scotty pushed the little red button on the transceiver. The small magnetic catches on the tube opened and a white piece of fabric unrolled. Gunn broke out in wild laughter.

"Come on over here boys, you gotta see this!" Gun ordered, wiping the tears of laughter from his eyes.

"WE COME IN PEACE?" said one of his team with a questioning look?

"Guy, you bastard! You crack me up!" cried Gunn in his thick Australian accent.

After Guy Lerner had saved Robert Gunn in combat, they started ribbing each other right before each mission with the phrase "We come in peace." They both found it ironic that they were often sent into a mission with guns blazing, all in the name of peace.

"No one but Guy Lerner would know that," he said to his men. "You know that this isn't an alien space ship, right?" he demanded from his team, the accent drawing laughter from his squad.

"Hello, Robbie, It's been a while."

"Okay, where is that voice coming from?" asked Gunn.

"There's a touch screen phone in a little compartment behind the sign, Robbie. Don't' touch the edges of the craft… they're razor sharp," Guy told him.

Robert Gunn stepped up behind the small craft, now locked in position, and easily retrieved the phone.

"How are you my old friend?" Gunn asked. He looked at Guy's face displayed on the small video screen.

"We're getting along Robbie," Guy stated as Kelt moved into camera view beside him.

"Oh my, you didn't get that bright kid into space, Guy?"

"No, my friend. The bombs were dropped as he was directing efforts dirtside and he was contaminated with the rest of the remaining ground crew. I did manage to get to space, but decided to drop down to ride it out with Kelt, and the rest of my men," Guy responded.

"Robbie, we need your help.

"Sure, anything for my old buddy," he answered.

"Robbie, I'm sure that you've got a team of scientists there working on the problem, right?"

"Guy, they were working on it before the government even acknowledged there *was* a problem. They assigned all their research staff to it. They supplied this facility like a fortress, and have at least 5 years of food. I think they will work themselves to death long before the food supply is gone.

They gave me a call just a couple of weeks after Aldo let us go. We were all rich from what he paid us. The folks here told us what they were working on, and why it was so important. We knew we had to jump in to help. We aren't getting paid anything. It doesn't matter anymore … the money thing, does it?" Gunn queried.

"No, I suppose it doesn't, Robbie," answered Guy. "How hot is your situation down there?" Guy asked.

"We get busy bodies from time to time. It has been very quiet the past few weeks. Everyone has gone right out to the coastline. Either they have ships, or they are trying to trade with those people on ships. There have been a lot of murders lately, Guy. It's heartbreaking to see all this go down. Look at this," Gunn said, pointing to a bush, "It's nearly all yellow now, it did produce seeds this past fall, but now, it's nearly dead.

Everything around here is dead or dying. We've been watching a wild boar rummaging in the dirt outside today, looking for mushrooms, I suspect. In any case, we were hoping to bag him for some roast pork. The frozen stuff in our supplies isn't very good. Some fresh meat…," and then Gunn's voice trailed off. "Guy, they are eating each other here. I know that it's been just a few months, but most people have nothing to eat. I see the little kids being snatched up … well… you can imagine," he said with great sorrow pulling down on his face.

"I'm sure glad to know that you made it, Guy. I didn't know that I had anyone left, you know?" Gunn asked.

"I know, Robbie. The same goes for all of us at the Nevada site."

"Don't tell me you are living in that crapper, Guy! That place ain't much more than a cave."

"We do what we have to do, Robbie," Guy admonished.

"That we do, Guy," Gunn responded sullenly.

"Robbie, can you get a message to those researchers? Tell them that we'd like to work with them. We have vital information and biological samples that they do not have. We can't evaluate them without contaminating our research facilities in space," Guy pleaded with Gunn.

"Give me five minutes. I doubt that it will take any longer than that for me to explain the situation. They are pulling their hair out in there and getting nowhere. I'm sure they will welcome the help," Gunn said.

"Robbie, if it is any consolation, we are very much in the same situation."

"Hold on Guy, I'll ring you back in five," Gunn said as he cut the link.

"Scotty, did you send them out our specialized communications equipment, yet?" asked Kelt.

"Yes sir, we sent it out with the peace sign," Scotty acknowledged.

"Good work Commander Scott," Kelt grinned.

Scotty nodded with satisfaction in return. Kelt could see that he was calm and somewhat subdued, but in very good spirits, this day. The specialized equipment included several black boxes that had been sealed in carbon matrix. All were identical and sported standardized interfaces on the back. Inside the black boxes were embedded DC's or dimensional conduits. If someone were to X-Ray the box, all they would see would be an array of cables coming into the box, and dead ending in the middle. Space Truck was still paranoid about losing its technology. Kelt wondered if the world would ever be able to work together.

"We're not all that different than the military, I suppose," he mused.

31- Back to the artifact

Kelt dove back into the streaming flow of threads in the never-ending turbulence of the system functions within the libraries. He had now been able to determine time. He could see when events happened. He still did not understand how the coding worked, and he had no idea how data was processed. He could only detect the things he had learned and a few that he was looking for.

The artifact had performed a miracle before they had been able to find it. The truth in that fact was self-evident, in the plants that were growing around it. That is how they had discovered the artifact. Active green plants growing in a desert, a radioactive death zone, and one filled with the killer virus, had miraculously managed to sprout and survive right above the protected embellished stone. Everyone had questioned the nature of this event. Everyone tried to figure out exactly what had happened. Every clue led nowhere. The artifact sent out no known signals, other than the simple video feed they were getting for the researchers up in the floating cities. Attempts to identify the differences in these plants with other known species had been thwarted, due to a lack of ability to do DNA sequencing.

That process could be done at Hughes in Malibu. The complete sequencing of the two plants under investigation would take several more days or weeks. Then, comparisons would be made with other similar plants to determine the differences. It could easily take months or years to complete the process. And, after all the effort, after all the work, worry, and stress, what would they find?

"They'll have some little difference in their DNA," Kelt thought, "And then what? What will we do when we find that difference? Can we make a similar change in all plants? How long will it take to manipulate individual DNA strands in multiple sets of genes, to create just one plant that can survive our new environment? If we can make one, then how about all the plants we have in inventory?"

196

The answers were truly staggering. Kelt had done the math considering the most favorable of outcomes. With the current crop of research personnel on board, it could literally take thousands of years.

The world was dying, in short order. Within the next decade, most humans living dirtside, would also perish. "And my name is on the list," thought Kelt.

In his mind, he followed the streams with the markers he had identified with Akhi, just a few nights before. He had been here several times since, but each path led to a place where he could not find what he was looking for. He had figured out how the time stamps were used. He could now read them.

"Every computer must have a system log, and this is a computer isn't it?" Kelt kept reminding himself. He was looking for that place that had molecular streaming dated within the past year. There would likely be nothing else to note in that place. He was looking for the "file folder" of system logs where the broadcasts had been logged.

"If I had to explain this to a lay person, I suppose that I'd call it the folder of emails," he thought as he gazed at the tremendous breathing machine in his mind.

Up and down, this side to the next, he followed Akhi's 45 tags that she had left by accessing the library those few nights ago. They were repeated in many places, as they carried his mind with them.

Everywhere he went, he looked for commonality, for matching sequences that he recognized, for those things, which matched formulae, he considered, might be useful. He *was* learning from an intuitive standpoint, the internal workings of the library. "It's sort of like memorizing a piece of music. Once you have learned it, the notes are in your head and no longer on that piece of paper," he sidetracked as he fondly remembered playing the cello. "That's exactly what this feels like. It's not just reading the notes and interpreting them, it's like memorizing the notes, and playing them with passion. This isn't a simple set of instructions, which are being processed with these complex functions and symbols. There is power of feeling and expressiveness here. That's what I've missed. Is that why music helps round out a person's education? Is that why love is expressed without words? Is this functionality built into our brains?" he wondered.

He had evidently just sent a passionate code sequence to the machine, for his mind was swept by a streaming thread to the place he had been looking for. The spacious place had only a few hundred streams moving and intertwining together. He noted the time stamps of them all, and found one that dated just a few months ago. This was what he had been looking for all these weeks. Nothing preceded it, for thousands of years. The most recent marker on a stream that he could find was over 5000 years old. What had happened those few months ago? This would be the puzzle he must solve. He realized that time was getting late and he was extremely tired. He took special note to remember all that had brought him to this place. He reduced everything he could see to Culinari equations he could easily remember. He noted the coding of sequences of the four special characters. The emotions of his passion must be carefully observed in order to return.

31- HRC

Shannon Liberty, Amanda Perry, Akhi Richmond and Gary Johnston, sat in video conference with Nevada Base. "Men and women, I'd like to give you some wonderful news. The research team at the Hughes Research Facility has agreed to work with us," Kelt proudly announced. The conference room onboard Pacificus suddenly filled with cheering and applause. Akhi quietly stepped into the room. She had already heard the good news and had to be there for the celebration.

Gary met with the biology team every morning for a quick rundown and reviews of any progress coming from the biological research. He was a physicist, but also a pragmatist. Kelt had noted his ability to stray from the pack, mind think, and speak his frank opinion.

"So far, I haven't accomplished much. I just send specs out for little robots now and then. I feel pretty useless, for the most part," Gary thought. This was indeed some great news.

"I'd like you now to meet the team at HRC," Kelt said as he opened the video feed from Malibu.

It was a bit disconcerting for so many people to work via video link, but this was the situation they had.

"I'd like to introduce Dr. Amanda Perry, microbiologist, Dr. Shannon Liberty, our virologist, Dr. Gary Johnston, quantum physicist, and finally, Dr. Akhi Richmond, quantum physicist. I am Dr. Kelt Nelby, molecular physicist," he finalized.

Dr. Jayne Thomas, virologist, at HRC introduced herself and three of her lead researchers to the team in Malibu.

"We've been working on this problem before the CDC in Atlanta even knew about it," started Dr. Thomas.

"That's where I should have applied for a job," thought Amanda to herself, but then chided herself for whining about the past.

"Initially we worked on solutions to eradicate the virus but soon realized that would never be a viable solution. Ever since we've been working on ways to produce new plant populations that are virus resistant," Jayne explained.

"Have you had any success?" asked Amanda Perry.

"I'm afraid that we have not," answered Jayne. "We've tried splicing telomeres, gene manipulation, and splicing DNA sequences from animals... we've gotten nowhere."

"We have pretty much been through the same exercise," Shannon Liberty spoke up.

"Do you have a virus free lab?" Akhi asked.

"For now, we do," Jayne said. "We have just one left. Nothing goes in or out. It is only a matter of time on that one. I can't imagine that the air supply and filtering systems we have will keep that bug out forever. We do have a healthy plant population that we've managed to keep viable. The care and feeding of the plants are taken care of by remotely controlled robotics. Six months ago, we had six virus free labs. The first we contaminated ourselves by just walking in. We had hoped that the three stage scrubbing procedures, which are severe at this facility, would clear the virus before entering the lab. We used harsh flash ultraviolet light, our own developed chemical wash, as well as the standard soaps, rinses, and scrubbing. The virus still contaminated the lab. In the others, we don't know how the virus got in.

"Jayne, generally speaking, has UV flashing been effective in killing the virus?" asked Amanda.

"Yes, Amanda, it has."

"So, all we have to do is let the world die and let the sun take care of this problem for the next 10,000 years or so," Amanda murmured softly.

"Excuse me?" I didn't quite hear you, Dr. Perry," Jayne said.

"Oh, I was just expressing some frustration to myself," Amanda explained.

"Well, Amanda, it may take some time, after all, we still haven't found cures for cancer," Jayne said in an effort to boost Amanda's moral.

"Actually, Dr. Thomas, we have managed to do that," Amanda admitted.

"Really?" Jayne said with a surprised voice.

"Yes, working with the telomeres, and RNA binding, we have been able to effectively treat nearly all types of cancers. It's rather odd that our research on this virus has led to a cure for cancer. We also have machines we call sniffers that can be used in diagnosing nearly any malady. So, even though we've had many failures, much good has come of all of our research. Unfortunately, it may never be useful.

"Why is that, Amanda?" Jayne asked.

Jayne thought of the apocalypse around her and realized her own answer. She slumped back into her chair.

"Okay, Amanda, you were going to speak to Jayne. Please, go ahead," Kelt said, obviously noting Jayne's visible emotion.

"Jayne and colleagues there at the HRC, have you done any estimates of how soon we'll need to repopulate the world with plant life?" Amanda asked.

"Well, not really. We do understand that it must be done soon, or the necessary micro ecology surrounding plant life will shortly be lost. Microbial life forms will be healthy for several years, but we are especially concerned about the insect life. For the species that are most helpful in the growth of food plant life, time is very short," she answered.

"Jayne, you have intuitively come to the same conclusions that we have estimated with real numbers? This coming spring, or possibly next spring, will be the tipping point for our planet. If we cannot repopulate plant life in a major way, we will be wiped out for hundreds or thousands of years," she concluded.

A wash of ashen faces filled the conference room at HRC. Hushed whispers attempted to mask the astonishment of this group of brilliant people.

"We had not considered it to be so soon. After all, this virus infection happened here, only last year," Jayne said.

"Okay, that's the bad news," Kelt said. "Let me tell you what we have been doing. We have been seeding very small plots of ground in the southern hemisphere with mats of these plants that we have found, along the Nile River. We realize that those plants do best under the conditions found there, but those plants are the only living species that survived the virus. We have watched these plots with our technology, and they are all surviving. We have attempted to replant some in moderate climates, and in locations where they are least likely to get washed out with heavy rainfall or run off. It is getting late in the summer season down there, so it probably doesn't make sense to continue the planting. We shall continue to expand our cultures until early spring and continue our efforts in the northern hemisphere."

"So, what is your total estimate of the plant life from your seeding efforts?" asked Jayne.

"I'm sorry to say that it is less than ten square meters in total," answered Kelt. "The plants are growing, but clearly not enough to save the planet in this decade," he added.

"In addition to that effort, we have created what we are calling an "algae-eco," which is essentially a small pond of nutrients, bottom feeding fish, and the necessary bacteria and other microbial life to make a small eco system work. The algae are harvested, and we have developed a process to make nutrition bars from the green slime. Once the fish lay their eggs, we can create a mix that fits in five two-liter bottles, that can populate a fresh water pond of 1000 liters. Each pond can sustain three individuals. Maintenance and harvesting time is minimal. The algae cracker tastes like cardboard, but it is nutritious. When the fish eggs hatch, we also have a form of protein.

We don't know how long a person can live on that sort of diet, but the Irish lived decades on not much more than potatoes. So, this is a viable step forward on at least one front," Kelt finalized.

"I know that it sounds like it is too little too late," Jayne said, "but you people are fighting. I am amazed at your tenacity. Even with what you have done so far, at least a few people may endure. Our species may survive due to your actions."

"We shouldn't give up on the people living at sea," added Shannon. "We don't know how sea life will be affected, but the population of sea going vessels, is currently harvesting one-tenth of that before the new era in the fishing industries. It may be that the fish will make a strong comeback. Unfortunately, areas around the shorelines have been or they will be stripped of nearly everything as the people continue to attempt to survive. We estimate the majority of shoreline ecosystems will perish within a year. The damage to the shorelines will take decades to come back. With those areas damaged beyond repair, and any positive effect that land-based plant life may have had on sea life, we have a very difficult time envisioning the future of our seas."

"How many have perished so far?" asked Jayne.

"We run the numbers every other day or so, to establish a fairly stable estimate... oh here we go," Amanda said. "Today, it looks like we've lost about 70 percent of the human population around the world. Our estimates vary slightly with each estimate, but we can see the sudden downward trend. No one could have ever realized that panic would have caused so many deaths. There certainly was enough food to last everyone thus far. Hoarding and raids have been directly responsible for more deaths than anything else has. Now we are seeing the worst of the worst," Amanda concluded.

"Do you have seed stock, frozen animal embryos, insects... biological samples or stocks of that nature, Jayne?" asked the young Shannon.

"Yes, we do. We have long realized that some sort of bug may threaten our species. We have large stores of seeds sealed in bunkers below us. We also have many samples of embryos and insects that could be used, if we could find a way around this virus. You know, we always thought that *the* bug would have come for us, not the world's plant life," Jayne said sadly.

"Jayne, I am assuming you have the capability to do DNA sequencing down there?" asked Amanda.

"Yes, we do," Jayne replied.

"I'd like Kelt's team to rush out a few samples of the plants they are growing. Can you prioritize the sequencing of those samples?" Amanda asked.

"We could if we had the power, Amanda. Our fuel reserves for our generators are running low, and we don't have the ability to turn on all the computing hardware for a sequencing run," explained Jayne.

"Now, we can help you with that particular problem," Kelt said, "We can give you all the power you need."

"Well... if we could fire up all our computers, we could manage to do two sequences simultaneously. I'm sure you know that even though we've come a long way in sequencing DNA, it may take a few weeks for each sample," Jayne warned.

"That's what we expected, Jayne. There is a difference in these plants and we need to know what it is. I would suspect that in the common DNA nucleobases sequences all plant life shares; there is uniqueness in these new plants. If we could figure that out, we'd at least have a new path to pursue," Amanda said.

"You get those samples out to us and a generator, folks. We'll get started on the sequencing as soon as we can get the new power hooked up," promised Jayne.

"Some of the equipment has already been delivered. Guy will come out with a couple of his troops to get you hooked up. They know your Mr. Gunn and his group. They'll be able to set up your new electrical plan and give you the samples we have," Kelt smiled as he thought of the huge generator they would be replacing with a small dimensional conduit box.

Kelt advised the committee to carefully prepare summaries of all the research done by both Space Truck and HRC so that both teams could not only come up to speed on what they had accomplished, but perhaps provide some idea or clue that one team had missed.

"Don't discount the dead ends from either team either," Kelt advised. "You just never know what little detail someone overlooked."

Amanda and Jayne came up with a quick list of action items everyone could accomplish for the rest of the day, and agreed to meet early the next morning, Earth time.

"This is going to seriously affect my sleep schedule," thought Shannon.

32- Nelby Station infected

"We're finally underway, making progress," Akhi thought as she showered and got ready for the day's activities. She had been buoyed up by the new paths they were pursuing, in conjunction with the Hughes lab in Malibu. Kelt seemed to be making progress with his interactions in the library. She had a long mental streaming talk the night before, where he told her what he had been up to.

"Who knows where all of this might lead?" she cheerfully reminded herself. "I think that I feel better than I ever have, since Kelt was stranded on Earth," she mused. "What a glorious day!" she screamed in her mirror.

Her thoughts turned to what might come.

"We'll find a way and turn this around. Kelt will be with me. We'll find new and exciting things to work on, together. Who knows where we can take technology now?" she asked herself.

Then the realization slowly flooded into her brain. New technologies required not only research, but also huge enterprises to bring them to fruition. They needed raw materials, machinery, and most importantly, people.

"And there aren't that many people left down there."

Current estimates place the number just under one billion survivors, but the anticipated death curve would leave fewer than 200 million, within just a year. Even if they could turn everything around, the spiral of death and destruction would continue.

"Now, I'm depressed," she admitted.

The past several months had taken its toll. She hardly ever heard anyone tell a joke. Everyone walked around with sullen faces, worried for the future. Hardly anyone could perform to their peak level, although everyone was doing their best. The morale had reached a new low in all the history of humanity. Even during the worst of conflict in the history of the world, there had been some happiness, some levity, a dance, a movie, or a concert somewhere, which would lessen the load, for those carrying the heaviest of burdens.

"And we have nothing except the hope that we can find some hidden secret in those new plants we found. And then what shall we do, if we find how they are resistant to the virus?" she asked herself. She quickly came to the same conclusions that Kelt had chosen not to share with her the evening before.

"I suppose that we'll find ways to survive upstairs. The world will be lost below. I'll lose my darling who's stranded down there with the rest of them."

"The oceans and the algae-eco, right?" she forced herself to remember. "There is a way that Kelt can live. There just has to be." Her passion and will to make it so, bolstered her spirits greatly as she finished dressing and checked herself in the mirror. "Breakfast time!" she told her image in the mirror. "Chanto, Freia, lie down and stay here." The cats quietly lay down in front of the couch.

Akhi left her quarters and instead of going down to the cafeteria, decided to pop in to the CIC first. It was closer than the cafeteria, and she always wanted to be on top of the action. As she opened the hatch to enter, she could see the solemn faces of everyone in the CIC. Everyone was bent over display monitors in hushed whispers.

Commander Barnes was currently in command and noticed her entry into the CIC. "Dr. Richmond, we have some disturbing news," he started.

"Well, what is it?" she demanded before he could finish his sentence.

"Dr. Richmond, Nelby Station has reported that they've been infected by the virus. Some of their plants are dying," he managed to say.

"Put me on video link with Dr. Amanda Perry, would you Commander Barnes?" Akhi asked in a measured tone.

"She's working on the problem, I'm not sure…" he started, "Ah, here she is Dr. Richmond," Barnes said.

"Amanda, what's going on over on Nelby Station?" Akhi asked.

"Akhi, I was about to contact you. We've been trying to isolate this thing for the past twenty minutes. Shannon and I just ordered a complete lock down of every sphere and section in the city, until we can get it all sorted out. One of the recycling engineers was going through a medical physical. The sniffer picked up the virus right away. We had the biologists over at Nelby check the status of the farms growing in several spheres.

They found very small yellow spots on some of the strawberries and wheat down in one of the farm spheres, about two hours ago. After we started checking closely, we found that all the plant farms have slight infections in every sphere where we grow crops. We've had them flush the contaminated crops into space, but you know as well as I do, that won't effectively deal with the contamination."

Akhi buried her face in her hands. "What should we do? What should we do?" she asked herself repeatedly. "Amanda, do you have any recommendations?" Akhi finally asked.

"Akhi, we are following every protocol in the book. If we can contain it, we will. We've also put the other cities on alert, in full lock down mode. We're moving all of our medical sniffers to the farms. Every person will be scanned. No one will be allowed to leave their spheres without a full scan and under special orders. There will be no more travel between cities, via shuttle. If you have anything that you can add, we would like to hear it."

"It sounds like you have it covered, Amanda," Akhi noticed as she heard the full lockdown command issued throughout Pacificus.

"Amanda, we can't remain in full lockdown for long. People need to eat. I realize that we designed and built habitats in all the farm spheres, but that's also where much of our frozen food supplies are located. How shall we proceed?" Akhi asked.

"We'll just need to wait and see, Akhi. I suspect that if we don't find any infections within the next several days, we'll be able to relax the lockdowns in the other three cities," Amanda explained.

"And what will happen to Nelby Station?" Akhi asked.

"For now, we have asked them to move outside the cluster by five hundred kilometers. I suppose that they'll live off their existing food supplies before they are ultimately forced to return to Earth, and do their best down there to survive," Amanda stated with great despair in her eyes.

"Amanda, we can do better than that. They just can't run out of food and then try to start life again, down along some costal area. They are going to have to have some time to build boats, learn how to fish, and grow the algae," Akhi stated.

"Let's not get too far ahead on this Akhi. There is still a chance that we can contain this," Amanda said.

"Amanda, how many people are locked down in the infected spheres?"

"I don't know, Akhi, we don't have an accurate count yet, but I suspect at least 20 percent of their population was on duty when we closed them off."

"Amanda?"

"Yes, Akhi."

"I just wanted to thank you for all your hard work. I know that you and Shannon have worked every waking hour for so many months, with so little progress. I want you to know that we appreciate all of your efforts. We know that if anything could have been done, both of you would have found a way to do it," Akhi noted.

Tears welled in Amanda's eyes. She wiped her nose with her blouse sleeve. "Akhi, thank you so much. I'll pass it along to Shannon. You can't imagine how hard it has been, with so many counting on us, to not discover a single clue that we could fight this thing with."

Tears streamed down both their faces as they finished the conversation. "And this was going to be a good day. I wonder what a bad day is like," Akhi wondered.

*****

"Commander Grayson?" Akhi addressed the commanding officer of Nelby Station, CIC.

"Yes, ma'am."

"I realize that you've got a lot going on over there."

"Yes ma'am, we're still assessing the extent of the infestation. I must tell you, that it's not looking good. Our testing indicates that at least 50 percent of the spire is infected, and it cannot be contained."

"I understand, Commander. I doubt that you'll be able to contain it. I don't want to be pessimistic, but that's how this bug works."

"Understood, ma'am."

"Once you finally decide that the infection is uncontainable... which I imagine will only take a few days, I'd like you to send out a few shuttles and bring in the survivors from the space elevator. Make sure, that if you find any provisions over there, they are retrieved as well."

"I'm sure that we'll be able to do that, ma'am. I have heard of the women over there. I understand that several have already had their children."

"Well, Commander, that's another reason to get them to safety. We have very few children onboard the stations and that's not healthy for our population in general. We will need children for the future."

33- A big question

"I'm sorry Kelt, but I've got some bad news to pass on," Rick Carter said over the video link.

"Rick, I know already. Akhi sent me a message… you know…," Kelt said pointing to his cranium.

"Oh yes, that," Rick said, "She told me about this telepathy thing, but I wasn't so sure that it really worked,"

"Well, it does, Rick. Only a half dozen of us can do it presently, but I suspect that most millenarians could learn to do it, if they spent time learning the old language."

"That may be true Kelt, but obviously, we don't have time for that sort of thing. We've got a freakin Greek tragedy being played out, up here," Rick said.

"I understand, sir," Kelt said, "What can we do dirtside to help out?" he asked.

"Assuming the worst, we need a plan to bring Nelby Station back to Earth in the not so distant future, and figure out how we are going to feed nearly five thousand people."

"I understand, sir. We've been wondering ourselves what we are doing in the middle of this forsaken desert. We're really worried that our algae ponds on the surface will expose us. If we don't get healthy plants growing around the world within the next year or two, well… I suppose we could easily hold out longer than that… but what I'm trying to say is that we are clinging to the fringe of existence. I feel like we aren't doing enough to ensure our long-term survival. There is nothing wrong with us physically, but we are mental wrecks, sir. The work we are doing isn't giving our little band of a couple hundred, enough mental challenge to make life worth living. We just seem to wander from one crisis to another," Kelt explained.

"I can understand that Kelt. We feel equally frustrated up here as well. It's like watching an endless funeral, if you catch my drift. The crisis hasn't come to a head over on Nelby Station just yet. We'll give it a week or two, to see if we have contained it or not. Meanwhile, we should make some contingency plans. Clearly, some of us are going to have to learn how to live dirtside. You and your crew have the most experience as far as that goes. You have the best contacts and you have covered the most territory. Can you get Guy on the link with us?" Rick asked.

"Sure thing, Rick. Just give me a moment to chase him down. I think that he's out prepping a shuttle for an algae-eco run," Kelt said as he rose from his chair and left the room.

Kelt and Guy returned to the open session. "I'm sorry Rick, but I felt compelled to personally ask Guy to join us. I could have used our coms, but...well, I just didn't want anyone to know about this until we think it through a bit. Guy, Nelby Station, formerly known as City A, has been infected with the virus," Kelt said.

"Holy pariah," Guy responded in a barely audible whisper. "There's just no getting away from this thing is there, Mr. Carter?" he asked.

"Gentlemen, I'm very much the pessimist today. I do believe that sooner or later one of the other cities will also be infected. Or, we could eventually lose them all. We need to start planning for that, my friends," Kelt noted. "Rick, people are still murdering each other dirtside for a meal. I'm afraid that will continue for some time. There is nowhere that is safe."

"I can't in good conscience advise a plan that brings down Nelby Station within the foreseeable future, for that very reason," Rick suggested.

"They don't have to do anything at the moment Rick. After all, they do have supplies that will last ten years," Kelt said.

"I was thinking long term strategies, Kelt. In a year or two, I'm hopeful that the violence dirtside will subside, and we'll have better opportunities. We should be able to find some good beachfront property with good fishing," Rick said cracking a small smile. It wasn't much, but the slight humor in his statement did raise morale just a tad.

212

"Yeah, sir… we could all just retire," Guy said grinning a little bit more.

"And fellas, we could sit out all day with a fishin' pole drinking cool ones with limes," Kelt added, finally laughing. The laughs spread around, and a bit of cheeriness permeated the conversation for a while.

"I'll build me a grass hut and bring in some dancing girls in hula skirts," Guy laughed.

"It's nice to see you two laughing for once," Rick said as he wiped a tear of joy from his right eye. "Fellows, we are not dead yet. Kelt, Akhi told me that you were following interesting clues within the library. Can you tell me what this thing actually is?" Rick asked.

"It's a computer, Rick. As you know, it contains the history of the world. I've been able to penetrate its shell, so to speak, and gain entrance to the operating system. But I haven't found out anything that can help us."

"You've done what? I haven't seen you near that thing. It's locked behind that place where we're growing those weeds, Kelt," Guy exclaimed.

"It's a mental exercise, Guy. I suppose if you studied long enough, you could do it too," Kelt said looking at Rick to make sure he hadn't let the cat out of the bag.

"You know about Guy, Kelt?" Rick asked.

"Sure, Rick. It's just one of those things that I can feel, if you catch my drift. Aldo taught me how it's done," Kelt answered.

"Know what about me?" Guy demanded.

"You deserve to know, Guy," Rick started. "Guy, do you know about the millenarians?" Rick asked.

"Why, no sir, I don't," he answered.

"Do you know Aldo, Guy?"

"Yes sir, I do know him," Guy answered.

"He's over two thousand years old. He's what we call a millenarian. Fewer than two hundred of us live in the cities and dirtside. And Guy, you are in the club with us. I'm afraid that's about the simplest way to put it, Guy. I

213

suppose I should have prepared a better explanation, but why waste the time," Rick explained.

"You mean I'm going to live two thousand years?" Guy asked with amazement in his voice and eyes. "Rick, I've known you for many years, and you haven't aged a day. Look at me, I've got gray hair," he said.

"Guy, you've lived a tough life, so far. You've spent a lot of time out in the elements, your skin is "tough as leather" as you once told me," Rick answered.

"Well, it's not so tough now. I'm going soft."

"I've noticed. Living the "soft life" down there for the past several months has done wonders for your face," Rick grinned knowing full well that his team had been working nonstop. Getting out of the sun for a few months really had changed Guy's appearance. "Guy, have you taken notice when you shave every day? I would swear that you look ten years younger than you did just a year ago," Rick explained.

"I have noticed. I was sort of worried that I had some sort of unknown medical condition. This is pretty hard for me to believe, sir. I mean, I've heard about people living a long time from the Bible, but I never really believed it. You are serious that I could live that long?" Guy begged assurance.

"Yes, Guy. It's true. We've run the tests on your blood. You are just like Kelt, my daughter, and me. In fact, the entire research team from the Stanford lab is in our little club. Now, you can still be killed, mind you. You are not immortal. You will likely never suffer from disease, and you will age gracefully over the centuries. Now, does this news give us all incentive to solve our problems?" Rick surmised.

"Why, yes sir!" Guy exclaimed as he started to bring his hand to a snappy salute and right in the middle of the action, realized who he was talking to, and withdrew his hand. Both Kelt and Rick smiled at Guy's instincts.

"Welcome to the club, Guy. I've only told one other person this news and that was Akhi. It is an amazing bit of news to learn about yourself, to be sure," Kelt said.

214

"Okay then, let's get back to the subject at hand. I have some ideas that I'd like to pass on to you, and perhaps we could draw up some long-range plans. We really will need some beachfront property. We'll need trained fishermen, well-experienced fishermen. We'll also need sunny spaces to grow the algae. And finally, I'm sure that we'll need boats of some sort to catch the fish with… hmm, we'll need floater powered boats, won't we?"

"Yes, we will. That should be a mandatory requirement. We had better leave fossil fuels out of the mix. I see where you are going with this line of reasoning. Guy and I can handle the details of the small stuff, Rick. I'm sure we can call in an expert or two from time to time, and I know of a few fishermen who might be willing to join us, if they survive. But, Rick, you have a much larger mission. We are going to need more floaters, DC's for power, and you need to make sure that we have a healthy supply of solar collectors in orbit around the sun," Kelt advised.

"Kelt, our hoppers are dry up here. What we need is my old plant just outside of Beijing. Thousands of tons of that processed carbon we use are just sitting there. No one has any interest in the plant. Hmm… the plant is located well inland from the shore. I'll check into that plant and see where we stand. We might be able to move in and start the operation back up. We'll place some floater cams over the site and see what's going on.

Um... Sorry. On second thought, I'm thinking we should advise the Chinese of our efforts. Without their support, that facility could be a death trap for anyone we send in. They still have a very active military presence. Well, my friends, I'm sorry to dump on you as I have with all the bad news, but we shared a good laugh together, Guy has some interesting things to think about, I'm sure, and I see that we have a plan forming to bring humanity back together. I'm feeling much better now that I've made this call," Rick finished.

"I feel better as well," Guy said.

"I wish that I could say the same, sir. Rick, may I speak to you privately?" asked Kelt.

"Guy, would you mind?" Rick asked. Guy returned with a lazy relaxed comical salute and left the room with a grin a mile wide.

"You made his day," Kelt said.

"I suppose I did. Not everyone gets to live hundreds of years. I only hope that he will. Say Kelt, we are going to make it. No matter how Mother Nature beats us, I have real hope that we'll make it.

"I believe that as well, sir. There is another matter, which I want to discuss with you. Actually, Rick, I'd like to ask your advice."

"Sure thing, Kelt. What's on your mind?"

"I would like to marry Akhi. I can't see how it would work out since we can't even be together. Still, I want it more than anything."

"Have you talked to her about it, Kelt? Ultimately, she will need to be in on this, you know," Rick grinned not knowing how it might injure Kelt's self-esteem. He quickly realized how serious the boy was from his facial expression. Obviously, this thing was tearing him apart. "I'm sorry, Kelt. I didn't mean to crack a joke at your expense. It wasn't even funny."

"Don't worry about it, Rick. I can't explain why I want this so much. It is extremely important to me."

"Then, Kelt, I suggest you ask her and see how she feels about it."

"There's one other thing that I'd like to ask of you Mr. Carter."

"Oh now, we're moving to formal language... I suppose I can guess what you will ask me."

"Yes, sir. I would appreciate your blessing," Kelt announced."

"So, you want to marry my daughter while you are down there dirtside and she is upstairs in space?"

"Yes sir, I do."

"Kelt, I love you like my son, but how will this ever work out?"

216

"I'm not sure, sir, but it is extremely important that you allow me to marry her. It would mean everything to both of us, even if we cannot be together," Kelt said.

"Kelt, my little girl loves you with more passion than I have ever seen in a woman. I know you feel the same way. You've always treated her with the greatest respect. You've been honest in your dealings with me. You are literally trying to save the world. I suppose that what I'm trying to say is this; I know you can't be together, but if it is her desire, it would be a defining moment in my life to have you be part of our family. I know that this tradition of asking the father first is an old and often ignored one... shoot, most people don't even get married anymore. I admire you for coming to me. You do have my blessing to marry my daughter," Rick said as his eyes welled with tears.

"Sir, can you please keep this a secret until I ask her? I don't want a hint of this reaching her. It is extremely important to me," Kelt pleaded.

"Not a word, Kelt, I promise."

34- Pi

Midnight at Nevada Base

"I want so much to share the sound of the waves lapping against the sandy beach," Kelt thought to himself, "Do you remember the gulls and the fresh wet scent of the ocean, the mists coming from those rocky crags? Do you recall how I embraced you with a kiss? I yearn for your touch, the sweet smell of your hair, the kiss you surrendered."

"I do too, my darling," Akhi answered.

"Akhi, I connected with you through my mind!"

"Yes, you did my darling. I never knew you to be a poet," she jibed.

"I'm afraid I'm not very good at it, Akhi," he granted.

"I love you all the more for it, but you should keep your day job," she answered with a wide unseen grin. "You've been studying haven't you, Kelt?"

"I have, Akhi. I've spent every spare minute going over the notes from Aldo's classes. I've craved physical contact. I seem to be infected with an insatiable case of heartache every day, Akhi. My abilities are impaired. I'm overworked, and I still can't seem to leave this feeling behind to get enough sleep."

"I feel the same way, Kelt. Say, can you get to a video link, so we can see each other?" she pleaded.

"Akhi, look in your mirror," Kelt demanded.

Akhi had been resting after 20 hours of dealing with engineering difficulties. The extrusion machine, down in the small forge, had miss stepped a gear. She had been working with the young mechanical wiz team, Dr. Lang Jin and Dr. Chung Chi, to retrofit some smaller spheres with miniature magnetospheres to protect the occupants from radiation exposure from the sun. The extrusion machine made the copper filaments that they were using to shield the craft. This had been an unfinished loose end, which she

218

had wanted to finish up ever since Dr. Uru Umbata had passed away. He had been responsible for the design of the magnetospheres for the solar collectors now orbiting the sun, and had helped Scotty significantly in the development of the dimensional wave splitter machines. He had been a most critical piece of the development of everything she saw around herself. Without him, she would not have been able to create the dimensional shift technology with their floaters, locks, and dimensional conduits. Everything they had was dependent on that technology. He had died of heart failure just three weeks before. She didn't know whether she was moving ahead with the project as a matter of dedication to him, or of an intense need to keep her mind active. She thrived on development.

Akhi threw on a sweatshirt and stepped in front of her full-length mirror. "I suppose I don't look too bad for just getting out of bed," she surmised.

"You look fabulous, Akhi," Kelt sent with a strange warm glowing sensation she had never felt before. It filled her entire being in a heated rush, sending the hairs on her arms to attention.

"You can see me?" she demanded?

"I can, my love, through your eyes. And you can feel my passion for you, correct?" Kelt gazed in amazement through her eyes, while that beautiful warm rush permeated her very soul.

"Kelt, how are you doing this?" Akhi demanded.

"It seems, I've discovered a variation on telepathy that you have missed upstairs, sweetie," Kelt sent.

"Okay, Kelt, video link right now! I have to know what is going on," Akhi demanded.

Kelt greeted his sweetheart in the usual way; they placed their hands together on the video monitor and smiled sweetly at each other. Kelt never grew tired of their video link sessions, but they were becoming most disconcerting, and he always felt absolutely frustrated after each call. They left him longing all the more just to be with her. He was tired of these puppy love feelings. They were a

219

significant distraction. They also interfered with his long relationship with Akhi. There was no doubt, the normal impulses of an active young man playing their dance with his natural hormonal urges. He could set that aside for the larger picture. Just to be with her, would satiate those other physical needs completely and fully. "Love has no bounds." The saying rolled around in his head. It was true, he knew.

"So, please, Kelt," Akhi started, "I have to know what you have discovered.

"Pull up the lesson notes for session 2076 section 43, Akhi."

"Okay… I've got it, now what?" she asked him.

"See that little squiggly thing that looks very much like the Pi symbol?" he asked."

"Yes darling, it is Pi," she stated with conviction.

"Akhi, it's not. Look in session 3313 section 10, third formula from the top. You will see the real Pi defined there. Notice how closely it resembles the symbol that we use in the modern age.

"Wow, Kelt, we won't get to that material for months," She noted as she scrolled through the material to find what he had indicated.

She perused a couple of pages of text and formulae in an attempt to pull it all in. She could not do it of course; she hadn't learned much of the basic structure for this material yet. Even so, she could put together bits and pieces with some understanding.

"But, Kelt, that equation doesn't do anything. It doesn't add up to any useful function. I would chalk it up to Aldo's faulty memory," Akhi said.

"Akhi, why does the character Pi exist in the Greek set of characters, but none of the other ancient symbols have survived?" Kelt asked.

"I've wondered about that myself," answered Akhi.

"I found this most curious, Akhi. I believe that one of the old millenarians managed to get it into the Greek alphabet as a clue to the past. As you know, I've been jumping around in the lessons finding paths of logic... well,

220

you know how I think… fragments here, fragments there. I need the macro view before I can delve into the straight forward thought as it is developed logically. Remember, that's how I solved the wave splitter problem in the Stanford lab. I didn't know anything about the specifics of what you were doing, but by spreading out all the problems in front of me, and "taking a picture" of the totality, I could see several paths of action. Fortunately, the first path led to success."

"Yes, but Pi is an absolute constant. Look, the equations work. We are able to communicate effectively by using Pi as part of this equation in our thought process,"

"I understand, Akhi, but it does not have to be the same value. Pi, as we currently understand it, is a constant of 3.14, with an infinite series of other numbers following. But, Pi in the old language can be a variable, with a completely different meaning. I've run through the studies and found this to be a valid conclusion. It is true that the value we have assigned will work in many cases. I have discovered through inventive curiosity that the meaning of Pi is not necessarily a constant. It is most definitely a variable. When I originally looked through the equations and this symbol, I thought it a fluke.

I know that Aldo was writing out the equations for this form of advanced thought from rote. He did not understand the equations; he had only remembered them from his mother's teachings. It is good that he did, for I noticed an interesting fit with unusual equations I'm working with, right away. I'm not sure that he ever knew the true meaning of the symbol. I cannot find equation examples in anything that can describe an adequate representation in his lessons.
I checked the equations in other lessons and, the symbol, Pi pops up regularly, yet I held a strong hunch that it was much more than just a constant. Do you know the name of Pi in the old language, Akhi?"

"Kelt, as far as we can tell, it is just Pi. It seems as though the name survived."

"Akhi, did Aldo tell you the symbol name for Pi?" Kelt asked.

"Yes, my darling, he did."

"But, he did not tell you that it was also a variable, did he?" asked Kelt

"No, why is this so important, Kelt?"

"Well, for one sweetie, not only can I communicate with you telepathically, but I can see what you see and smell, I can hear what you hear. In fact, I can fully experience all of your senses," he said.

Akhi blushed at the thought of someone else rumbling through her brain, seeing her thoughts, and feeling *her* sensations.

"Kelt can you feel and sense everything?" Akhi asked in the most embarrassed fashion.

"Only what I choose, Akhi. Some feelings and sensations are yours and yours alone. I shall never invade them," he promised.

"The Pi constant is truly a constant in the evaluation and mathematics of a circle, but not necessarily viable for our thought processes," Kelt said. "And Pi is not the only symbol that has multiple meanings. Look at this one, for example," he said as he brought it up on his monitor to share.

"Yes, I know that one, Kelt. Translated it means "human" but it literally means "Culinari," the speakers of the old language."

"Ahah! Not quite so absolute, my dear."

Akhi stared him down in unqualified concentration. Had they been together in contact, Kelt was sure that the piercing gaze from her emerald eyes would have brought him to his knees.

"Okay, Kelt, I give. Give me a clue here."

"It also means "name" or specifically a string of characters or a formula that substitutes for the symbol. Many other symbols, even formula fragments that I've discovered have several meanings. It's one of the reasons that the Culinari had so few symbols in their language in addition to their standard character set. The symbols have context, and they can be subtle."

"Why, this could be an incredible breakthrough, Kelt! We've run into this in several of Aldo's classes. So many things just don't seem to mean anything. As I said before, we surmised that Aldo had forgotten much over the centuries, and we'd probably never make any sense of those sections in the lessons."

"Sweetie, you have no idea. Remember, Aldo learned this without a full understanding of the nuances of the language. He simply memorized much of what his mother could write down for him. Believe it or not, Akhi, I believe his memory is impeccable. Here, I'd like you to replace this particular constant with this formula snippet." He sent to her mind a fairly complex formula that created a new constant. He told her to use that constant in the formula for thought, instead of the standard value for Culinari.

She worked it through her mind quickly. Triggers opened ancient unprogrammed genetic synapses and neurons in her mind. She focused her thoughts on this newfound ability to develop the new mental connections. She repeated the calculations in normal speech, as would one of the old ones. It took her five minutes of concentrated effort before she finalized the programming in her brain, to accept the new formula as a single mental word. She could now see through Kelt's eyes, she could smell the dark damp heated odor of 221 bodies in Nevada's bunker, where there should be only 100. Her senses reeled as the shock of stench burned her nose.

"What's the matter, sweetie, don't you like the smell in our bunker?" Kelt asked.

"Oh Kelt, it is terrible, how can you bear it?"

"We get by. Yes, the stench down here is pretty hard to get used to. We do our best to keep things clean, but our air handlers aren't quite up to the task, and we haven't had time to work on them."

"This is remarkable, Kelt. Can you imagine the possibilities?"

"Akhi, I already have."

"Join me in thought," he said, "with this variable substitution in this equation." He picked up an old trucking invoice from the stack of used papers that they used for writing paper, and turned it over and wrote his name in the old language symbols. Not only were there characters that had phonetic sounds, but there was a formula interwoven within. "Akhi, this is my name," he said as he finished writing and held up the paper so that she could see.

Akhi noted down the formula, which took four entire lines of written characters and symbols and processed it through her mind as she had just done previously. This time, it was more difficult for her. The calculations were so complex, and she had a splitting headache from pushing symbols forward, performing the calculations, and resetting functionality in parts of her mind that had never been used. In the process, she felt a guiding hand, a whisper of presence, the help of Kelt's complex thoughts. It took her considerably longer this time.

"Now, contact me with my name, Akhi" she heard him say as if he were in her room.

It was a great mental effort, but one she could master, she somehow understood. The constant was replaced by the variable created by the equations in Kelt's old language name. Neural networks sent tiny energy bursts throughout her thoughts, forming thousands of sets of synapses to make the connection. She suddenly understood why so much of the human brain had gone unused for so many centuries. It may have evolved for this purpose, and, perhaps, humans had forgotten how to use it over the millennia.

"Perhaps, we never learned. I wonder if that could really be the case?" she mused in the back of her mind. She finished the process and virtually stood in awe of her surroundings.

Akhi and Kelt stood in the ancient agricultural village created by the old ones 16,000 years ago. Kelt

224

grabbed her hand and pulled her around the crowd gathered to hear the old woman speak.

"Kelt!" Akhi's heart throbbed to be with him finally. "I am with you!" she squealed.

"Yes, my love, we are finally together, and I don't want to diminish this moment a bit. We will find other times to make similar connections.

"Can they see us, Kelt?"

"No, Akhi, this is the history from the library."

"You mean the *libraries*, don't you, Kelt?"

"No, Akhi, it is a single library, the history of the Earth. Look, I want you to gaze upon this little girl as she listens. Her mind is completely open. Her entire thoughts and memories have been recorded. I have searched through the crowd, and her mind is the only one who has been left completely open for us to access," Kelt said. "I don't think that this was meant to be. I believe it to be an oversight on their part. The millenarians have kept themselves withdrawn from all things through the ages. They were merely observers to record the history of humankind," Kelt added.

Kelt saw Akhi turn her head to look up at the wise woman speaking from atop the platform, that of the small wooden structure, which had held the ancient artifact; the one he had come to know as the history of the Earth.

"Akhi, please don't worry about her yet," Kelt said as he drew her attention from the speech and looked at the ten or eleven year old porcelain skinned girl, with beautifully braided black hair. "Now, concentrate on her mind. I want you to learn the name of her father who is holding her hand." Akhi was now nearly fading as her ability to control the pain in her head intensified. She had never exercised her brain to this level, ever, in her short life. However, she did recognize the name of the girl's father through her thoughts.

"Okay, Akhi, I can see that you have the name. Now, access his mind."

"Oh Kelt, this is giving me such a headache. I have never experienced such agony. I don't know if I can keep this up," she cried with tears streaming down her cheeks.

"I understand, Akhi. I've been doing this for the past 10 days, to track down this single piece of information."

Akhi focused again, thinking through the equation, melding new synapses in her mind to perform a link to this man's historic memories hidden in the ancient artifact. She focused on the name and felt her mind laser focused to the contemplation of his thoughts.

"Are you connected, Akhi?" Kelt asked. Of course, he knew that she was, he was with her now, as they traversed the history of what this man had seen and done, during his entire life.

"Yes, darling, I'm here. I understand what I'm seeing too," she said as the man looked down to gaze into his adoring daughter's face.

"Okay, Akhi, I've tagged a moment in his life when he teaches his daughter the meanings of these symbols. The library becomes incredibly easy to search, once you know how to use the right variables and key words. Okay, take note, sweetie, as we move forward in time in this young girl's life," Kelt instructed.

The young father was teaching his daughter of 15 to 16 years of age, how to use the symbols as he taught her the full ancient language. He had drawn the Pi symbol in the dirt. In his explanation to his daughter, he used a different word than what they had understood to be Pi. In English, it translated to Pi variable. Akhi understood the spoken word significantly more than Kelt, for she had been practicing with Aldo, Amy, and the others for some time. Aldo had missed many things, as he had not understood the language or those notions of usage that had been passed down incorrectly. Here, they were getting a firsthand lesson on how to use the newly discovered variable.

"Akhi, this again is a fluke, for I can find it nowhere else in the library. I don't think that the Culinari had meant to pass down this particular piece of knowledge… of course, I'll never be sure, but certainly it has not survived past the generation we are seeing here in this piece of ancient history," Kelt finalized.

Kelt broke the link with the father and daughter, yet stayed in the small village to spend a few minutes with Akhi.

"Akhi, the "Pi variable," led me to look at other snippets of the equations. I spread them out on several monitors, and I saw an interesting pattern. Many other variables exist that even the ancient ones unknowingly accepted as constants. But, indeed, they are variables. It was through one of my macro view exercises, that I saw the patterns merge. I gleaned intuitive understanding that I'm sure no one has ever divined. I brought us here with those other variables. Akhi, I am taking the old language forward. I am reinventing things that they could never imagine. I am inventing another new form of mathematics, and other than being here with you, I still don't know where it all leads. I only know, that the physics and biology, or whatever you call telepathic abilities, work," he told her.

"Akhi, that little girl knows the names of everyone in the village. We can access their minds to find out more about our heritage. I must tell you that I doubt we will find anything previous, to the moment of the speech from their leader. That was when the recordings started. We have considered this artifact we found to be the libraries, as in the plural form of library. Akhi, it is a single library. It is our history. There may be other libraries yet to find, but I find no clues to their existence.

"But, throughout the ages, they have been mentioned by other millenarians. Now, they could be referring to the Earth history, for it does contain literal libraries of information, but somehow, or at least I feel, there is more for us to discover. It may not be a stash of information. It might come in the form of our abilities to develop new technologies. I'm not sure. But, the clues I've discovered have given me newfound hope."

"Kelt, shall we find them? Perhaps I should be asking if they actually exist."

"I don't know. I want you to share this information with your study group," he said.

"Oh Kelt," she said with amazement for his unimaginable advancements, we'll get right on it," she said.

"Good, Akhi. I want you to know that I have not been sleeping well. I've spent full nights going out on missions, planning events and projects, and then trying to put as much time as possible to unravel this puzzle. I know that this is important. We can mentally access the Culinari history. I must find out what remains a mystery to us. It may be significantly important. Then, perhaps I may get some peace," he concluded.

"Okay, my love, but can we take a walk along the beach for a few moments? I've not seen you for months, and I have endured a never-ending ache in my heart, to be with you," she said.

"Well, sweetie, this is a gift that I wanted to share with you. We need time together, and now we have found a means to do so. Look, there's the beach over there. Isn't this beautiful?" He asked as he pointed to the gulls soaring in the air currents over a sandy beach lined with reeds and grasses.

"The air has such a fresh clean bite in my nose," she giggled, "Kelt. I can smell the rich life of the living ocean and the wet grasses growing; I've never experienced anything so pleasant.

"I have."

"And what would that be, my darling?"

"Spending time with you, sweetie."

35- President Crawford

"President Crawford, we need to know about the nuclear attack capabilities of the Chinese," Rick addressed the president.

"Why is that, Rick? The world is dying, why would they even care about attacking anyone?" Crawford queried.

"We've been monitoring several of their ICBM launch pads, in northern China, and it seems that there is some activity around those sites. We thought it prudent to collect as much knowledge as we can, Mr. President."

"I do not like this man. He is a political hack, a sleaze ball…" Rick had slipped to a brief thought as Crawford interrupted.

"Why, we don't know anything of their ICBM program," Crawford said.

"Look, Crawford, do you think I'm stupid?" Rick demanded, "I know you've got details on every one of those damned launch sites. We may need it too, so that we can save your sorry hides down there. Frankly, I don't really care what the Chinese do. They might feel like you led them down the path to self-destruction, by convincing them to nuke the Suez and the southern regions of Africa. Maybe they think it's time for some payback. My daughter insisted that I talk to you about this.

Crawford sat pensively staring at the monitor of his video link, trying to ignore the presence of Carter, glaring back.

"We'll get you the details of all their missile launch sites, Carter," he finally said stoically.

"What about their boomers?" Carter asked.

"You mean their nuclear missile submarines?" asked Crawford.

"Of course, Mr. President. Those are the most likely threat to you. We can very likely take out the land-based missiles if we know where the launch sites are. We can't do anything about the submarines. Besides that, Mr.

President, I'm very worried about your nuclear volley in return. We're teetering on the edge with all this ecology business and adding more nukes to the mix just doesn't make sense. We're already seeing dozens of unattended nuclear reactors melt down, as their cooling pools evaporate. As hard as we try, we won't kill mother Earth, but she can wipe us out. We don't need any more bombs going off." Rick finalized.

Crawford was at first struck with indecision, but then replied. "Rick, we can get you the Chinese launch site details. We know of five of their boomers, and we have attack subs on their tails," Crawford said.

"How many boomers do they have?"

"We think they only have five, but we don't know for sure. Our nuclear capable ships have been at sea, as you know, since the New Era began. They are running very low on food and supplies. But, our men and women on those ships are disciplined and will follow our very strict code as far as nuclear weapons are concerned. They will not use them," Crawford assured.

"I agree with you on that point, Crawford. I just want to make sure that you are onboard. You are the one that has the authority to launch those weapons. If the Chinese were to attack, do you have any assessments as to what their primary targets might be?"

"Well, the Pentagon and Washington would be at the top of the list," Crawford answered, and then continued, "We don't know much more than that, but we would anticipate that they'd have some of our military bases in their sights. They know we have dismantled our land based missile silos, so I'm confident they wouldn't go after those," he finalized.

"And how are "we" getting along with the Russians," Carter asked as a side note.

"Thanks to your help in reestablishing our relations through your communication satellites, Rick, I have spoken to the Russian president several times. We'll have no problems with them," Crawford answered, "the same goes for India and Israel. We think that Pakistan unloaded what

230

they had on Africa. So, I suppose, according to what you've told me, China is our only nuclear threat right now," Crawford concluded.

"Mr. President, I want to make this abundantly clear. We cannot work with you blind. We must know everything. We expect you to send us up all the locations of those launch sites, as well as your current intelligence on those boomers. We need to be updated when you are. I have some excellent ex-service men and women up here that are still loyal to *our* country. They know the lingo and the operational procedures. I want to set up a communications link for them to be in constant contact with your military staff. Can we agree on this?" demanded Rick.

"Hold on a minute, Carter, while I check with my advisors," Crawford said, as he momentarily stepped away from the video feed. Rick could hear whispered concerns and several sound-bytes of distrust. Crawford came back to his desk and sat down.

"My advisors are against it, Carter. It's time someone made a few decisions around here that make sense. I'll make sure that your people are advised properly. We aren't exactly sure how you manage your technology, for we've seen no weapons on your part, but perhaps we might help with some of the tactical decisions in setting up a defensive plan with your people," Crawford suggested.

"I like that idea. We welcome cooperation now. I'd rather have all of my people working on solving this other problem caused by the virus. I really hate to put my people on duty, to swat mosquitoes."

"I agree with you," President Crawford admitted.

"Before we set up our contact information, I have a personal request from my daughter. She wants to know if you have preserved the artwork and other valuable artifacts from the Smithsonian and other museums in the Washington DC area. I suppose it doesn't matter all that much to the people who are starving, but she is adamant about this. She feels that those treasures must be preserved."

"We took care of that long before the food riots, Carter. Tell your daughter that the artwork and most of the other historical artifacts have been carefully stored well away from the area in bombproof bunkers. It will be safe," Crawford assured.

"Thanks, Mr. President. I'm sure that she will be relieved to hear that. I have a retired admiral on board one of our cities, John Hickman, I believe he commanded one of your carrier groups shortly before he retired. Do you know him?" Carter asked.

"Yes, I do. He's a good man. I've known of him and he was well respected," answered Crawford.

"He'll be your contact point up here then, if that suits your advisors," Rick said. Rick watched Crawford look around his room behind the video monitor for acceptance from his commanders.

"That is quite acceptable. My staff thinks that Hickman is an excellent choice. Many here know him personally."

"Say, I didn't know you had any older people up in those cities. The impressions we have down here is that you've got a bunch of teenagers doing everything."

"No, sir. We have many people here who are masters of their skills. We do have a few very gifted young people, but that accounts for only a fraction of our general population. We know that we need the experience gained from years of work in various disciplines," Rick answered.

"So, you do have older people up there, I'll be damned… and here we thought we were fighting a bunch of teenagers," Crawford said.

"You have been misinformed, Mr. President. We still have a lot to learn about each other don't we?" said Rick as he terminated the video link.

"Yes, we still have very much to learn about each other," Rick mused to himself as he thought about all of the technology, the libraries, the biological experiments, and finally, the knowledge of the millenarians' existence. The

232

general population in the floating cities still did not know about the millenarians.

36- Cradle of civilization

"Do you have some time, sweetie?"

Akhi had just retired to her quarters and had planned to review project plans during her down time. She still had a slight headache from her mental connection with Kelt the night before. Kelt's mental query had a similar effect, of listening to someone banging a large bass drum.

"Video link or telepathy?" she asked him through her mind. "I still have a headache from last night. I'm not sure I'm up to brain exercises tonight, my love."

"You'll get used to it, Akhi. The more we connect, the less of an effect it should have on you. This is a learned talent. How many times did you fall on your bum when you learned to walk?"

Akhi definitely sensed a smirk on his face, even though she could not see it.

"I was too young to remember that!"

"Really? Have you tried? You should, because those memories are still there. I'm surprised what I can remember now. It's been a wonderful thing for me to remember my parents in my early years. I've been pretty happy today, with these newly discovered memories. Akhi, that's not what I want to talk to you about. Link with me," he demanded.

"Okay, let me get out of this hemp flight suit and climb into a comfortable sweatshirt."

She quickly unzipped and stepped out of the flight suit and donned a super-sized sweatshirt that had been lying on the foot of her bed.

"Lay down, it may help with the headache," Kelt sent.

"Sounds good. Okay, I'm on my bed. Can you make the link? I'm afraid that I can't quite put my name together."

"Akhi, you must remember your name. It's important."

"Oh Kelt, you are right. It's rolling around up here somewhere," she sent as she retraced the pathways in her mind. She found it surprisingly simple to remember the long series of characters and formula snippets that represented her real name. "It's easy! I thought I'd never be able to remember without looking at it."

"Good, sweetie. Now, last night I connected with you. I'd like you to concentrate and connect with me."

Akhi focused her thoughts on Kelt. She dove into the pathways of recent memory looking for the record of his connection. There she discovered his name and sent the string to him.

"How's my girl?" Kelt asked as he put his arm around her. "What's with the giant sweat shirt?"

"Um, it's what I put on just as soon as I have a moment to relax. I really like to wear clothes that are loose and warm at the end of the day. I feel comfy and it helps me calm down. What's wrong, don't you like it?"

"You look good in anything. Seriously."

"I'd bet you'd rather see me dressed differently, though, wouldn't you?" She thought about it a moment and within an instant she was wearing the yellow dress she had worn so long ago, when they had their first real date in San Francisco.

"Wow, sweetie, you look better than I remember!"

"I thought you'd like it better than an old sweatshirt."

"Right now, Akhi, I want to see you. Your clothes are not important to me."

"So, where are we?" she asked as she looked out across the waving grasses of open plain. Deciduous trees spotted the landscape and two large rivers to her right and left, joined into a single channel to her rear as she looked around.

"It's beautiful isn't it, my love?"

"I've never seen a place more tranquil. I smell flowers. Where are they?

"I don't know. Somewhere close by I'd suspect."

A pair of orange and purple butterflies flitted in front of them. The male obviously was intent on self-propagation. The female attempted to avoid him. Her flight path was erratic as she flew up and down and from side to side.

"I haven't seen butterflies in years, Kelt! They are beautiful! You still haven't told me where we are."

"Turn around, Akhi, and I'll explain."

"At this time in our ancient history, the place bears no name. In fact, no humans live here yet. If you turn around, the river on your left is in our modern time called the Tigris. The river on your right is the Euphrates. We are standing in what we call the cradle of civilization. This region has had several names over the centuries. Basra, Ur, and Qurma are our most recent references. I prefer an ancient one, the *Rivers of Babylon*."

"So, why have you brought me here, Kelt?"

"Oh, I have a couple of reasons. First, I wanted to spend a few moments with you. I realize that what I see, smell, and feel is of our own construction built from the memories stored in the library. But, it's the next best thing to actually being with you in the real world."

"You just want to kiss me, don't you?" Akhi chided.

Kelt swept her off her feet and gave her a passionate kiss.

"Does that answer your objection? The kiss was meaningless, for I felt what I wanted to feel and not what you wanted to give. It does not fool me."

"It was sort of weird, Kelt, I must admit. I can only explain it as kissing someone else. It wasn't you at all. Now, I understand why you didn't kiss me last night. I didn't realize the limitations of this experience," Akhi noted. "So, why are we really here?"

"I really wanted to show you this place, sweetie. This is where civilizations began. It is where people first started to learn and pass their knowledge to their children. The first creation myths started here. Our ancient ancestors

236

started here… and you know which ones I'm talking about."

"The Culinari?"

"Yes, Akhi. It's where I'd like to build a new life if we can ever solve our problems. I'd like to see this land restored as we see it. I want a small farm, right over there, where we can grow some crops and live a quiet life together.

"You're no farmer, Kelt, and neither am I. You do realize that this is just a pipe dream of yours, don't you? What is located in this place in our current time? I bet that it's covered with a dirty city and oil refineries."

"You are right, of course," Kelt admitted with some sadness. "If we ever solve the Earth's problems, this would be a good place for us, for the millenarians. I don't want to sound racist or anything, but we are a new species, Akhi. I'm sure of it. I know human nature well enough that we could quickly be exterminated, once the rest of the population learns of our existence.

"I may be a romantic, but this place is also worth saving. In the real world, no humans live within a thousand miles of this place. The radiation clouds destroyed the native population. No one will venture here… not even for the oil. The reserves were vastly depleted over the past few decades. There are still untapped reserves in this region, but no one knows about them. Anyone looking for oil will do so somewhere else. Additionally, this location is a fairly good distance from the coast where prying eyes will not see us.

I believe that we could make a good living here. A peaceful life… I can't imagine abandoning our technologies for any reason. But, I do yearn for a peaceful life in a place like this."

Akhi took Kelt's hand in hers and they both absorbed quiet tranquility among the grasses and butterflies.

"It is beautiful, Kelt. Perhaps we can make it beautiful again someday."

"We'll have the opportunity to conquer this place. It will take a lot of work to clean up the mess our predecessors made of it, but we can do it. Share my dream, Akhi."

"I shall, my darling."

37- Devin Sharrod

It was hard to believe, but several hundred million humans yet survived on Earth. Many had been housed in secure locations stocked with many years' worth of provisions. No one ever conceived that the virus would succeed so thoroughly. The threat of radiation exposure had greatly diminished over the past several months, but the virus still covered the land, lay dormant, and waited for new crops to devour. The greatest number of deaths had been caused by people in fear and not by starvation. The riots and gangs killed humanity off at an alarming rate.

Kelt had just landed his shuttle on a large tanker at sea, off the coast of California. The tanker originally had a crew of only 21 individuals, but had taken on 13 others during the past few months.

"So, how are you getting along?" asked Kelt.

Captain Devin Sherrod, now in his late 40's replied, "I think that we are doing pretty well, all things considered. We've been able to pull most of our food from the sea, as you know. The fishing has been good here. We had thought that we might move down to Monterey in the next few days to see if we could scare up some different sorts of fish, but from what I hear, there's no point. It's stripped clean. All that is left there is anarchy and pirates. We received warning from one of my fellow tanker captains. He's out thatta way, about 12 nautical miles or so," Sherrod said as he pointed his finger southeast.

"I want to thank you for helping us to set up our algae-eco ponds. The nutrition bars made from that goo kind of grows on you after a while... but they still sorta remind me too much of eating cardboard, to really enjoy a meal of them."

"We have to do what we have to do." Kelt replied. "How is your fuel supply?"

"If we just hang out around here as we have been, we could make it last for several years. It all depends on where the fish are biting, and how long we'll need energy to run our freezers. We've been perfecting methods of flowing with the current, whenever we can," replied Devin.

"You're better off than most of those out on the sea. Many are completely out of fuel and they are barely hanging on. Those doing the best are the sailors on the smaller craft." Kelt told Devin.

"The smaller craft will have a hard time setting up these algae eco-ponds with any success though. They just bob up and down too much in the sea swells. Sooner or later, you folks might be able to barter with the algae bars."

"I hear you Kelt. We've had a couple of storms where we thought we might lose those ponds on our deck. I did want to let you know that we have been passing out some of our harvest to other large boats, as you asked in your instructions. They too, are now actively harvesting and preparing these … ah…wonderful morsels," Devin grinned as he pulled one from his pocket and took a bite from one of the bars. "It still tastes like cardboard," he said.

Devin was showing clear signs of skin cancer and thought his days were numbered. At the time of the nuclear attacks on the Suez, his ship had been close by, only 500 nautical miles away. He had been in his prime at the time. He was fit, well groomed, and a highly desirable catch for some lucky woman. His lady had been the sea, however. He had never spent more than a few days in any port, and had not been able to form any long-term relationships. That had changed shortly after the Suez bombing when he had rescued survivors from a smaller pleasure boat, out of the United Arab Emirates. He met the girl he would marry in the group rescued. As captain, he had married himself to his wife. "Hey I'm the captain, and I determine how things work around here." He had said at the time. His crew took it all in good humor. The couple now had a son, four months old. There were only two other families on board.

"I hope that this medicine will help control the skin cancer, Devin. Our biologists upstairs can produce as much as we need, and I have my crew out delivering it to everyone we can locate who has been affected. We discovered the technology as an accident in trying to contain the virus. Our geniuses tried this technique called DNA binding, to castrate the virus genetically. It didn't work on the virus, but since the technique had been developed, one of our other researchers tweaked it to fight the cancers so many are suffering. I hope you don't mind that it hasn't been through the FDA approval process," Kelt grinned, "I think that you will find it most effective."

"I am most grateful to you, Dr. Nelby. I'm sure that the rest of the crew will be equally happy to get this. We've all dreaded that this cancer will kill us, long before anything else will."

"How about your fresh water supply? Are your solar units providing enough?" asked Kelt.

Kelt referred to the simple distilling units that Scotty had come up with. "All you have to do is build another bathtub like we use for that algae scum, and put an angled top on it," Scotty had demonstrated. The angled top usually was a piece of plastic or glass, anything that was waterproof. The tubs were manufactured from any useable wood, forms, whatever could be found, and home store plastic was used to line them. In the sunlight or just the heat of the day, water would evaporate and condense on the underside of the top, and form tiny rivulets that would run to the lower end of the top where it was collected as salt free distilled water. It was certainly not high-tech and didn't produce that much fresh water, but the design had saved countless lives. As Kelt scanned the deck of the gigantic tanker, he noticed only ten algae eco ponds and literally hundreds of smaller distillers.

"Yes, they are. And I want to thank you for helping us with them. Until you came along with those simple engineering ideas, we were just getting by. I'm not sure we could have gone on much longer," replied Devin. "We're getting close to two hundred gallons a day out of those things," he said beaming with pride for his crew.

"So, how is the rest of the world doing?" asked Devin as he noticed Kelt's urge to get on his way. Devin craved some connection with the outside world.

"We've managed to transplant some of the new vegetation that popped up in the Nile area around the world. It does seem to take well. I sometimes feel it to be an exercise in futility. I doubt that those efforts will bear fruit for thousands of years. Our biologists at the Hughes Research Center in Malibu are doing some experiments with some of the grass varieties, to see if they can't come up with grains that we can eat. They have had moderate success, but still nothing of any consequence. I've lost touch with our island base near New Zealand. We don't dare go near the large bunkers where people are holding out, because my small team of commandos just can't control the crowds, if hostilities erupt... If I lose control of a shuttle... I too could become stranded. Hopefully, those people hunkered down are all still alive," Kelt replied as he stared at the deck.

"Yes, I remember the day you floated out aft of our deck and your security team quickly appeared with arms at the ready. We were scared to death. I'm glad that we've been able to work with you Dr. Nelby. You have literally saved our future," Devin said.

"Please Captain, don't call me doctor. Kelt is fine. Those in my command call me doctor, or sir, and I put up with it. I know that command requires a hierarchy, but I really don't need the formalities with you," Kelt pleaded.

"That's fine with me, Kelt. It's nice to see a few niceties still left in the world. What else is going on?"

"We still have had no progress in killing the virus. That's nothing new I suppose. We've actually abandoned all hope in that line of thinking and are pursuing other possibilities. Killing a virus around the world is quite impossible as you may surmise." Kelt said. "The Mars stations are doing fairly well, all things considered. Man oh man would I hate to be cooped up in those steel tanks we built for them," he continued.

"We have been able to send them very few and precious supplies from time to time with our unmanned flitters, but our space locked cities are running low on raw materials," Kelt informed the captain.

"We've used up a great deal of what we put up there in our cargo train. We could not anticipate just how difficult it is to provide for so many thousands of people in space. There is very little left in metals, carbon, and other things that we so desperately need to keep the store open," Kelt said.

"Are they going to get by up there? I'd hate to think that not only humanity, but also its accomplishments could be lost. It would be a shame, not to mention a disaster, for those of us still left on Earth," Devin spoke softly. "We did it to ourselves," Devin said as he scanned his arm across the deck. I was part of it. I carried this poison around the world for years."

He referred to oil, of course. Humanity had managed to use so many fossil fuels and create so many harmful chemicals that many believed this to be the source of the virus. While it was clear that artificial greenhouse gasses had been responsible, at least in part, for the climate changes, it had never been proven that the virus attack had been created by the pollution.

"Don't blame yourself, Devin. We never did come up with a real reason for the viral infection of land based plant life. We've never been able to figure out why the virus never spread to the seas either. We just can't explain it all. I suppose that good ole Earth has some sort of reset clock that goes off every few million years. Let's just chalk it up to that," Kelt said trying to bolster Devin's mood. "And let's not forget that the very worst of the radiation problems are behind us," Kelt added.

"I suppose you are right. We'll never know about the virus and we can take heart that the seas still retain life."

"Well, sir, I've got a few more stops to make today and then we need to get back to our base. It's a long day for

243

me and my crew," Kelt said as he scanned the rapidly aging faces of his commando squad. The stress was well lined on their faces.

Kelt and his team returned to the Nevada bunker shortly before midnight. At their last stop, the people on board the large yacht had insisted they stay for dinner. Kelt regretted the delay, because he had been running on very little sleep for so long. The meal of fresh fish had been worth it.

38- Thar be plants Cap'n!

"Kelt, wake up!" Scotty said as he shook Kelt from his restful slumber.

"I was just having a great dream, you slimeback," Kelt moaned as he rolled over to face the blinding lights. "What time is it?" Kelt asked as he fumbled to see the clock. "I was just having a great dream with…"

"Yeah, I know, Akhi. I tell you Kelt, we all know that you love her and all, but your pining is getting to be old hat down here. Your dilithium crystals are cracked" Scotty said.

"Okay, okay, what's up, buddy?"

"Kelt, you've got to see this to believe it! Hurry and get dressed. We need to go topside."

Kelt started to dress, having a very difficult time shaking the sleepiness from his head. "I would be a lot happier if you'd just tell me, so I could get back to sleep, Scotty."

"Some things you have to see to believe. Come on, just come on up with me topside. And hurry!" Scotty said with excitement.

"Okay, okay, I'm coming, Mr. Scott." The pair joined nearly the whole crew in front of the elevator door. A quick glance at the status lights indicated that the elevator was descending from the surface.

"It's almost here," announced Guy.

"What's going on, Scotty?" Kelt asked, as the entire base population seemed to push into the elevator. Over two hundred people moved in quickly, filling a small section of the large elevator floor.

"I just came in on a shuttle from a run out to Malibu. You will not believe what I saw," Scotty returned.

"The sun isn't even up yet, what could you possibly see in the dark?"

"Thar be plants, Cap'n!" Scotty exclaimed.

"What do you mean… plants?"

245

"They are growing all around the base, Kelt. I'm not kidding you. It's a huge circle of plants sprouting all around the base!" exclaimed Scotty.

"I'll believe it when I see it," Kelt said as the elevator reached the top of its run.

The large hangar door opened, presenting an early dawn with a clear sky. The cold morning fresh air, flooded the warehouse and those who hadn't been topside for some time, felt a sudden sense of clean in the freezing rush. It had been too long, living down in the old mine.

The morning air smelled sweet and the early hour, calmed the breeze that constantly swept the site during most other times during the day. The crowd stepped out in awe. A carpet of greenery surrounded the base. Small seeds had sprouted in the past few days, and were now showing their color.

The small crowd roared with cheering laughter and a sweeping, clapping of hands swelled within the space of the warehouse.

"People, stay in the hangar, please," yelled Guy. Everyone responsibly complied and spread out along the edge of the concrete slab. The huge opening let them all be on the front row, for the most hopeful moment of their lifetimes. Smiles and cheery talk of wonderment filled their short conversations, as they stood and stared at a miracle.

Kelt stood in bewilderment. "How big is it, Scotty?" Kelt asked as he looked out to the horizon.

"Kelt, I don't get it, it's mostly round, and we're right in the middle of it. It's a circle and almost four kilometers in diameter. What do you suppose happened?" Scotty asked.

"I'm not sure, Scotty. I want to check this out. Walk with me," Kelt said.

"Where are we going? We never walk out here. That's Guy's first rule, buddy," Scotty answered.

"Hey Guy!" Kelt yelled to summon his commando leader. Guy was fully outfitted with his armor and weapons. "Guy, grab five or six of your men. Scotty and I are taking a walk. We need some company," Kelt commanded.

"You know my opinion on taking daylight walks here, Kelt. So far, I've been able to keep you safe. I don't feel right about taking a walk during daylight hours," Guy advised.

"I understand," Kelt started, "It's an order, Guy," he finalized. Kelt had never explicitly given his commando squad an order like this. It was not his style. Guy felt Kelt's intensity and seriousness immediately, as the command left his lips.

"Yes, sir, I'll get a couple men right away," he answered crisply.

Kelt, Scotty, Guy, and two well-armed troops walked west on the dirt road. To everyone looking, the plant life seemed like a velvet carpet on each side of the path, and there were many plants popping up through the compacted Earth of the road as well. In reality, the plants were fairly well spaced apart. Yet, the desert hadn't seen this much plant life in recent human history. Two commandos flanked each side with weapons ready. Guy unslung his weapon and gripped it in iron fists, as his eyes continually scanned the horizon for threats.

"Does anyone have a com unit on them with a video screen? I didn't bring mine," admitted Kelt.

"Sure thing, Kelt, you can use mine," Scotty said as he passed him the device.

"On second thought, Scotty, why don't you call up an image from one of our floater cams up there," Kelt asked, "I want to check out this circle you described." They had gone less than a few hundred meters. Kelt stopped and pulled out a pencil from his jacket. "Does anyone have a piece of paper I can use?" One of the commandos passed him a shipping invoice he had nearly filled on the backside with his "to do" lists. Kelt neatly folded the page and tore it into small narrow strips. He stepped to the roadside and selected five different varieties of the more common plants.

"Scotty, can you please take some pictures for me?" Kelt asked.

"Sure thing, Cap'n."

Kelt knelt down and held one of the strips of paper behind each of the plant varieties he had selected. He then marked the height of the plant, and marked each strip in the middle giving it a number. Then, he checked the height of several other plants of the same variety, and marked their heights. Each variety was measured and photographed.

"Okay, let's continue our walk," Kelt said as he finished his measurements.

As the team walked down the road, Scotty could see their progress from the floater cam above. They appeared as small ants on the road in the large green circle.

"I've got that image you were asking for, Kelt," Scotty said.

Kelt paused in mid step and grabbed Scotty's com to check the picture. He held a strip of paper on the com, with one end of the paper against the left edge of the paper and creased the paper with his thumbnail, on the opposite side of the green circle. He then used the same piece of paper to measure the height of the circle.

"It's not a circle," Kelt said. "What's the image orientation Scotty?" Kelt asked.

"North is up, that puts left as west and right as east as the camera sees it, Kelt," Scotty answered.

"Hmm, so that makes it wider going from east to west," Kelt observed. "If I use the dimensions of our hangar as a reference, this circle of vegetation looks to be … about… three and a half kilometers from north to south and just short of four from east to west. Okay, men and women, let's continue," Kelt said, reminded that two of the commandos with them that morning, were female.

After thirty to forty minutes, with several stops to make measurements, they arrived at the edge of the greenery. "Take some more pictures of this, Scotty," commanded Kelt. "Look. There is a broad circle containing plants and then suddenly we see none. It's like an invisible barrier of sorts," Kelt mused out loud.

He retrieved his little paper strips that he had made earlier and asked Scotty to take images as he made comparisons of the plants progress, against those nearer the

248

center of the field. "They are decidedly the same as far as I can tell, Scotty," Kelt said, "let me take another look at that image." Scotty handed him his com unit, and zoomed in on the image. The edge of the east side was as dense as that of the west side. Kelt's eyes went wide with a sudden realization.

Kelt walked west a few more paces and stepped off the road. He knelt down and placed his face right onto the ground in the mud. There he saw very tiny sprouts.

A train of thought flooded his mind and he drunkenly stood, stepped back onto the road into a barren area, and sat down.

"Are you okay, son?" asked Guy.

"Yeah, just give me a few minutes to think," Kelt answered.

Kelt needed more than a few, as he sat there with his hands in his face and his eyes closed. Scotty and Guy backed off so they wouldn't bother Kelt in his thoughts. Kelt thought back to his most personal contact with Akhi just a few days before.

"Is this related in any way?" he asked himself, "If so, how did it happen?"

Kelt started reviewing his memories of the equations he had compiled to complete the communication. He had to admit to himself that several of the functions held no real meaning to him. He had merely used snippets from the library's transmission record to wrap around his codes to contact Akhi. Kelt examined and recalculated the variables that he had used, trying to assign some function to those, which had not made sense. He drew a complete blank. He momentarily lost concentration as his temples started to throb. "Come on Kelt, you can figure this out," he told himself and he buried himself deeper into his thoughts, attempting to trace the synapses he had formed the night he had spent with Akhi in the ancient farming village.

"What's going on, Scotty?" Guy asked.

"He gets like this when he's putting puzzle pieces together, Guy. I've seen him do it several times. He usually wanders off to some room to be alone, but as you can see, there's not much privacy here. He has squirrels running around in his head. I don't know what, but he's working on a problem of some sort."

"Do you think he's got this thing figured out?" Guy asked.

"He's definitely thinking about it. I can't imagine what's going through his head, but it certainly boggles my mind to see how effective he can be. He's not always right, but his batting average is pretty high, if you know what I mean. It is also wise to recognize that success is sometimes measured by the number of failures," Scotty answered. "He might come up with ideas that won't mean much. Sometimes he comes up with nothing.

"While we've been working our butts off for the past several months, I can't say that we've had a whole lot of success," Guy commented.

"That's all a matter of perspective, Guy. We've managed to save a few lives, fend off the military, develop means for people to produce more food, and made important inroads with Hughes Research. I wouldn't call that failure," Scotty advised.

"While that may be true, it really hasn't made much of a dent in the problem has it?" Guy said.

"I suppose not. It has been the most frustrating time in my life. And we're the lucky ones," Scotty surmised with some degree of sadness. "You know, Guy, sometimes we need to measure success by the number of failures. Edison experimented with thousands of filaments before he found one that would work in a light bulb. And look at our experience at the Stanford lab! We thought we had the process nailed with all of our fancy equipment and simulations. It took over a hundred long and costly runs, before we were ultimately successful."

It had taken him twenty minutes of thought until Kelt let his hands drop and raised his face. White marks gripped his face where his hands had been.

"Scotty, do this quickly while I'm still thinking through the process... 1- Send those images to Jayne at the

HRC and our microbiologists Shannon and Amanda. 2-
Ask them to identify closely related genus and species. 3-
Ask Jayne at Hughes if they have sequenced the DNA of
any plants closely related. 4- Set up a meeting with Akhi,
HRC, and our biology team," Kelt ordered as he removed
his jacket and lay down on the frost-covered ground. He
threw his jacket over his face to keep the rising sun from
invading his closed eyes.

Scotty quickly made the calls and sent the data.

"What's going on down there, Scotty?" Akhi,
asked.

"You can see our crop can't you?" Scotty asked.

"Yes, we can, Scotty. We're picking up a live feed
from the floater cams above you. The news has spread
throughout the cities. It is amazing to say the least," she
answered with an ever-broadening smile.

"Well then, you can see what's happening, Akhi. It
looks like Kelt has decided to take a nap," Scotty said.

"He's thinking," Akhi reminded him.

"I know. He always gets sullen, when he's
resolving a problem or daydreaming about you. It has
become a bit unnerving lately," Scotty added.

With his face shielded from the early morning sun,
Kelt could think more clearly. He formulated his equations
and symbols, not forgetting the strange sequence of four
unique characters. He wove the pattern in his mind,
following not new, but not well travelled synapses of the
transmission. Kelt felt the warmth of his inner being swell
within his chest. He was not in the artifact, nor was he
interfaced with it to any degree. This effort was his alone.
The task was daunting, the amplification felt as though it
would seer his brain cells, as he brought forth his own
heaving throbbing molecular strands of parallel
computational thought to the process. He could now clearly
see that everything was set up properly, and he tried to
make a connection with Akhi in the never-ending night of
Earth's shadow. The Earth was difficult to penetrate.

"So, is he waiting for sand worms or something?" Guy asked after fifteen minutes or so.

Scotty laughed at the reference to one of his favorite novels. "I would say it is the "something," Guy," Scotty smiled, "so, Guy, you liked Dune too?"

"I never read the books. I only saw an old TV miniseries, but I do know about the sandworms," Guy answered. Scotty merely smiled in return. While Scotty loved to play the Star Trek clown, he had also read many of the great science fiction works. Dune had been at the top of his list.

Kelt felt only the hint of acknowledgement with Akhi. He could strongly feel her presence, but he lacked the necessary skills to concentrate his abilities through the mass of the Earth. "Akhi, are you there?" he asked. He may have heard her voice, but he definitely felt her presence. Kelt kept trying, reevaluating and refining the equations, and pushing his mental telepathic abilities to the extreme. Sweat eked from every pore. His back, covered only with a light tee shirt, lay on the frost covered ground and he still sweat with the effort he exerted attempting to control mind and matter. He lost all sense of time and felt weakened in the knowing his conceptual understanding was not complete or effective. The process needed further study. He needed to understand better the various components that were required to make the connection. He quickly surmised that the mass of the Earth was blocking the landscape of Akhi's mind. "I must understand what is going on here. What do these unknown values mean? What are these four character sequences? Why are they repeated so often, but seem to have no function other than to make this mental stuff work?" Kelt deliberated.

"Scotty, it's been nearly an hour. I really hate to be out here in the daylight," Guy said with increasing concern in his voice. One of the troopers signaled to Guy that he had an emergency of a personal nature as he pointed toward his crotch and waved his hands. "Outside the circle! Don't piss on the plants!" Guy shouted before turning back to Scotty.

"Give Kelt his time, Guy, it's not like it's the end of the world or anything like that is it?" Scotty said, quickly realizing how stupid his comment had been.

"Well, …" Guy started a thought and let it trail off.

Kelt continued to follow his excruciating journey through the unknown landscape of the mental transmission. He had not been successful in making the connection. He was quickly coming to a realization concerning the four-character sequence. "I know what it is."

"Scotty, we're going on sixty five minutes here and we're right in the…," Guy stopped in mid-sentence as Kelt removed his jacket from his face and stood dazed with his back to the sun. It was wet from the melted frost and drenched with sweat. He was chilled as the light desert breeze engaged its engine, blowing across his wet body. Kelt mindlessly dropped his jacket and fumbled for the remaining scrap of paper in his right pocket. Before he could lose his train of thought, he had to get this information written down. He quickly scribbled a long set of integers. Scotty ran up to him.

"Are you okay, Kelt?"

"I'm fine. Let me borrow your travel pad," he ordered. Kelt was regaining his breath and his ability to stand. Scotty handed him the small touch pad device as Kelt gazed at the integers.

Guy grabbed Kelt's arm and tugged at him until he started walking down the road. In his focused state of mind, Kelt did not realize that they were returning to the warehouse. He just plodded along as he stared into the small com's vid screen.

"Akhi, get this info to Hughes and our teams up there," Kelt started.

Akhi interrupted, "Kelt, we are all on video conference waiting for you. We have been waiting for nearly an hour," she said.

"Good, then, let me just show you these numbers. Someone snap a shot of this paper. On the paper, he had written 02113021002131102, the base four sequence he had manipulated in his transmissions. He had assigned an integer to each of the old symbols. "Does anyone recognize this as anything meaningful?" Kelt asked. No one spoke up for a minute or two.

"They could be DNA nucleobases, Kelt. Where did you get the numbers?" asked Amanda Perry.

"I can't explain right now," Kelt said "I believe they could be nucleobases as well. I'd like our folks over at Hughes to see if they can find a common sequence that matches one of our little plants' cousins here. I assume you can put your DNA sequencer to work there, Jayne?" Kelt asked.

"Yes, Kelt, and we have already sequenced a plant variety very close to one of the plants we see in your pictures. It's a grass common to most of the western states. It would be helpful to know which integers match the four base types," Jayne said.

The DNA molecule, while very complex and very long, had only four bases; A for adenine, C for cytosine, G for guanine, and T for thymine. It was the long sequence of seemingly random base sequences, which determined the building blocks of all life on Earth. DNA was responsible for blue or brown eyes, blond or auburn hair, and all other unique characteristics of life. However, only a small percentage of those sequences determined the uniqueness of each individual life form. Most DNA in all forms of life shared common sequences. And in plant life, that percentage of commonality was extremely high. Kelt was looking for a common denominator. He had a base sequence, he was sure of it now. The sequence he had, must be the transmuted sequence in the DNA of the plants growing before him. How he had reached these conclusions, he would only divulge with Akhi.

"We'll have to match each of your numbers to one of the four nucleobases, and by trial and error see if we get any matches," noted Jayne as she fidgeted with aimless doodling.

"Look, you've only got 24 permutations to work through for each nucleobase," Kelt said, "it shouldn't be that complicated. You have plenty of processing power out there. Just assign different bases to each integer. I'm sure that a solution will pop, sooner or later."

"Akhi, are your sleeping quarters near one of the spheres that contain seed stock?"

"Yes, Kelt, what do you need?" she asked.

"Can you please drop us samples from anything that matches the native plant life in this desert region? Throw in some samples of vegetables and grains as well. We need to get it to Hughes in Malibu," he said.

Kelt felt constrained using this tiny video screen to hold a proper meeting. He wasn't aware that they had almost approached the large hangar door when he asked Akhi, "Can you also find someone on this base that has their pad with them?"

"Uh Kelt, they are right in front of you, from what we can see up here," she laughed, "You are really focused today aren't you?"

"It's a good day to be focused Akhi, a very good day. I think that we're on the verge of discovery." Looking out to the crowd, Kelt continued, "Okay folks, we'll get some of these live samples out to Hughes." Referring to the HRS team highlighted on the com unit he asked, "Jayne, do you have any questions?"

"No, Kelt, we're good here," she answered.

"We're good up here as well Kelt. We'll get a shipment dropped right away," Amanda added.

"Amanda, use a flitter and send it directly to Hughes," Kelt ordered.

"Kelt, that flitter will be contaminated and we won't be able to use it again. We'll have to leave it down there with you," she advised.

"Just do it, okay, Amanda? It will save us some time," Kelt ordered. "Akhi, join me in a private video session as soon as I can get to my room," Kelt ordered with a more subdued voice.

"What's up Kelt? Why aren't the others involved?" she asked.

"It's personal," he said. With so many others surrounding him, he didn't want to talk about this business with her. He wanted to let them think that he wanted to talk *his* business with her.

"Let's get some of the plants that look like these pictures ready to go in a flitter. Make sure you get the rootstock as well. And boys, use a real pressurized container this time. Some of those soda bottles exploded with our last set of samples, we sent out a couple days ago," Scotty commanded.

A few civilians started out the warehouse door with squares cut from aluminum cans, to serve as digging tools and some old paper bags for the samples. If an observer didn't know any better, they might think we have an odd compulsion about using garbage for everything," Scotty mused, "We need to do some more midnight requisitions at the home store.

"Is Dr. Patel here?" Kelt yelled.

"Yes, Kelt, I'm over here," she responded from a few meters away pinned in a throng of people.

"Meet me over there," Kelt commanded as he pointed to the sidewall of the hangar.

"Okay!" she yelled back.

"Guy, with me."

"Yes sir."

"Can anyone pass me a piece of paper and pencil?" Kelt yelled to the crowd. He was quickly passed an old Space Truck memo and a pencil. As he walked to the side of the hangar to meet Dr. Patel, Kelt drew a circle. He hadn't finished his drawing by the time he reached the good doctor.

"It is nice having a biologist with us, Padma," he said looking at Dr. Patel. I felt terrible when you didn't make it up to the cities, but it's been a pleasure working with you under the circumstances. Your sister worries about you very much. It's not hard to see a strong connection between the two of you."

"Life brings us many surprises, Dr. Nelby. It's how we deal with them that counts."

"I should write that down and post it on my wall," Kelt grinned. "Look, Padma, I'd like you to go out and study the field with some of your people. Your only priority will be to determine the size and shape of the area of plants growing in these two areas." Kelt drew a partial ellipse just outside the western side of the circle around the hangar. "I want the dimension of this ellipse. These plants are younger. See if it extends to the north and south of the greenery as well. I'm not interested in their growth cycle." Kelt said as he retraced the half ellipse extending west of the circle for emphasis. "I'd also like measured dimensions of the more mature plant life surrounding the hangar in this circle. Padma, take the time you need, but be quick... okay? Remember, all I want right now is the dimensions of these two areas."

"I'll be happy to do so, Dr. Nelby. Many of my people haven't been topside since the bombs were dropped. They'll be delighted to do some brief fieldwork. I'll make sure that they do it quickly. But later, if we may, we'd like to spend some time to do a proper investigation."

"Guy, please assign a couple of riflemen to each of her people. Dr. Patel, we'll make sure that you get as much time as you need under Mr. Lerner's protection. Work with him for the scheduling."

"Yes, sir."

"Padma... thanks," Kelt said.

Dr. Patel had been a bit confused about the two areas she was to measure, but now understood the urgency under which Kelt was thinking. She would step up the measurement activities and at the same time be extremely careful. There would be no time to enjoy being topside for her crew.

39- You've done it!

"You've done it, Kelt!" Akhi squealed on the video screen as soon has Kelt had made the connection. "How did you do it Kelt? Did you find some way to activate the libraries? How did you start all the plants growing around the base?" she continued with her excited and continuous string of questions. Kelt hadn't seen her so happy for months. She was, absolutely adorable today. Kelt stared into her emerald eyes and listened patiently as she rambled on with her endless list, until he could bear it no more.

"Akhi, hold on for a minute will you?" Kelt asked. How long do you think that it takes for seeds to sprout?" Kelt asked.

"Oh, I don't know. If I were to guess, it would be anywhere from two to seven days or so? Honestly, Kelt I don't know how long. Do you know?" she asked.

"No, I don't, Akhi. But, I'm guessing that you have it pegged."

"Kelt, I could ask one of our biologists up here, if we need that information."

"Don't bother, Akhi, it's not all that important."

"Why isn't it all that important? I can't tell you how much hope this event has generated. I haven't heard anyone joking around for weeks. I never see a smile anymore. Everyone has been moping around with a somber look that nearly puts me in tears. We know that the world is changing for the worst. We can see so many murders every day from our floater cams. Within a year, we believe that there will only be a few million survivors left, Kelt. Somehow, humanity may survive down there by harvesting the oceans but we see little hope for those of us up here. Shannon and Amanda keep telling us that we don't have the experience yet in complex ecosystems, to survive more than a couple decades at best. And with the infection of Nelby Station, we have enough gloom and doom to nearly lose all hope.

"Kelt, we've had seven suicides this week. The news of plants growing around Nevada base has generated a tremendous amount of excitement in the floating cities. I haven't seen smiles for so long, I was afraid that everyone's face would crack by letting one out. We are beyond belief to see growing plants down there. Everyone seems so positive this morning!"

"Akhi, were those suicides all on Nelby Station?" Kelt asked.

"No, Kelt, they were in the other cities. The people on Nelby Station seem to be holding up somehow, in full battle mode, and are doing their best to contain the virus. Even people that were trapped in locked down areas with the virus, seem to be getting along as best they can. I suppose that the loss of Nelby Station was just too much for so many of us in the other cities. Kelt, twenty five percent of our population is over there!" Akhi cried with a somber burden in her eyes.

"Akhi, we've taken the responsibility of the world's survival on our shoulders. A task so great, should never be given to so few. I'm not just talking of the couple hundred or so here in Nevada, but all of you upstairs as well. I know how you can see all that is going on in the cities. We watch the video feed from time to time as well. But, we are here. We see it wherever we go. We smell it. The stench of death reeks in every city. All of the animals have been cleaned to the bone. We see dog and cat skeletons. In the farmlands, we see livestock skeletons. And we haven't seen any large game in the old forests for weeks. It has been wiped out by the hunters. And worst of all, we see evidence of cannibalism everywhere we go. That evidence just a few weeks ago had been hidden. Now, those committing this heinous act are all to brazen, leaving the skeletons right out in the open. Sometimes we find them in heaping piles. We know how unbearable this situation is. I am continually amazed at how well we are holding up here in the bunker. I suppose that with so much activity, we seem to be able to push on, hoping for a solution of some kind.

Akhi, we are working toward a solution here. I'm still staggering at the thought, trying to run down all the ramifications. This wonder, this supposed miracle, may be the beginning of a much larger solution. I can envision it. It is so front and centered in my mind that it is totally consuming. I do see a future for us. I hope that you can pass that along to everyone upstairs."

"Yes, Kelt! It is amazing! We are all dying to know how you did it. How did you get those seeds to sprout around the Nevada Base? Was it the artifact?" demanded Akhi.

"Akhi, it was you," Kelt answered softly.

He felt a swell of love rise through his chest as she listened to his words. His dearest Akhi, sat in front of her video screen bewildered with the announcement. It began with a curious look, and then her face lost its color with a lifetime of questions burning in her eyes. The brief pause seemed to drag on for an eternity, as Kelt watched his lovely soul mate absorb the seemingly impossible. Finally, she asked a simple question.

"How?" she softly asked through pale lips.

"Akhi, do you remember our personal mental link five nights ago?" he asked.

"Oh, how could I forget? The moment was intense… it was heartfelt… it was you, Kelt. I will never forget those precious moments together. How could that have anything to do with the plants around the base? We were just sharing a moment in history, weren't we? We were in the library, right?" she asked.

"No, sweetie, we were not in the library. We were linked in thought. Those events we saw originated in the library. The three-dimensional aspects of what we saw, what we heard, everything that we smelled and touched, were of our own making. How was it, do you suppose that we could walk barefoot along the beach, and feel the sand beneath our feet? Or, how could we watch the waves wash ashore and the gulls circling overhead, without one of the

260

millenarians watching the scene, recording all he or she saw? Akhi, it was our creation, one that I planted in your mind," Kelt explained.

"Kelt, I still can't understand how I made the plants grow. That is what you are telling me, isn't it?"

"Yes, I am telling you that."

"Please, tell me how. I don't understand this. I can't tell you how frustrating it is. I don't understand."

"I've told you that I've been investigating the library. You also know how I look at things and how I learn. I can't start at the beginning of any book. Even when I was studying calculus, I started looking through the book from the back, before the semester even started. I had no idea what I was looking at, of course, but the perusal of the material generated unanswered questions that I could remember. As we progressed linearly through the material in classes, I could sort of see ahead and answer those questions as the methodology unfolded. I understood how the calculus worked long before my classmates did, because I could envision it. That is how my thinking works. That is how I put my education on the fast track and finished my doctorate so early in life. Unlike you, I was twelve or thirteen before I recognized my special talents. I had always considered myself a failure in school when I was a child. My teachers told me that I couldn't learn anything, and I was an underachiever in grade school. It wasn't until I saw my learning habits for what they were, and learned how to utilize them, before I could do well in a structured learning environment. I've always looked at things from the top down instead of the bottom up. Procedures and methodology are at the end for me, where those things are the beginning for most."

"I know, Kelt. That's why Daddy hired you to work on the spheres and to come in and help us develop the dimensional shift technology at Stanford. Daddy sort of thinks through things in a similar way, but he'd never seen anyone like you, who was so proficient at it."

261

"I realize that now, Akhi. He kept me in the dark, which was such a frustrating experience. I need the total picture, so I can work backwards, as I move forward. We did manage to succeed, didn't we?"

Akhi gave him a nod of acknowledgement as he continued.

"I believe that most people who study the text on the ancient artifact, can access the library, Akhi. All they need to know is the language, the symbols, and the mathematics. When I first examined the artifact, looking at the instructions for direct access, I was certainly baffled. I had to retrieve enough information from Aldo's archives to make that first direct access, which turns out to be a mental connection.

"Then, I had to break loose from the information stream, so that I could observe the inner workings of the device. Once I had done that, Akhi, I was able to move throughout the system, fashioning questions, finding equations that fit, doing what I do… working from the top down. I have no idea how the device actually functions. I can't tell you how it is powered or how the programming codes actually work. I've managed to figure out enough, with your help, to access a very important "folder" of transmission logs. Thanks to your help, I could find and identify the time stamps on those files. I now know what they look like, and can readily detect their true date. Before just a couple of years ago, the last transmission had been thousands of years old, from my interpolation of our little experiment. I figured that the next transmission, made just a few months ago, before we found the artifact, was the one that triggered the plant growth around the artifact site. I see many new transmission records, as our historians are looking, searching the database, or whatever we call it. Those video transmissions they are receiving are so simple in comparison to the time that we spent together.

"I still do not recognize what that transmission, now two years old, was or to whom it was made, if anyone. Within that stream of data, I extrapolated the differences between it and those mental connections I have made with the device. A set of four single character constants stood out quite conspicuously… and these really are constants, Akhi. In this "first" transmission, the first in eons, there was a string of these four characters included in the equations that helped boost the signal in my way of thinking. I worked for days trying to determine what these constants were. They were clearly associated with each other. I thought that it might be a base four numerical sequence similar to the binary or base two, functions of our own computing devices. This notion was quickly dismissed, for what we could call a processor, works with long molecular strands, represented in the old language's formulas, in a massively parallel fashion. This sequence of base four numbers, characters, or whatever they really are, baffled me. Then, I realized that each one of those values very likely could represent a sequence of nucleobases within a DNA strand. Upon realizing the potential significance of this discovery, I made somewhat of a rash decision to contact you.

"I don't know how the connection works. The side effects… shoot… I didn't really know what they might be. I only knew that I had to try. I wrapped this string of constants in the formulas required for transmission that the machine made, some two years ago, in my own mind and asked you to do the same. You absorbed the information, reformed synapses in your physical brain, and we connected telepathically, as Pacificus floated overhead the base at midnight.

"I was stunned at the reality of our experience, Akhi. I had been to the old village, listened to the older woman speak, and had managed to scan the recollections of a young girl. The world was so fresh and real with you. It had not been so in my previous ventures to that historical record. What I saw before was a two dimensional image in my mind, much like watching a monitor. With you, just a few nights ago, it was so realistic. We could touch each other, go where others were not watching, we spent a few precious moments together in the world, we made in our minds. I honestly believe that the artifact had no influence on us. Otherwise, we could not have spent those moments together, in a full sensory environment like that.

"I made a connection; one that I felt might work by observing what the machine had done. I wrapped my own equations around a string of constants that held no known meaning and brought you into my own thoughts with it. Your projection to me was not entirely focused; it covered the area that is now thriving with plant life. Akhi, I believe that the seeds in the ground were modified with the new DNA sequence, and "inspired" to grow with the strong emotional bond that we share. I have discovered that the artifact, factors emotion, perhaps love, into its equations. I know that it sounds difficult to believe, but that is what I have been able to surmise.

"The plant growth pattern is also worth noting, Akhi. I notice the shape of this circle, is not a true circle. It tracks the movement of the Earth below Pacificus, while we were entrenched in thought. Additionally, there is no attenuation of the number of plants toward most of the edge of this area. The only part where it is thinner is when we started the mental link. One might think that attenuation would be the natural case of an energy dispersing. Your thoughts affected this area in full strength for; there is no attenuation near the edges. I've also seen seeds sprouting to the west of the circle….

"Hold on… yes, here it is. I've just received a preliminary study from Dr. Patel, of the dimensions of the circle and the sprouts that are about a day younger. The smaller sprouts lie in a partial ellipse to the west of the circle, and extend slightly to the north and south. Those are the seeds, which were affected by our connection, the next afternoon. Since I contacted you at sunset, as we down here were on the apparent limb of the Earth from your perspective, I had anticipated this very phenomenon. Your broadcast is like a cone, on to the Earth. When we are under your position, the cone is more or less a circle. When we are on the edge of the Earth, it forms an ellipse."

"Wow…" Akhi managed to say. All of this made little sense to her. Her life and thought processes had always been very structured, in her way. The thoughts of this telepathic session with Kelt actually altering the DNA in plant seeds, and then motivating them to grow with… love? She could not comprehend, yet the results were self-evident. The Nevada site was surrounded by active plant life.

"That's not all, Akhi," started Kelt "If you were able to do that down here, what of the seed stock in the cities? I believe that my transmissions to you have altered the yet unborn seeds in a similar fashion. Do you recall if any of the other cities were within a two kilometer radius of Pacificus that night, or the next afternoon?" Kelt asked.

"Let me check our logs, Kelt. Do you think you really were able to change our seed stock? Kelt, I can't imagine anything greater or more hopeful!" she exclaimed. "Okay… Um… I'm sorry, Kelt, but no. We've been spread out more, since Nelby Station was infected.

"Akhi, please have Shannon and Amanda perform some testing on the seed stock on Pacificus in addition to those you'll be sending to Hughes. Send the other samples over to the dirty lab, where they run samples from Earth. Have them pick seeds that sprout quickly," Kelt said. "Oh, and one more thing, Akhi…regardless what I may have asked before, please don't tell anyone about our mental links, and how they are associated with this plant growth. Let it be a mystery. I know that I asked you to tell Aldo about our connection. Tell him to play it down. He'll understand.

"Why should we keep it a secret, Kelt? This is knowledge that should be shared. I did mention it to Aldo, but I gave him no details," Akhi replied.

"Akhi, I've just now realized that what we have done could be very dangerous. If someone were to use the incorrect sequence in a transmission, the results could be devastating. We have a very powerful weapon at our disposal, and it must be kept secret. This must be kept between us."

"I can do that, my darling. I understand. If this does in fact, alter DNA, someone might learn to use it as a weapon against people. I'll contact our biologists, as soon as we are finished here to conduct the tests you requested."

"Akhi, I need a sphere. I'd like to take one out with the new magnetic shielding," Kelt said. Akhi looked at his eyes, and the most serious look stared back at her.

"We've been flight testing a small sphere with the new magnetosphere. It is nearly ready to go. The testing is complete, but the ship isn't fully outfitted yet," Akhi said.

"Does it have basic life support systems?"

"Yes, and they are fully tested and functional. We haven't been able to get all the crew quarters, galleys, and the like fully outfitted. All we have operational is the bridge," she answered with a look of understanding, now growing in her smile.

"Great, Akhi, we'll need it pretty soon. Again, please don't tell anyone. Just make sure I get the codes as soon as you can get them sent down to me securely," Kelt said.

"I completely understand, my love. We can have it ready to go by nightfall, if you'd like," she answered.

"Great! Let's do that," Kelt said sounding like he was in a rush to finish their conversation.

"Wait Kelt, before you go, I want you to know just how much you mean to me. I've told you so many times before, and I don't ever want it to get old. I love you so very much," Akhi expressed with the look of obvious affection in her face.

"I love you too, sweetie," Kelt answered with a big smile cracking his face.

40-Secretary Tse

The Chinese hadn't constructed conventional missile silos. Those were too easy to spot from orbiting spy satellites and take out with a variety of weapons. Instead, they had constructed a labyrinth of tunnel systems in the mountains of northern China. Intelligence reported that they had dug in thousands of kilometers of passageways and storage facilities. The Chinese constructed standard concrete pads in a variety of locations, along the mountain range where the missiles could be configured, fueled, and launched. This made it much more difficult to take out their nuclear capability effectively in a single strike.

Jiang had just finished meeting with his hawkish military advisors. They were insistent that they take out the surrounding countries that may pose a threat to the reconstruction of China, after the current problem had been resolved.

"Gentlemen, there is no end to the current problem," Jiang had pleaded. "We have always been isolationists. I see no advantage in preemptive strikes."

His generals were not convinced. Here they had no plan to keep themselves alive, and were insisting on striking the countries around them with nuclear weapons. "All sanity has left the planet," Jiang thought as his face sagged into his hands.

"India and Pakistan have nuclear weapons and we must destroy them, Mr. Secretary," the leading general demanded.

"General, these countries don't even have functioning governments at this point. Why should they even bother to shoot at us?" Jiang asked bluntly.

"That makes it even more imperative that we take them out first, Mr. Secretary. We have our bunkers in the north. We have a fighting army of half a million. We have enough food for them for two years. We must protect ourselves."

"Yes, general. We know what we have, but do they? Now, think carefully general about who *they,* actually are at this point. I would imagine that the few still alive are those that managed to make it to the coastal waters, and are fishing for a living. *They* have been reduced to simple fishermen gentlemen."

The meeting droned on for hours and Tse Jiang had managed to stall his military from taking nuclear action, yet another time. He wondered if he might need to resort to violence, to get rid of the internal conflict he perceived. He did have a private guard of some thirty highly trained troops at his disposal. He wondered how many were loyal to him, and not his generals. He may need to find out soon.

*****

Rick Carter knew better than to contact the Chinese General Secretary by conventional means. Even if the lines were still active, right now, he would not dare talk to him directly. His old acquaintance, Tse Jiang, had risen to the top of the ladder in the recent unrest.

"I imagine his hold on the government is tenuous at best," Rick imagined. With activity around the Chinese missile sites, he had to have a conversation.

Rick knew where the Secretary General's office was. It was standard intelligence data. He had planted a wide-angle micro camera on the office window nearest the General Secretary's desk. From the inside, it looked like a small piece of dirt. On top of the building, sat a cutter with articulated arms, hiding between two large air handlers waiting for the right moment.

As Jiang's office cleared, the floater's remote pilot waited for five minutes watching Jiang stroll through paperwork on his desk. Convinced that no one else was in the room, the pilot lowered the floater from the rooftop to the window.

"Ping, ping, ping..."

"What's that noise?" Jiang asked himself as he glanced toward the window. There he saw the small flying saucer disk. Below the disk dangled two mechanical arms. One held a Space Truck com; the other had been used to

268

knock on the window. Between the arms dropped a sign, which read in English: Rick Carter is on the line, will you please talk to him?

Jiang smiled broadly. He knew that it could be no other Rick Carter, than his longtime associate. He acted tired as he stood up from his chair, and walked to the window. As he opened the window, the floater pilot extended the arm, handing the com unit to him. Jiang quickly pocketed the phone and closed the window. He knew this room was bugged. Every room in the facility was bugged. He didn't even know who the watchers were. He did know where the bugs were, however. He doubted that the video bug in his office saw him retrieve the com unit. The curtains jutting out from the wall hid him well in this situation. For all anyone knew, he had opened the window for some fresh air.

Jiang made expressions as though he were tired. He yawned and slapped his face. He sat down at his desk and pretended to fall asleep for a moment. He yawned again hoping that those watching fell for the ruse. After feigning the need for rest, Jiang pushed himself away from the desk, and retired to the bedroom through a side door in his office. Jiang worked many hours throughout the days and nights. It was common for him to take a nap. Jiang moved his portable music station to his bed stand and propped up the pillows against the hidden microphone/video bug in his bed's headboard. He turned on some classical music and threw himself into the bed. After checking that the pillows completely covered the bug, Jiang quietly left the bed, and tiptoed to the other side of the room, where he hid behind the window curtains to take the call.

*****

"Mr. Carter, we have the General Secretary on line for you."

"Thanks Jen," Rick responded as he retrieved his com unit.

"Mr. Secretary! It's been a long time. Say, I never was able to thank you for giving me the heads up to leave

269

your fair country. And I'm doubly grateful for your help in uncovering the fact that I had been framed."

"You are most welcome," Jiang responded in his lowest whisper.

"I hope you are not taking any unnecessary risk in talking to me."

"I believe I have taken the necessary precautions, Rick."

"Say, Jiang, we've been noticing activities at your missile launch sites. You aren't planning to actually launch any nuclear birds, are you?"

"Right now, they are only performing exercises. My generals want to assure China's preservation by launching preemptive attacks on India and Pakistan."

"And the United States?"

"Our land based missiles do not have that range. Only our ballistic submarines could deliver atomic weapons to the US mainland."

"And those submarines are patrolling the coasts of the US, Mr. Secretary. Let's see here. We have four of your Jin-class boomers patrolling waters of the west coast and one on the east coast of what was the United States. Hmm. Each one carries twelve JL-2 multiple warhead missiles. Am I right so far, Jiang?"

"Right on the money, as you would say, Rick. I know that I'm not divulging state secrets, you know where they are, don't you?"

"So does the U.S. Navy, Jiang. Every one of your boomers is being shadowed by a Virginia class attack sub, propelled by what is popularly known as worm drives. Pump-jet propulsors is their official designation. Jiang, the U.S. military is practically non-existent. All that remains are the loyal crews on those subs. They will attack your boomers at the first sign that your missile bay doors are opening. Those subs of yours don't stand a chance. Order them home."

Jiang paused to think of the implications of what he had just heard. Either the US was working with him, which he doubted, or he had capabilities to track them from space.

"You are right, Rick. There is no reason for them to be where they are. I will find a way to recall them."

"We need to start working together, Jiang. There aren't all that many of us humans left. If we ever get the planet fixed, we'll no longer be able to have individual countries. We tried that and it didn't work. We need to plan for that future. We need it to work. Look, I don't want anything to do with the government. I may help it get started, but I want out at the first opportunity."

"Rick, you must understand…." Jiang started and trailed off as he considered his tenuous position. He was constantly watched. He felt like a puppet answering to his subordinates. He honestly did not know what to do.

Rick heard it in his voice. "You aren't in control are you, Jiang? They're breathing down your neck and they'll blame this portending nuclear strike on you, won't they?"

"Yes, Rick, I am afraid that is what is happening. I am not in charge, and I am constantly being watched."

"Well, let me give you a suggestion, Jiang. Hold a general assembly and invite everyone that can fit in the largest hall you can find. Line the walls with your personal security guard…"

"Rick, I don't trust my security guard."

"Hmm…. Well there has to be at least a few of them who you trust, right?"

"Yes."

"Well then, make sure they have live rounds and extra clips for their weapons. Give everyone else blanks. If someone tries to shoot you, you'll be covered. Those that don't try to shoot you, should be given the extra live round clips."

"You make everything sound so simple, Rick."

"It's the only way to get things done, Mr. Secretary. Now, let me finish. Prepare an inspirational speech. Tell everyone that China has come out on top of this mess. Tell them that China has the only functioning government left in the world... You won't be lying, my friend... Pump them up. Make them feel proud. Let them know, you are responsible for this success.

"Then gently move them to where we need to go... that we need to work with other people of former nations to solve this crisis and build a new world together. Tell them that China will lead the way, but ultimately, a new world government will be necessary to allow humanity to survive. If they support you, it will be the right moment to bring down those hawks, which are trying to nuke the world. Do you think you can do that?"

"I've seen the game played. I'm sorry, Rick. I've been wondering for some time, what I might do, and this is better than any idea I've come up with on my own. I might die trying, but I'm already a dead man as it is."

"That's the way I see it too, Jiang. Keep the com unit hidden if you can. If not, give it back to the robot. We can monitor your window if you like."

"I think that is the safest route for now, Rick. I can't be caught with this thing."

"Okay, come to the window and blow your nose. We'll send down the little robot. That will be your signal from now on to contact me... blow your nose at the window. I'll have someone watching our monitor 24 hours a day. I wish you the best Jiang."

"Thank you very much, my friend."

41- HRC responds

"Dr. Perry?"

"Yes, Jayne," Amanda responded.

"We ran into a bit of luck. The string of constants that you provided us … well, we think we've solved the DNA riddle. Oh, I'm all befuddled. Let me start over.

"If the sequence were to alter many plants at once, it was a logical step to consider only those DNA nucleobase sequences that all plants have in common."

"Yes, that is exactly what I would do. Please continue," Amanda requested.

"We've sequenced several species and have them on file. We had already developed some macros that helped find the commonalities. The commonalities in DNA structure, runs well above 90 percent in plants.

Our computer whiz here then compared Mr. Nelby's string using permutations of the different nucleobases assigned to the numbers, and looked for commonalities within that string. The process could take weeks or months, but we thought we got a possible hit within just a few hours of computing time. Within the string, there can only be one match. We've got the samples from Nevada and started the sequencing focused on that area, in the DNA strands. I'd like to report that we can confirm there has been an alteration of just two nucleobases in that common segment.

We'll continue the complete sequencing of the sample, but upon hearing how this data came to us, I'm nearly compelled to throw our strict procedures out the window, and give you two thumbs up!" Jayne grinned.

"I know that you'll not leave it there, Jayne. You are very thorough in your work. For now, I'll just pass along confirmation of our assumptions to the others with the caveat you are doing a complete sequence on the DNA samples," Amanda explained.

"Before the infection, I would never have done things so sloppily, Amanda. Sometimes in a crisis, early information can be a determining factor. That's why I called you to pass on the good news."

"Thanks Jayne, I appreciate it."

42- Space journey

"Guy?"

"Yes, sir?"

"Walk with me."

Kelt headed down into the tunnels away from the CIC, in the Nevada bunker.

"Where are we going Kelt? No one comes down here."

"I wanted some privacy. You and Scotty are the only two that I absolutely trust."

"So, why didn't you bring him along too?"

"I couldn't find him. You'll have to bring him up to speed on a need to know basis."

"Oh… alright. So, what is it, sir?"

"Do you know what caused the plant growth around the base?"

"No one does, sir. We have all assumed it was related to the artifact, but no one has been able to figure it out for sure. Those eggheads have been monitoring that thing ever since, to see what they can discover."

"I know what caused it, Guy."

"Well, why haven't you told anyone, Kelt? This is big news!"

"What I will tell you must never be passed to anyone else. Tell Scotty if you must. But, give him the same warning."

"Okay."

"I've been experimenting with the artifact…"

"But you haven't stepped near it for weeks. The geeks have it."

"I know, Guy. I've learned how to get inside it with my mind. I figured out what it did to make those weeds grow, where we originally found it along the Nile. It sent out some sort of transmission coded with a base four sequence, which I believe is a portion of the seeds' DNA nucleobases…"

"I'm sorry, sir, but please, use smaller words. Remember, I'm just a grunt."

"Okay, Guy. I got inside, figured out how the plants were changed through a transmission. Then I made a similar transmission to Akhi on Pacificus. It was her mental energy focused on the Earth around the base that altered the seeds and encouraged them to sprout."

"Holy mother... she did that?"

"Yes, she did. I suspect that my energies focused her way, equally changed the seed stock for any of the floating cities within my mental cone of influence. We'll find out in a day or so from Hughes, but I'm already quite confident that I'm right."

"So, why are you telling me this, Kelt?"

"Because we want to try it on a planet wide scale... tonight or tomorrow. I'll be taking a small sphere out four times the distance to the moon, a little more than 1.5 million kilometers from the Earth. It'll take me 10 or 12 hours to get out that far with a comfortable acceleration and deceleration. Then, Akhi and I will make a similar mental link, and we'll alter the seeds in the same way as the world turns below us."

"Again, Kelt, why are you telling me this?"

"Because it is potentially dangerous. We've not spent much time together in a mental link. It is strenuous and leaves us with a throbbing headache."

"Oh, man, I do NOT want to be in the middle of this. Do you realize that Carter expects me to protect only two people in this world? That's you, mister, and his daughter. And you are going to put both yourselves at risk, for a dream together?"

"No, Guy, to save the world."

"You're serious, aren't you?"

"Dead serious. And so is Akhi. We are doing this, Guy and I want to enlist your confidence and help. Just think! We've done it already on a small scale. I've proven it to the strictest of my standards. We received confirmation from Hughes that my numbers match up with the altered

DNA, from the plant life around this base. I believe that Akhi and I can literally save the world."

"Okay. I'm not in yet. I want to understand the risks… and I mean all of them, Kelt. You give it to me straight."

"Very well. I owe you that. The first risk is not a threat to either Akhi or me. The threat is the means by which we do this, might somehow be discovered. Since we've already made the link twice, I doubt that should be an issue."

"And, why should making a link be a risk?"

"Think of it, Guy, we are manipulating DNA. Could it not be used as a terrible weapon? Quite frankly, I don't know how to configure it as a weapon, but it is certainly a possibility."

"Okay, since the horse is already out, I can live with that one," responded Guy.

"The next, is that it caused us to have severe headaches. Neither of us has sought medical advice to see if we've had any damage. I'm thinking that longer sessions, like we are planning, could pose a threat."

"Now, this one, I'm having a hard time with. Once we're done here, we're headed right off to medical where we'll get you a brain scan."

Guy lifted his com from his belt.

"Oh Guy, please," Kelt begged.

"This one is for your best girl, sir. Amanda? Yeah, Guy Lerner here. You are now in on a big secret. You can't tell anyone, and that includes Rick. Get Akhi down to your medical lab. She needs a brain scan right now. If nothing is wrong, great. Let me know how it turns out either way."

"What's this about, Guy?" Amanda asked.

"I'll let Akhi tell you. You deserve to know. Don't let her out of the scan. Tell her I want it done, now. If she doesn't, I'll bring her father in on our secret."

"Affirmative, Guy." Amanda said.

Guy cut the connection and clipped his com back to his utility belt.

"Okay, what else?" Guy demanded.

"I believe that the process can become addictive. Although not probable, we might get stuck inside the connection."

"This just gets better and better, kiddo. What can pop you out, if you get stuck?"

"I'm hoping that you would, Guy."

"And just how would I accomplish that?"

"I would think you could deliver me to the medical lab where they could figure it out."

"Beyond giving your life for your country, you haven't thought through this much, have you, son?"

"Believe me, Guy. It's not as if I haven't tried. I just haven't had the time to find solutions to the last two risks. I could spend the time. It could take decades. How much time do we really have? Spring will be upon us here in the northern hemisphere very shortly. Believe me, Guy, if we can alter the seeds just waiting to sprout, we might save the planet."

"Okay, now I understand your rush to get this done. The seeds that are growing topside around the warehouse… did they sprout early because of this?"

"Yes. But, the other seeds won't be but a week or two behind. The seeds farther south are already starting to sprout and die. We need to alter them immediately."

"Let me think about this for a moment, Kelt. I really have great affection for you and Akhi. Believe an old soldier when he says that… because quite frankly, you practically never hear anything like it from an old soldier."

"You know, I had thought that we would just do this, consequences be damned. That didn't set well with me. I decided I needed your help with this effort."

"I'm glad you ran into me first, instead of Scotty. I'm sure he wouldn't contest your will to do this like I'm doing. And for sure, he wouldn't be thinking of protecting your hide like I do."

"You are right, of course," admitted Kelt.

"C'mon, let's get up to medical and get your head examined."

278

"Clean bill of health," Dr. Masurwosky nodded to Guy. His brain looks excellent. He seems to have areas that are more active than most people, which is curious, but he is a genius, after all."

"Thanks, Doc," Guy offered.

"Yes, thank you doctor," Kelt followed.

Kelt and Guy took another walk down the long hallway.

"Akhi's tests came out fine as well. Fortunately, for her, she has records up there and her "unusual areas" have already been documented. I suppose you are both okay. So, how do you want to do this, Kelt? Before the issue even comes up, I'm telling you that Dr. Masurwosky and I are coming with you."

"There is plenty of room on the ship. But, this is a very intimate thing, Guy. I don't think I can do it with people looking at me."

"Well, we'll leave you alone for a while to make the link. Once you're under, we'll come in and monitor you. The same goes for your pretty little girl up there in Pacificus. Amanda has already promised me that she'll follow through with whatever instructions I give her. The doctors need to be in on this as well."

"Can we trust them, Guy?"

"I don't see any choice, Kelt. We'll give them a slimmed down version of what's going on. There will be no getting around the fact that, *if* the seeds start sprouting around the world... well, they'll know."

"They can never speak a word of what happens."

"Dr. Masurwosky has already agreed to go with us, to monitor you, and has promised on forfeiture of his life that he'll not breathe a word to anyone. He promised *me*, Kelt... and I carry a pistol," Guy grinned.

"All right. It's a plan. The ship is coming down as we speak and should be here in just a few minutes. Please have the good doctor prepare the supplies he might need,

279

let's take a sniffer, and get the kitchen to prepare us meals for four days."

"Okay, son, I can handle that. Say, is the ship shielded?"

"They just finished up the magnetosphere last week. The ship has a cockpit, but not much else. We should be suited up the entire time. The plumbing hasn't been installed yet."

"Man, I hate space diapers," Guy grunted, shaking his head

"I do too, Guy. It's a minor price to pay to save the world though. Don't you think?"

*****

Kelt advised Scotty as to what was going on as he suited up. Scotty was unexpectedly more concerned with the situation than Guy.

"Guy is smart, Kelt, but he hasn't the mental facilities he should have developed by now."

"That's because he's been taking care of us instead of studying books."

"Kelt, are you off your rocker?"

"No. Scotty, I want you to look after our ship while we're out. I trust you more than I trust anyone else, and should we have a malfunction, or the automated macros fail to return us. I want you to man my flight center."

"Alone?"

"Do you need anyone else?" Kelt grinned.

"No, not really. These things practically fly themselves!"

"They do, don't they? I've got macros preprogrammed into the system to take us out and bring us back in. Here are the codes to override them. Guy will have them as well."

"So, all I can do is watch, then." Scotty said despondently.

"Yes, Mr. Scott, and it's going to be a long stretch for you too. You'd better have a pot of coffee set up by your station."

"It's not that I've never stayed up that long before. We went five days once at Stanford before you came on board."

"Well, it shouldn't take that long, my friend."

*****

"All aboard?" Guy asked.

"All present and accounted for," answered Kelt.

"Okay, let me do my preflight check," Guy grinned.

There was really little need to do a preflight check. All that needed to be done, was to check pressurization of the cabin, assure that the magnetosphere was operational, and to make sure everyone was buckled in. Other than the safety belt check, macros had already checked the other systems.

"This sure is an odd looking space ship, Kelt. I mean, it is butt ugly."

"Well, Guy, we weren't after aesthetics. A sphere is the easiest to build, the easiest to protect with a magnetosphere, the most efficient to…"

"Yeah, spare me the gobbelty gook. I know there were good reasons. I just hope that someday, once we get through all this, we can design a craft that looks elegant."

"I'm looking forward to it," Kelt started, "I've been working through some conceptual ideas in my free time."

"I'm sure you have. I can't imagine how you have much free time to consider things like that."

Kelt grinned wickedly, "Well, certain times during each day, every man has a private moment or two to consider his paperwork."

Guy got it immediately, potty breaks. The comment went right over the good doctor's head.

"Huh?" was his response.

"Okay, Guy, take off!"

"No countdown?"

"Okay, 3, 2, 1 go!"

Guy moved some icons around on his pad and then with his special new flight stick, nudged the craft upward.

281

After giving the ship a few moments to clear the warehouse, he gave the stick another thrust forward to climb at two g's. The doctor was totally befuddled by his new apparent weight and Kelt could see how uncomfortable he was.

"Hey, Guy, back off a bit until Dr. Masurwosky gets used to the acceleration. We've got some time to spare."

"Aye, aye, sir."

"Guy, as soon as we pass the spires, I'm going to prepare to make my first mental link. We'll catch all the floating cities in a cone of thought. It's our backup plan just in case the whole world thing doesn't work."

"As planned, sir. Get ready to bed down."

"Dr. Masurwosky, please give me 10 minutes, then come and check on me. Akhi?"

"I'm here and waiting for you."

"Are you alone?"

"Yes, my darling. I'll press a hospital bed button just as we start the link. Amanda and my doctor up here will come in five minutes later."

"See you in five, then."

Kelt descended to the lower deck where a reclining car seat had been installed. A shoulder harness would keep Kelt in the chair. A sniffer was placed around the headrest. Akhi had a similar setup on Pacificus, but she had a real bed and didn't have to bother with an EV flight suit.

Kelt buckled in and performed a mental relaxation exercise to calm himself. He then started thinking through the formulas, the symbols, and the myriad of complexities that would allow him to join Akhi in the mental space of their own creation. The required quotient of love, emotion, charity, whatever one chose to call it, was unconsciously woven naturally by Kelt's mind. When he was ready, he called her by her true name.

"Hello, my love," she grinned at him.

"Hi sweetie. You look great today!"

"Kelt, I wanted to ask about that. Are you seeing what I want to look like, or what you want me to look like?"

"Well, you're wearing a standard gray hemp flight suit and no makeup."

"That answers that question, then," she smiled.

"So, where are we? Oh, look over there! Is that a missile?"

"Akhi, we only need to spend a few minutes in this link. I wanted you to see what I feel was one of the most important of the Apollo missions. That, my sweet, is the Apollo 8 spacecraft and it's about ready to lift off."

"Wasn't the moon mission Apollo 11?"

"Yes, it was. But Apollo 8 actually went to the moon and orbited it. It was the first manned flight out of the influence of Earth's gravitational pull, and into the gravitational pull of another solar system body. I consider it the most significant. Do you know that they used slide rules in flight to make their calculations?"

"What's a slide rule?"

"It's basically a sliding stick marked logarithmically. You can multiply and divide very quickly with one. They also had basic trigonometric functions. I have one in my things on Pacificus. Go ahead and look when we finish this thing. There's a manual you can use as well. Oh look, they're starting up the rocket motors!"

The crowd hushed and huge bino cameras zoomed in on the rocket as the motor crackled and roared to life. Huge plumes of smoke and superheated steam seemed to thrust up from the ground as the large Saturn V rocket slowly lifted from the launch pad.

"Oh Kelt, this is so exciting!" Akhi yelled into his ear.

He could not hear her. The sound was truly mind shattering. The rocket quickly gained speed and within moments was out of visual sight. The telescopic binocular cameras were able to track it for a few more minutes, but the event was now over for the casual spectators.

"Okay, sweetie that marks our moment to sever the connection. I'll be seeing you again in a few hours."

She pecked him on the cheek and the connection broke. Kelt woke up with a splitting headache, but it soon subsided. Dr. Masurwosky was already performing a brain scan and was nearly finished. The results popped up on the monitor to the right of the flight couch."

"Looks good, Kelt, how do you feel?"

"I had a really bad headache at first, but it's feeling better already."

"Okay, that's fine. How much longer until our next exercise?"

"We'll reach altitude in about nine hours. At that time we'll be able to catch Asia, Europe, and Africa. After that, we'll do three more overlapping links six hours apart, to make sure we get the whole world. Remember, don't let me stay under for more than twenty minutes."

"It's in the plan, Kelt, I've got that part memorized and my watch is very accurate."

"Thanks Doc."

Kelt and Dr. Masurwosky returned to the flight deck and strapped in to keep Guy company. There wasn't really anything to do. The ship was accelerating at a constant rate, giving them a good solid feel of gravity. They had passed the Moon's orbit just a little over two hours into the flight.

"It's really too bad that it's new moon," Kelt said.

"Huh?" Guy asked.

"It's on the other side of the Earth. We can't see it. I sure wish we could have seen it up close is all."

"Kelt, we don't even have windows. All you'd see is an image on the monitor. And you've seen that before."

"You're not much of a romantic are you, Guy?

"No, I suppose I'm not."

"You call Amanda a lot, though."

"I do not."

"Yes you do. You got a thing for her, Guy?" Kelt teased.

Guy sat solemnly in his seat, obviously not wanting to answer the question.

"You do have a thing for her! And I was just jibing you! Who'd a thunk?" Kelt laughed.

"Kelt, I'm afraid you've caught me with my hands in the cookie jar. I do like her very much. I have to tell you that it was very hard for me to jump from Pacificus to take care of your sorry …"

"I get it, Guy. I understand. Do you suppose, that once we get these problems resolved that we'll be able to put our own lives a little higher on the priority list? Won't we deserve it?"

"You both deserve it," Dr. Masurwosky said.

"Hey Doc, what's your first name?" Kelt asked.

"It's Harold, Kelt."

"Mind if I call you Harry?"

"Yes, Kelt I do. My name is Harold."

"Well then, can we call you Harold? I mean, just for this trip. I promise we'll call you doctor when we get back," Kelt offered.

"That's fine, Kelt. I can surrender my dignity for your cause," he grinned in return. "After all, you too have earned an esteemed title. I should have been more mindful. So, tell me Kelt, what is your full name?"

"Oh please don't ask."

"Come on," Guy jabbed, "What's your full name, Kelt? Tit for tat."

"You guys let this out and I'll…"

"Your name, Kelt," Guy demanded.

"It's Gerald Kelty Nelby," Kelt said softly.

"So, what do you think Dr. Masurwosky, shall we just call him… Kelt?" Guy laughed uncontrollably. "I'm sorry Kelt, but I could never call you Gerald or Jerry or anything like that. It just doesn't fit you."

"Why do you suppose I like, Kelt?"

"Okay, Guy, your turn," Dr. Masurwosky demanded.

"I shouldn't have started this. I'm in deep doo doo now," Guy smirked. "Okay, this is top secret, even more so than this mission. My full name is Stacey Gomez Lerner," he finished with a blushed face.

Kelt nearly swallowed his tongue. "Really?" he asked.

"Why do you think I go by Guy?" he responded flatly. "Okay, enough of that. If I hear "Stacey" from any of the crew, I'll be looking for you two.

"I'm hungry," Dr. Masurwosky said.

"We've got another hour or so before you can eat, Doc," Guy advised.

"Why is that?" Dr. Masurwosky asked.

"Because when we do the flip to decelerate, you'll feel weightlessness for the first time in your life, and if you've got fresh food in your belly, it's likely it will end up on the walls."

"Oh, I hadn't considered that. I suppose I can wait," he said as his stomach protested loudly.

The three men sat silently for the next seventy minutes.

"Okay, time for the flip, Doc. Kelt and I have done this a hundred times. Just try to hold your breath and scrunch your stomach muscles. That's what worked for me the first time."

Guy cut the acceleration and flipped the craft. It only took a few seconds. The good doctor was certainly looking a little green as his computing pad and glasses floated into the cabin.

"Okay, Doc, I'll start this deceleration slowly so your glasses don't break when they hit the floor. As the craft slowly decelerated, the objects softly landed on the floor. When they had reached one g, Guy told Dr. Masurwosky that he could unbuckle and retrieve his possessions.

The rest of the trip out was uneventful. Guy and Kelt passed the time with idle chitchat about old times. The doctor felt out of the loop and mostly just studied some journals on his pad.

"Okay Doc, decelerating time is up. We'll be without gravity for the next day or so. Get your barf bag ready," Guy advised. The admonition turned out to be very good advice.

*****

"Sit down Akhi," Kelt said as he pushed her into her seat.

"Kelt! How rude!"

"I'm sorry, but he's about ready to start playing."

"Who?"

"Sergei Rachmaninoff, sweetie. We are going to hear him play the first two movements of his second concerto. Remember, you played it for me once?"

"It's my favorite, Kelt! But why must we only listen to just two movements?

"No more than twenty minutes, sweetie."

The music was perfect; his timing was just slightly different than she had heard it played on several recordings. It was magical to hear the original beautiful melodies the master had crafted, played by his own hands. She held Kelt's hand and drifted into his eyes as he sat spellbound by the performance.

"How did you get these great seats? The auditorium is packed?" she asked.

Kelt looked at her with an annoyed look. "I edited them out," he curtly replied.

Akhi got the message. The first two movements were just about twenty minutes long. And she should be enjoying this! She paid attention to the artist, his hands, the attack to the keys, his use of the pedals to sustain the notes. She was quickly caught up in every aspect of the orchestral accompaniment. She now saw the wisdom in Kelt's care, to keep these moments together short and well timed. She wanted this moment to never end. However, it ended, all too soon.

"The second movement is over, sweetie, time to break contact."

Akhi awoke to Amanda pinching her on her arm.

"Owe! What are you doing to me?"

"Trying to wake you, Akhi. You're nearly overdue by a full minute," Amanda gasped, "We thought that we had a serious medical problem on our hands. Look, you are sweating."

Akhi looked at her arms. Beads of sweat covered her. Amanda had already cleared her forehead and handed her the towel.

"Do you have a headache?" asked her doctor.

"No, I feel wonderful! I got to hear Rachmaninoff play his very own concerto! Can you imagine? And I was with Kelt too!"

Amanda sensed a change in Akhi she felt was a little off. And this was just the first of four twenty- minute sessions. She was very worried that she had been unable to waken Akhi at the time limit. She sent for Aldo and asked him to sit outside Akhi's room.

Kelt met with considerably more of a scolding. The doctor had been frantic in his attempts to arouse Kelt, even though just a few seconds had passed for the time limit.

"I'm sorry, guys," Kelt said. I timed it a bit wrong. We went a few seconds over," he explained.

"You can't do that to us," Guy said. "We don't know how to handle it. We could not wake you."

"Yeah, I was afraid that might happen. Look, if we go a little over, don't sweat it. I've tried to find events that last only twenty minutes. I'm sorry this one went over, but we did break at the right time."

"Okay, Guy said. We'll just deal with this as it comes."

*****

Six hours later, the craft hovered over Western Europe and Africa. Kelt and Akhi formed another link.

"The Mona Lisa! You have to be kidding me, Kelt!"

"I know, sweetie. I wish that we could spend the day here together, but I figured you could spend twenty minutes staring at this one painting."

"I've never seen it before!"

"Very few have seen it in this condition at the Louvre, sweetie. Look, see how there is no security. For the past hundred fifty years or so, it has been locked in a glass case. Here in this time of our human history, it hangs in its glory with nothing between it and us. The colors are also much richer, for they have not had time to fade and crack."

Akhi gazed on in wonder. DaVinci's style was certainly unique, beyond realism. The unfinished objects in the background only highlighted the beauty of the oddly misshapen face. Kelt kept his eyes forward, trying to enjoy the view while he waited for his signal. He tried not to think of the woman approaching from behind in red. He dared not think of the ability he might have to slow her progress. He'd never edited on the fly, in an unconscious way, but he still worried about altering their perceived timeline.

"Oh Kelt, I can't imagine a more beautiful gift than you have given me today. First, Rachmaninoff, and now, da Vinci's most famous painting. It is extraordinary."

"I think that our time is just about up, sweetie," Kelt said as he put his arm around her shoulder and gave her a squeeze. "Yup, there's the woman in red." He had timed her precisely before she was in full sight. He decided that leaving a few seconds early might make the new Doctor Guy Lerner, a bit happier. Besides, Kelt had no idea how long the sessions needed to be. "Okay, Akhi, time to break the link," he said.

"I love you," she said as she was whisked away and Kelt lay gazing into Guy's eyes.

"Now, that's more like it, son! You're even a few seconds early. You are sweating a little more this time though."

"How's your head, Kelt?" Doc asked.

"I've got a headache, that's for sure. But it is quickly dissipating."

"Let me run a quick scan and then let's get a sandwich to eat. I'm really hungry."

"You'll hold it down this time, Doc?" Guy demanded.

"Yes, I feel much better now. I could really go for one of those chicken sandwiches. We don't get much of that in the bunker and I cherish every morsel."

"Make sure you do cherish every morsel doc, I don't like crumbs floating in my airspace," Guy winked.

"My, aren't we persnickety?" Dr. Masurwosky replied.

Guy smiled back to assure the doctor that he was only joking. The doctor was not amused.

"Pass me a couple of sandwiches, would you, Guy?" I'm feeling weak," Kelt said.

"You do look a bit pale. Let me check your blood sugar," the doctor said as he pricked Kelt's arm and sucked the blood into a tester. "Hmm, it is a bit low. Here, drink some apple juice."

"We have apple juice? I didn't know we had any left!"

"I saved my rations, Kelt, for a special moment. You deserve it. Enjoy," Guy said.

Kelt drank slowly and savored every sip with pleasure. It had been over two years since he'd had an apple juice.

*****

"We're going to run over a little bit this time… again. I've advised everyone to expect it. I've asked them to give us 22 minutes," Kelt said as he pushed Akhi into her seat. "It's Rostroprovich playing the Saint-Saëns cello concerto. I've always wanted to play it and may never be able to do so," Kelt explained as the famous cellist attacked the intro with absolute conviction.

This time Akhi just sat in wonder as Rostroprovich's hand moved so gracefully up and down the fingerboard, as the notes shot out in quick sequence. The tone of his instrument was deep and mellow. Both Akhi and Kelt were mesmerized by the passion of the music. And all too soon, it ended.

"I love you too, sweetie," Kelt said as he broke the link.

*****

Kelt awoke in a full sweat. Guy was wiping his forehead.

"One more time, Guy, just once more. We have five hours and twenty minutes and just one more time. Then we'll be through and can go home," Kelt said with an almost drunken stupor.

"Look, kiddo, if you don't start talking normal within five hours, we're putting a stop to this. You've already hit the entire globe with this mind ray thing of yours."

"We haven't a solid hit on China and Australia, Guy. The cone has hit the Earth at an oblique angle. I want to be sure that the Chinese and Australians survive too!"

"Five hours, kiddo."

*****

Akhi was soaking wet from perspiration. She awoke to discover an IV drip had been sunk into a left arm vein.

"Her brain scan still looks pretty good," her doctor said.

"Akhi, are you okay?"

"Daddy, what are you doing here?"

"I'm your father, pumpkin and I'm worried about you. Look, I'm not here to give you a lecture. I'm just concerned. I know you have one more session left. Do you feel up to it?"

"Not now, Daddy. Perhaps I'll feel better in a couple hours."

"Well, let's make sure you feel okay, before you do this again, okay? Promise?"

"Okay, Daddy. Now everyone, please leave the room. Amanda, please stay." Everyone filed out as Amanda lingered by Akhi's bedside. "Why did you tell him, Amanda?"

"He's your father, Akhi. He needed to be with you, to support you, to worry for you. Most of us should be so lucky. It was my call."

"Thanks Amanda. You are a good friend."

"Aldo is also here. He's in the next room. I haven't told him everything, but I've asked him to step in just in case you can't break the link. He's become very gifted in telepathy, from what I've been told."

"He is. Amanda, I'm so sorry we didn't bring you in sooner when we hatched this hair-brained plan. We don't even know if it will work. Kelt says we'll get our greatest success if we act now."

"He's right Akhi. We know of many biological reasons for seeds to lie dormant. Some have been dormant for centuries. Some get stuck in a dry place, others need certain temperatures and combinations of moisture and sunlight... I imagine that there will be many such dormant seeds in the southern hemisphere. The spring crops will be sprouting shortly in the northern hemisphere. In fact, they've already started in the lower latitudes and just as soon as they sprout, they wither and die from the virus. Kelt was right to try this. I know that it sounds highly improbable that a mental connection can alter DNA in this fashion. I certainly can't get my head around it. The results are self-evident, around the base in Nevada. Hopefully, you two will succeed. I'm wishing for it with all my heart."

*****

"Oh Kelt, this place is ugly! Where are we?"

"Remember when I took you to the waters of Babylon two nights ago? Well, this is what it looked like ten years ago."

"How could it be so ugly? Why have you brought us here?"

"I had planned on a casual trip on the Nile by the newly constructed pyramid of Kufu. This was my backup plan. I figured we could be here, talk about my dream of settling here, and then leave. I figured that you wouldn't want to stay here too long. I agree that it is pretty ugly."

"I thought there had to be some logic in your choice," she grinned showing her perfect teeth.

"I figure we can start some farming north of the city. The land is already cleared there. They've been farming for centuries after all. The canals are in place and are easy to operate. The Tigris and Euphrates rivers will provide all the water we'll need. It's simple farming without all the hassles."

"I suppose that I can envision it, Kelt. What will we do with the ugly city, the refineries, and the cement walls?"

"We'll build some giant crunching machines of course. I've actually got some solid ideas for robotics that will demolish the ruins, extract the metals and grind everything else to dust. We can dig big holes in the desert and bury it. Akhi, we can bring this place back to the beautiful grasslands I showed you."

"With farms," she added.

"Yes, with some farms."

"Akhi, I've wanted to ask you this for some time."

"Not here, not now, Kelt," she responded bluntly.

"But, you don't even know what I want to ask," Kelt asked, obviously hurt.

"This place is not real, Kelt. Ask me when we are together for real. I do know what you want to ask. Now is not the time."

"You are a woman of astute wisdom, my love. Even though this may be our last chance to spend any resemblance of time together for a few years. I can wait."

Akhi smiled at him. She realized how he must feel. He was more emotional than she was. It wasn't that she was detached and he was in puppy love heaven. She could see his emotions ran very deep and sincere. He had told her that this process worked because of heartfelt emotions.

"Is it your love for me that made the seeds sprout, Kelt?"

"I can't say that it is love, sweetie. I know that my emotions play a strong role in the outcome of the equations.

I don't discount your feelings at all, either, Akhi. For they strengthen mine significantly. Perhaps I'll learn enough to know why this all works. For now, we'll just have to accept that it did work twice, and hope that this current venture does the impossible."

The two sat in silence, watching the landscape. Kelt could envision what could be created here. Akhi wondered if she had been too harsh with Kelt.

"Kelt, my legs sting!"

Kelt scanned the horizon for the blue truck that was to have appeared on the road at the twenty-minute timeline. Only the cab was visible through the shimmering light of the summer heat. It had stopped!

"Break the connection now, Akhi! Do it now!"

"I can't Kelt. I want to stay here with you just a little more. My legs sting, Kelt!"

"Someone is trying to wake you, Akhi. Break the link!"

*****

"Akhi, this is Aldo, can you hear me?"

"I'm here with Kelt, Aldo. I am safe."

"No you are not Akhi. You are sweating profusely and we see swelling of your brain. You must break the link."

"Really?"

"Yes, my dear. Open your eyes and come back to me."

"Okay Aldo," Akhi said verbally as she opened her red eyes. She was soaking wet and shivering cold to the bone. She looked down at her legs. Her flight suit had been removed and red welts covered her skin.

"Wa... wa... what happened?"

"You wouldn't wake, Akhi, we were slapping your legs hoping that you would come out of it. The link lasted 90 minutes. We were afraid we had lost you!" Amanda sobbed.

"Is Kelt okay? He could have left me, but he didn't. He kept trying to get me to break off, but I wouldn't listen."

"Listen honey, Guy left their position in space well over an hour ago. They are on a fast track back to Nelby Station. They should get here within three hours."

"Did Kelt come out of it?"

"No, he's still unconscious, Akhi. Dr. Masurwosky says he has an embolism and brain swelling. We'll get him back here and under the best medical care we can offer."

"Oh Daddy, it's my fault. I insulted him and then kept him when we should have broken the link." Akhi's red eyes flowed with tears. Her nose filled with mucus. She sobbed uncontrollably. "Why did I not let him ask his question? I know he wants to marry me. I want to marry him. What difference would it have made?" she quietly sobbed to herself.

As she sat crying on her bed surrounded by her closest family on Pacificus, someone opened the bathroom door to let the cats out. They had grown considerably in recent weeks. They both jumped onto the bed, tipping it from the floor momentarily on one side with their weight, Chanto to her right, Freia to her left. Each cat tried to comfort her in its own way. Akhi swatted at them to go away, but they refused in beloved confusion. Freia laid her head in Akhi's lap. Chanto snuggled her ear. She relented and pulled both of them closer to herself, one in each arm, and continued her sobbing lament.

43- Wake up!

They tried for several minutes to wake him with no results.

"Strap yourself into your flight deck couch, doctor."

"I have a patient to take care of!"

"Listen Doc, we're taking the fast track home. You'll not even be able to lift your arms. Strap yourself in now!" Guy commanded.

While the doctor struggled with his harness, Guy made a quick check on Kelt to make sure he was strapped in securely, and that the medical equipment was firmly attached to the floor. Guy pulled the IV drip and stowed the supplies in a locker. He knew that the fluids might be critical, but so was time and he didn't need anything falling on Kelt's head during the trip back. After making sure everything was secure, he quickly pulled himself to the flight deck. He set the coordinates into the controlling pad and commanded the vessel to move to an acceleration of 4 g's. The welcome return of gravity was of some comfort to the doctor for the first minute or two, but when the craft reached the intended acceleration, he was screaming that he couldn't breathe.

"Here," Guy slapped a button over the flight couch and an oxygen mask fell down. "You can breathe now," Guy said with an irritating scratch in his voice. He then took the flight pad and secured it to the Velcro straps in front of the doctor on the dash. "This is our X-Y vector. Make sure we stay on this highlighted path. This is our Z vector. Make sure this green triangle stays over the red circle. See the numbers on each graph? Those indicate our range and should remain identical. If they change and become different, let me know."

"What are you going to do?"

"I'm going to take this spare flight couch apart."

"Pacificus, this is Dr. Masurwosky, can you please give us an update on Dr. Richmond?"

"Yes, Dr. Masurwosky, this is Amanda Perry. Akhi appears to be in a coma, we cannot awaken her. We've been slapping her legs, making loud noises, and pinching her. She seems to react to these efforts, but she remains comatose."

"Please keep us posted, Amanda. We have a similar problem with Dr. Nelby."

"We will, Doctor."

Guy had relieved the flight couch of four bolts in the backrest. The backrest clunked to the floor. Guy took a box cutter to the fabric and began tearing away at the stuffing. He glanced at the control pad, and recalled he hadn't given the good doctor instructions on the deceleration phase of their flight.

"Crap," he thought as he pulled himself toward the flight pad where he could see. "I've only got five minutes." He pulled himself back to the demolition in progress, and secured the jumble to the seat of the flight couch, which was still bolted to the deck. He managed to climb back into his couch and strap in, just as he felt weightlessness overcome the deck. The ship flipped and started the deceleration process.

Guy fumbled at his harness, trying to gain advantage before the increasing deceleration made it harder for him to move. The harness clicked open, and he fell to the floor of the flight deck. Guy crawled back to the chair he had been taking apart. 13 minutes later, he finally had what he wanted. Two steel tubes held up each side of the seat back, he held one in his hand.

"What are you going to do with that?" asked Dr. Masurwosky.

"You don't want to know," Guy said curtly.

He pulled himself to the ladder to go down to the next deck where Kelt was strapped in. He wondered if he could get himself down without falling. He also considered the trip back up the ladder. He had to try. He slipped his legs over the hole and they fell with great weight against the ladder, nearly sucking him into the hole. He managed to grab the top rung securely with one hand, while he held on to the steel tube. He descended slowly and carefully.

"I feel like I'm carrying 800 pounds," he thought, but acknowledged that it wasn't *quite* that much. After his grueling trip down, he managed to stumble slowly to Kelt's side. The sniffer showed an active image of his brain. Guy was no doctor, but he had seen several images of Kelt's brain today. It was obvious that it was swelling.

*****

Akhi's visage changed slightly. She warmed up to Kelt and touched him in a more intimate manner.

"No Kelt, I just want to be here with you. I want to hold you and share your vision."

Akhi had left the connection. What remained was what Kelt wanted to see. His desire to leave his waters of Babylon diminished. All he wanted was to hold her and talk about the future.

"Look we can plant some fig trees right over there."

"Yes, that sounds lovely."

"And we'll build an adobe house. It will be cool inside."

"I like that idea too."

"You'd live in a mud house, Akhi?"

"Yes, my darling."

Kelt had doubts about her answer.

"Will you marry me?"

"Of course, my darling."

Kelt now knew he was trapped. This was not Akhi. He knew that's what he'd want her to say. It's not what she would say. What had happened to her? Had she successfully cut the connection? If so, was he trapped in his own mind? He reached out to contact Aldo, but he received no response. He was ensnared in his own imperfect vision from which he could not escape.

"Guy! Help me!" Kelt screamed at the top of his lungs. They were virtual lungs, not those of his own. His own lungs struggled to breathe under the crushing weight of deceleration.

Guy approached Kelt. He considered briefly, what he was doing. He looked at the sniffer monitor and Kelt's brain had continued to swell, in just a few moments since he had last checked the monitor. "Yes, I must do this," he thought as he raised the steel pole above his head and brought it crashing down on Kelt's left shin.

Guy was sickened by the snapping of Kelt's leg. The fracture split his skin and the bone protruded several centimeters. The bleeding was light, but still pooled around his foot on the floor and the old car seat.

"Owe, that hurth!" Kelt said drunkenly as he slowly opened his eyes. "Did you hith me, Guy? My leg hurth."

"Don't look at it son."

"It hurth, Guy. Oh, ith really hurthing now. I can hardie stan the pain. Oh please, Godth, Guy, hep me, thith hurth so bath! I canth stan ith!" As Kelt regained his consciousness, the magnitude of pain assaulted his reality.

Guy opened the compartment where he had stowed the medical supplies. The doctor had prepared a syringe of Demerol in case of an emergency. Guy slammed the syringe into Kelt's thigh above his injury.

"Lay back, Kelt, you are going to be okay. Hold still okay?"

"But Guy, there's some ting serrrealosly wron I hur so bath."

"Lay back, make yourself comfortable. We're on our way to Nelby Station. You'll be fine Kelt."

"Pwomiss, Guy?"

"I promise, son."

Guy pulled a long bandage from the medical kit and tied Kelt's head to the headrest of the seat. He checked the sniffer feed. It looked like the swelling was in check. He then made the long laborious climb up the short ladder, and back into his flight couch.

"What did you do to him, Mr. Lerner?"

"I broke his leg."

"How could you be…"

"Drop it Doc, he's come out of it. It worked."

"I'll be dashed," the doctor managed to say through his sagging jowls.

44- Kelt is back

"He's going to be alright, baby," Rick said as he shooed Freia aside and embraced his daughter from the side. He was in surgery for quite some time, and they'll keep him sedated for a couple of days."

"Did they do brain surgery, Daddy?" Akhi asked in a trembling voice.

"Yes, sweetheart. He had a slight embolism, and they had to release some of the pressure. That is looking good they say. He also had surgery on his leg. It was shattered pretty bad, right about here," Rick explained as he pointed to his own shin.

"How did he break his leg, Daddy?"

"Guy broke it to get his attention, and it worked. He was under your spell for a half hour after we got you back, Akhi."

"Oh Daddy, I was so mean to him before I left. I can never forgive myself."

"He had a brief moment of consciousness after the surgery, Akhi. He told the doctor that was how he knew he had to escape. The Akhi he was with was acting differently, submissive. He knew it wasn't you. So, my little one, you helped save his life, in some sense."

"Is his brain okay? I can't bear the thought of hurting him like I did. Oh please, there can't be any brain damage."

"There is some swelling, but like I said, they'll keep him sedated for a couple of days to give him a chance to let that swelling go down. And as far as his leg goes, well, he'll be up hobbling around in a week or so. Within six weeks, he'll be as good as new."

Akhi started to cry. Tears flooded her cheeks as she embraced her father.

45- Plants

Kelt had not been healing as well as had been expected. His brain was still swollen. He had made progress to be sure, but he was still kept under sedation and careful observation. Guy sat in a chair near his bedside, where he had spent most of his four days since arriving at Nelby Station. He spent time reading stories aloud, checking the monitors and the image of Kelt's brain constantly shown above his headboard. Guy sought no entertainment for himself. He was heartsick. He wondered if Kelt would ever be the same again. Guy had seen the effects of concussions in the ranks of his own men during his military years. Kelt's injury was similar to a concussion. Some of his guys never seemed right, some were totally disabled, and a few died. He felt that he'd never be able to forgive himself if Kelt didn't pull through.

"Guy, pick up your pad," Amanda commed.

"Hey Amanda, what's new?"

"Only the most glorious sight mankind has ever seen, Guy. Have you seen what's going on dirtside today?"

"Did it work?" Guy managed to ask.

"In full luxurious living color, Guy! The world is rebounding. Plants are growing on every continent. Even South America and get this, Antarctica has thriving plant life. South America isn't as lush as the other continents to be sure, but I'm told that many of the wonderful rare woods *will* return. We'll have crops this year too, Guy!"

Kelt mumbled a few unintelligible words, which grabbed Guy's attention.

"Hold on Amanda, Kelt is awake."

"What did you say, Kelt?"

"I toll you it wud worth," he managed to say before he fell back to sleep.

"Amanda! Kelt just told me that he knew it would work! Then he fell back asleep. I think he's still got good ole Kelt in there, Amanda!"

"I'm so pleased, Guy. I'm so proud of you," she said somewhat seductively.

Guy liked this. He could learn to love this woman. "Who knows? Perhaps? … someday," he thought.

Kelt stirred yet again and opened his eyes.

"Hey Amanda, thanks for the update, Kelt just opened his eyes. Update Akhi for me… and Kelt, I'll talk to you later."

"I toll you it ud worth, Guy," Kelt tried to say again more clearly as he blinked his eyelids in an attempt to move some of the sleepy time crud out of the way.

"Here, let me help you with that," Guy said as he grabbed a tissue and cleaned Kelt's eyes.

"Thanes, Guy. Tha heps alaw."

Over the next two hours, Kelt came around fully and his speech became clear. He asked for a cranberry juice. He received reconstituted powdered orange drink instead. He didn't care. It was cold and it was sweet. It picked him up.

"Guy, I've got one splitting headache!"

"Yeah, kid, you've been down four days and sedated. You nearly killed yourself on that little expedition."

"But we saved the planet didn't we, Guy?"

"It looks like it, son."

"Is Akhi okay?"

"She's just fine, son and she's aching to talk to you. Do you think you are up to it?"

"I don't care how I feel, Guy, I'm awake and she's the first person I want to talk to… well, I'm glad you've been here. I've known you were with me the whole time Guy. Did you know that?"

"No, Kelt, I didn't," Guy answered, as his eyes got blurry.

"You're not going soft on me are you…? Sta… Guy?"

"I told you that I'd never forgive you, if you used *that* name… I'm glad you got your thoughts straight."

303

"Thanks for reading to me. I enjoyed the stories."

"You actually heard them?"

"All four days' worth. Thanks again. Now how about that video link with my sweetie?"

"Right away, sir," Guy responded with the greatest respect.

46- Looming OAE

"I'm sorry Kelt, but Shannon and I aren't trained for this. Our climate expert, Dr. Nathan Andrews didn't make it up before Africa was bombed. We've literally been figuring this out as we go. But, facts are facts. We have some serious problems. I wish that we would have known sooner," Amanda advised.

"So, you're telling me that even though we've got new plant life around the world, the Earth is still self-destructing?" Kelt asked incredulously as he moved his leg to release some of the building pain.

"Um, yes. There have been all sorts of scientific papers published over the past five or six decades. Some of them are quite bogus, but many reach similar conclusions, and they are based on real science, Kelt. The oceans are becoming anoxic."

"Does that mean that they are losing their oxygen? I remember that from somewhere. I thought that the problem was global climate change."

"Yes, Kelt, anoxic means that the water can hold no more oxygen. And no, global climate change is not what we are worried about here. Climate change and an anoxic event like this can be related, but don't' have to be. Both can be related to excessive CO2 levels, however. Shannon and I are concerned that we are facing a world-wide OAE or Oceanic Anoxic Event caused by excessive CO2 in the atmosphere."

"And the fish will die and all the survivors who depend on them will perish." Kelt thought aloud. "How is this happening?"

"Yes," Shannon answered, "We are now faced with an Extinction Level Event. There is no question. We had anticipated huge amounts of carbon dioxide released from the decaying humus on forest floors and the rest of the land's biomass. We had also predicted that at some point, within just a few years, the atmosphere could no longer sustain human life. We had not considered the fact that people down there would burn the forests to drive out the wildlife. Neither did we anticipate wide ranging ecological effects until we started seeing large dinoflagellate blooms in the oceans."

"Dino flagettes?" Kelt asked for clarification.

"Dinoflagellates, Kelt. These dinoflagellates are little plankton that consume CO_2, much less efficiently than other types of plankton. The last time these plankton were dominant, was 55 million years ago, for a period of about 225,000 years, a time of massive extinctions. It didn't take long before we saw the connection with CO_2 levels in our research. Shoot... anyone could have looked it up online if they wanted. It's just that we don't use our "online" so much anymore... So much is missing now. In any case, we totally missed it. Amanda and I focus on little bugs not ecosystems. It was logical that we'd miss the implications to some degree. I must admit, we've screwed up big time on this one, Kelt. I'm very sorry."

"Shannon, I don't want you and Amanda to beat yourselves up on this. I don't consider it a screw up, in any way. So puh-lease, set your minds at ease and let's deal with this. Okay?"

"Yeah, thanks for the pep talk," Shannon replied.

"Okay, go ahead, I'm sorry for interrupting," Kelt grinned slightly.

"CO_2 levels need to be well above current levels before humans will start displaying physical distress. At 6000 ppm (parts per million), we would only last 30 minutes or so. At the time we first performed our measurements, the atmosphere had an average level of just over 600 ppm. We are now topping 900 ppm of CO_2. I don't have to tell you that you are in for some incredibly bad weather systems down there."

"Yeah, we're already experiencing them. We've had a lot of rain in the Nevada desert. Lately, it's been like a bloody rain forest here without trees," Kelt added.

"We've used some of your floaters with instruments and checked oxygen levels in oceans and other bodies of water around the world. The results are staggering, Kelt. Some of these water systems are completely anoxic in several areas and completely devoid of all animal life," Shannon told him.

"We just can't get a break, can we? What more can we do to save this damned planet? You know, sometimes I think it might just be easier to shoot myself and be done with it." Kelt had been on a constant high since recovering from his trip into space, even though he was still hobbling around on crutches. It appeared as though everything would turn around, now that the planet had been repopulated with newly sprouted seeds. This new revelation brought his intellectual prowess to its knees. "So fill me in on the details… and please, give me the armchair version."

"Well," Amanda began, "I'm not sure exactly where to start. Hmm, let's see… Well, we already know that the CO_2 count was more than 600 ppm before the infection started. For most of mankind's history, it had leveled around 270 to 280 ppm. We were on our way to poisoning the atmosphere and the oceans all by ourselves. Many researchers considered the tipping point at around 960 ppm."

"Tipping point for what?" Kelt asked.

"We are about to find out, Kelt," Amanda admonished. "The problem is made worse by the water runoff from the land masses which no longer can keep their topsoil. The new plant life is not mature enough to hold all the topsoil in place. Phosphates and nitrates which we've been using as fertilizers for decades, will run into the oceans and further increase the explosion of plankton growth near the surface The existence of these plankton and their waste products will create anoxic conditions lower in the seas. Not only that but the anoxic waters will become colder and the oceanic conveyer belts will shut down. I'm sure you know that they have been key in keeping our weather patterns stable, for as long as mankind has lived on the Earth."

"So is it all our fault… I mean did we cause this?" Kelt asked.

"To some degree, Kelt. Had we, as a species, been more careful, this would have been delayed a year or two after the viral infection. So, yes, we've had a part to play. We should keep in mind that if it were not for the virus, we would have had a few more decades to work through the problems and provide solutions. Now, we don't have that luxury," Amanda advised.

"If we can bring CO_2 levels down, will the problem go away?" asked Kelt.

"Not immediately. We may arrest further anoxic conditions in the Earth's waters. We should be able to keep the oceanic conveyor belts running if we act in time. We've also been reviewing research on seeding the areas covered with that plankton with iron dust. We'll do some testing on that… the key thing we need to do is lower the CO_2 levels. Even if we accomplish that, we still believe that a cooling trend will ensue for at least a few years."

"We're in a cooling trend? I thought that it was getting warmer. It's supposed to be winter time in the Southern Hemisphere, but it is unseasonably warm there."

"Kelt, with the loss of plant life, the Earth's surface has become warmer and will become warmer still for a while. The heat will cause more water evaporation, which means more cloud cover, which means sunlight will be blocked and that will ultimately lead to cooling. That's why you are having so much rain there in Nevada. So yes, we estimate a cooling trend will take place. We aren't experienced climatologists, remember. This is only our best guess."

"This is all very convoluted to me. Up is down and black is white. I'm used to numerical answers that make sense and there seem to be none here. Can we bring Akhi in on this conversation? I'd like her perspectives," Kelt asked.

"I'm already online, Kelt. I didn't want you to get distracted while Amanda and Shannon explained the problem," Akhi said as she enabled the video portion of her link.

"That's sneaky," Kelt said.

"I know how you think," Akhi said grinning. "I didn't want to distract you."

"How can you grin at a moment like this? This bloody mess is worse than the viral infection."

"Not quite, love."

"Really?" Kelt asked in astonishment. "It seems to me that this problem is much larger than the viral infection."

"It is, Kelt," Amanda started, "This time we just might be able take immediate action. We already have the science. Remember, to keep it simple, we need to knock down the CO_2 levels to mean historic levels. The Earth will hopefully resurrect its pleasant environment we have enjoyed for thousands of years… in time."

"But the scope... It's just as big or bigger," Kelt whined.

"Indeed it is, Kelt," Akhi started, "but we have someone up here that thinks we have a chance to turn it around. We have to try."

"Who is it? Do I know this person?" Kelt demanded.

"Our primary chemical engineer, a Dr. Paul P. Einstein." Amanda informed with some trepidation knowing the name might spark jocularity.

"Einstein? Really? You've got to be kidding me," Kelt said with great astonishment.

"That's his name, buddy," Akhi admonished, "he thinks that we can build atmospheric processors that will crack CO_2 into its constituent molecules, oxygen and carbon. We could harvest the carbon for our Buckyball projects and release the oxygen back into the atmosphere. He's had a draft design finished for years. He can send it down to you within a few minutes."

"How could he just happen to have a CO_2 cracking plant design ready to go?" Kelt asked bewildered.

"Unlike most of us, this guy knew what would eventually happen. He planned for the future, Kelt," Akhi flatly stated.

"Well, that's nice to know. Okay, I've just received the design. Give me a moment or two, ladies, if you don't mind. Kelt opened the folder and picked the three key files he wanted to view. All he wanted to see for now was the cracking engine and power requirements. He was sure that they'd have to redesign everything else, so that these plants could be made by robotics.

Amanda privately commed Akhi. "Is this normal? Does he do this often?"

"Yup. Amanda, he's a genius, just let him spin in his chair as long as he needs to. It's better to watch that, than to wait for him when he lies down... that is incredibly boring," Akhi smiled.

Kelt took in the design, compartmentalized its constituent components, disassembled it, and reassembled it in modules easily produced by robotics. He then visualized a support structure to support the cracking plant vertically. Yes, the spinner technology could do this. All they needed were more solar plants in orbit around the sun and three or four tons of his carbon matrix per plant. The metals, copper, steel, gold, and silver could be easily scavenged, now that no one cared about such things. They would need over five hundred thousand plants. "Holy crap," he thought.

Kelt stopped spinning and rubbed his eyes. Intense thinking had given him a slight headache. He had still not recovered fully from his venture into space a few weeks before. His leg itched.

"We can do this," Kelt announced. "The biggest problem that I can envision, is that we'll need a half million of them, right?"

"Ah, yes, Kelt. That's a bit high perhaps," Akhi said solemnly.

"And how much time do we have to get them built?" Kelt asked.

"We don't know, Kelt. I'd have them up and running tomorrow if I could," Amanda started, "We can waste no time on this."

"I understand. Let me spend some time with our Dr. Einstein. I need to make significant changes to his machine so they are easier to build. I'll need to delegate tasks to others though, so someone please take notes on this and pass them around.

"We are going to need millions of tons of my carbon matrix hopper mix. We have nearly a thousand tons at the old plant in China. Have Rick call the Premier and get him onboard. We'll be building these things all around the world, I suspect, so they'll be needing them as well. We need that hopper mix to get the project started.

"We'll not be getting enough carbon out of the first several plants to do squat, so we are going to need another easy carbon source. Akhi, I'd like you to check into sending out a sphere to Phobos or Deimos, and see if you can bring back a load of some of that black gold on the surface. Perhaps one of the Mars colonies can help. We'll see if there's any oil sitting in any of the big refineries dirtside.

"Ask Rick to call the President and advise him that we will be liquidating the gold from Fort Knox. We'll need it for the collectors.

"We need to start building solar collectors in unprecedented numbers to power these crackers. We will also need several hundred shuttles

"Get your logistics teams together and have them draft up a plan to feed work crews. We are going to need lots of labor, and we'll need to feed them. There's not a person alive on this planet that will not accept a job for food. We'll need boats and experienced fishermen.

"Get Jin and Lee working on robots to disassemble buildings, to extract the copper pipe. We'll see if we can't find some supplies dirtside, but we'll need those machines.

"Get the logistics team to select 10 sites where we can start construction. We'll need people, food, standard construction supplies, like cement, rebar, steel studs, and the like. And don't forget heavy construction equipment like backhoes, tamping equipment, trucks, etc.

"I think that's a good list to start. We can add details as we go. I'll feed the logistics team exactly what we'll need within... let's say... 24 hours or so, assuming our Dr. Einstein can pull an all-nighter with me. Oh... one more thing. I don't want to be in charge of this project. I'll be working on the CO_2 crackers. Assign the logistics team to work through all the details. I don't want anything to distract me," Kelt finalized.

"I knew I could count on you, Kelt."

"Rick! You sneaky... guy!" Kelt had another word in mind but could not find it within himself to call the big guy a bastard. "I'm not surprised though. It saves me a lot of time and an extra video link. Can we get this organized or not?"

"It's certainly a project greater than the spire program by at least an order of magnitude. We'll pull in workers from around the world. Provided we can keep their bellies full, we might pull it off. I don't want to rain on anyone's parade... it's a real long shot. It will be a worldwide effort," Rick cautioned.

"Perhaps we will finally pull the peoples of the world together in a common cause," mused Kelt. "Now, wouldn't that be a miracle?"

"Indeed it would," Rick agreed.

"Well, team, let's get busy!" Kelt ordered just before he closed his link.

"Wait," Amanda started. "We may be jumping the gun here. I recall a research assistant working on a bacteria project down in the biolab."

"What was she working on, Amanda?"

"HE was working with bacteria, stimulating them with a small electrical current in an attempt to separate potassium from waste products. We use potassium in our crop production."

"So, what's significant about that?" Kelt asked.

"Someone accidently dropped a pencil in his electrically charged fluid tank. When he retrieved it a day later, the writing end of his pencil had a fat bulb of carbon on it. I remember him making a remark to that effect when he pulled it out."

"I'm not sure I understand where you are going with this, Amanda. What is the significance of a fat pencil end?" asked Rick

"Isn't that what we are trying to do? Pull carbon out of the CO2 molecule? You know... make oxygen?"

"Duh," Kelt said as he slapped his forehead. "How could we have let this slip by?"

"Well, it isn't a given, but it's worth a look. Why don't you all continue with your planning? Don't start any real work. Let me drop in and talk to Greg. Does that sound okay? I just don't want to send what's left of humanity to work on massive building projects, if we could more effectively deal with this problem."

"Great, Amanda, you work on that idea and I'll get together with Dr. Einstein."

Kelt knew that he could not get wrapped up in anything else for this project. He quickly made some notes and some rough CAD drawings of his proposed changes to Dr. Einstein's CO2 cracker, and sent them upstairs.

Amanda quickly hurried to the biolab, lower down in the Pacificus spire.

*****

"Akhi"

"Yes, my darling! I didn't expect to hear from you so soon!"

"Yes, sweetie. I've noticed activity from hardened farmers in the Midwest of the US mainland, who are out tilling the soil. We should get them together... in one or two areas where they can be defended. Have the logistics team put areas like these on the highest priority for the cracking facilities. That way we can watch both at the same time, if you know what I mean. If you would, have someone else seek out active farming around the rest of the world. Let's organize this project intelligently. Maybe it's possible to get the crops growing again, and I don't want those people attacked. I hate to be giving you orders, sweetie, and I promise I'll ask nicely next time."

"Kelt, you amaze me. How do you organize so many things in your head, at once, so quickly?"

"You know, Akhi, I don't know if you realized it or not, but I just stuck my foot in my mouth in our meeting. I was too quick to assess without all the facts. I've just learned a valuable lesson. I should take just a little bit more time to gather more information. Sometimes, I wish that I could slow down a bit, and I wish that someone else had these abilities. I feel that I'm at a breaking point at the moment. Somehow, I know I'll get through it. I do have your support, after all. You can't imagine how that keeps me going. Have you changed your mind about my question?"

"When we meet in person, Kelt. Just like I told you before," she answered. "I have to give you a little uncertainty in your life," she said with a bright smile.

"As if I didn't have enough of that already," he grinned back. "I don't know why, but this looming disaster actually has me pumped up. I feel overwhelmed and ready to break, yet... I'm excited. Does that make sense?"

"Not much, Kelt. But I understand. Understanding doesn't need to make sense."

"I love you sweetie."

"I know, Kelt."

47- Dr. Einstein and Greg

"Greg, it's nice to see you again!" Amanda exclaimed as she approached him in the lab. "And who is this?"

"Amanda, I would like to introduce you to Dr. Paul Einstein. Dr. Einstein, this is Dr. Amanda Perry, one of our biologists."

"You do realize that Kelt is going to be looking for you, Paul?"

"Yes, I know. I took a quick look at his sketches and ideas and they are quite good. Greg had given me a call, just moments before Kelt did. I asked Kelt to hold his horses for a couple of hours. I think that we might just have a better solution here."

"Well you know how we discovered this process, accidentally?" Greg asked.

"I was here when you pulled the pencil from the tank, Paul," Amanda grinned.

"Oh, yes. I remember."

"Well I've been working on the process here for the past month or so. I figured that it might provide a redundant solution to our CO_2 scrubbers onboard. I've got a prototype working here," Greg said as he pointed to a lab bench. "After drying out my pencil and sharpening it, I hadn't given it much thought. During the next month, I just couldn't get it out of my mind. I felt that there had to be a practical implementation for this process. It is sort of odd how so many inventions come from mistakes, you know? Remember sticky notes? That was a mistake due to a chemical mix-up in making glue. Since the glue didn't stick very well, someone very bright found another use for it."

"I understand, Greg. Gasoline was another. The primary effort at the time was to produce kerosene to provide fuel for lamps. Gasoline was a byproduct. It wasn't until the automobile came into production that there became a real need for it," Paul added. "So, show us what you have, if you will."

"We are working with variations of photo synthesis based bacteria here. This particular variety occurs in nature and goes super active when given a mild jolt of electricity. The crib notes version is that they crack CO_2 and deposit carbon. If we give them a column of carbon to live on, they deposit the carbon there. The column approach also makes it easy to apply a small current to the population. For some reason, they actually can conduct the current to their little friends and they have a big party, cracking CO_2. As they party on, the column of carbon grows in thickness. Here's my prototype."

Greg pointed to the 25 centimeter tall slender mountain, or was it a tree trunk, growing in an aquarium sized tank?

"You've got to be kidding me," Amanda said with clear astonishment.

"No, Amanda, all we have to do is provide some carbon and a little juice and these things go crazy."

"Can they grow uncontrolled… can they get out of hand and cause other unforeseen problems?" queried Amanda.

"They will pretty much become disorganized, once their electrical current supply is removed. They go back to their own little way of life, if you know what I mean."

"Amazing," commented Paul.

"They'll need a water source, won't they?" Amanda asked.

"Nope, they can pull the water they need right out of the air. If there's any humidity, they have their water. And the way things are dirtside, there isn't anywhere on the planet where the humidity is below ten percent."

"You mentioned photo synthesis, Greg. Does this mean that they will require sunlight?"

"No, Amanda, the electrical current takes care of their energy needs. That means they'll work at night and in very extreme environments. If given enough juice, they can work in extremely cold environments."

316

"What about the heat?" Amanda asked.

"If we can survive it, so can they. They can be cooked if it gets too hot, just like us. The juice can warm them up, but can't cool them down."

"So, how do you provide them with the current?" Amanda asked.

"I've just got a couple of bare wires... Um "electrodes" going to each side of the carbon column, see? I suppose I really should get my scientific jargon in line. Too many people don't take me seriously up here."

Amanda and Paul noted the wires embedded in the monolith from each side. The wires, on the other end, were connected to a small battery.

"They are growing like coral, aren't they?" Amanda stated more than asked.

Greg pointed at some minute dust particles around the base of the black pillar. They were very difficult to distinguish from a day's worth of ordinary house dust.

"Sort of, Amanda. See this dust? It is the corpses of dead bacteria. The column sloughs off everything, but the live bacteria and the carbon they produce."

"Greg, this falls outside the norm of most photosynthetic organisms. Usually, they will store the carbon in their bodies. When they die and are oxidized by bacteria and fungi, the carbon is released back into the atmosphere in the form of CO_2."

"Amanda, it is a fluke. These things literally poop carbon with electrical stimulus. Well maybe it isn't literal. I don't really know where the carbon comes out of 'em, if you know what I mean. They do have a favorite place to do it... on more carbon. I know you've never seen it before. Neither has anyone else. Here, before your very eyes, you can see the evidence."

"How tall could we grow these things?" Paul asked.

"From my experiments with the range of current these little critters need and how much they can share, I'm thinking anywhere from 25 to 30 meters tall."

"Can we look at your notes on that, Greg?" Amanda asked.

"Sure thing."

Greg opened a drawer and pulled forth an engineering notebook, opened it to the right page, and handed it to Amanda and Paul. The notes were exceedingly well organized. Greg seemed a little goofy from the way he talked, but his notes and calculations were impeccable.

"So let's see," Amanda started as she reviewed Greg's estimates of carbon production from a fully developed carbon mound, comparing them to her estimates of the compounding CO_2 disaster looming. She ran the numbers quickly through her head. "We're going to need at least 50,000 of these things to keep the current growth of carbon dioxide in check. How can we build so many?"

"I think that perhaps you missed a decimal," offered Paul. "I've been running the same mental exercise. I'm probably running with a different set of assumptions, and my number is significantly higher than that."

"Please hand me a pencil and paper," Amanda asked Greg politely."

"No need, Amanda, I've got a simulation program I've written. All you need to do is give me the base values. I'm afraid I'm not up to speed on that part of the mix. I've been worried about problems here, on the station and not those of what's going on dirtside."

Greg pulled a computing pad from the top of a loose stack of books and asked Amanda to give him her assumptive numbers.

"Yes, you lost more than a decimal, Amanda. According to the estimates you gave me, we'll need 501,000 carbon piles."

"Ah, but Greg, there is another variable here that we missed," Paul noted

Greg handed the pad to Paul.

"Okay, let's take a look at what I was considering as our base measurements. This value can be decreased and this one needs to be enlarged. There you go, my number is nearly double that of Amanda's estimation."

"Staggering. One million?" Amanda hushed, "Paul, how many of your cracking plants would need to be constructed with your same variables?"

"I figured somewhere in the range of 300,000, Amanda. Those would be very large complex structures with machines consuming large quantities of power."

"Hold on, gentlemen, I'd like to get Kelt in on this. I just can't fathom the scale of this project. Greg, do you have a monitor we can use for video feed? I'd rather not have to use your pad."

"Sure… just over here on the next aisle. Why don't we take a picture of the carbon experiment before we wander over that way, so we can share a visual?"

Paul pointed the pad toward the experiment and snapped a picture, then forwarded it to Kelt.

The three stepped around the end of the aisle to where the monitor was, and keyed in a request for video conference with Kelt. There was no answer. Amanda unclipped her com from her utility belt.

"Kelt, Amanda here, can you share a video feed with us right away? We've got some interesting developments."

"Sure, Amanda, just give me a minute, pass me your station number, and I'll find a quiet spot here and call you back," Kelt answered.

For the next fifteen minutes, the three scientists on-board Pacificus related the information and their impressions about the experiment. Amanda raised concerns over the significant number of CO_2 cracking piles that would be required.

"Amanda, you've got the wrong perspective here. Yes, that's a lot. I can't fathom doing this with Paul's machines. I may have sounded upbeat on getting started on *that* project earlier, but I had great doubt that we'd be able to succeed. I've been running some of my own numbers down here as well. Although my assumptions vary from both you and Paul, my estimations come in around 700,000 units or so. We haven't considered what it will take to bring

319

atmospheric levels back to where they should be. That could take millions."

"We haven't factored what the new plant life might bring to the mix," Amanda said.

"I would say that is unimportant, Amanda, for this reason. We know we need to do this. We know we need hundreds of thousands of cracking stations. Fortunately, this experiment has resolved many manpower issues. We can do much of the work with robots, floaters, and Buckyball Fullerine line. Shoot, for now, let's just drill some shallow holes and drop a Buckyball line from a floater, provide some battery power, and coat those lines with Greg's slime. We can probably get ten of them up and running by the end of the day tomorrow, provided you can drop us some of your goo, Greg. Can you do a simple unmanned drop?"

"With floaters or parachutes, Kelt?"

"We'll need the floaters for the cracking piles, so let's plan on those."

"Yes, we can pack up enough to get 10 stations started. An insulated package will make it down just fine. Just make sure to give our goo some air as soon as you retrieve it."

"We're familiar with the procedure, Greg. We've been growing algae goo down here from a similar drop."

"Really, what for?" Greg asked.

"For food, Greg."

"I'm sorry, Kelt, I didn't know things were that bad for you down there."

"Well, whatever you can imagine, it's a lot worse than that, for most people dirtside. Let us know as soon as you can make the drop. Amanda, can you ask Akhi to set up two potential drop sites? One for Nevada Base, the other for our friends in the military base, up north. The military base will be our most likely site if I can set it up. They have some heavy machinery where we don't. They've also been treating us really nice lately. And Greg…"

"Yes, Kelt?"

"Make sure you send us some instructions as soon as you can, okay?"

"The process is new, Kelt. I'm afraid that I've only constructed one of these, and it is just a few centimeters tall."

"Send me what you've got, Greg... okay?"

"Right away, sir."

There was that sir thing again. Greg had been calling him Kelt just a few moments before.

48- China commits

"Rick, we need to start up our Buckyball production facility in China," Kelt said over the video link.

"I've received a short brief on the CO2 cracking piles that are being proposed. I think I see where you are going with this. You need carbon lines. You need floaters to hang them from. Am I correct?"

"Yes, sir. That's exactly what I had in mind. As you know, our other choice is massive construction projects to build Einstein's cracking towers. They'll consume an inordinate amount of resources and quite frankly, I know for a fact that we'll never be able to come up with the manpower to build them. We have to learn how to do this with robotics. I'd like to set up a few manually, as soon as possible. The robotics can come later. Before we can get this thing going, we need some carbon line to hang from floaters…"

"And that's where the production facility in China comes in," offered Rick.

"We've got thousands of metric tons in carbon sitting in stock there. From what I've been able to find out, the factory is for the most part still intact. All that has been destroyed are the food court vending machines."

"That video is a few month's old, Kelt."

"What might have changed since then? The factory isn't near the coastal areas. There is no recent evidence of people around from what we can see from our floater cams. I think it's worth a shot. I'd like permission to send in a team and start it up. We can take in a bucket load of Dimensional Conduits and have the plant powered up within an hour after we get there."

"Kelt, I'd like to go through the Chinese government to enlist their support. I've wanted to get this done for some time. I don't want a firefight down there. You may not know it, but there is still a very well organized army in China. You might just get away with firing up the plant. But, then again… well who knows.

Besides, this may be a first step in working together. The entire world has never agreed to work together on anything. This could be a first."

"I hate politics," Kelt murmured.

"I do too, Kelt. But, I've learned they are a necessary part of getting anything done. I've never told you this, but when you were first assigned to work alone, I made a conscious decision to keep you away from all politics to keep you focused. That's why you worked in an isolated office. Looking back, I suppose that I should have brought you in sooner on the bigger picture. In the beginning, you were prodigious in your output."

"Now, I finally understand your decisions, Rick. I suppose I should thank you. I've always wondered why you didn't trust me. It's nice to learn that was not the case."

"Kelt, give me a few minutes. Let me see if we can get into that Beijing facility with the full blessing of the Chinese."

"Sounds good, Rick. Say, while you are pursuing that path, I'm going to check and see what's left out on the space elevator, that might give us an earlier start."

"Excellent idea, Kelt."

"Thanks. Let me know as soon as you can about what the Chinese say."

"Will do, Dr. Nelby," Rick smiled.

"Hey Rick, before you go… how's Akhi getting along? I talk to her every day, but I'd like to know what her father thinks."

"She's fine. I think that those cats were a blessing in disguise. She's happier now than she has been in months."

"I'm glad to hear that, Rick. Thanks."

"Kelt, let me cut this feed, and I'll see if I can't contact Tse Jiang, who just happens to be the new General Secretary and a personal acquaintance from way back."

*****

"Mr. Secretary, Rick Carter here. I'm glad to have been able to contact you!" Rick said.

323

He had placed a call through the Chinese Politburo network, which was still up and running. The fact that Jiang could take the call also meant a couple of things. First, he wasn't worried about the bugs and second, he was still in power.

"It's good to talk to you, Mr. Carter. I want to thank you for your advice. All went well. I did gather the assembly together. There was no violence. My generals succumbed to my pleas for peace. The submarines have been recalled, and our forces are no longer performing missile exercises. I must have made a "helluva speech," as you Americans might say."

"I knew you had it in you, Jiang. You're a good man."

"Thank you, Rick."

"Say, Jiang, we have a situation developing that is a further complication presented to us by the plant killing virus."

"But Rick, the seeds are sprouting around the world, are they not?"

"Yes, they are, but this new plant life will not mature quickly enough to prevent our next ecological disaster. The oxidation of the world's dead biomass is happening much faster than the new plants can compensate. The oceans are turning anoxic."

"What exactly does that mean, Rick?"

"Essentially, in a nutshell, it means they can no longer sustain life. The water cannot bear enough oxygen for most animal life to survive."

"So, what does that mean to us?"

"It means a second Apocalypse, Jiang. I realize that we aren't even through the first one. Millions more will starve before we can ramp up food production. Animal life in the oceans is beginning to die from what they are telling me, is an Oceanic Anoxic Event. We won't recover if our atmosphere is poisoned. We'll still be able to breathe, but if there is no food in the oceans and none from the land... well, you can certainly envision the inevitable outcome.

"This sounds hopeless, Rick. We have one disaster after another. Is there anything that can be done?"

"We'd like to try a new process, Jiang. We don't know if it will work yet. But, if it does, I can assure you that your country will share in the technology. We have made a single prototype of what we're calling a CO2 cracking pile. We'd like to move to our second stage where we construct production models. We will of course, set up several in a populated area of your choosing in our first tests. We need access to my carbon plant just outside of Beijing. It was shut down shortly after I left the country. It has raw materials that we desperately need to get this project started. As you know, we could probably move in and start up the facility without anyone knowing. No one is alive in that area. I wanted to talk to you first. Not only am I asking for your permission, but also for your assistance."

"Can you send me some supporting materials, Mr. Carter? I'd like to review your request with the committee. I assure you that it will not take long. I can call a meeting together right away. I would also like you available on video link to answer any questions."

"Yes, Mr. Secretary, that sounds most appropriate. I'm sending you copies of our notes right now. I'm sorry they are not in the form of a more formal presentation. We are in a hurry to get started, if you understand."

"Very well, I'll get back to you in a few minutes," Jiang responded.

49- Buckeyballs

"This timetable is astonishing," Kelt thought as he reviewed the figures and projections from various sources on Pacificus. No one quite agreed on all the variables. To begin with, it was nearly impossible to establish a baseline for the rotting biomass on the planet. All the projections, however, pointed to one simple fact; there was no time to wait.

Kelt called up the codes to access the hoppers aboard the defunct space elevator. He quickly scanned the inventory levels, capacity, and operational status of the spinners. Only a few tons of carbon remained on board in the hoppers. The ceramic steel inventories were of little import, for the moment. All he really wanted was a few meters of Fullerine cable made from the Buckyballs, and there was more than enough carbon in the hoppers for that.

He scanned the schematics and wondered if he could remotely configure the machine to produce product in a more unconventional means. The machine was configured to provide filaments to the spinners as they climbed up and down the cable holding the large hotel in orbit. All Kelt wanted was a few meters of thick line that could be retrieved by a shuttle.

"Hmm… yes. Let's see. I can manage this. The spinners can be reconfigured and work with short lengths within the station." Kelt knew that working with longer lengths might only provide knots, which the spinners could not manage. He didn't need cables any longer than that in any case. "Oh, what a piece of luck! A couple of robots are still in action that I can use to move the cable to the dock." He configured the machine to weave three- dozen cables, 45 meters long and four centimeters thick. The robots could roll them up and tie them off in neat packages. A few spare containers lying about were perfect to pack them. "Now, all I need is a shuttle and crew."

"Nelby Station," Commander Grayson answered the video link."

"Wow, right to the top. I like that," Kelt grinned.

"You folks down there get top priority, sir." Grayson smiled back.

"I appreciate that Commander. I do have a priority request."

"Yes, sir. What can we do for you?"

"I need you to send out a shuttle with a crew of two men to the hopper station of the space elevator. I placed some crates just inside the primary dock. I need them delivered to the Nevada site as soon as you can get them here."

"I suppose that the ban on shuttle flights dirtside is now of little consequence, since we already have the infection on board."

"Correct, Commander. I am officially rescinding that mandate. Your crew can return to the station if they'd like. They are welcome to stay with us too."

"I think I'll let them decide, if you don't mind, sir."

"It isn't going to matter in the long run, Commander. They'll be back down here soon enough. We're going to need a lot more help within the coming months."

*****

Several hours later, Nevada Base had secured the cable shipment from the space elevator, and the cracking bacteria slime, sent down on the back of a floater. Two shuttles had been taken out to the space elevator and were ready to load.

"C'mon gentlemen, get those shuttles loaded!" Kelt commanded to Guy's squad. Kelt pitched in to get the final two cable crates loaded.

"You sure we can trust those guys up north, Kelt?"

"Hey Guy, those troops are surviving on the algae ponds we provided for them. Now, we are telling them that they are crucially needed in getting our world back up and running. What do you think? Come on, split your squad, and load 'em up."

Scotty stepped forward. "Kelt, I'm not going to let one of those commandos fly my shuttle."

"I suppose you need a break as well as anyone else, Mr. Scott. Okay. You know where we're going. You've been there before."

"I'll see you there," Scotty grinned.

The shuttles quickly ascended high into the sky and dropped to north of the military base within a few minutes.

Two squads of unarmed soldiers stood at ease as the shuttles landed. A young lieutenant approached the shuttles as Kelt dropped the rear hatch.

"Good afternoon, lieutenant... Kavinsky," Kelt said as he referred the soldier's nametag on his khakis.

"Good afternoon to you, sir."

"Did you prepare the site for us like we asked?"

"Yes sir, step this way," Kavinsky motioned.

"So, how are your algae farms getting along?"

"We had been supplementing our rations with them 50/50 up until a few weeks ago. Now, that's what we eat, along with a fresh carp every once in a while," the lieutenant grinned. "It sure beats the alternative, if you know what I mean, sir."

"Yes it does, Lieutenant. So, let's see, you have the holes far from the algae farms and close to your barracks. That looks good. How deep did you go?"

"We only got down a little over 12 feet, sir. That's the extent of the auger on that back hoe over there."

"That should be fine."

Kelt motioned to the shuttles, and the men quickly disgorged carrying crates, floaters, and a couple gallon cans.

"Okay, men, gather round. I want to show you how to set these up. I don't want to do every one of them myself. My leg is killing me, and I'd rather be at home with a good book," Kelt smiled, "Besides, if these things work, you'll be teaching others how to do it within the week."

The men looked at each other in wonder. Few knew exactly what was going on, other than this was a project to crack carbon dioxide, a naturally occurring gas, which was poisoning the planet.

"Scott, pass me a floater."

Scotty had reviewed the procedures. With his com unit, he commanded the device to float mode and gently moved the device in front of Kelt, directly over the hole in the ground. Kelt attached a short length of steel cable to the underside hook mounted to the floater. To that, he attached one of the Buckyball/fullerine cables.

"Okay, Mr. Scott, take her up 26 meters and hold her in place."

Scotty raised the floater precisely 26 meters and issued a command for a soft lock. Kelt attached leads to an AA alkaline battery, and to the end of the cable. He then dipped the end of the cable in a gallon of goo.

"Okay, drop the floater by 12 feet."

"Kelt, are you going to make me do the metric conversion?"

"Yes, Scotty. Make it close too."

"Affirmative."

The floater dropped to the correct height, leaving the dangling end of the cable just touching the bottom of the hole.

"Okay, Scotty, hard lock that floater."

"Okey, dokey."

"What happened to affirmative, or yes sir, or even Cap'n?"

"Hey, you got the message," Scotty smiled.

Kelt smiled in response as he continued, "Now this is our primary, gents," Kelt said as he attached two uninsulated leads from a battery to the cable at ground level. This real "battery" was made from a Dimensional Conduit buried in a carbon matrix block. The power source to the conduit was of course a regulated connection to one of the solar collectors orbiting the Sun.

"Pass me the paint if you please, Mr. Scott."

Scotty handed Kelt the can of paint made from mostly carbon, water, and some weak binders. Kelt painted the contact points with the paint and blew on it as it dried quickly.

"Okay, gents, the goo is the last step."

Kelt picked up the bacteria laced goo and painted it around the cable where the leads met at ground level.

"Now gents, let me explain what we've done. We want to get the CO_2 cracking bacteria going nice and healthy at the outset. That's why there's a battery in the bottom of the hole. That alkaline will provide enough excitement for them to fill the hole with carbon, I'm told. Once the hole is filled with carbon, we'll need help from a second electrical source. That's what this bigger battery is for. Now, set up the others just like this one. Hang one of those cables just off the ground... don't put it down a hole. The people upstairs want a standard to examine. We can drop it in a hole later on."

The group split up into several teams and split the supplies. They had all set up their CO_2 cracking piles within the hour.

"If this works," Kelt thought, "we'll also harvest the carbon for our technologies. No more distilling from oil or cracking carbon from coal. This could work out really well for us."

50- Leo Galt

"Mr. Carter, I'm sorry to bother you," offered the ex-president Murlough. "I'd really like to return to Earth and spend what time there is left with my wife and family. Is it possible that you can forgive me and grant me this request?"

Carter realized that the people trapped in the lunar Tycho base had not been informed of recent events on Earth. They did not know that plant life had returned, and they knew nothing of the advances in controlling the CO_2 in the air. Murlough was requesting a death sentence, as far as he knew, to spend his final days with his family.

"That's very noble of you, Mr. President."

"It is my last wish, Carter. I can't atone for what I've done. I realize that. But my wife and kids… well I'm not sure if they ever want to see me again, but I'd like to give it a go, if you'll see fit to release us."

"It wasn't any error on the part of your commandos that they were stuck with you, either, Mr. President. I've been thinking about that for some time. I realize that it isn't fair. Still, you have been protected from the worst humanity has to offer. It is entirely likely that many of them would have perished had they been dirtside, during the past couple of years."

"I can only imagine. I know I had a large part to play in the disaster."

"I suppose that under most circumstances, you'd have been given the death penalty, Mr. President."

"I suppose that I would. I'm grateful to be alive."

"Well, Mr. President, I pretend to be no judge. I don't know if it would have made any difference one way or another, depending on whom you talk to of course. Many innocent people were murdered in the nuclear strikes in Africa. I know you ordered it too, in an offhand way. We've all been under great duress. I've had the terrible responsibility to select who gets to live. In my mind, I have a hard time separating our actions. I'd like to think that you were foolish, and that I was not. We've both been guilty in some way for the deaths of far too many. Many people still alive dirtside, have also committed great atrocities. Normal people have become mass murderers and cannibals. What shall we do with them? Do we have a choice?"

"I sense great grief in you, Mr. Carter."

"That, there is. It's been very difficult during these past few years to keep my vision intact and my morals in some sort of bizarre order. I can't say that I've been successful."

"You've done better than anyone else, Mr. Carter. Some 22,000 people, including me and my family, owe you great consideration."

"I suppose."

"Rick, I should have brought this up with you long ago, but I too have been burned by Leo Galt. I should have told you earlier, but ever since I arrived here, I felt we both deserved our banishment."

"Oh please don't talk about him. I really had hoped he would disappear. And you, Mr. President? Quite frankly, I agree with your assessment."

"I've been negligent in passing on to you the real facts concerning the incidents for which you blame him."

"Really? Don't tell me he wasn't involved."

"The shenanigan in China was his doing. He freely admits it and the records prove his story. He wanted control of the space elevator, and you kept dumping money into it. Because of that, he could not gain a controlling interest in the project. He figured your legal team would have you out of China in a month at the most. He only needed a week or two to force you out of the consortium."

"Yeah, well, that incident... I don't' even care about, Mr. President. He kidnapped a little girl, came after my daughter, and nearly killed me! That's what I'm upset about."

"And for those things, he is not guilty, Mr. Carter. I have not been forthright with you on various occasions, but I give you my solemn vow. He did not do these things."

"I don't believe you."

"Well, let me explain. The attempt on your life at the television studio was by a fundamentalist religious sect. They believed that you were trying to crown yourself as God, or some such nonsense. They tried to take your life as a result. I was briefed on the sect and its attempt to murder you. We made a decision not to reveal all the facts. We felt that the best way to quell terrorism was to take away the terror. That's why it was described as a murder plot, by unknown assailants on the newscasts. The story died quickly, as we hoped it would. The terrorists got nothing out of it."

"Okay, go on. What about the kidnapping of that little girl at Stanford?"

"Your commandos shot the lead instigator in that fiasco at his apartment. We found numerous files and data sets on his home computer. He was looking for your daughter and he thought he had found her. The ransom demands led to his cell phone. He had absolutely no connections to Leo Galt. You can't imagine that Galt would have been so stupid, as to try a plan that inane would you? He didn't need the money, and he didn't need to irritate you. It just didn't make any sense that he would be involved in such an overt crime.

The attack on your island in the Mediterranean was not of Galt's doing either."

"Hey, now there you are wrong, Mr. President. We caught him with the goods!"

"Not so quick, Mr. Carter. That attack was planned and executed by a Corsican family. That's family spelled M O B. They had overflown that island and collected recon for months. Many of those who attacked were actually related. Once they stole the disk drives, they sold them to Leo Galt for a very large sum of cash. Mr. Galt, here, really didn't care too much about getting his intellectual property through industrial espionage, through the work of his own employees, or anyone else, for that matter. All he cared about was getting his hands on new tech he could patent.

Clearly, he would never get far with your technologies. You were a dangerous man to him, Mr. Carter. He didn't even know the materials were stolen from you until he saw your little video worm at the end of his presentation."

"That explains them all except for the attack on my daughter and her team in the Stanford Lab, Mr. President. Explain that one away."

"I'm quite embarrassed about that one, Mr. Carter. It was a rogue squad from one of our secret agencies. I assure you I had nothing to do with the assault. Somehow, they had acquired enough knowledge about your machine down there, to think that you had developed a new weapon of mass destruction. They believed that the research team, protected by well-armed mercenaries, were terrorists, and had to be brought to justice. Mr. Carter, I did not know about them, I did not authorize their attack, but I do take full responsibility for them. They were rounded up and prosecuted, if it makes any difference to you."

"I'm assuming you can prove these things?"

"I don't know what condition the world is in, Mr. Carter. I know there were a significant number of records for all these events. I'm sure that they exist somewhere. I'm sorry that all I can offer you at present is my word."

"Frankly, Mr. President, I've never really trusted you. You've been a self-serving politician for as long as I've known you. If there ever were a cause you believed in, I'm sure you sacrificed it, just to get elected."

"You're not far from the mark. I've made many mistakes, Rick. Please let me see my family before I die."

Rick rubbed his chin pensively for a moment.

"Let me talk to Galt."

Murlough looked surprised by the request, but motioned to his servicemen.

Two commandos brought Galt to the camera. His hands were bound, and his mouth gagged. One of the commandos released the gag."

"Mr. President, please give Leo a headset and leave the room."

"But…"

"Look Murlough, this is important, and I don't want to explain. Close the door behind you on your way out."

"Okay people, Carter wants to talk to this jerk alone. Let's leave the room and let him have his say."

Rick waited until he could see the room clear, and the door closed. "It doesn't look like you are doing all that well up there, Leo."

"Life sucks. I wish they'd just shoot me."

"Perhaps they should... Leo. I have a question for you. Back in the beginning of the civil war, Adalardo came to visit you."

"Leo's jaw dropped. So, you know about *us*?"

"Some. How long had you owned that place?"

"I'd just moved in, Rick. I bought the place complete with silverware, furniture, and the slaves. It was a nice place, Rick."

"So, I understand. Tell me about your slave managers."

"What do you want to know, Rick?"

"Just tell me whatever comes to you first."

"Ah well, they weren't very good. The slaves wouldn't work. It turns out they were beating them up pretty bad every day. I caught two raping one of my house servants about a week after Adalardo left."

"And what did you do?"

"I shot them, of course. No one treated my slaves badly, especially like that."

"Hmm... you didn't pay your employees well in your companies, Leo."

"Rick, come on! Who did? You were the only idiot I knew of, who thought his employees should be paid more than they were worth."

"That's one of the reasons why I had loyal employees."

"I know. I only got to one of them."

"The one drilling holes in my disks?"

335

"What disks, your disk drives? I was talking about the one who helped me frame you, so you'd be arrested in China. Hey, Rick, whatever happened to those women in the space elevator? Are they okay?"

"What is it to you, Leo?"

"Well, I'd befriended their pastor years ago. He managed to contact me just before I hijacked your shuttles. I couldn't let those women suffer. So, I gave him the security codes to the elevator and told him how to use it."

"A moment of compassion, Leo?"

"I know it's hard to believe, Rick, but I am cursed with them from time to time."

"They and their pastor are safe, Leo."

"Thanks, Rick. I've been worried sick about them. I couldn't stand the thought of those young girls stuck in South America, on what they considered a compassionate mission… and getting… well you know."

"Yeah, I suppose I do, Leo. For once, you and I are thinking along similar lines."

Rick seriously wondered at Leo's motivations. Perhaps some of those children were his. Perhaps, just perhaps, Leo might be showing a side of himself that no one had ever seen before.

"Leo, tell your president there, that I'll think about his request."

"Yeah, sure. Will you ask him to shoot me for payment? I'm sick of living here. I can't stand it anymore."

"I'll think about it, Leo."

*****

Rick sought out Amy Prichard on Pacificus. She had just finished a lesson with Aldo, and Rick found her in the hallway.

"Amy, may I ask you some questions?"

"Sure. I'd be happy to help with anything."

"Remember when Aldo visited you in the south just as the civil war was getting started?"

"Yes, I do."

"How long had Galt lived there?"

"He had purchased the house that very week."

336

"I only ask because when Aldo related the story to me, he said that you were terrified to talk with him."

"I was, Rick. The slave managers were ruthless. There was good reason to fear them. They had rules, which could not be broken. In fact, they were raping me for speaking to Aldo a few days later, when Leo walked in."

"What did Leo do, Amy?"

"He shot them in the head. Then he said, "No one treats my slaves like that.""

"Did he ever molest you, Amy?"

"He offered companionship a few times. I told him that I wasn't interested. He quit trying."

"So, as a slave, he treated you well?"

"Rick, slaves were never treated well. We were slaves! After that, I was well-fed and never punished under Leo's management if that's what you mean."

"Might you ever forgive him for being a slave owner?"

"I suppose that it was common practice back then. I might be able to forgive him, if it weren't for all those things he has done to you and your family."

"What if it turns out he didn't do those things… could you forgive him?"

"Maybe. I don't know. I'd clearly have to devote some time to think about it. I suppose that there must come a time of reconciliation. At some point, revenge makes no sense. No one knows who started what, for which reason. Yes, I would say that I would have to try to forgive him. Logically, I could. Emotionally, perhaps not so much."

"Thanks, Amy. You've been a big help," Rick said shortly before rushing back toward his office.

Amy stood in the hallway dumbfounded. "Is he really going to let Leo Galt go? I bet that's what he's thinking."

51- Beijing excursion

"Kelt, the Chinese are on board. They'll send out some armed guards to protect you while you bring the plant online."

"Can we trust them, Rick?"

"Do we have a choice, Kelt?"

"I suppose not. I've been reviewing the estimates from our biologists upstairs, and this thing could cascade out of control very quickly. We really can't spare a few weeks or even days. I'll be taking Guy and a squad along with me, just in case."

"I was going to advise that, Kelt. But, make sure during the initial contact, they don't provide an aggressive profile, okay?"

"I'm going to leave that up to Guy, if you don't mind Rick. He's got a lot more experience at this sort of thing, than either of us."

"Good point, Kelt."

"Say Rick, we set up a dozen of the lines at that military base north of us yesterday."

"So I've heard. Are they working?"

"Our biologist, Dr. Patel is up there right now. She informs me that the bacteria have multiplied like crazy and have populated the full lengths of the cable. She has noted some measurable carbon deposits already near the base."

"That's excellent progress, Kelt."

"Yeah... now if we can get cooperation with the Chinese, we'll have access to our old production facilities."

"Kelt, you don't need to give them floaters. Tell them to hang the cables from rope stretched between buildings, from trees; you get the idea. Does that sound like it will work for you?"

"Yes, Rick. I was pretty concerned about letting the cat out of the bag too soon. That will help significantly."

*****

"Mr. Secretary, I understand that our joint mission was a success," Rick said over a standard video link. The monitor and related equipment were given to him by the team sent in to start up the Beijing production facility.

"Yes, Rick. I understand it was a tense moment at first… two squads of highly trained commandos armed to the teeth… but your commander Lerner easily broke the ice with his excellent Mandarin. Did you know he has no English accent?"

"Yes, I know, Jiang. That's why I sent him in. So, we've got a couple dozen CO2 cracking piles set up around your offices, correct?"

"Indeed, we do and they are getting very fat as we speak. The flowers are lovely too. You did that didn't you? You restarted the world's plant life. How did you do it, Rick?"

"I'm not a good liar, Jiang. You know that. Yes, my people were responsible. Let me just say that if I told you how they did it, you'd never believe me. Can we let it go at that?

"I suppose some things we are not meant to know, Rick. What really matters now is that we are on track to save our planet."

"That's good to hear, Jiang. I hope that we can get along together. It looks like it's just you and me, for the time being. And believe me; I do NOT want to be in charge."

"I know you too well, Rick. You don't want to be in command, but you always will be. Your people will make sure of it."

"Perish the thought! Let me get to the point Jiang. We need to set up somewhere in the neighborhood of a million of those CO2 cracking piles around the world. We're going to need significant help. I also need to outfit our Beijing production facility fully with workers. Can you see where I'm going?"

"You want me to build and install them."

"Well, in China, at least. We'll start with that. Can you feed your people?"

"We've seeded many of our fields within the past few weeks. The crops are thriving. We've also set up many of your algae ponds. We can manage on algae crackers and fish, for a year, while we build our seed stock."

"It should only be another year until we can plant enough crops to feed whoever is still alive, Jiang. You and I can manage that, can't we?"

"All we can do is try."

"There is one other thing I wanted to talk to you about, Jiang. And it is most delicate. Please tell your people not to worry about what we are doing in our production plant. For now, we will be making the carbon rope and other devices used in our technologies. Please tell them that. You can come watch the process. It is very important that we operate the facility around the clock without hindrance. I will tell you that there is life-saving technology in what we are doing, but that is between you and me. Someday, if we can bring the world together, we'll share the technology with everyone. For now, they will reap its rewards."

"You and your dreams," Jiang grinned. "I understand. If you can produce the materials for the CO2 cracking piles, we'll get them planted. We won't bother you or your employees in your facility. I understand that you have enlisted Chinese personnel for your plant. It's good for us and good for you too."

"Do you think you can manage Asia?"

"Like you said, Rick, let's start with China.

"And Space Truck, my friend, will enlist the rest of the world."

52- New trends

From dirtside enclaves within the Nevada Base organization, the news was good. Violent gangs were trending down. They did not have the organizational skills or strategic minds for success. Algae-eco ponds were popping up all over the world, defended by well-armed, organized, and generally peaceful people. Kelt had been thrilled when he noticed a group of large pond farms, organizing in California's central valley. The central valley had been one of the premier agricultural areas of the world. Although getting the resources together to manage its water systems was clearly a plan for the future, Kelt felt it absolutely necessary that the farming community there be reconstituted as soon as possible.

"I hope they are receptive, Guy," he said as he watched the ground come closer. An additional transport sphere and three Space Trucks accompanied their descent to the largest of the farms.

"Well, if they're not, Kelt, we'll just have to leave. I really don't like your plan to expose yourself like this."

"Yeah, I'd rather send you, but you'd take your rifle, and I'd rather not piss them off with our first hello."

"We've got your back in any case," Guy responded as he took mental inventory of his well-armed troops on the five craft descending on the farms.

"Take us in slowly, Mr. Garner," Kelt advised the pilot. "We don't want them to think we are attacking them."

"Yes, sir."

Kelt watched the monitors as an armed group of civilians gathered below them. He hated these "first contact" situations. People were generally receptive to them, for they still had a memory of what the Space Truck craft looked like, from before the virus attack. Some had taken pot shots at them, all the same. This group was ready for the worst, but still had not taken an aggressive stance.

341

"They're well organized, Kelt. Look, they've got sharp shooters moving into strategic positions to cover their people," Guy noted.

As planned, only the command sphere touched down. The others stopped some 100 meters above ground, while Kelt managed the negotiations.

"Okay, sir," we're down," Captain Garner advised.

"Mount up! Guy ordered his team. They lined the corridor, out of sight, to back up Kelt as he lowered the ramp and exited the craft alone.

Kelt stood near the sphere, in case shooting started. He held his hands high in plain sight.

One of the armed farmers cautiously approached him.

"What do you want?" he asked with some disdain.

"We're here to help. My name is Dr. Kelt Nelby."

"Yeah, I recognize you from the television broadcast. You're a little late to help, Mr. Nelby. We're doing fine here. Now get lost."

"You're growing algae for sustenance, I see," Kelt said as the farmer had just turned to retreat.

The farmer turned back to face him. "Yeah, no thanks to you."

"Where do you think that technology came from?" asked Kelt. "Yes, it came from the floating cities, and we provided instructions to everyone who got it, to pass it on. It's no accident that you have it, sir."

The farmer seemed to warm up a bit. "My name is Samuel Woodsworth," he said as he shouldered his weapon and extended his hand.

Kelt gave him a warm handshake.

"So, what's in those spacecraft?" Samuel asked.

"I told you that we are here to help," offered Kelt. "We have things that you need."

"Such as?"

"We have various varieties of non-hybridized crop seed, and a technology that we'd like to have your people implement to help resolve the mounting CO_2 problem in our atmosphere," Kelt replied.

342

"Crop seed?"

"Yes. We need to get real crop production scaled back up in this valley, and we figured that you are better to do that task than we are. I told you Samuel, we are here to help. It's also extremely important to get the carbon dioxide problem under control. The world is still dying, and we need your help too. We are learning to help each other again," Mr. Woodsworth.

Samuel had been joined by two others, who had heard what Kelt had just said.

"Holy pariah, they are going to save the world after all," one older man exclaimed to Samuel.

A broad grin spread across Samuel's face. "We're just local farmers who've managed to wipe out the local gangs. We banded together to survive the holocaust. We shared all of our resources to get by, and we've done pretty well for ourselves. Unfortunately, we've eaten most of our seed stock. Without those scum ponds, it's likely we would all be starving by now."

"Well, Samuel, we're seeing pretty much the same wherever we go. May I have your permission to land our other craft? We do have an armed escort. They will shoulder their weapons and remain onboard. We'd like to distribute these supplies, show you how to set up what we are calling CO_2 cracking piles, and leave you in peace."

"Sure… but give me a minute and let me tell the rest of the group, so no one gets trigger happy."

"I'd appreciate that, Samuel."

Samuel stepped away from the ship and yelled to the gathered group and the sharpshooters hidden in the background. "Space Truck is here, and they've brought us supplies! Hold your fire!"

A rousing cheer erupted from the survivors. Many ran to greet Kelt with happy faces, many with tears in their eyes.

"Bring down the Space Trucks!" Kelt commed.

53- Waters of Babylon

"I'm sorry about the long wait, Kelt. You know how I was worried about reintroducing our people dirtside before they could adequately and safely take care of themselves."

"Yeah, I know, Rick. We've been through it about 5,000 times over the past five years. And every time I've agreed with you."

"So Kelt, Aldo is still looking for the libraries. Do we have them in that artifact of yours or don't we?"

"I don't know, Rick. It's a history of the world, and as such, is an incredible treasure. And... it did help us save the world," Kelt answered as he made sure no one could overhear him. "I don't know what to think of Aldo's ranting. I'm not so sure that he's wrong, but I can't say he's on the mark on this one, if you know what I mean. I don't mean to change the topic, but I heard the strangest rumor."

"What would that be, Kelt?"

"Rick, are you out of mind? I heard you let President Murlough and Leo Galt go."

"It's a time for reconciliation, Kelt. I think we blamed Leo for more than he was guilty. He's no doubt a scoundrel, but he's not a murderer. I'm very sure of that now. We've already brought the Tycho base people on board Nelby Station. The president has been reunited with his family."

"You've got to be kidding me. I can't believe it," Kelt said in amazement. "I was wondering why the president's family was rotated upstairs. I figured that with all the people coming down from Nelby, it was a way to relieve us from the responsibilities of taking care of them."

"Don't worry, Kelt. They've been here a while. Leo has had quite a bit of privacy, if you know what I mean. I have an assignment or two in mind for his talents. He's been spending a lot of time studying. I expect a lot from him, and I'm pretty sure that he'll rise to those expectations. As far as President Murlough goes, well, he's not the President any more. There seems to be no government control anywhere. I'm sure that will change as we rebuild our civilization."

"I understand, Rick. I too am hopeful. It's been tough dirtside, we've been able to release the people in bunkers, build nearly two million CO_2 cracking piles, rebuild our industries with robots, develop new Dimensional Shift production facilities, and create trading partnerships around the world."

"It does sound like you've been busy. You haven't been in contact with Akhi much. Do you still want to marry her?"

"Rick, there is one everlasting truth in this universe. I love your daughter dearly. I most certainly will marry her, if she will accept."

"Why the lapse in communication, then? It's been quite troubling for her."

"Like I said, I've been busy. I've been building us a home."

"Oh, you mean that sleek craft you came up to Pacificus in? It is a beauty to be sure. I love the sleek flattened look with two levels of ports all around the edge. It is absolutely stunning."

"Well, that's part of it. I'm afraid it's not much of a space-going vehicle. Our inability to provide gravity and adequate shielding are the primary reasons. The best surprise for Akhi is dirtside. And for that, I need her. I assume she's coming down to meet me here on the flight deck?"

Rick chuckled. "She can't figure out what to wear. She's beside herself with joy, Kelt. I can't tell you how proud I am for both of you. When's the wedding?"

"I told you Rick, I haven't asked her yet. Should she accept, I'm sure that she'll want to take care of those arrangements herself."

"Ah, here's my girl," Kelt beamed with pride as Akhi strolled on to the flight deck in a bright red cotton sundress and matching heels. She had matured significantly since Kelt had seen her last. She was *definitely* no longer a skinny teenager. His heart skipped a step, as he scrutinized her glamorous form glide in feminine grace onto the flight deck.

She caught him staring at her, and smiled wildly with anticipation. No longer able to contain herself, she ran toward him and jumped into his welcoming arms. After an intense kiss, she hugged him in a crushing embrace. Chanto and Freia, now fully grown, paraded around the happy couple, wagging their tails in acknowledgement of Akhi's joy.

"Akhi, you look absolutely stunning. I had no idea just how beautiful you really are. Are you ready to go back home?" Kelt grinned.

"Yes, my darling," she beamed. "The cats come too, right?"

"I'm sure they'll behave. I've heard you have quite a way with them."

"I talk to them," Akhi rolled her eyes up toward her forehead... you know what I mean?"

"I don't doubt it, sweetie. I have a surprise for you and can't wait for you to see it."

"Oh, Kelt, it's beautiful!" she said staring at his sleek lined two level craft.

"That's not it, Akhi. That's just where I fix my meals and sleep. We need to go dirtside. Please, step into my conveyance," he said as he politely motioned her through the hatch.

"This is lovely inside as well, Kelt. It's so unlike you to furnish rooms so elegantly. I would never say this to anyone else, my darling... but when it comes to decorating, you have no taste."

"Hey, now that's not fair," he grinned. "I like this, don't I? No, I didn't design it, but I did pick it out."

"I suppose, I'll have to catch up a bit, Kelt. Seven years is a long time to be separated."

"As long as it's just the simple stuff, I'm not at all worried, Akhi."

The cats split up and went exploring, carefully checking out every nook and cranny of the living space.

"Some Scandinavians are doing this in trade for crop seed and power conduits. They do really nice work, don't they? Here, Akhi, let's retire to the den, while the ship takes us down." Kelt motioned down the hall and pulled her into a windowless room lined with books.

"Real books! I haven't seen one forever! But I'm not even going to look at one, Kelt. I'm not taking my eyes off you for one second!"

"I like what you're saying, sweetie. Here, let's sit down for a few minutes. I have some fresh lemonade on ice."

Akhi hadn't had fresh lemonade for years. She had heard that lemon trees were making a return on their own. It was a good thing too, because, the lemon trees and seed stock aboard the cities had perished over the years. Amanda and Shannon had been right. The floating vessels and their crews did not yet have the experience to maintain viable ecosystems.

"Oh, Kelt, this is so delicious! May I have another?"

"Of course, sweetie. Here you go," he said as he poured out the last, for his own refill. "Drink up or it will go bad. But it's the last for a while. We only get a few lemons, and everyone in the community gets their turn."

"It's been seven years, Kelt. We've been separated for *seven* years. And just think, we only knew each other for just a little less than two years before you were left behind. I am filled with incredible joy to be with you again finally. I am so happy."

"It's a big moment for me, as well. I've worked very hard for this moment. To us, Akhi," Kelt said as he raised his beverage in a toast, his face beaming with elation.

Akhi raised her glass in response. Kelt leaned over her and gently kissed her on her forehead. The cats purred in happy response from the emotional high she was sending.

Mindless romantic chitchat between two long lost lovers easily filled the three-hour descent to the Earth. Akhi thought that it was taking a bit too long to drop to the Nevada Base. It was after all, directly below Pacificus when they had started their descent. Perhaps Kelt was just taking it slow to share time with her before meeting the crew.

"Oh, we've arrived!" Kelt announced. "This way, my love," he said as he lovingly took her hand and led her to the descending hatch.

They stepped out into the warm moist morning of the desert air. Before them, lay fields of waving grasses, grains, pens of sheep, hundreds of deciduous tree saplings, and mammoth thick fluorescing CO_2 Cracking piles. Akhi stood in awe at the simplistic beauty.

"So, what do you think sweetie?"

"It's lovely Kelt! It takes my breath away. You did this?"

"Well, I can't take all the credit. This is our new home for the millenarians and the Nevada crews. The Nevada personnel made this happen, and they are here with us."

"Where are the buildings, Kelt? Where is everyone?"

"We won't ever have any buildings here, Akhi. We all live in spheres now, or other floating craft, like mine. There's no need to pollute the countryside with buildings that will just get old and disintegrate. This is our place now. It is our home."

"My darling, where, exactly are we?"

"So soon, she forgets," he mumbled. "Look around, sweetie, you'll figure it out."

Akhi stepped further from the ship and took in as much of the 360-degree view as she could. To the side of the ship, she quickly recognized the Tigris and Euphrates where they joined, in the distance. Although the paths of the rivers had changed, she easily assessed where she stood. A large smile spread from ear to ear.

"I should never have doubted you, my love. The answer is **YES**!" she squealed as she gripped him around his neck in a hug that he had waited a lifetime to share.

"But Akhi, I haven't even asked the question!"

Waters of Babylon

Michelle Stone

I've spent many years wanting to write. I've worked as an Electrical Engineer in the computer industry for two decades. I served in several capacities as a software engineer, systems analyst, to project manager. I also served as a marketing manager in a medical company that built lab equipment. During the last eight years, I designed, built, and sold large portable telescopes, enabling amateur astronomers the ability move to a mountaintop of their choice, for a night of casual observing. Out of all the work I have done in my life, the telescope endeavor was the most meaningful to me. I also run a private, non-profit astronomical observatory, and play in our local community, Mariposa Symphony Orchestra, here in the Sierra next to Yosemite National Park.

Feel free to contact me at litebkt@gmail.com. Please make sure to put "Dimensional Shift" in the title so that I'll be sure to read it.

You can find me on facebook:

http://www.facebook.com/LightBucket

I value all feedback. I sincerely want to get to know my readers!

I would like to sincerely thank Frankie Sutton for her splendid job in the copy edit of this book. She was very helpful.

120227A

Made in the USA
Lexington, KY
05 March 2012